D0210816

PERFECT

ON

PAPER

ALSO BY SOPHIE GONZALES

Only Mostly Devastated
The Law of Inertia

PERFECT

ON

PAPER

Sophie Gonzales

W

WEDNESDAY BOOKS
NEW YORK

This is a work of fiction. All of the characters, organizations, and events portrayed in this novel are either products of the author's imagination or are used fictitiously.

First published in the United States by Wednesday Books, an imprint of St. Martin's Publishing Group

PERFECT ON PAPER. Copyright © 2021 by Sophie Gonzales. All rights reserved. Printed in the United States of America. For information, address St. Martin's Publishing Group, 120 Broadway, New York, NY 10271.

www.wednesdaybooks.com

Designed by Anna Gorovoy

Library of Congress Cataloging-in-Publication Data

Names: Gonzales, S., 1992– author.
Title: Perfect on paper / Sophie Gonzales.
Description: First edition. | New York : Wednesday Books, 2021. |
    Audience: Ages 13-18.
Identifiers: LCCN 2020048635 | ISBN 9781250769787 (hardcover) |
    ISBN 9781250769770 (ebook)
Subjects: CYAC: Bisexuality—Fiction. | Dating (Social customs)—
    Fiction. | High schools—Fiction. | Schools—Fiction.
Classification: LCC PZ7.1.G6532 Pe 2021 | DDC [Fic]—dc23
LC record available at https://lccn.loc.gov/2020048635

Our books may be purchased in bulk for promotional, educational, or business use. Please contact your local bookseller or the Macmillan Corporate and Premium Sales Department at 1-800-221-7945, extension 5442, or by email at MacmillanSpecialMarkets@macmillan.com.

First Edition: 2021

10 9 8 7 6 5 4 3 2 1

To Mum and Dad, who showed me the beauty of words when I was only a baby, and held my hand as I fell in love with stories

ONE

Everyone in school knows about locker eighty-nine: the locker on the bottom right, at the end of the hall near the science labs. It's been unassigned for years now; really, it should've been allocated to one of the hundreds of students in the school to load with books and papers and forgotten, mold-infested Tupperware.

Instead, there seems to be an unspoken agreement that locker eighty-nine serves a higher purpose. How else do you explain the fact that every year, when we all get our schedules and combinations, and lockers eighty-eight and ninety meet their new leasers, locker eighty-nine stands empty?

Well, "empty" might not be the right word here. Because even though it's unassigned, locker eighty-nine ends most days housing several envelopes with almost identical contents: ten dollars, often in the form of a bill, sometimes made up of whatever loose change the sender can gather; a letter, sometimes typed, sometimes handwritten, sometimes adorned with the telltale smudge of a tearstain; and at the bottom of the letter, an email address.

It's a mystery how the envelopes get in there, when it's

rare to spot someone slipping one through the vents. It's a bigger mystery, still, how the envelopes are collected, when *no one* has ever been spotted opening the locker.

No one can agree on who operates it. Is it a teacher with no hobbies? An ex-student who can't let go of the past? A bighearted janitor who could use some cash on the side?

The only thing that's universally agreed on is this: if you're having relationship issues and you slide a letter through the vents of locker eighty-nine, you will receive an email from an anonymous sender within the week, giving you advice. And if you're wise enough to follow that advice, your relationship problems will be solved, guaranteed, or your money back.

And I rarely have to give people their money back.

In my defense, in the few cases that didn't work out, the letter left out important information. Like last month, when Penny Moore wrote in about Rick Smith dumping her in an Instagram comment, and conveniently left out that he did it after finding out she'd coordinated her absent days with his older brother so they could sneak off together. If I'd known that, I never would've advised Penny to confront Rick about the comment during lunch the next day. That one was on her. Admittedly, it *was* kind of satisfying to watch Rick perform a dramatic reading of her texts to his brother in front of the whole cafeteria, but I would've preferred a happy ending. Because I did this to help people, and to know I made a positive difference in the world; but also (and maybe even mostly, in this case), because it pained me to drop ten dollars into Penny's locker all because *she* was too proud to admit she was the one in the wrong. Problem is, I couldn't defend myself and my relationship expertise if Penny were to tell everyone she didn't get a refund.

Because no one knows who I am.

Okay, I don't mean *literally*. Lots of people know who I am. Darcy Phillips. Junior. That girl with the shoulder-length blond hair and the gap between her front teeth. The one who's best friends with Brooke Nguyen, and is part of the school's queer club. Ms. Morgan-from-science-class's daughter.

But what they don't know is that I'm also the girl who hangs back after school while her mom finishes up in the science labs, long after everyone else has left. The girl who steals down the hall to locker eighty-nine, enters the combination she's known by heart for years—ever since the combination list was left briefly unattended on the admin officer's desk one evening—and collects letters and bills like tax. The girl who spends her nights filtering strangers' stories through unbiased eyes, before sending carefully composed instructions via the burner email account she made in ninth grade.

They don't know, because nobody in school knows. I'm the only one who knows my secret.

Or, I was, anyway. Up until this very moment.

I had the sinking inkling that was about to change, though. Because even though I'd checked the halls for stragglers or staff members like I always did barely twenty seconds ago, I was thirteen-thousand percent sure I'd heard someone clear their throat somewhere in the vicinity of *directly the fuck behind me.*

While I was elbow deep inside a very much unlocked locker eighty-nine.

Crap.

Even as I turned around, I was optimistic enough to hope for the best. Part of the reason why I'd gotten by without detection for so long was the locker's convenient location, right at the foot of a dead-end, L-shaped hallway.

There'd been close calls in the past, but the sound of the heavy entry doors swinging closed had always given me plenty of notice to hide the evidence. The only way someone would be able to sneak up on me was if they'd come out of the fire escape door leading from the pool—and no one used the pool this late in the day.

From the looks of the very wet guy standing behind me, though, I'd made a fatal miscalculation. Apparently, someone did use the pool this late in the day.

Well, fuck.

I knew him. Or, at least, I knew *of* him. His name was Alexander Brougham, although I was pretty sure he usually went by Brougham. He was a senior, and good friends with Finn Park, and, by all accounts, one of the hottest seniors at St. Deodetus's.

Up close, it was clear to me said accounts were categorically false.

Brougham's nose looked like it'd been badly broken once, and his navy-blue eyes were opened almost as wide as his mouth, which was an interesting look, because his eyes were kind of bulgy to begin with. Not goldfish-level, but more like a "my eyelids are doing their best to swallow my eyeballs whole" type of bulgy. And, as aforementioned, he was wet enough that his already dark hair looked black, and his T-shirt stuck to his chest in damp, see-through patches.

"Why are you soaking?" I asked, folding my arms behind my back to hide the letters and leaning against locker eighty-nine so it closed behind me. "You look like you fell in the pool."

This was probably one of the few situations where a sopping wet, fully clothed teenager standing in the school hallway an hour after dismissal *wasn't* the elephant in the room.

He looked at me like I'd said the stupidest thing in the world. Which seemed unfair, given I wasn't the one who was wandering around the school halls literally dripping.

"I didn't 'fall in the pool.' I was swimming laps."

"With your clothes on?" I tried to shove the letters down the back of my skirt without moving my hands, but that was a more complex task than I'd anticipated.

Brougham surveyed his jeans. I used the brief distraction to ram the letters inside the band of my tights. In hindsight, this was probably never going to go far in convincing him he hadn't just seen me digging through locker eighty-nine, but until I had a better excuse, denial was all I had.

"I'm not that wet," he said.

Today was apparently the first time I'd heard Alexander Brougham speak, because until just now I'd had no idea he had a British accent. I understood his wide appeal now: Oriella, my favorite relationship YouTuber, once dedicated a whole video to the topic. People with perfectly good taste in partners historically had their senses addled in the presence of an accent. Setting aside the messiness of *which* accents were considered sexy in which cultures and why, accents in general were nature's way of saying, "Procreate with *that* one, their gene code must be varied as fuck." Few things, it seemed, could turn a person on as quickly as the subconscious realization they almost certainly weren't flirting with a blood relative.

Thankfully, Brougham broke the silence when I didn't reply. "I didn't get time to dry off properly. I'd just finished up when I heard you out here. I thought I might catch the person who runs locker eighty-nine if I snuck through the fire escape. And I did."

He looked triumphant. Like he'd won a contest I was only now realizing I'd been participating in.

That was, incidentally, my least favorite facial expression. As of right this moment.

I forced a nervous laugh. "I didn't *open* it. I was putting a letter in."

"I just saw you close it."

"I didn't close it. I just banged it a little when I was sliding the, uh . . . the letter inside."

Cool, Darcy, way to gaslight the poor British student.

"Yeah, you did. Also, you took a pile of letters out of it."

Well, I'd committed to this enough to shove them down my tights so I might as well follow this through to the end, right? I held my empty hands out, palms up. "I don't have any letters."

He actually looked a little thrown. "Where did you . . . I saw them, though."

I shrugged and pulled an innocent face.

"You . . . did you put them down your stockings?" His tone wasn't accusing, per se. More "mild, patronizing bafflement," like someone gently questioning their child on *why,* exactly, they thought dog food would make a great snack. It only made me want to dig my heels in further.

I shook my head and laughed a little too loudly. *"No."* The heat in my cheeks told me my face was betraying me.

"Turn around."

I leaned against the lockers with a rustle of paper and folded my arms across my chest. The corner of one of the envelopes dug uncomfortably into the back of my hip. "I don't want to."

He looked at me.

I looked at him.

Yeah. He wasn't buying this for a second.

If my brain were functioning properly I would've said something to throw him off track, but unfortunately it chose that precise moment to go on strike.

"You *are* the person who runs this thing," Brougham said, confidently enough I knew there was no point protesting further. "And I really need your help."

I hadn't settled on what I believed would happen if I ever got caught. Mostly because I'd preferred not to worry about it too much. But if you'd forced me to guess what the person catching me would do, I would've probably gone for "turn me in to the principal," or "tell everyone in school," or "accuse me of ruining their life with bad advice."

But this? This wasn't so threatening. Maybe it was going to be okay. I swallowed hard in an attempt to shove the lump in my throat down closer to my thudding heart. "Help with what?"

"With getting my ex-girlfriend back." He paused, thoughtful. "Oh, my name's Brougham, by the way."

Brougham. Pronounced BRO-um, not Broom. It was an easy name to remember, because it was pronounced all wrong, and that had irked me since the first time I'd heard it.

"I know," I said faintly.

"What's your hourly rate?" he asked, peeling his shirt away from his chest to air it out. It thwacked heavily back against his skin as soon as he let go of it. See? *Overly* wet.

I tore my eyes away from his clothes and processed his question. "I'm sorry?"

"I want to hire you."

There he went again with the weird money-for-favors language. "As . . . ?"

"A relationship coach." He glanced around us, then

lowered his voice to a whisper. "My girlfriend broke up with me last month and I need her back, but I don't know where to start. This isn't something an email's gonna fix."

Well, wasn't this guy dramatic? "Um, look, I'm sorry, but I don't really have time to be anyone's coach. I just do this before bed as a hobby."

"What are you so busy with?" he asked calmly.

"Um, homework? Friends? Netflix?"

He folded his arms. "I'll pay you twenty dollars an hour."

"Dude, I said—"

"Twenty-five an hour, plus a fifty-dollar bonus if I get Winona back."

Wait.

So, this guy was seriously telling me he'd give me fifty dollars, tax-free, if I spent two hours giving him some advice on getting back a girl who'd already fallen for him once? That was well within my skill set. Which meant the fifty-dollar bonus was all but guaranteed.

This could be the easiest money I'd ever made.

While I mulled it over, he spoke up. "I know you want to keep your identity anonymous."

I snapped back to reality and narrowed my eyes. "What's that supposed to mean?"

He shrugged, the picture of innocence. "You're sneaking around after hours when the halls are empty, and no one knows it's you answering them. There's a reason you don't want people knowing. It doesn't take Sherlock Holmes."

And there it was. I knew it. I *knew* my gut was screaming "danger" for a good reason. He wasn't asking me for a favor, he was telling me what he wanted from me, and throwing in why it would be a bad idea to refuse. As casually as anything. Blink-and-you'll-miss-it blackmail.

I kept my voice as steady as I could, but I couldn't help the touch of venom that seeped through. "And let me guess. You'd like to help me keep it that way. That's where this is going, right?"

"Well, yeah. Exactly."

He'd stuck his lower lip out and widened his eyes. My own lip curled of its own accord as I took him in, any goodwill I'd been feeling toward him evaporating in one puff. "Gee. That's so thoughtful of you."

Brougham, expressionless, waited for me to go on. When I didn't, he circled a hand in the air. "So . . . what do you think?"

I *thought* a lot of things, but none of them were wise to say out loud to someone who was in the middle of threatening me. What were my options here? I couldn't tell Mom someone was threatening me. She had no idea I was behind locker eighty-nine. And I really, *really* didn't want everyone to find out this was me. I mean, the awkwardness of how much personal information I knew about everyone alone . . . even my closest friends didn't know my involvement. Without anonymity, my dating advice business was a bust. And it was the only real thing I'd ever achieved. The only thing that actually did the world any good.

And . . . god, there was the whole Brooke thing from last year. If Brooke ever found out about that she'd hate me.

She couldn't find out.

I set my jaw. "Fifty up front. Fifty if it works out."

"Shake on it?"

"I'm not done. I'll agree to a cap of five hours for now. If you want me for longer, it's my call to continue."

"Is that everything?" he asked.

"No. If you say one word to anyone about any of this,

I'll tell everyone your game is so bad you needed personal relationship tutoring."

It was a weak addition, and nowhere near as creative as some of the insults I'd thought of a few moments ago, but I didn't want to goad him too much. Something flashed so slightly across his blank face I almost missed it. As it was, it was hard to define. Did his eyebrows rise a little? "Well that was unnecessary, but noted."

I simply folded my arms. "*Was it* now?"

We stood in silence for a beat as my words played back in my head—they'd sounded bitchier than I'd intended, not that bitchiness was unwarranted here—then he shook his head and started to turn his back. "You know what? Stuff it. I just thought you might be open to a deal."

"Wait, wait, wait." I darted forward to head him off, hands up. "I'm sorry. I am open to a deal."

"Are you sure?"

Oh, for god's sake, was he going to make me beg him? It seemed unfair to expect me to accept his blackmail terms without any pushback or sass at all, and I was liking him less and less by the second, but I'd do it. Whatever he told me to do, I'd do it. I just needed to keep the situation contained. I nodded, firmly, and he took his phone out.

"Okay then. I'm at practice over at my swim club before school every day, and Monday, Wednesday, and Friday afternoons we do dryland training. Tuesdays and Thursdays I swim here at the pool. I'll grab your number so we can organize this without me hunting you down at school, okay?"

"You forgot 'please.'" Damn it, I shouldn't have said that. But I couldn't help myself. I snatched the phone from him and entered my number into it. "Here."

"Excellent. What's your name, by the way?"

I couldn't even *begin* to stifle my laugh. "You know, usually people find out each other's names prior to making 'deals.' Do you do it differently in England?"

"I'm from Australia, not England."

"That's not an Australian accent."

"As an Australian, I can assure you it is. It's just not one you're used to hearing."

"There's more than one?"

"There's more than one American accent, isn't there? Your name?"

Oh for the love of . . . "Darcy Phillips."

"I'll message you tomorrow, Darcy. Have a wonderful night." From the way he surveyed me, lips pressed together and chin raised as his eyes drifted down, he'd enjoyed our first conversation about as much as I had. I stiffened with annoyance at this realization. What right did he have to dislike me when *he* was the reason that exchange had gotten so tense?

He slid his phone into his damp pocket, electrical failure be damned, and turned on his heel to leave. I stared after him for a moment, then took my chance to rip the letters out of their extremely uncomfortable position by my underwear and shove them in my backpack. Just in time, too, because Mom emerged around the corner not ten seconds later. "There you are. Ready to go?" she asked me, already turning back down the hall, the clack of her low heels echoing in the empty space.

Like I was ever not ready to go. By the time she packed up her stuff, answered her emails, and got some sneaky paper marking in, I was the last student to leave this area of the school—everyone else was way down at the other end hanging around the art room or the track field.

Well, except for Alexander Brougham, apparently.

"Did you know students stay back this late to use the pool?" I asked Mom, hurrying to meet her stride.

"Well, we're in the off-season for the school team so I daresay it wouldn't be busy, but I know it's open to students Vijay gives passes to until reception closes. Darc, could you text Ainsley and ask her to take the spaghetti sauce out of the freezer?"

By Vijay, Mom meant Coach Senguttuvan. One of the weirdest parts about having a parent work at school was that I knew the teachers by their first *and* last names, and had to make sure not to slip up in class or talking to my friends. Some of them I'd known practically as long as I'd been alive. It might sound easy, but having John around for dinner every month, and at my parents' birthday parties, and hosting New Year's Eve for fifteen years, then suddenly transitioning to calling him Mr. Hanson in math class was like playing Minesweeper with my reputation.

I texted my sister Mom's instructions as I hopped in the passenger seat. To my delight, I found an unread message waiting from Brooke:

I don't want to do this essay.
Please don't make me do this
essay.

As usual, getting a message from Brooke made me feel like the law of gravity had declined to apply to me for a beat.

She was obviously thinking about me instead of doing her homework. How often did her mind wander to me when she started daydreaming? Did it wander to anyone else, or was I special?

It was so hard to know how much to hope.

I sent a quick reply:

> You've got this! I believe in
> you. I'll send you my notes
> later tonight, if it'll help?

Mom hummed to herself as we pulled out of the parking lot, unbelievably slowly, so as to not bowl down any unexpected turtles. "How was your day?"

"Pretty uneventful," I lied. Best to leave out the whole "I got hired and also blackmailed" thing. "I got into an argument about women's rights in sociology with Mr. Reisling, but that's normal. Mr. Reisling's a dickhead."

"Yeah, he *is* a dickhead," Mom mused to herself, then she gave me a sharp look. "*Don't* you tell anyone I said that!"

"I'll leave it off the agenda at tomorrow's meeting."

Mom glanced sideways at me, and her round face broke into a warm grin. I started to return it, then I remembered Brougham, and the blackmailing, and I wilted. Mom didn't notice, though. She was too busy focusing on the road, already lost in her own thoughts. One of the good things about having a perpetually distracted parent was not having to dodge prying questions.

I just hoped Brougham would keep my secret to himself. The problem was, of course, that I had no idea what kind of person he was. Wonderful. A guy I'd never met properly, who I knew nothing about, held the power to throw my business—not to mention my relationships—into havoc. That wasn't anxiety inducing at *all*.

I needed to talk to Ainsley.

TWO

Hi Locker 89,

So, my girl has been driving me fucking crazy. She doesn't know what the word space means!! If I fucking <u>DARE</u> to not text her one day, she'll blow my phone up. Mom told me not to reward her for being psycho, so I make sure I don't reply til the next day so she knows going off on me isn't gonna make me wanna talk to her. And when I do reply, suddenly she's all 1-word answers and passive-aggressive bitchiness. Wtf? Like do you wanna fucking talk to me or not? Now I have to feel fucking guilty because I didn't check my phone in bio? I don't wanna break up because she's actually really cool when she's not being psycho. I swear I'm a good boyfriend, but I can't constantly text her just to keep her from losing it??

Dtb02@hotmail.com

Locker 89 <locker89@gmail.com>   3:06 p.m. (0 min ago)
to Dtb02

Hey DTB!

I recommend you look up different attachment styles.
I can't say for sure, but it sounds like your gf might
have an anxious attachment style. (There are four main
styles, and to summarize: one is secure, where people
learned as babies that love is reliable and predictable.
Another is dismissive-avoidant, where a person learns
as an infant that they can't rely on others, and grows up
finding it hard to let people in. Then you have anxious,
where a person learned that love is only given sometimes,
and can be snatched away without warning, leaving
them constantly afraid of abandonment as adults. And
finally, fearful avoidant, where someone is both afraid of
abandonment and of letting others in. Confusing!) Long
story short, she's always going to be super sensitive to
anything that feels like abandonment, and she'll go right
into panic mode when that happens. We call it "activating."
It's not "psycho" (FYI that's not a cool term), it's a primal
fear of being alone and in danger. But in saying that, I
totally get how it'd feel smothering when she activates.

I recommend setting boundaries, but also taking steps to
reassure her you're still into her. She might need that more
than some others. Let her know you think she's amazing,
but you want to come up with a solution to make sure she
doesn't panic if you don't text. Come to an agreement
you're both happy with, because your need for space is
valid! Maybe you'd be happy to text her before school

every day, even just to say good morning, have a good day? Or maybe you think it's reasonable to send her a quick text reply in the bathroom like, "Sorry I'm in class at the moment, I'll message you when I'm home tonight so I can reply properly, can't wait to talk." Or if you're not in the mood for talking, message her to say, "Having an off night, nothing to do with you, love you, can we chat tomorrow?" The key is, it should be something you both think will work.

It'll take some compromise, but you'd be surprised how easy it is to talk an anxiously attached person down from their spiral if you don't leave them in silence to imagine the worst. They only want to know there's a reason for your distance that isn't "they don't love me anymore."

Good luck!
Locker 89

At home, Ainsley had not only taken the spaghetti sauce out to defrost, she also had a fresh loaf of bread cooking in the bread maker, filling the house with the delicious, yeasty smell of a country bakery. A sloshing, watery sound told me the dishwasher was halfway through a cycle already, too, and the linoleum floor had a "newly mopped" gleam. Even scrubbed down, though, our house was generally too full of clutter to look clean, and the kitchen was no different. Every counter surface was occupied by decorative knick-knacks, from succulents in terra-cotta pots to boxes full of baking utensils to assorted mug racks. The walls were covered in pots and pans and knives hanging from various wooden displays, and the fridge was adorned with magnets to celebrate every big moment in our family's lives, from Disneyland trips to a Hawaii beach vacation to my kindergarten graduation to a picture of Ainsley and Mom on the courthouse steps the day of Ainsley's legal name change.

Since she'd started community college, Ainsley had become preoccupied with "earning her keep" around the house, like Mom hadn't inundated her with reasons to go to college here instead of L.A. all of Ainsley's junior year. Mom, it seemed, wasn't ready to have the house totally empty every other week when I went to my dad's. Not that I was complaining; not only was Ainsley a much better cook than Mom, but she was, incidentally, one of my best friends. Which was one of the weapons Mom had had in her "convince Ainsley to stick around" arsenal.

I dumped my bag by the kitchen table and slid onto one of the benches, trying and failing to catch Ainsley's eye. As usual, she was wearing one of her personalized altered creations, a cream sweater with three-quarter sleeves and winglike frills running down the sides.

"Are you thinking of doing garlic bread, love?" Mom asked Ainsley, opening the fridge to get some water.

Ainsley glanced at the humming bread maker. "That's a good idea, actually."

I cleared my throat. "Ainsley, you said you were gonna alter one of your dresses for me."

Now, to clarify, Ainsley had said no such thing. She was good for a lot of stuff, but sharing her clothes and makeup was not, and never had been, her strong suit. It did the trick, though. She looked at me, finally, albeit in bewilderment, and I took the chance to widen my eyes at her meaningfully. "Oh, of course," she lied, tucking a lock of her long brown hair behind one ear. Her tell. Lucky Mom wasn't paying much attention. "I have a few minutes now if you want to look."

"Yep, yep, let's go."

I didn't visit Ainsley's room nearly as often as she made the trip to mine, and I had a good reason for it. Where my bedroom was relatively organized, decorations where they should be, bed made, clothes hung up, Ainsley's was organized chaos. Her green and pink candy-striped walls were barely visible through the posters and paintings and photos she'd stuck up haphazardly (the only photo that'd been placed with any care was the large, framed picture of the Queer and Questioning Club, taken at the end of her senior year). Her queen-sized bed was unmade—not that you could tell, with the four or five layers of clothes she'd thrown on top of it—and at the foot of the bed, a trunk she kept stuffed full of fabrics and buttons and bits and bobs she was sure she'd find a use for one day sat open, its contents spilling out onto the plush cream carpet.

As soon as I got through the door, I was olfactorily assaulted by the thick caramel-vanilla aroma of Ainsley's favorite candle, which she always lit when she was planning a new YouTube video. She claimed it helped her concentrate, but my muse didn't come in the form of a scent-induced migraine, so I could not relate.

Ainsley pulled her door shut. I threw myself onto the bundle of clothes on her bed, gagging as dramatically as I could. "What's up?" she asked, opening the window a crack to let in some sweet oxygen.

I crawled closer to the window and sucked in a breath. "I was caught, Ains."

She didn't ask what I was caught doing. She didn't have to. As the one and only confidante in the world who knew about my locker business, she knew very well what I did immediately after school every day.

She sat heavy on the edge of the bed. "By *who?*"

"Finn Park's friend. Alexander Brougham."

"*Him?*" She gave me a wicked smile. "He's a snack. He looks like Bill Skarsgård!"

I chose to ignore the fact that she'd compared Brougham to a horror movie clown as a compliment. "How, because he has puffy eyes? Not my thing."

"Because he's a guy, or because he's not Brooke?"

"Because he's not my *type*. Why would it be because he's a guy?"

"I dunno, just you usually go for girls."

Okay, just because I'd *happened* to like a few girls in a row now did not mean I couldn't like a guy. But I did not have the energy to go down *that* rabbit hole right now, so I switched back to the topic at hand. "Anyway, he snuck up behind me today. Said he wanted to figure out who was in charge of the locker, so he could pay me to be his *dating coach.*"

"Pay you?" Ainsley's eyes lit up. Presumably as visions of MAC lipsticks, purchased with my sudden windfall, danced in her head.

"Well, yes. That and *blackmail* me. He basically said he'd tell everyone who I am if I didn't say yes."

"What? That asshole!"

"*Right?*" I threw my hands up, before hugging them to my chest. "And I bet he'd do it, too."

"Well, let's face it, even if he only told Finn, everyone in town would know about it by tomorrow."

Even though Finn Park was a senior and a year younger that her, Ainsley knew him—and, by extension, his friendship choices—well. He'd been part of the Queer and Questioning

Club since Ainsley founded it in her junior year, the same year she started transitioning.

"So, what are you gonna do?" Ainsley asked.

"I told him I'd meet him after school tomorrow."

"Is he at least paying you well?"

I told her, and Ainsley looked impressed. "That's better than I get at the Crepe Shoppe!"

"Count yourself lucky your boss isn't extorting you."

We were interrupted by my phone vibrating in my pocket. It was a message from Brooke.

> Have a new sample haul. I could
> come around before dinner?

Everything inside me started flipping and tumbling like I'd knocked back a glass of live crickets.

"What does Brooke want?" Ainsley asked lightly.

I glanced up halfway through texting a response. "How did you know it was Brooke?"

She raised an eyebrow at me. "Because only Brooke makes you go—" She punctuated the sentence with a gooey, exaggerated smile, complete with crossed eyes and a lopsided head tip.

I stared at her. "Wonderful. If I look like that around her, I can't imagine why she hasn't fallen for me yet."

"My job is to give you the harsh truth," Ainsley said. "I take it seriously."

"You're good at it. Very committed."

"Thank you."

"She's got some samples for us. Are you filming before dinner?"

"Nope, I was going to later. Count me in."

Even though the Crepe Shoppe paid Ainsley's bills, for the last year she'd been putting all her free time toward building her thrift-flip YouTube channel. Her videos were actually really impressive. Dealing with the same pressure to fit in at a rich private school as I did, but amplified by the added pressure of working within the limited new wardrobe Mom and Dad could afford to give her at the time—much of which wasn't designed with her proportions in mind—Ainsley had adapted by developing her sewing skills. And, in the process, had discovered she had a natural creativity. She could look at the ugliest pieces of thrift store clothing, and where the rest of us saw something we'd never wear in a million years, Ainsley saw potential. She'd rescue items and take in the hips, add in panels, add or remove sleeves, and cover them in crystals or lace or patches, and she'd absolutely transform them. And it just so happened that the transformation process, along with her self-deprecating voice-over commentary, made for quality content.

I sent back a text to Brooke. What I wanted to say was abso-fucking-lutely she could come over, as soon as possible, and in fact, she could also move in, and marry me, and mother my children while she was at it, but my extensive study in relationships had taught me wild obsession wasn't cute. So I went with a simple "sure, we'll be eating around six." Same overall message, less terrifying intensity.

While Ainsley headed back to the kitchen, I changed out of my uniform, then fished today's letters out of my bag and started working my way through them. I had a real system going after doing this roughly twice weekly for two years. Dollar bills and coins went into a Ziploc bag to be deposited into my bank account (I figured the easiest way to get myself caught would be to be seen with a purse stuffed full of small bills one too many times). Then I'd speed-read all of the letters and sort them into two piles. Pile one: letters I could answer off the top of my head. Pile two: letters that stumped me. I was proud to say these days that pile two was almost always smaller, and sometimes there was no need for a pile two at all. There were very few situations that threw me anymore.

I did worry sometimes that this whole process would become too time consuming to continue in senior year. But, hey, plenty of students had part-time jobs. Why was this any different? Apart from the obvious answer: I enjoyed this. A hell of a lot more than most people enjoyed their minimum wage jobs bagging groceries or collecting dirty plates from ungrateful customers.

By the time Ainsley wandered back in so she could procrastinate from her own responsibilities, I'd finished pile one—the only pile today—and moved on to YouTube research. Over the last couple of years, I'd cultivated a subscription list of who I considered to be the very best relationship experts on YouTube, and I made a point of never missing their videos. It was a Tuesday, so that meant a new upload from Coach Pris Plumber. Today's video was a review of the latest research behind the biology of the brain in love, which interested me far more than my actual biology homework. Coach Pris was one of my very favorites, second only to Oriella.

God, how to describe the enigma that was Oriella? A twentysomething influencer who practically founded the corner of YouTube devoted to dating advice, she uploaded a video every other day. Could you imagine coming up with that many topics to cover? Unbelievable. And no matter how many she released, how many times you thought she'd surely talked about everything there was to talk about, boom: she blew your mind with a video about how to use artful shots of food in your Instagram stories to make your ex miss you. The woman was a goddamn genius.

She'd also pioneered one of my favorite relationship-advice tools, not-so-creatively called "character analysis." Oriella figured every problem could be labeled, and that to find the correct label, you had to run a diagnostic. Under her prerecorded instruction, I'd learned to list everything relevant about the person in question—in my case, always a complicated locker-letter writer—and once it was all written out, things would almost always become clearer.

Ainsley came up behind me and watched the video silently for three or so seconds, then she moved to my bed and sat heavily on the edge. My cue to stop what I was doing and pay attention to her.

I looked over to see her sprawled in a starfish pose on my bed, her straight brown hair fanned out over the blanket. "Any good ones today?" she asked when I caught her eye.

"Pretty standard," I said as I paused Pris. "What *is* it with guys calling their girlfriends psycho? It's an epidemic."

"If there's one thing guys love, it's an excuse to avoid accountability for their own role in causing the behavior they don't like," Ainsley said. "You're fighting the good fight."

"Someone's got to, I guess."

"Pays the bills. By the way, Brooke's just pulled up outside."

I slammed my laptop lid down and jumped to my feet to douse myself in perfume. Ainsley shook her head. "I've never seen you move so fast."

"Shut up."

We reached the living room as Mom opened the front door and greeted Brooke, which meant I had at least fifteen seconds to prepare while they embraced and Mom asked after every family member Brooke had.

I dove onto the couch, kicking various decorative cushions onto the floor, and arranged myself in a way that hopefully looked like I'd been chilling casually for ages, unconcerned Brooke had arrived. "How's my hair?" I hissed to Ainsley.

She studied me with a critical eye, then shot her hands out to tousle my shoulder-length waves. With a nod of approval, she threw herself beside me and took out her phone, just in time to complete the picture of relaxed nonchalance as Brooke appeared.

My chest compressed. I swallowed my heart, which had lodged itself somewhere behind my tonsils.

Brooke glided into the living room, her stockinged feet silent on the carpet. She was yet to change out of her uniform, to my secret delight.

Our school uniform consisted of a navy blazer with the school logo on the breast, and a white button-down shirt, both of which had to be bought from the uniform shop. Outside of that, there was still a code, but it was a little more lax in terms of how we interpreted it. Bottoms had to be a beige, khaki color, with the choice of pants or a skirt, but we could buy them wherever we wanted. Guys had to wear ties, but the color and style of tie was up to them— barring any explicit or inappropriate prints. That rule had been added back in my sophomore year when Finn got his hands on a tie covered in marijuana leaves.

So, we'd come to a compromise that stopped the students

from revolting. Uniform enough to keep the majority of parents and staff happy, but with enough expression that we didn't feel like we were trapped in some stuffy British boarding school where individuality was illegal.

Now, it might sound like I was complaining about the uniform, but let the record show I was not. How could I complain, when Brooke looked like this in it? With her slender legs shown off by her flippy skirt and black tights, her gold locket pendant dangling in front of her buttoned collar, and her straight dark hair tumbling over the shoulders of her blazer, Brooke was a goddamn vision. I was quite sure that until the day I died, the sight of the St. Deodetus girl's uniform would send my stomach into rollicking butterflies. All because of how it looked on Brooke Amanda Nguyen.

"Hey," Brooke said, dropping to her knees in the center of the room. She dumped the canvas bag she'd carried in with her upside down on the carpet and dozens of sachets and tubes bounced out.

One of the great benefits of having Brooke as a friend—other than, you know, having her around to bring light and joy into my life each and every day—was her department store sales job.

It was hands down the coolest job any teenager could have, if you ignored my job, which was arguably cooler. She got to spend her shifts talking to people about makeup, recommending products, and getting sneak peeks of new stuff. And best of all, she got a staff discount and could take home any samples she wanted. Which translated to me inheriting more than my fair share of free makeup.

With a shriek of happiness, Ainsley dove off the couch and onto the ground to grab a sachet before I'd had the chance to process the selection. "Oh, yes, yes, yes, I've been *wanting* to try this," she said.

"Well, I guess you're claiming that one," I said, pretending to be put out. "Hi, Brooke."

She caught my eye and grinned. "Hey, you. I brought gifts."

Somehow—thankfully—I managed to stop myself from making a cringey one-liner about how her presence in my house was the real gift. Instead, I made just the right amount of eye contact—which she unfortunately broke before we could have any kind of moment—and kept my tone carefully casual, but not so casual I sounded disinterested. "How's the essay?"

Brooke wrinkled her nose. "I got the outline done. I was waiting on your notes."

"You've still got until next week. That's plenty of time."

"I *know*, I know, but it takes me *forever* to do them. I'm not a fast typer like you."

"Why are you here, then?" I asked her teasingly.

"Because you're so much more fun than working on my essay."

I shook my head at her, in a pretense of disappointment, but the look of elation on my face probably gave me away. For a second there, she'd given me what seemed like a meaningful look. Sure, it might have been platonic affection, but it *also* might have been a hint. An opening. *I would rather be around you. I have fun with you. I'd sacrifice a good grade so I could snatch an extra hour with you.*

Or, maybe I was reading into it and hearing what I wanted to hear. Why was it so much harder to answer my own relationship questions than everyone else's?

While Brooke and Ainsley gushed over the product

Ainsley had swooped in on—a chemical exfoliant, from what I could gather—I crawled over to the haul and found a mini liquid lipstick in the most perfect peachy-pink shade I'd ever seen. "Oh, Darc, that'd look beautiful on you," Brooke said, and that was it, I needed this more than I'd ever needed anything in my life.

But as I was swatching it on my wrist, I noticed Ainsley giving me puppy-dog eyes in my peripheral. I glanced up. "What?"

"That's the lipstick I was gonna buy this weekend."

I pulled it into my chest protectively. "You got the exfoliator!"

"There's like a hundred things here, I'm allowed more than *one thing*."

"You're not even blond! You can't pull off peach!"

Ainsley looked affronted. "Um, excuse you, I'll have you know I *rock* peach. And your lips are perfect bare. Mine need all the help they can get."

"You can borrow it whenever you want."

"*No,* you get cold sores. If I hold onto it, you can borrow it if you use an applicator, how about that?"

"Or I could use an applicator all the time, and *you* can borrow it."

"I don't trust you. You'd get lazy and rub your herpes all over it to claim it."

I threw my hands up and looked at Brooke for support. "Wow. *Wow.* Are you hearing this slander?"

Brooke shared an amused look with me, and all the fierceness flooded out of me. She sat up straighter and laid her palms out. "Okay, chill, this doesn't need to end in blood. How about rock paper scissors?"

Ainsley looked at me.

I looked at her.

She shrugged.

Damn it, she knew I was going to crack. She *knew* it, and had *zero* shame in taking advantage of that fact, and only for her, *only for her.* Winning, knowing Ainsley wanted it so badly, would feel sour now. "Joint custody?" I offered. Good-bye, beautiful lipstick.

"Oh, *Darc,*" Brooke protested. She knew as well as I did if it disappeared into Ainsley's room I'd probably never see it again. But I had to set terms regardless, otherwise I looked like I was easy to walk all over. Which I was, when it came to Ainsley, but that wasn't the point.

Ainsley held up a hand to shush her. "I have full custody. You get unlimited visitation rights."

"And if you go away for the weekend? Or if I need it on a Dad weekend?" While Ainsley did sometimes join me in visiting Dad every other weekend, I was the only one of us bound by the family court to see him so regularly. Once Ainsley turned eighteen, it became totally her call when to go to Dad's, and as a college student, packing up a suitcase and traipsing across town twice a month was usually too much of a hassle for Ains.

She hesitated. "Case-by-case basis. If one of us has a special event that weekend, it goes to that sister."

We turned to Brooke as one. She tented her fingers and looked between us, frowning. I was glad to see her taking the role of adjudicator seriously. After a couple of seconds pondering, she spoke. "I guess I'll allow it, on the condition that Darcy gets to pick two more things, now, and they're automatically hers. Deal?"

"Deal," I said.

"Don't hold back, Darc," Brooke warned.

I stuck my hands in my lap. "I won't."

"Oh, but not the Eve Lom," Ainsley said, lifting a hand. Brooke shot her a *look*, and Ainsley stuck her lip out. "Fine, deal. No conditions."

I was sorely tempted to snatch up the Eve Lom cleanser just to make a point. But I settled for a tinted moisturizer that was more my shade than Ainsley's anyway, and a perfume sample, ignoring Brooke's side-eye.

What could I say? Something about having Brooke nearby made me want to spread love.

It was a good thing she was so often nearby.

And damned if I was going to let Alexander Brougham mess with that.

THREE

Self-Analysis:
<u>Darcy Phillips</u>

Have known I was bisexual since I was twelve and I got so invested in a female character from a kids' show my stomach fluttered whenever she was on-screen, and I used to think about her when I fell asleep.

Despite the above, have never even kissed a girl. To be fixed.

Have kissed a guy, once, in a Target parking lot. He flicked his tongue in and out of my mouth without warning like it was a hole he'd been assigned to jackhammer.

Despite the above, still definitely get crushes on guys, too.

Almost-definitely in love with Brooke Nguyen.

Believe love can be simple . . . for other people.

———————

The Queer and Questioning Club—or Q&Q Club, as anyone who didn't have time for seven syllables called it—held meetings every Thursday lunch in classroom F-47. Today, Brooke and I were the first ones to arrive, and we set about pulling the chairs into a semicircle formation. We knew the drill.

Mr. Elliot burst in a minute after we had things set up, looking frazzled as usual, carrying a half-eaten rye sandwich. "Thank you, ladies," he said, shuffling through his messenger bag with a free hand. "I got held up by a crazed fan. I told him I didn't have time for autographs, but he started raving that I was his 'teacher' and I needed to 'sign his pass' so he could 'access the music room.' The demands of fame, am I right?"

Mr. Elliot was one of the youngest teachers in the school. Everything about him screamed "approachable," from his twinkling eyes, to his deep dimples, and his soft, rounded edges. He had dark brown skin, a pigeon-toed gait, and a chubby baby face that probably got him carded about as often as the seniors. Also, not to be dramatic, but I would have killed for him.

One by one, the rest of the club trickled in. Finn, who'd been out as gay for a year now, made a beeline for Brooke and me. Today, he wore a tie in a shocking yellow shade consisting of, upon closer inspection, rows upon rows of rubber ducks. Apparently, he was still testing the boundaries of how "appropriate" should be defined. Against his impeccable grooming, from his tidy black hair to polished black shoes to his high quality rectangular-framed glasses, his tie choice only stood out more. I'd both hate and love to see what would happen if boys were allowed to wear printed socks. Anarchy would be renamed Finn Park.

Raina, the only other openly bi member, came in next, scanned those of us sitting with a disappointed expression, and took a seat at the head of the semicircle. Raina was the student council leader, and had run against Brooke for the spot last semester (our school allowed both juniors *and* seniors to apply to hold the position). It'd been a tense race, and there was no love lost between the two girls. For a hot minute I'd thought Brooke had a chance of beating Raina, too.

Lily, who was somewhere on the ace spectrum but she wasn't sure where yet, came in with Jaz, a lesbian like Brooke, and Jason, gay. Finally, Alexei, pan and nonbinary, brought up the rear and we closed the doors to start the meeting.

We took turns running meetings, rotating every week, and this week was Brooke's turn. She sat up a little straighter, with her legs crossed at the ankles. When I first met her in freshman year, she'd hated public speaking to the point where I'd had to leave class to talk her through breathing techniques in the hall before she had a presentation. Then, after a year of working with the school counselor, she gained enough confidence that sometimes she even volunteered to speak. Like today, and when she ran for student council president. I didn't think she loved presenting, even now, but she was much harder on herself than she was on everyone else, so the less she wanted to do something, the more she forced herself to do it anyway.

"Let's start with"—she scanned the notepad she held between her shaking hands—"check-in. Clockwise, from me. I've had a generally good week, my mental health is in a good place, and everything's great at home. Finn?"

One by one, we went around the room, Mr. Elliot included. During these meetings he tried not to take on too much of an authoritative role. He said as long as the door was closed, we could view him as more of a queer mentor than a teacher, and it was a safe space to discuss inappropriate behavior or comments from other teachers without having to feel uncomfortable around him.

This week, check-in went fast. Some meetings we weren't able to get past check-in, because someone would bring up something they were struggling with, and the rest of the group would jump in to problem solve, offer support, or listen. It wasn't unusual for check-in to end with the whole group in tears.

"Next on the agenda was going to be the multi-school mixer, but we've postponed the date to next month because Alexei's going to Hawaii . . ." Brooke said in a voice so small it was like she was speaking to herself. I gestured for her to speak up, and she got a little louder, a small smile spreading. "Mrs. Harrison has given approval to do a presentation to the freshmen about how to contribute to safety in schools. Does anyone have any suggestions for specific topics to touch on?"

Finn cleared his throat. "I was thinking we could try and lean into this as a recruitment session," he said in a serious tone that didn't quite match the glint in his eyes. "I'm picturing all of us in glitter and feathers, choreography, maybe some laser lighting if we do well at the bake sale, that kind of stuff. By the end of it, if membership doesn't go up by two hundred percent, you can put me in solitary confinement."

Mr. Elliot jumped in. "Once again, Finn, we are not a cult, and we do not have recruitment targets."

"But sir, think of the children. Us. We're the children. We want more friends to play with."

"Make it sound creepier next time, Finn," I said, and Jaz snorted from across the semicircle, tossing her hair over one shoulder.

"Does anyone know any queer icons?" Finn pushed on. "I'm thinking a celebrity appearance could really add a wow factor here."

"Do I count?" Mr. Elliot asked.

"With respect, sir, that's a hell of a loaded question."

Right about now, Brooke should be jumping in to steer the conversation back to business. But she sat with a stiffened posture, raising her hand off its place in her lap every now and then, before lowering it, apparently losing her nerve.

Raina rolled her eyes, let out a sigh, and crossed one leg over the other, running her hands down her tight beige riding pants. She had a hard face to begin with, thin lipped and wide jawed, made all the harder by the sleek ponytail she scraped her straight, mouse-brown hair into. Today I was surprised her narrow eyes hadn't turned Finn into a gargoyle. Finally, she broke. "Okay, thank you, Finn," she said in a firm voice. "Lily, name a topic."

Lily blinked large green eyes and blushed a deep red at being put on the spot. "Um . . . harsher punishments for using queer terms as an insult?"

"Wonderful," said Raina, and she pointed a finger gun at Brooke. "Brooke, write that down."

I bristled as Brooke scribbled notes. Raina *did* know this wasn't student council, right? But Raina continued. "Alexei? Your thoughts?"

"Could we spend a couple of minutes on pronouns and why it's important to use correct ones?" they asked.

"Perfect, love that. Jaz?"

My phone buzzed in my skirt pocket—helpfully sewn in

post-purchase by Ainsley—and I pulled it out to peek at it surreptitiously. It was from Brougham.

Still on for later?

A feeling of dread flooded through me and clenched my chest. After stressing all yesterday, and tossing and turning all night, I'd finally managed to block out the thought of Brougham and his threats by focusing on school and normality. Now the whole thing came rushing back. I texted a quick reply.

Yup. 3:45.

Without quite meaning to, I leaned my arm against Brooke's a little, seeking comfort. She didn't lean back into me, but she didn't pull away, either.

And so the meeting continued, with Raina at the head, barking orders to Brooke every now and then. Mr. Elliot did look over at Brooke a few times, to see if she seemed upset, I guess, but he didn't intervene. He didn't usually unless things got out of hand.

A couple of times I almost, *almost* said something, but I wasn't brave enough to start an argument with Raina in front of everyone. It didn't stop me from simmering with a quiet outrage on Brooke's behalf during the rest of the meeting, though. Finally, the bell rang, and everyone headed back to class. As the leader, it was up to Brooke to stay behind and put the chairs back where they should be. Notably, Raina didn't take over *this* particular task.

As soon as the room emptied, Brooke let her distress show.

"Did you notice that?" she asked, throwing herself backward to sit on the edge of a desk and folding her arms in a huff.

"Raina's attempted coup? Yeah, she's not super subtle."

Brooke shook her head in disgust. "She thinks just because she's student council president that gives her authority over everyone, in any context. Next she'll be overruling the ref calls at football games."

"She's always had a big head," I said. "You get everyone's attention because they like and respect you. You don't have to fight for it."

"What, you think she's threatened by me?" Brooke asked.

"I don't think shit. I *know* she's threatened," I said, sitting on the desk across from her.

She pressed a hand against her chest. "Of *me*?" Even though she seemed skeptical, I got the feeling she sort of liked the idea.

I nudged my foot against hers. "Yes, of you! You gave her a run for her money during the election. I bet that girl's never been beaten at anything in her life."

"Yeah, but I *didn't* beat her."

"Which is a *travesty* I'll honestly never get over. Anyway, who cares? She made herself look stupid today. Everyone knows you're the one with class."

"I know, I shouldn't mind," Brooke said, looking down at her hands. "Usually I wouldn't."

That was true. She was practically the human version of a Care Bear. "What's up? You okay?"

Her face softened. "Yeah, yeah, totally. Just, argh, stressing about this stupid essay."

I burst out laughing. "You *still* haven't done it?"

She groaned and tipped backward. "Not even halfway!"

"What about those essay-help sessions they run in the library after school? Actually, I'm pretty sure it's Thursdays, right? Go today."

"*I can't*, Darcy, I have work tonight."

"Can't you call in sick?"

Brooke rolled her eyes back so far I could only see the whites, her eyelashes fluttering. "Negative. It's the launch of a hyped palette today, we're expecting a full house. They had to roster on five more of us to be safe. They low-key hinted that if anyone skips for any reason other than a coma, we might as well not come back."

"Harsh. All that over a palette?"

"It's pressed pigment," Brooke said, like that somehow explained everything.

"Oh, right, pressed pigment, of course."

"I have to work Saturday and Sunday, too. How am I going to get this done?"

"Do you want me to come over and help?"

She straightened and gave me an apologetic smile. "Darc, I love you, I do, but I want to get a *good* grade."

Laughing even harder, I pretended to double over in pain. "Ouch! *Ouch!*"

Brooke started giggling now, too. "Oh no, that came out so much harsher than I meant it to."

"Tell me how you really feel next time."

A movement in the doorway caught my eye, and the spell between us was broken. Brooke seemed to have noticed it at the same time, because we sobered up and turned as one.

Raina hovered in the doorway, looking hesitant. "I think I dropped . . . my phone."

We watched silently as she stalked by us to the semicircle.

Sure enough, her iPhone, cased in a leather wallet, lay on the floor by one of the chair legs. The silence was getting louder by the second, but it had gone on too long to break it. It must have been obvious I was irked by Raina's presence. The moment she'd interrupted had felt special.

Not so special it couldn't be shattered, though, apparently.

The closer it came to my meeting with Brougham, the more nervous I felt.

As much as I didn't want to admit it, I had no idea what I was doing. Giving advice from my computer was one thing. I could choose my words precisely, and I could always consult one of my books or YouTube coaches if something took me by surprise. Face-to-face? Different ball game. What if I stumbled or couldn't be sure of myself? Or I misremembered a piece of advice and made the wrong call? Or, most likely of all, what if I let Brougham's grating personality blind me from approaching things systematically and logically?

Stop it, I scolded myself. *You've given advice hundreds of times. You know this stuff inside out. Don't let a stupid, presumptuous guy intimidate you. You're the expert here.*

Still, my heart jumped and tumbled when the last bell rang.

I gathered up my stuff and headed to the library to get a start on my homework. I could've used Mom's classroom, but the thing is, she couldn't help but chat at me about her day when I sat in there, even if I told her I needed to concentrate.

The minutes trundled by like time itself was coated in

molasses, until *finally*, the clock ticked over to three twenty-five, and it was time for me to pack up, head to the pool, and get this the hell over with.

I got to locker eighty-nine a few minutes before Brougham was due to meet me, and I took the opportunity to check for witnesses and collect that day's haul. Three letters. Not bad. Prom was coming up in a few months, so this time of year always saw an influx of pleas for help from senior students. At the start, it'd given me a giddy thrill to give advice to students so much older than me, who'd never look twice at me in the hallway, let alone treat me with any measure of respect or deference. Now the thrill was long gone, and it was replaced by a new level of empathy.

There was nowhere to sit in the hallway, and honestly, I'd never been overly fussy about getting a little dirty, so I plopped right on the linoleum floor with my back against the lockers and settled in to scroll through my phone while I waited.

And waited.

And waited.

Three lifetimes later, I was perfectly done with waiting, thank you very much. Fucking Alexander Brougham. *Meet me at three forty-five*, he'd said. Well, here I was. And he was where, exactly?

Muttering a few choice insults under my breath, I got to my feet and stomped down the hall, through the double doors, and into the aquatic center. I didn't love it in there; the air always felt sticky and humid, thick with chlorine, and sound echoed in a way that didn't feel quite right. Like it weighed more, somehow.

It was quieter today than I was used to, which made sense, given I usually came in here when I was dragged in during swimming blocks in gym class. While the acoustics were usually choked with screams and splashes and the squeak of shoes on nonslip rubber flooring, today it was eerily calm. Just the steady drone of . . . something—the HVAC, I guessed—and the rhythmic slap of water from a single swimmer.

Brougham didn't notice me walk to the edge of the pool. His head was mostly submerged, and when he tilted it to the side to breathe, he faced the wall. His body moved down the length of the pool with impressive speed. I tried to walk along with him, but had to break into a jog to keep up. "Brougham," I called, but he didn't seem to hear me. Or, if he did, he ignored me. Which I wouldn't put past him, to be perfectly honest. *"Alexander."*

He hit the end of the pool, then flipped underwater. The change of direction made him tilt his head my way when he took a breath now. He stopped short after one stroke and shook his head like a dog that'd been dunked. "Is it quarter-to already?" he panted, treading water and pushing his wet hair back out of his face. He didn't even bother greeting me, which didn't do wonders for my patience.

"It's four o'clock." I gestured at the clock on the wall behind the starting blocks. His eyes followed where I pointed.

"Oh. So it is." Without apologizing for keeping me waiting, or thanking me for giving up my afternoon, he paddled over to me and lifted himself out of the pool with his arms in one smooth motion, causing his lithe muscles to bulge. Show-off. If I tried that maneuver I'd end up flopping on my side like a beached whale.

I scuttled backward to get out of his way, and he nodded at me. Apparently, that was my greeting. He strode over to the benches where he'd stashed his crumpled uniform, backpack, and towel, pulling his skin-tight, above-the-knee swim shorts so they loosened their grip on his thighs. "I still need to shower real quick," he said to me from an upside-down position as he haphazardly scrunched the towel around his hair. "I'll meet you outside in ten?"

"Oh *sure*," I said with as much sarcasm as I could inject into my voice.

If my sarcasm was noted, it wasn't acknowledged.

I stomped back to my waiting spot in the hallway, pulled my half-ponytail out lest it contribute to a stress headache, and plonked myself down on the floor. Might as well start to make my way through this week's questions, I figured.

The first letter I picked up was written on flower-bordered, pink notebook paper in handwriting that was refreshingly easy to read. Scanning the letter, I instantly caught an issue with the way this writer kept using the word "need." They "needed" texts from their boyfriend. They "needed" his attention.

I didn't adore the word "need," because it carried this heavy sense of expectation, and it made any letdown so much worse. I'd gotten a few bullet points into the Notes app on my phone, jotting down thoughts for my response email, when Brougham came out into the hall. He'd ditched his uniform for a clean pair of pants—black, although just as ankle-hugging as the tan ones he wore with the uniform—and a simple white T-shirt, his damp hair towel dried and sticking up at every angle. At least he was semi-dry today.

"Ready?" he asked, slinging his backpack over his shoulder. He was unsmiling, as usual. Now that I thought about it, I'd never seen any expression more cheerful than "careful nonchalance" on his face.

"*I've* been ready for about forty minutes."

"Great, let's go."

He started walking down the hall, and I had to scramble to catch up with him while simultaneously folding the letter back in its envelope. "Brougham?" He ignored me. *"Alexander!"*

He stopped short. "What?"

I reached him and stood still, folding my arms. I had to tilt my chin to face him down; I might have been tall, but he was taller. "I'm not your employee."

"What?"

"Just because you're paying me for my time doesn't mean you get to boss me around. And if you're late, you should apologize."

"Oh." He looked taken aback. "I'll still pay you from the time we agreed?"

"That's—Alexander, that's not the point."

But he still looked puzzled. Well, money did not buy common decency, that was for sure. "Um, what's your point then, sorry? And it's Brougham."

Well he *said* it was Brougham, but "Alexander" clearly got his attention. "My point is, don't be a dick. And it wouldn't kill you to say hello to me when you see me. I have other things I'd rather be doing right now, so a little friendliness wouldn't go astray."

I *swear* he almost rolled his eyes. I could practically see him fighting with his eyeballs to keep them in place. *"Hello, Phillips."*

His sarcasm game was as strong as mine. "It's Darcy. *Hello*, Brougham," I shot back, my tone equally as terse. "How was your *day?* It's good to *see* you. Where would you like to *go* to *do* this?"

"My house will work fine," he said, on the move again.

I stared after him, swallowing my outrage. Twenty-five dollars an hour. Twenty-five dollars an hour. If I'd had the chance to meet him before we struck our deal I would've applied an asshole tax and never agreed to less than fifty.

FOUR

Dear Locker 89,

I don't know whether it's time to break up with him. I keep trying to communicate, but it's like he doesn't hear me. I've told him about 20 times I need him to text me more, I need him to pay me more attention, and to come sit with me in the cafeteria at least SOMETIMES. But the more I communicate my needs, the more he avoids meeting them. One of his friends actually called me demanding the other day! Am I being demanding? Is it unreasonable to know what you need and to communicate that? Serious question. Be honest with me. I can take it.

Strangerthings894@gmail.com

Locker 89 <locker89@gmail.com>   5:06 p.m. (0 min ago)
to Strangerthings894

Hey strangerthings!

Let's do some redefining. It's totally reasonable to communicate your needs. But you seem confused about what your needs are. You don't *need* anything from your boyfriend. You want it. Saying we *need* something from someone else makes us feel like we can't live without them, or they completely control how we feel, which is not true. When you say you *need* him to do xyz, what I'm hearing is that your real need is to feel loved, and special, and wanted. And you can get that need met from people other than your bf! I recommend rewording the way you explain your needs to him. Tell him your real needs, and then let him know what kind of things he *could* do to help you feel loved, special, and wanted. People respond better to encouragement than criticism. Then it's on him. Once he understands that it's not about him and what he's doing wrong, but about you and how he can make you feel awesome, he might step up to the plate! And if he doesn't, that's when you ask yourself if you're satisfied getting those needs met through platonic relationships, or if maybe this isn't the right guy for you.

Good luck!
Locker 89

I swallowed hard in the driver's seat of Ainsley's car—she'd lent it to me for the day so I could fulfill my extortion requirements—as Brougham pulled off the road ahead of me into what I assumed was his house. To put it lightly, though, this was no house. It was a mansion. A fuck-off enormous mansion.

There were about a million different sections, room after room after room, dormer windows and bay windows and balconies and columns and cornerstones, fancy French windowpanes and a mixture of curved and boxy rooftops. The brick was a cool, calming shade of purple-gray, which, paired with the bluish roof and cream detailing, gave it an overall fairy tale feel. The front yard was immaculate, with trimmed hedges bordering a sprawling, two-lane driveway.

Come *on.*

There was no way I was taking my car up that driveway. It felt like eating a work-of-art cupcake. This driveway was meant to be observed, not used, right?

So I pulled over to the curb outside the gate instead. Brougham, who had driven straight up the driveway to park near the entrance, leaned against his car and watched me trek up the winding path with raised eyebrows. *When* I finally reached him, he gave me a pointed look, then led me to the front door.

"Do you have a butler?" I asked as we entered, suddenly excited. "Or, like, a chef or something?"

Look, it's not that I could necessarily be bribed with food, but let's just say if Brougham had a chef who could bring us tastefully presented after-school snacks like crustless sandwiches or dragon fruit salad, I'd be a lot more amenable to afternoon mansion visits.

But to my boundless dismay, Brougham gave me a look of disdain. "No, Phillips, we do not have a butler."

He was really not in a rush to forgive me for calling him

Alexander, was he? *"Sorry,"* I said. "Just, it seems like a lot of work to clean a mansion by yourself, that's all."

Brougham had the nerve to sigh at me. "Well, of course we have *cleaners,*" he said, the same way someone might say "of course we have a roof," or "of course we have a kitchen sink."

I hung behind to make a face at the back of his head. "Well of *course,*" I muttered. "Naturally. Who doesn't have cleaners? *Pfft.*"

"And it's not a mansion."

"Bull*shit* it isn't a mansion," I said with a flash of irritation. How was it Brougham managed to come across equally grating when he was bragging about his wealth *and* when he was underestimating it?

"It's not. Maybe it'd be considered one in, like, San Fran. But it wouldn't cut it in a town like this."

The look on his face was half pitying, half judgy. Well, excuse me for not being well versed on mansion politics before speaking, ever-so-sorry about that.

We'd entered a sweeping open space in the way of a grand foyer, complete with a wrought-iron balcony over our heads—I guessed so people could gaze patronizingly upon visitors from the great heights of the second floor—cream marbled flooring and a chandelier dripping crystals from the impossibly high ceiling. I bent my neck at an angle that was too close to ninety degrees to be safe, but right now my neck muscles had to take a backseat to taking all of this in. When we crossed into the hallway, my shoes slipped on the marbled floors, and I adjusted my pace to keep control. The last thing I needed was to go careening off track and collide with a mahogany desk or priceless Ming dynasty vase.

Brougham walked slightly ahead of me, making no real effort to match my slower speed. It was almost like he was trying to hurry me through the house. Probably to protect the vases, in all fairness.

The first indication we weren't alone was the clacking of heels against marble, an extra percussion element to Brougham's and my already out-of-sync footsteps. A woman sauntered into the hall ahead of us, through an archway to our left, in a cloud of French perfume. She was confident, she was sleek, and, unless I was reading her face entirely wrong, she was irritated to see us.

Mrs. Brougham, I assumed.

She looked something like the female Snapchat filter version of her son. Slender and fine boned, she shared his protruding navy-blue eyes and thick, chocolate-brown hair, although hers had subtle, warm highlights through the layers. She was dressed in an outfit that by all means should've looked completely uncoordinated, but on her looked like it came straight out of a *Vogue* streetwear editorial. She'd tucked a crisp white T-shirt into wide-legged pants made out of a black pleather kind of material, paired with black kitten heels and a black woven bracelet.

Brougham came to an abrupt halt, and I copied him. His mother surveyed him with a flat look, and narrowed her eyes. "Alexander, your father will be working late again," she said to Brougham without even acknowledging me, "so I have a friend over. We'll be in the renovated wing. Don't bother us unless it's an emergency."

Brougham didn't seem surprised at his mother's hostility. "Okay."

"If he tells you he's coming home early, text me."

"Okay."

They faced each other down, and I felt a weird sort of chill. It was obvious I was missing something between them, but for the life of me I couldn't pinpoint what. All I knew for sure was that the vibe was extremely uncomfortable, and I wanted to get out of there, pronto.

With a sharp nod, Mrs. Brougham glided out of the room. And I do mean glided. If it weren't for her heels' rhythmic clacking, I would've insisted she was carried out on some sort of invisible conveyer belt.

"Sure, nice to meet you, too," I whispered, before I could stop myself. It probably wasn't the *best* thing to say with her son still in earshot.

But if Brougham was offended he didn't show it. He just tore his eyes away from the door she'd left through and pursed his lips. "With my parents, you'll be better off lowering your expectations," he said. "We can go into the back room."

On the way through the maze that was his house, Brougham made a pit stop in the glossiest kitchen I'd ever seen. Everything was shiny and reflective, like someone had taken Photoshop to real life. Gleaming white countertops, pristine glass cabinets built into the walls guarding crystal plates and glasses. A mahogany island counter so reflective I could make out my awed expression on its side. The floor so polished I felt rude to be tracking my school shoes over it.

Brougham, still oblivious to my wonderment, dug around in his refrigerator—which I was sure contained only the very most expensive, fanciest, organic, locally sourced produce— and then emerged with a bunch of grapes and a small wheel of Brie. He set about arranging them on a plate, along with some water crackers, and only then did he glance up and notice my face.

"Sorry, will these do?" he asked.

Truly, a personal chef couldn't have whipped up anything

that would've delighted me more than the sight of a whole wheel of Brie. It's not like I'd never had cheese before, but it wasn't exactly a staple in either parent's house. This was all so *fancy*.

"It'll do, I suppose," I allowed.

In the back room—a second living room that smelled like rosewater, with floor-to-ceiling windows looking out over a groomed, unnaturally green backyard—Brougham flopped into a cream leather armchair, resting the plate on the glass end table with a clink. "So, how does this work?"

I shucked off my backpack, tucked my skirt under my thighs, and lowered myself into the matching chair. "It doesn't. I usually write emails, remember?"

"Okay, so, what do you do when you get a letter?"

"Depends on the letter."

Brougham's face was thoughtful as he pulled a grape off the bunch. He held it up with a questioning expression, and I nodded with a bit more enthusiasm than I meant to, and snatched it from midair when he tossed it my way. He was still a blackmailing asshole, so I didn't want to be too grateful, but it was nice to be fed.

Brougham watched me patiently, and I realized he was waiting for me to initiate. Part of me wanted to insist I had no idea what I was doing, because I kind of didn't, but that might be poking the beast here. Maybe the best thing I could do right now was tackle the familiar, hoping the unfamiliar would come as a natural next step.

Wordlessly, I fished today's three letters from my backpack. I scanned them all, and, thankfully, one of them was vague enough I was certain it wouldn't give the writer's identity away to Brougham. "Okay, so," I said. "'Dear locker eighty-nine, I'm really into this girl, but we're ac-

quaintances at best. She's a year below me so we don't have
any classes together or share any friends. Sometimes I feel
like she might be sending me signals when I do see her
around, but I'm worried I might be seeing what I want to
see. How do I ask her out without putting my foot in it or
coming across like a massive creep? 'Hey, you're hot, wanna
go out with me?' is a weird hallway icebreaker."

Please help, ray_of_sunshine001@gmail.com, I finished
in my head. Just in case Brougham happened to know who
the email address belonged to.

Brougham popped a grape in his mouth and rolled it into
his cheek. "That doesn't give us much to go off," he said.

I held my hand out palm up, and he dutifully picked off
another grape and threw it to me. "It gives us enough," I
said. "You just have to break it down. We know they're at
least a sophomore, because they're a year above this girl.
We know they don't share friends, so we don't have to worry
too much about someone being off-limits. We know they're
at least on speaking terms, because they called the girl an
acquaintance, not a stranger. We know the writer is at least
a little self-aware, because they've thought about this girl's
hypothetical reaction to being asked out without any warning. That also tells us the writer probably hasn't done anything rash to scare the girl off previously, which helps a lot."

Brougham looked thoughtful. For a brief moment I
wondered if I'd impressed him. But then he narrowed his
eyes. "You think the writer's a girl," he said. Statement, not
question.

"Not necessarily."

"You were avoiding pronouns. How come you don't think
it's a guy? Or did the email address give it away?"

"I don't think it's a guy or a girl. I literally have no way of knowing. Why would you think they were anything right now?"

He didn't seem to realize the question was rhetorical. "Well, because statistically, straight guys outnumber girls who like girls. And," he added, before I could interject, "people with other genders."

He looked smug for some reason. Like he'd somehow bested me. I flared up. "So?"

"So, if you had to put your money on anything, you'd put it on this being a guy, with the information we have. Right?"

"But I don't have to put money on anything." My voice was thin.

"Now you're just being stubborn," he said. "You don't have to take it personally. I'm only talking facts."

"So am I. The fact is, I have nothing to gain by putting bets on a gender, so statistics don't matter. I don't know their gender, so I'm not going to guess it. There's no reason to. We have words for not knowing a person's gender. Isn't it more stubborn to use pronouns we don't know, when our language caters to neutrality?"

I stared him down. He held my gaze. Then, to my amazement, he shrugged a single shoulder. "That makes perfect sense. You're right."

This sudden surrender made me suspicious. "But?"

"But nothing. You made a good point."

I kept waiting for the dig, but it didn't come. After a beat, I had no choice but to accept it wasn't *going* to come. But I still felt snippy for being challenged over something so stupid, so I couldn't resist pressing a little more. "Aren't you best friends with Finn? What does he say about stuff like that?"

"Stuff like what?"

Okay, now he was being willfully obtuse. "You know it's rude to assume pronouns, and you know I'm part of the Q and Q Club, and you picked a fight over it anyway. Why? To irritate me?"

Brougham had the nerve to look shocked. "I'm sorry. I wasn't trying to be rude. I was just interested in your thought process."

"Well, now you have your answer."

"Yes, now I have my answer." He didn't quite smile, but for a moment, I swore I saw amusement in his eyes. "You do realize I'm agreeing with you here?"

"I guess I've never had agreement feel so much like an argument," I shot back.

"Maybe you shouldn't classify a respectful dialogue as an argument, and you'll feel better. And to answer your question, Finn doesn't have any issue explaining why he feels something is right or wrong."

"Oh, I bet he *loves* explaining to you why his sexuality is right or wrong," I said dryly.

"I never said anything about his sexuality. And I guess he must be fine with explaining things to me, because he keeps hanging out with me." Brougham raised his eyebrows. "And *he* does it for free."

"You aren't paying me to hang out with you. You're paying me to help you."

"You're right. Maybe we should get back to business, then."

He passed me another grape. I snatched it from him with a huff, a little more harshly than I meant to, and crushed it between my teeth. "Gladly. So, let's start with the most important thing. Who broke up with who?"

"Isn't it obvious?" Brougham asked. "I'm the one trying to get her back."

"You'd be surprised."

He looked unconvinced, but played along. "She broke up with me."

"What happened?"

Brougham squinted his eyes like he was recalling a far-gone memory. "Something about me being too handsome and talented."

"Gee, that's so believable, tell me more."

"Why does it matter, anyway?"

"Why does the reason for the breakup matter?" I asked in disbelief. "Did you really just ask me that?"

"I mean, not every letter includes *everything*, every little detail, right? You still manage to get a lot correct, though, yeah?"

"Almost always."

"See? So, you must not need everything."

I hesitated, picking my words. "Usually I can tell what the theme of the issue is. People generally have a good sense of the problem, they just don't necessarily know what caused it, or how to fix it. Then I match the problem to a theory, and give advice based on the one that fits best."

"Theories?"

"Relationship theories. Like attachment style, how to deal with commitment phobia, the no-contact rule, men are from Mars, how oxytocin is triggered at different times in different people . . ."

A blank stare. "You've always known all this stuff?"

I couldn't help but sit up a little straighter. "I've built my knowledge base. But I've always been interested in it. Since middle school, at least."

"Where did it start?"

I had to think for a minute to pinpoint the original theory I'd stumbled on, the one that'd kicked off my whole fascination. "Do you know the book *He's Just Not That Into You*?"

"With Scarlett Johansson? Sure, but I don't know what it's about."

"That's the movie, not the book, but anyway," I muttered under my breath. "The general idea behind it is if a guy doesn't reach out to you or make an effort, he doesn't have feelings for you."

"Groundbreaking."

"Well, for a lot of people, yeah, it was. I read it years ago and I loved it, and I started reading as many relationship self-help things as I could. Then I found YouTube, and podcasts, and it kind of went from there."

"But what about the locker?"

This was the first time I'd ever shared this secret with anyone. (Ainsley didn't count, because she'd followed the whole saga in real time.) As much as I wasn't exactly Brougham's biggest fan, it was actually nice to be able to spill it all to someone. Two and a half years was a long time to keep a secret. "I started it at the beginning of ninth grade. I had all this relationship knowledge, but no one to apply it to." Honestly, I didn't know if I wanted the rush of being able to help people, or simply to experiment on others to see if these theories had any basis in reality. Maybe it was a bit of both. "And when you're around the offices after hours as much as I am, it's not as hard to find . . . certain information as you'd think, so I happened to find which of the lockers was unassigned, and its combination. Our school still uses hard-copy records for that stuff, go figure, so it was easy enough to just remove number eighty-nine from the assignment sheet. Then one afternoon while I was waiting for my mom, I made some flyers and stuck them in random lockers, saying if they wanted free relationship advice, they could put an anonymous letter into locker eighty-nine with an email address."

"And people did it?" Brougham asked.

"One person did it. And I guess my advice worked, because they told some friends the flyer was legit, and it snowballed. Later in the year, someone dropped a tip in the locker with a thank-you note, and it occurred to me half the kids at our school were millionaires. Or their parents were, anyway. So I gave people a few weeks' warning that advice wouldn't be free anymore by putting it at the bottom of every email. And the whisper network did the rest for me. I started out charging five, now I charge ten. I could probably do even more, but I don't want business to drop."

Brougham watched me intensely, not reacting, but not breaking eye contact, either. For the first time, I understood why Ainsley found him attractive. That stare made me feel like I was telling the most interesting story in the world. "But why anonymously?" he asked. "Why don't you just do what we're doing with everyone? People would pay."

He wasn't wrong about that. People would pay. That meant more than even Brougham probably realized. In a school where seven-figure family incomes were the norm, it really was a lucky break for me that we had a uniform. Without it, my status as a scholarship student would've been abundantly clear to anyone who looked at me. But even with the uniform, kids found a way to flaunt their wealth. Fendi bags and camel Gucci skirts and Cartier watches decorated every second ensemble. Each time a new iPhone was released, it was all you'd see in the hallways by the next Monday. People usually didn't make comments about older models, per se, but anyone who lagged in upgrading would find themselves on the receiving end of lingering, pointed looks anytime they checked their phone around other students.

There was no way in hell my parents would be able to keep up with all that. My locker income was the only thing that gave me even a fighting chance at fitting in with the other students here. Obviously, ten dollars an email wasn't going to get me Fendi and Gucci, but it was enough to cover a decent iPhone plan and the odd thrift store haul. Add in Ainsley's skills with a sewing machine, and on a good day I could pass for upper middle class. And, thankfully, that was enough to get me by.

So, yeah, some extra income would *not* go astray.

But if people found out it was me running the locker, all the fancy clothes in the world couldn't protect me from the awkwardness that would follow. How would I have a normal conversation with someone in English class when they knew I knew all about how they lost their virginity? Or that they'd secretly cheated on their boyfriend? Or that they sabotaged their sister's relationship so they could have a shot in her place?

And a million times more pressing than that, the reason I would never, *ever* admit to being behind the locker, was that I'd used it to do something awful to Brooke. If she ever found out about that, who knew if she'd ever forgive me again. She'd *definitely* never trust me again. I wouldn't, in her shoes.

Locker eighty-nine couldn't become a real person.

I could've opened myself up and explained all that to

Brougham. Problem was, I didn't really like him, let alone trust him.

In the distance, a door slammed. I made out the murmur of voices, then footsteps that grew closer, but not so close I could see who they belonged to. One of the voices was male. And angry. Was this the "friend" Brougham's mother had mentioned? Or his father, home early?

I shifted in my seat, suddenly overtaken by the urge to make myself small. My home life was happy, by all accounts. It'd been years since my parents divorced. But still, the sound of adults stomping and yelling was enough to make me feel eight years old again, crawling into bed with Ainsley to seek reassurance I never really believed.

Brougham was totally unruffled. The only sign he'd noticed anything was a blink, and the slightest tilt of his chin toward the voices. Then he grabbed a cracker and nibbled on it thoughtfully. "Well," he said. "I think it's pretty clear we're not getting anywhere today."

"What?"

At first I thought he might be kicking me out because of the nearby argument, despite the fact that he barely seemed to have heard it, but then he continued with, "You're obviously not prepared, and so far, I've learned nothing useful."

I gaped. "You barely gave me a chance—"

"How about we call it for today? Let me know when you have something prepared, and we can regroup then."

My lips tightened as I fought the urge to tell him to call this whole thing off. How was it even humanly possible to teach your child such shitty manners? If his parents hadn't been so obviously preoccupied with an argument down the hall, I'd have had half a mind to tell them off for letting their son develop *this* for a personality.

But I somehow managed to keep my cool. I just folded my arms and followed Brougham silently out of the room, back through that hallway. The closer we got to the front door, the louder the man's shouting got—something to do with a lie he'd caught Brougham's mother telling—and the more I shrank into myself.

Truthfully, I was glad Brougham chose this moment to lose faith in my abilities. All I wanted to do was get out of this spotless, charmless mansion with its echoing halls and unwelcoming vastness. How had I thought it was beautiful when I first got here?

If this was where Brougham was raised, no wonder he was so cold.

FIVE

Locker 89 <locker89@gmail.com>   6:45 a.m. (0 min ago)
to ray_of_sunshine001

Dear Ray of Sunshine,

You're right. Asking someone out without a foundation
might be the preferred mode for some, but for the rest of
us, it's a little too confronting, and the risk-to-benefit ratio
is too big! It sounds like you fall into the latter category.
In that case, I would approach things gradually. Find an
excuse to spend time with this person—one-on-one is
great, groups work too in a pinch. Your best bet is finding
something you have in common, then using that as a
jumping-off point. "Oh, you love Stephen King, too?
I've been wanting to stream his new movie for ages,
but none of my friends are brave enough to watch with
me." Or "I've seen you at the game the last few weeks,
are you hitting up the next one? My friends bailed
on me." Or "I love baking too, I'd love to share tips
sometime."

You've got to have *something* in common (and let's be tough but fair, if you don't, maybe she's not the best match for you anyway?). Once you're hanging out, you can take the opportunity to a) develop your friendship, and b) scope out your chemistry. Rest assured, the "friend zone" is *not* a real thing. There is nothing wrong with pursuing a platonic relationship for now while you figure out the next steps, and, in fact, the chances of any romantic relationship working out will be increased if you both know you get along, have things in common, and are comfortable around each other. Just keep it consensual, and remember just because she agreed to hang out, does not mean she's agreed to a date with you.

If you want to figure out if it's safe to ask her about her feelings, body language is your friend. Look for prolonged eye contact (if she holds it long enough to feel *too* long, it's a good sign), casual physical contact (the arm touch), a prolonged hug hello or good-bye on her end, lots of leaning in, if she's spending a lot of time looking at your lips . . . these are all possible indications she might be receptive to you asking her out. I believe in you, Ray! It's much easier to ask someone out once you've had the chance to gauge their interest and to show them how much fun you have together.

Good luck!
Locker 89

"Now, don't forget about the paper due tomorrow," Mr. Elliot said. It was Monday afternoon, and the seconds were ticking closer to the final bell. "There will be no extensions granted for anyone without an extremely valid excuse, and 'I was too tired' is not one of them. Please note, I am not your father, and I don't love you, so appealing to my humanity is a waste of time you could be spending on your homework. Clear?"

A few halfhearted murmurs from the class, but nothing too enthusiastic. I glanced up and caught Brooke's eye one row ahead of me. She gave a dramatic grimace. The bell rang, and everyone shot to their feet, chairs scraping and shoe soles squeaking and friends calling to each other across the room. Mr. Elliot raised his voice to be heard over the cacophony. "This isn't an exercise in paper conservation, so I encourage you to *meet the word count*. As much as I appreciate your thoughtfulness in giving me less work to grade, which I might add I do *on my own time* after dinner, if you can't write more than half a page on symbolism it makes me look bad. And I *hate* looking bad, because Ms. Georgeson always manages to slip in a dig my way about it at the staff Christmas party. Do you want to ruin Christmas for me?"

I stopped outside the classroom and pressed myself flush against the wall to avoid the flood of tan-and-navy-clad students pouring into the halls while I waited for Brooke. She'd warned me before class she wanted to hang back to ask a question about the essay, and she was my ride home that day, because Mom had to stay behind for a staff meeting and Ainsley was at class until four thirty.

I zoned out while I waited, until suddenly my attention caught on Finn and Brougham joining the main artery from one of the smaller capillary halls, along with two of their friends, Hunter and Luke.

Brougham and Finn seemed to be the unofficial leaders of their pack of four. Together, they resembled what I imagined it'd look like if a puppy made best friends with a particularly cranky cat. While Brougham stalked the halls with sharp eyes, barely reacting to the jokes and chatter of his friends, Finn bounded, clapping Brougham on the shoulder, snatching Hunter's phone from his grasp, and reading something aloud from it to Luke's delight.

I didn't mean to stare as much as I was, but I couldn't help but wonder what on earth the puppy saw in the cat. Then the cat spotted me, and I froze, caught red-handed in my goggling.

He held eye contact with me, and I felt like maybe I should be waving, or something? But what if Finn noticed, and asked how we knew each other? And then what if Brougham told him, and Finn told literally everyone he'd ever met, and then my whole life fell apart?

I didn't wave. Neither did Brougham.

My stare was ripped away from him when someone threw their arms around me from behind, and Brooke's musky vanilla perfume filled my vicinity. She swung me from side to side, chanting my name.

"Yes?" I laughed, wriggling out of her grip, and turned to face her. She looked especially magnetic today, with her long, dark hair falling in loose waves, a swipe of eyeliner, and a mischievous sparkle in her deep brown eyes. My stomach kicked up, and a grin spread as wide as my cheeks would allow. She hadn't needed to touch me, but she had. Did that mean something? Had she wanted to hug me as much as I wanted to hug her?

"So," she said, tipping her head and tapping one foot behind the other in the way she did whenever she had a favor to ask.

"So?" I folded my arms and leaned against the wall.

She stepped in to keep the space between us close, and a mixture of hope and delight jolted through me like a shock. Everything in my periphery had vanished at that point, so the only thing that existed was Brooke.

"So, I know I was crappy and insulted your essay-writing abilities," she said. I could feel her body heat.

"Correct, it was very hurtful. I've been crying myself to sleep every night since."

"Right, super sorry about that. Anyway, I'm desperate, for real. Is it too late to take you up on your offer to help?"

Wow. If Brooke was admitting defeat—or at least, impending defeat—she must be seriously struggling. My mouth was open to say "of course I'll help" before she'd even finished her sentence, then I remembered I couldn't. Brougham and I had agreed to take two tonight, after he finished dryland training. I mean, I *could* cancel, but my parents had raised me to consider bailing on someone at the last minute pretty damn rude.

The problem was, I couldn't exactly tell Brooke what my plans were tonight.

"Um, I, well . . . I'm busy," I said weakly.

Brooke's face fell, and everything shattered. Fuck Brougham, fuck Brougham, fucking, fucking *fuck* Brougham. "Oh," she said.

"I promised Ains I'd help her with a video."

I'd just lied to Brooke. I didn't need to lie. I could've left it at "I'm busy." But just saying I was busy felt like a blow off, and I couldn't stand it if Brooke thought I didn't want to see her, when that couldn't be further from the truth.

"That's fine. I'll be fine. I just, yeah, need to sit down and *focus*, I guess."

She didn't sound certain. But of course she didn't. She wouldn't have asked for help if it wasn't a last resort.

"If you need help, English is my best subject."

The voice came from behind me, and Brooke and I both looked up to see who'd spoken.

It was Raina. She stood awkwardly, looking at the floor and pulling on the ends of that too-tight ponytail. This alone was unlike her. She was usually forceful and confident—when she pushed her way through a crowd, it was a little like experiencing the running of the bulls. Here and now, though, she seemed almost hesitant.

If I was shocked to hear an offer of assistance from her, Brooke sounded even more so. "I, uh, oh. Hi, Ray."

"Hi." Raina's eyes flickered up briefly at this, but she didn't smile. "You're reading *The Kite Runner*, right? Mr. Elliot assigns that every year. I'm not doing anything tonight, so. I'd be happy to help." It sounded like the words themselves pained her to say them.

"Help . . . me?" Brooke asked dumbly. I didn't blame her. Raina's attitude toward Brooke ranged from mild disdain at best to outright disgust at worst. This? This was close to a cease-fire.

"Why?" I asked shortly.

Raina looked at me directly now, her gaze icy. "Because it looks terrible if someone on the council fails a major assessment piece," she said.

Well, that did make more sense for Raina.

"I'm not going to *fail*," Brooke protested, but she sounded unsure.

"Do you want a hand or not?"

Brooke hesitated. Good. She wasn't falling for whatever

ploy this might be. For a second, I'd—"I have to drop Darcy home now," Brooke said.

"Well, I'm free whenever. How about if you decide to take me up on it, you shoot me a message on Insta?"

She didn't even wait for Brooke's reply, just turned on her heel and all but sprinted down the rapidly emptying hall. Brooke and I stared after her.

"Do not message her," I said.

"You don't think?"

"I do not think. That was *way* too weird."

"It was, wasn't it?"

"Do *not* message her."

"Okay. I won't."

Brooke looked at me, and I looked at her, and we burst out laughing at the ridiculousness of it all. Raina offering to help Brooke out for no gain. What was next? Brougham developing a soft, warm disposition?

After that random-ass display, nothing could surprise me too much.

I had about half an hour before Brougham was due to arrive for round two. Even though he'd given me way less time to prepare than I would've liked—while simultaneously ruining my potentially romantic night with Brooke—at least I'd been able to grab a notebook from the staff supplies closet at school. That was a start, right? Now, to work on the personalized plan for His Lordship of Demands and Condescension, Alexander Brougham the First.

I shoved my laptop backward on my desk to make room for the notebook, then opened it to page one. After some thought, I settled on a title page.

THE EX-GIRLFRIEND GETTER-BACKER EXPERIMENT

STARRING:
DARCY PHILLIPS—A LITERAL MIRACLE WORKER
ALEXANDER BROUGHAM—SINGLE, BUT NOT QUITE READY TO MINGLE

I devoted a few minutes to decorating it with hearts, lips, sparkles, and stars, until I felt too guilty to keep procrastinating. Okay, all right, focus. I decided to start with a list of things I knew about Brougham. That seemed like a good bouncing-off point.

Character Analysis:
Alexander Brougham

Thinks he's much hotter than he is.

Total entitled asshole.

No wonder Winona left him.

No ability to problem solve, because he usually solves issues by throwing unlimited cash at them until they go away.

Doesn't care about anyone but himself!

After a moment's thought, I ripped this page out and crumpled it up. Better not let Brougham see that one. But this helped. Well, helped in that I now knew what we had to devote today's session to: information gathering. A relationship assessment, or postmortem, if you will. I couldn't begin to help Brougham until I knew what went right in the first place, as well as what went wrong.

Energized, I darted down the hall to Ainsley's room. Again, the air was clogged with vanilla and caramel. Kneeling on her plush carpet, surrounded by scissors and scraps of fabric and sewing patterns, was Ainsley. Apparently, she'd started work on her next creation the moment she got home from class.

A lot of the time she kept her door closed so she could film her next YouTube video in peace. Once I'd burst in on her during what was meant to be a time-lapse take, and she'd raged at me so dramatically our neighbor poked her head over the fence to check no one was hurt. But her open door now was my green light, so I went in without hesitation, carefully stepping around the bomb site of material and errant clothespins. "What are you working on?" I asked.

Ainsley was halfway through tracing a pattern onto the back of a pale blue strip of cottony fabric, so she didn't take her eyes off it while she answered. "I found a hideous bag of a lace dress at Jenny's," she said, referring to Jenny's Thrift Store, one of Ainsley's favorite haunts, "that I think'll work well as a two-piece crop and skirt set. I'm making a new lining for it because it's practically see-through right now, and then"—she grabbed a pair of scissors—"I'm thinking like an elastic, frill trim on the bottom of the top part."

"Nice. That'll look awesome."

"I hope so. Will you be my model?"

"For a crop top?" I cringed. "I think I'll pass. I can't wait to see you in it, though. I bet you'll look incredible."

Ainsley smiled to herself, pleased at the compliment.

She had always been thin, narrow hipped, and tall, taking after Dad's side of the family in height and figure. Her hips and chest had gained gentle curves over the last few years, but she was still very slim by all measures, more like our paternal aunts. I was tall, too—at five foot nine, I towered over most girls my age—but I had Mom's bone structure. "Child-bearing hips," Mom had commented when I was still a child myself, an eleven-year-old who'd just gotten her first period and suddenly exploded outward with hips and breasts that couldn't be contained by any of my old school clothes.

At the time, I couldn't have cared less if my hips were ideal for sliding out babies with ease and grace, I just didn't want to be the only kid in the grade who had to go up two uniform sizes in a year to accommodate puberty's offerings. These days, I liked my hips, and I liked my boobs. Even if they meant that I couldn't get away with borrowing any of Ainsley's old size-six school clothes.

But the above did *not* mean I wanted to model a crop top on a channel with thousands of subscribers, thanks all the same. Loving my body didn't make me magically immune to stage fright, or to comments from nasty, sexist strangers on whether girls should or should not be wearing revealing clothing to begin with. I didn't know how Ainsley did it. Anonymity was a warm blanket, wrapping me in a safe cocoon free from personal attacks.

"What's up, anyway?" Ainsley asked as she dug around in her wicker sewing kit for measuring tape. "How was Q and Q Club?"

"That was yesterday. They moved it to Thursdays for Mr. Elliot this year. I *told* you."

"Okay, but counterpoint, I'm resistant to change and repress that kind of stuff."

"To answer your question, they're all missing you desperately."

"Oh, wow, I almost believed you with *that* tone."

"They've erected a statue in your honor."

"It's the least they could do."

"That's what I said. Hey, can I borrow your bulletin board?"

"Sure, it's behind my desk. What for?"

I crawled across her bed to her desk and stuck my hand down the gap to retrieve it. "Brougham's coming around soon. I need equipment."

Ainsley, who was well informed about my Brougham experiences following yesterday's meeting, snorted. "What kind? Pepper spray?"

"Just the board will do. Thank you!"

"Hey, can you guys make sure you keep it down?" Ainsley called out as I retreated with her bulletin board. "I'm gonna be recording my voice-over in thirty."

"No problem."

Back in my room, I propped the bulletin board up on my bed, then arranged some pages of blank paper, some Sharpies, and my trusty new notebook on my desk. Right as I was finishing up, there was a knock at the front door.

"You play nice now, Darc. No murdering!" Ainsley called out from her room as I went to answer it.

I ignored her.

When the door swung open to reveal Brougham, my first thought was how out of place he looked on our eclectic front porch. I'd expected him to come straight here after dryland training, but he'd obviously gone home to clean up first. His silhouette was neat and preppy, skinny chinos under a pressed, bottle-green shirt with the sleeves carefully folded to his elbows. His hair had been swept into a side part and styled in waves so fluffy and careless they had to have been placed and held with a ton of product. Beneath his spotless, polished brown boots, weathered, chipped floorboards creaked and splintered. Then, surrounding him, a mess of garden gnomes and flowerpots with plants spilling out in every direction, dirt scattered on the boards from the last time Mom attempted to garden. Above his head, tinkling wind chimes and hanging planters overflowing with flowers, some thriving, some dry and withered. Behind him, our porch railing with its layers and layers of Christmas lights, left in place so we didn't have to put them up all over again every year.

Brougham's arms were folded tightly over his chest, his glower even more pronounced than usual. "Well, you look like a summer's day," I deadpanned, and he moved forward to enter without waiting for a proper invitation. I jumped aside to get out of his way. "Sure, absolutely, make yourself at home."

"Ta." He stepped into my living room, glanced around with an unreadable expression, then nodded at me. "Shall we?"

Like he owned the damn house. "We're in my bedroom, upstairs."

At least he let me lead the way to my own bedroom. Once we had the door closed, I felt a little calmer. The rest of the house had its fair share of mess, thanks to Mom and Ainsley, but at least my room was neat. It felt like Brougham had less to judge in here.

I pointed at my desk chair. "You can sit there."

He obeyed, rested one arm on the desk, crossed one leg over the other, and put on a pair of dark brown, square-rimmed reading glasses that probably cost more than Ainsley's car. They suited his face shape perfectly, somehow softening the sharp edges of his jaw and cheekbones, and the straight line of his eyebrows. He flipped open the notebook. "A literal miracle worker?" he asked, looking at the title page.

I leaned over him to pick a Sharpie. This close to him, I could smell his cologne, a heady combination of musk and something sweet. Not nearly as nice as Brooke's perfume. "Yes."

"There's *so* many sparkles."

I cleared my throat. "Yup. Okay. So, step one: your personality."

Brougham sputtered. *"Pardon?"*

"You"—I pointed at his chest—"need to stop being so *serious*. I don't mean to sound like a random man on the street, but you should smile more. If you smiled, like, *ever*, you might make the person you're talking to feel warm and comfortable. Which some people report to be nice, when on a date."

Brougham was blinking quite rapidly. "She did date me once."

"Yeah, and then she dumped you." Well, *now* we had a real emotion on his face. Acidic loathing, to be precise. "So, let's practice making Winona feel warm and comfortable. Go on, tell a joke, I'll show you."

"I like my dignity."

"Come on, a knock-knock joke or something, it doesn't have to be good."

"Ah, no. No, thank you."

"Okay, fine. I'll tell the joke, and you pretend I'm Winona."

"My imagination isn't vivid enough for *that* feat."

"Fuck you and try!"

A stony glare, then a slight head dip that was apparently a go-ahead.

"Brougham, what's a pirate's favorite letter?"

He stared at me. "You're not serious?"

"I'm not feeling very charmed right now, Brougham, so play along, would you?"

He let out a sigh sufficiently loud and long enough to let me know *just* how he felt about this exercise, then rolled his eyes and offered, "R?"

I hopped on the spot and clapped my hands. "Ahh, you'd *think* so, but his true love be the C!" My pirate voice was good enough to be on Nickelodeon voice-overs.

Brougham blinked and scrunched his mouth up in a pitying sort of way. He didn't laugh even a little bit.

"Like, 'sea,'" I said.

"Oh, don't worry, I got it."

"*Brougham!* You're not even trying."

"Trust me, if a girl makes a joke like that on a date, any inclination I have to flirt with her will evaporate."

"What if she's nervous?"

"Wouldn't blame her," he said mildly. "I *am* intimidating."

"Then, when you're *laughing*"—I raised my eyebrows at him, pointedly—"you can grab their arm and act like it's just because you found them so funny. Like this," I demonstrated, buckling forward in sudden, fake laughter, and gripped his toned bicep.

He surveyed my hand on his arm with a look of mild alarm. "You know what?" he asked, removing my hand delicately. "I think I'll be okay without the flirting tips."

"Fine." I wasn't thrown. I came *prepared* today. "Next, we're going to do a timeline of your relationship with Winona."

"Why?"

My head whipped up, and I damn near shot flames from my eyeballs. "Because I said so, Brougham, god*damnit.*"

"Darcy, no *murdering*!" Ainsley's voice sung out from down the hall.

Brougham's eyes flickered toward the door. "Okay, sorry." He didn't sound sorry. "Go on."

"Right," I stuck the marker in my mouth and pulled the lid off with my teeth. The tinny smell of the Sharpie cleared out my sinuses. "Wew wid you guysh meet?"

"On a field trip bus. I accidentally knocked her backpack off her seat."

I nodded, leaned over him, and drew a stick figure round-kicking a backpack into midair, next to a shocked-looking stick figure gaping on a vague imitation of a bus seat.

"It was absolutely nothing like that," Brougham said.

"It's called artistic expression, Brougham, look it up." I finished off the drawing with a flourish and stuck it to the board with a thumbtack. "Perfect. First date?"

"It was actually a group thing, and we—"

"Doesn't count. First real date."

Brougham regarded me like he was hoping I might combust. "We went bowling."

I drew two stick figures gazing into each other's eyes, gently caressing a bowling ball between them.

Brougham sighed when he saw the final product. "Sure. Put it up."

It joined the board. "How long were you two together?"

"About six months."

"So, what made you work? It must have been good for a while."

Brougham took a moment to answer, and in that time his face softened. Without his trademark expressionless mask, his eyes looked bluer, somehow. They'd gone from navy to almost azure. Like this, they looked dramatic, maybe even expressive, rather than bulgy. His fingers lightly traced the corner of his mouth, in a way that seemed unconscious. "We had fun," he said. "She made me feel like a little kid. Sometimes we'd drive to the ocean and just hang out for hours, talking and mucking around and shit. Climbing trees, playing truth or dare, that sort of stuff."

"Is that your best memory of being with her? Going to the beach?"

His eyes locked somewhere in the distance. What was he seeing? "No. No, the best memory was when we went to Disneyland."

"Yeah?"

"Hmm." His voice was low, barely above a whisper. "We got there at opening and spent the day going between the parks, and we had a competition going over who could get the most ridiculous PhotoPass picture. Then we watched World of Color, and I told her I loved her."

An excursion that could be extended or cut short depending on how it was going. Lots of things to do. Memories to talk about to stir up nostalgia. Plenty of opportunities to change pace, and do something distracting if things turned awkward or the conversation died. Lots of chances for physical contact and intimacy.

It was perfect.

I lowered the pen. This didn't need to go on the board. I could visualize it all now. I had the whole plan in my head. "How long has it been since you talked to Winona?"

Brougham went back to staring into the distance. When he replied, he spoke slower than usual, enunciating carefully. "I *may* have been acting petty."

"Can you be more specific here?"

"I decided if we were going to speak again, she'd have to

reach out. Because she was the one who dumped me, you know? At first, I hoped she was bluffing and she'd crack, or regret it or whatever. But then I realized she's not gonna reach out, and I probably blew it by going silent for a month, so I asked you for help."

Usually, when I got a letter, I accepted everything the writer told me at face value. There was a certain freedom that came with spilling your guts anonymously, and people often confessed to some pretty bad behavior. But face-to-face was different, and something wasn't adding up with Brougham's version of events. He and Winona had shared a great relationship, then she dumped him out of nowhere, and he decided to stop talking to her for a month in response? Nope. My bullshit meter was red-hot.

There was one possible explanation, though.

The first time I'd read about commitment-phobes, I'd been surprised to find they didn't present as loner, anti-commitment types. In fact, I'd learned that often, they were romantics, who believed in "The One," but would inevitably decide the person they were with didn't meet their criteria around the time the relationship started settling in for the long haul. Then they'd grow cold and distant, push their partner away, and—even stranger—often idolize their partner in hindsight and want them back after the breakup. Until, of course, things got too serious again.

It was textbook. But hey. I wasn't Brougham's therapist. He'd hired me to help him get Winona back. What he did after that was on him. And in terms of winning her back, he'd accidentally done exactly what I would've wanted him to.

"You didn't blow it," I murmured.

Brougham's eyes lit up. "I didn't?"

"No." I whipped the notebook out from underneath him and scrawled a title on the next page.

STAGE ONE: DISNEYLAND.

Brougham's brow furrowed as he watched me write, and he played with the rim of his glasses. "You want me to go back there?"

"With Winona."

"I'm sorry, you must have missed the part where I said she dumped me."

But I was too busy deep breathing to react to his petulant tone. This wasn't Brougham anymore. He wasn't sitting beside me, acting like everything I said was the stupidest thing he'd heard in his life. This was just someone dropping a letter into the locker. I had the background information. This person in front of me was lost, and they needed me.

"You keep it casual," I said, writing notes down as I went. "Since you haven't been talking since the breakup, you have a clean slate. Reach out with a text that's friendly, but not intense. You want the tone of it to let her know you have no hard feelings, but nothing that's gonna make her think you have ulterior motives, either. If you have an inside joke or something, use that. Like, 'Oh my god, X happened and I knew you'd appreciate it.'"

"Her favorite *Bachelor* contestant got into the final two, last episode?"

Alexander Brougham: rich egomaniac, rude know-it-all, reality TV connoisseur. Interesting. "That's actually perfect. Use that to get back in touch. Be pleasant."

"You keep repeating that. Do you think I'd struggle with being pleasant?"

We sat within a long, long pause. "I'm sure you'll be fine," I said at last. Honestly, I was proud of my diplomacy. "Love makes people softer."

"Am I hard?" he asked, with his trademark blank expression.

I went on like he hadn't spoken. "As early as you can, segue into Disneyland. Say something like you've been wanting to go, then ask her if it would be weird to go with her as friends, and say she made it more fun or something. If she doesn't absolutely hate you, you'd have a good shot at her being down, I think."

"Tell her I want to be friends when I don't?" Brougham asked, his dark eyebrows flying up into an arch of judgment and superiority. "That seems manipulative."

"Well, no. Because right now, you *are* aiming for friendship. And it might stop there. But honestly, it's *never* going to go from total silence to back in a healthy, revamped relationship. You need an in-between point."

I handed Brougham the notebook, and he scanned the steps I'd written down for Stage One. When he looked back up, he'd set his jaw in determination. "You know, Phillips? I can work with this." He blew out a breath. "When should I text her?"

I locked eyes with him and grinned, the excitement of it all hitting me. I'd get to see how my advice worked in real time. And I might just be able to bring love back into Brougham's frozen, emotionless life. "Tonight. Do it tonight."

SIX

Character Analysis:
Alexander Brougham

~~Thinks he wants a relationship, but is actually terrified of opening up, because he has godawful parents.~~

Scratch that, that's an awful thing to say. His relationship with his parents is strained, and this affected his views on the stability of relationships. Says he adored Winona, but went silent on her for a month despite describing the relationship as good.

Is a commitment-phobe!

Therapy needed?

Pretty eyes, I guess. We can work with that.

A knock on the door an hour after Brougham left made me swing around to see Mom, still in her clothes from school.

Her sunflower dress had splatters of blue goop on it—presumably from one of the day's experiments—and her hair was frizzy and coming out of its bun, but overall, she still looked awesome.

Mom had always shunned the clothes available in the plus-size section of most stores. Her philosophy was just because a woman was fat, it didn't mean she had to dress in clothes designed to make her blend into the background. If society wanted her to take up less space, Mom made a habit of taking up extra to spite it. So she got most of her clothes online, in a style best described as *loud*. Everything she owned came in vibrant prints and popping colors, from A-line dresses covered in cupcakes to peplum tops in a red and orange zigzag pattern to knee-high boots in raspberry pink.

"Still working, huh?" she asked. Because she had no idea about my whole locker venture, she figured whenever I was hunched over a notebook or papers or a Word document, I was studiously making my way through the week's assignments. I was more than happy to encourage this misconception.

"Yup," I said. "I had a friend over after school so I'll be going for a while yet."

"A 'friend'?"

I saw her point. The only "friend" I usually brought over was Brooke, and I'd never referred to her so distantly in my life. Brooke was *Brooke*. Brougham was *a friend*. And that was being extremely generous. "Yeah. Alexander Brougham?"

Mom blinked in surprise. "He's in my class."

"My condolences."

She folded her arms. Oh god, here it came. "And is he perhaps someone you hope to be *more* than friends with?"

"I'd pay good money to avoid Alexander Brougham ever seeing me like that."

Mom laughed. "Strong feelings."

"To put it lightly."

"Well, we'll see how that goes," she said. She had that annoying tone, though. The all-knowing, wise bringer-of-enlightenment tone adults got when they thought they knew you so much better than you did.

I was about to retort, when my phone buzzed against the wood of my desk. I glanced at it, assuming it was Brougham updating me on the Winona situation, but it was Brooke. I snatched my phone up and opened the message.

Soooooo I have a lot to tell you.
Long story short, Ray came around
to help me write my essay. A Lot
Happened. When can I call?

"Oh my god," I murmured. I half-expected Mom to ask what was wrong, but a brief glance up told me she'd already left. I reread it silently once, twice, three times. Each read-through, my stomach sank lower and lower, and my heart started a funeral march thud.

No. No, no, no, no, no.

I tried desperately to think of another explanation for "A Lot." A Lot Happened, we got the whole essay done? A Lot Happened, Mom got into a fight with Ray over her bad attitude and stupid face? A Lot Happened, we got to talking about our family trees and realized we're cousins?

I told myself any of the above could be true. But I didn't really believe it. Because something that should've occurred to me much earlier had finally become obvious.

Ray.

Ray of Sunshine.

Ray of Godforsaken Sunshine had found an excuse to talk to "her," the her in question being Brooke, *my* Brooke. To hang with her. Realistically, there was only one thing A Lot was likely to be. Ray of Sunshine had made her move, like I'd instructed her.

And I *rarely* had to give people their money back.

With trembling hands, I started to bring up Brooke's number, then I paused to breathe. I didn't know if I was ready to hear what she had to tell me.

Seven months or so ago, at the end of sophomore year, Brooke had written in to the locker gushing about a girl she'd kissed. She wrote that it happened suddenly, while the two of them were setting up for an after-school event, and they hadn't had the chance to debrief because others came into the room. And then in Brooke's familiar, bouncy, cotton-candy handwriting, came the words *"I think I really like her. What do I do next?"*

I remembered the feeling that'd come over me all too well. Like someone had just run a bulldozer into a room filled with puppies and kittens right in front of me. Shock, and panic, and a rising nausea that threatened to force itself right out of my throat. And my heart tried to escape through my chest, screaming bloody murder. Because right around the time all this happened, I'd started wondering if maybe there was something going on with Brooke and me. There'd been a lot of meaningful glances, and loaded pauses, and casual finger brushing while we walked. And eye contact that went on, in my opinion, for way too long.

But I was sure as hell I hadn't kissed Brooke without realizing it. So who the hell had?

I'd given Brooke a call, as casual as I could. Led the conversation toward the Q&Q Club fundraiser we'd put together earlier that week. The one Brooke had gone in with Jaz to prepare for. And she confirmed everything I already knew was true. Yes, she'd had a crush on Jaz for a while. Yes, they'd kissed. Yes, Brooke wanted it to go somewhere.

No, no, no. But then, why the lingering looks with me? The flirting with me? Had I misread the situation? Or could she like both of us, but Jaz was the one who'd made the first move? And then, filled with grief and jealousy and fear and panic, I did a thing I wasn't proud of. I sent Brooke a response from the locker.

Dear BAMN765,

The best thing to do in this situation is act like it didn't happen. Don't bring it up, don't flirt, and especially don't let yourself get in a one-on-one position with this girl for a while. I know it sounds counterintuitive, but if you end up one-on-one, things can get awkward, and nervousness makes us act flustered and weird. She might pick up on your vibes and feel like there's an expectation—or, worse, desperation—there that would be majorly off-putting. Nothing kills a budding relationship faster than someone feeling pressured to keep things going too fast.

Don't worry about putting her off: if she likes you, she'll find a way to contact you and let you know her feelings. Just make sure she's the one doing the pursuing. Be cool, be casual, act platonic.

Brooke didn't bring up the letter to me. She didn't bring up Jaz again, either. I didn't hear another word of it until a week later, when another letter ended up in the locker.

Dear Locker 89,

I'm a lesbian, and last week I kissed a girl I know and I thought she was into it. I happen to know she's a lesbian as well so this isn't a "was she just confused" letter. Since we kissed, though, she's been avoiding me, and acting like it didn't happen. She's being friendly but only when we're in groups, she hasn't been close with me, hasn't texted me, hasn't *mentioned* the kiss. I'm like did I fucking imagine this? Should I assume it wasn't as good for her as it was for me, or should I try and reach out to her? I would've already but I lost confidence when she started acting all distant.

And, god help me, I replied.

Dear hellsbells05,

I know this isn't what you want to hear, but it does sound like she probably wasn't into it. It's unusual behavior to act as though a kiss didn't happen—especially if you've seen her around since—and if your gut tells you she's avoiding being alone with you, you're probably reading the situation right. In this case, my advice would be to move on unless she changes her behavior miraculously. You'll have many first kisses in your life, and I promise most of them will turn out better than this one. You deserve someone who's psyched to kiss you, and who can't get enough of you, and who will call you immediately after to set up a time to hang out. Don't lose your dignity by chasing after someone who's made it clear they're not psyched. You're too good for that.

I'm sorry I don't have better news.

And that had been that. Brooke made it clear she didn't want me to bring up her kiss with Jaz when I tried to check in on her, so I kept quiet on the topic. And over the summer, Jaz met a girl at church, and they started dating seriously.

And it was only following this that Brooke and Jaz began to feel comfortable enough around each other again to debrief on the whole kissing situation. And that's when they found out.

"It was almost like the locker sabotaged us," Brooke had raged the next time we caught up. "I understand whoever answers the letters gets a lot of questions every week, but would you *really* not catch on that Jaz and I were talking about each other?"

"I don't know," I'd said, swallowing. "Maybe they were distracted."

"Maybe," Brooke had said, but she'd glowered.

The rest of the week I had guilt nightmares every night, from Brooke finding out I was behind the locker and never speaking to me again, to Jaz sobbing to me in the girl's bathroom that she'd lost the love of her life.

As awful as this was, as much as I *hated* what I knew I was about to hear, I had to make up for what I'd done last year. This time, I was going to be supportive. I was going to be happy for Brooke. I was going to have her back in this. Even if it made my insides rot. I just had to make it through this phone call, then I could cry as much as I needed to.

As soon as she picked up the phone, Brooke started babbling. "Okay, so, Ray came over and we were working on the essay and it was all casual and fine and then Mom and Dad invited her to stay for dinner, so she did, and they got along super well and she was being really nice and she's actually really funny which I was *not* expecting, then we hung out for a while after and we were looking at something on my phone and she, holy shit, Darcy, she *asked me out.*"

I'd braced, I'd braced, I'd braced, but I still stumbled. Gut shot. She mistook my gasp for a gasp of joy. "I *know,*" she said. "And I said yes! We got along weirdly well outside of school, and it was really sweet and generous of her to help me with my essay, don't you think? And then she said she's been into me for ages now, and she always catches herself staring at me in Q and Q Club and council meetings, and have *you* noticed her staring at me? Because I never did, and now I'm wondering if I'm just oblivious, or what."

Talk. Speak. "Um, I'm not sure." *Speak happier than that.* "But wow, that's incredible!"

"You think so? I think it might be! I didn't see this coming, I mean, *Ray.* I thought she *hated* me. Darcy, hanging out with her was *nice,* can you imagine?"

Oh, I could imagine. I didn't *want to,* but I could, and, oh god, now it was burned into my brain and I couldn't stop thinking about them laughing and touching fingertips and sitting in each other's personal space. How could this happen? With *Raina?* Of all the people I could've seen as a threat . . . "Are you, like, together now?"

"Don't jinx it. I don't know what's going to happen now, I just needed to tell you."

Okay. Well, they weren't together.

But who knew how long it would stay that way for?

So I swallowed the sob that lurked somewhere in my throat, took a deep breath, and forced a smile. "Where are you guys going?"

All I knew was if they fizzled out, it wasn't going to be because of me.

Not this time.

Brooke was a veritable bundle of excitement and sparkles the next day. She laughed—too loudly—at everything, floated around the halls, and grinned at everyone who walked past.

My own feet had never felt quite so heavy.

"She was really nice to my mom, and Mom *loves* that she does so many extracurricular things," Brooke had gushed to me in homeroom.

"Did you know how smart Ray is? I mean, obviously she's smart, but her grasp on language is just mind-blowing," Brooke had whispered while I tried to take notes in math.

"I thought we were going to kiss when she said good-bye, but then we chickened out," Brooke had recounted for the fourth time as we walked to history.

Every time I'd put on a tight smile, and "hmm"ed and "wow"ed when appropriate, all while hoping my agony wasn't written on my face. It was getting to be such torture to be around her, and to know her lit-up face, and giggles, and swinging feet were caused by Ray, and not me, I was grateful to get a text from Brougham to meet me in the halls halfway through history class. I'd rather be around his drizzle and storm clouds than Brooke's rainbow right now.

I got a pass for the bathroom and headed in the direction of the science labs, where I found Brougham hovering, keeping an eye out for teachers or other potential eavesdroppers. He'd paired his blazer with tan, skinny chinos and a dark maroon tie. Though his outfit was coordinated and neat, his posture was stiff and he was bouncing on his heels, frazzled.

"Hey, walk with me," he said as soon as I got close enough, heading down the hall.

"Yes, sir."

He ignored my tone. "I did what you said, and *she* was the one who brought up taking a day trip there as friends, so right now I'm convinced you're either a witch or a genius."

"And I'll never let you know which one it is. That's great, when are you going?"

"Saturday."

"Did you wanna catch up beforehand so we can make a plan?"

"Definitely. Also, I really need you with me on the day."

I stopped in my tracks. "At *Disneyland?*" He wanted me to drive an hour each way to Anaheim for him, just casually?

"I can't do it without you, I'm pretty much stuffed if things start going wrong, and if you can't see her body language how are you supposed to know what happened and help me fix it?"

"She'd notice me."

"I trust you. You're not an idiot."

"Glad to know you trust my stalking skills, I guess?"

"Bring Ainsley with you if you want. I'll give you gas

money, I'll get your tickets, pay for your food, whatever you need. I just . . . I need you. I can't do this alone."

We were walking again now. Conveniently, we were at least heading in the direction of the girls' bathroom, where I was supposed to be. I thought about his proposal for a moment, then shook my head. "No. Definitely not. Sorry."

Brougham slowed his pace, crestfallen. "Is there anything I can do that'd make you change your mind?"

"No."

He took a deep breath, then set his jaw and nodded. "Okay. Fair enough."

I waited, but he didn't follow up with sly blackmail references or a reminder of the bonus waiting for me. Nothing. "That's it?"

"Um, I guess?"

Okay, well, that was a bit better. "You'd pay for all our food and drinks?"

"Yeah, within reason."

I didn't press the issue. Brougham hadn't historically shown himself to be particularly bothered about the cost of things, so I had a feeling his "within reason" was more generous than my "within reason."

"Okay."

"Okay what?"

"I'll do it."

Brougham rested a fist on the back of his neck and tipped his head back. "*Fuck*, you're confusing."

"I just wanted to know you were asking me to help out and not telling me I had to."

He rolled his eyes. "*Obviously* you don't have to."

"Then, *once again*, might I remind you favors are usually accompanied by a 'would you please?'"

He barreled past the lecture. "So, Saturday's okay? Any particular time?"

I sighed, resigned. "I'm free all day."

"Okay. Good. You can go back to class now."

"Thank you, sir." I curtseyed.

"What'd I say this time?" he asked indignantly.

There was simply no point with him. "Message me," I said with a grudging smile, before heading into the bathroom.

I checked myself in the mirror, fluffed then redid my messy bun, and rubbed some smudging eyeliner from under my eye. Then, given the stalls were empty, I called Ainsley, leaning against the sink. If I was going to stalk Brougham and his girlfriend for the day, I at least wanted some company. And Ainsley could almost certainly be persuaded by the offer of free food.

SEVEN

Dear Locker 89,

My girlfriend dumped me. I don't know what to do. It was a week ago, and it felt out of nowhere. We were fighting a little, but nothing huge, just little arguments we solved after a few hours. She says she's not ready for a relationship, but she's also been really obviously flirting with one of the girls in our Spanish class, and I don't know if it's to make me jealous or if maybe she wants to be with her. I haven't stopped crying. I'm constantly going to the bathroom because I know I can't get through the next five minutes without bawling. I feel like I'm dying. All I want is for her to love me again. We were supposed to be forever. We were going to room together at college. This can't be happening. What do I do?

Junkmailll@gmail.com

Locker 89 <locker89@gmail.com>   6:35 p.m. (0 min ago)
to Junk

Dear Junk Mailll,

I'm so sorry this has happened. Breakups suck, there's no way around it. There's a biological reason for it! When we go through a breakup, our brains have some of the same activity as someone going through drug withdrawal. Almost like you were addicted to this person, and now you're having to detox. So, for a start, be kind to yourself. And second, I can't promise your girlfriend will want you back. But I can absolutely give you some advice that's foolproof.

A) Stop reaching out for a while. You don't have to totally ignore her, but for at least a few weeks, don't start conversations. If she speaks to you, be polite and friendly, but don't engage. And do *not* spam her phone apologizing or saying you miss her! My reasoning for this is twofold: one, it gives her a chance to miss you, and process the reasons she broke up with you, and remember some of the good times. The second reason is it gives you a chance to detox, and remind yourself who you are without her. You are a whole person with or without a partner, and it's time to reintroduce you to yourself. You presumably had a full life before you met her, and you still will now you're not with her anymore.

B) Focus on yourself. Take up a hobby, spend time with your friends and family, read some books, go for long walks. Whatever makes you feel good. Not only will this help you to find yourself again, and make you happier and more confident, but your ex will probably notice how well you're doing!

So why do I say it's foolproof? Because this method can only go one of two ways. Option one, your ex misses you, and sees you doing well, and remembers the reason she fell for you to begin with, and is open to trying again. Option two, that doesn't happen, but you've given yourself so much space to work on your own happiness and abilities, that you honestly move on from your ex and find yourself happier and more successful than ever. Either way, you win.

Good luck!
Locker 89

My weekend started bright and fucking early as my phone buzzed, and buzzed, and buzzed, and buzzed against the wood of my bedside table. I opened bleary eyes and checked it. It was Brooke, who was one of those people who pressed enter after every few words, causing havoc to the recipient's notifications. I was in love with a chaotic neutral.

Hey!

I'm up early and I'm bored!

Wanna do something!?

Omg I looked at the movie times
and there's four I want to see.
Movie date???

I'll buy popcorn?

Wake uuupppppppPPPPPP

Movie date?

What did that mean? Like, a date-date? She'd had her real date-date last night with Ray, and she'd told me they still hadn't kissed. Was there a reason for that? Why was she asking me, and not Ray? Everything in me tightened with hope and trepidation and—

Crap. Today was Saturday.

Okay, so, obviously I couldn't go to the movies. Fuck, fuck, fuck, I *really* wanted to—even though Brooke's taste in movies was terrible and she hated horror movies—but I couldn't. Goddamnit, Brougham, why did his life have to complicate mine so much? Could I bail on him? No, nope. He'd asked first. I *hated* people who canceled already-made plans because something better came up. I was not going to be that person. So, I'd tell Brooke I was going to Disneyland with Ainsley.

Oh, but no, I couldn't, because she'd want to come. So I'd lie to Brooke and say I was busy doing something else . . . And that'd work for an hour, until one of our mutual friends saw me there. Half the school had an annual pass to the place. This was like a game of Russian roulette, if every canister had a surprise bullet.

I settled for:

> I'm so sorry, but I already
> promised Ainsley a sister
> date at Disney. She told one
> of her friends she couldn't

come, so I kind of can't turn
around and bring you, even
though I really want to .
Tomorrow?

I can't tomorrow

Work.

Gah fine. I'm jealous though.

Don't send me any photos, it'll fuel
my FOMO and I might cry.

Was I *sure* it wasn't okay to bail on Brougham? *"No,"* I
said to myself out loud, throwing my phone down on the
bed. As much as I hated it, I needed to consider this my
own not-up-for-negotiation shift at work. I was getting
paid for it, after all.

So, my heart breaking and my mind grumbling, I did
my hair and makeup (mostly using sample spoils scored
from *Brooke's* not-up-for-negotiation job), got dressed (a
lightweight knit copper sweater over a short-sleeved shirt
and a denim miniskirt Ainsley had altered for my hips), and
put on perfume (a half-used bottle of Dior Poison Mom
had passed down to me when I told her I loved the smell of
it). It struck me, as I looked at the finished product in the
floor-length mirror stuck to the back of my door, that today
I'd been dressed by the three most important women in my
life. Cheesy, but also kind of special. Special in a way that
an outfit bought on a Platinum Mastercard probably didn't
feel.

Okay, I had forty-five minutes to go before Brougham was due. That would give me enough time to get through the letters I'd shoved in my backpack yesterday, so I didn't have to spend all day dwelling on them. Perfect.

With Dad clattering around down the hall, and the smell of toast seeping under the crack in my doorway, I set my laptop up on the empty wooden desk and started working through the letters. It seemed like I'd barely sat down when Dad knocked on my door, but a glance at the time told me I'd been going for thirty minutes already. I knew it was Dad, because Ainsley, who had joined me in sleeping at Dad's last night so we could drive over together, didn't knock and wait, she knocked and opened. "Come in," I called.

I didn't bother hiding the letters. Dad was . . . unperceptive, to put it kindly, and if he noticed them at all he would probably just assume they were homework.

He poked his head around the door and screwed up his mouth so his mustache went lopsided. "There's a boy here."

"Oh. He's early." I still had one letter reply to go. Guess Brougham would have to entertain himself up here while I finished. I wasn't going to fall behind on my locker duties just because Brougham thought three forty-five meant four thirty and nine a.m. meant eight forty-five. Maybe in Australia time was but a vague concept but in America when we said nine we meant *nine,* damn it.

Dad pushed the door open farther and stood blocking the doorway, even when I got up. "Who is this boy? What does he want with you? Why haven't I heard of him before?"

I met Dad's eyes—and given I'd inherited his height, it wasn't so hard to do—and folded my arms. "Um, the real question here is why don't you quiz me like this when girls come to the door?"

Dad, who'd only recently stopped referring to me "turning" straight or lesbian depending on which gender he thought I had a crush on that day, surprised me by saying, "Because teenage girls are sweet and responsible and understand consent, and teenage boys are every father's nightmare come true."

I hesitated, then shrugged. "That's actually a fair answer. I'll allow it."

"Our dad, the ally," Ainsley sang happily from her bedroom, where she'd been apparently eavesdropping. Oh, good, she was awake. She'd had to drive back to Mom's late last night, after I'd already climbed into bed, because she'd accidentally left her hormones behind. One of the many hazards of being children of divorce.

Dad followed me to the front door, and hovered suspiciously behind me while I greeted Brougham. When I introduced them, even though Brougham was all firm handshake and polite words, Dad barely managed to give him more than a brief "hi, how you doin'." Brougham didn't seem overly ruffled—and, to be fair, compared to his mom's reception of me, Dad had practically rolled out the red carpet—so I didn't bother trying to make group small talk. Besides, it was probably the last time Dad was going to have anything to do with Brougham, so it hardly mattered.

"I'll just be a few minutes," I said to Brougham as we got to my room. "I'm finishing up an email."

I sat at my desk, and Brougham hung back, looking around the room. "It's really different here," he said.

"Hmm?"

"It's bare. Doesn't really look like your room."

"I'm only here a few days a month," I said without turning around. "It does the job."

"Looks more like a guest room."

"Well, when I'm not here," I said, typing away at my response, "it is."

"Oh, of *course it is*. Now I sound like a dickhead."

"'Sound' like one?" I muttered, before stealing a peek at him.

He glanced over his shoulder. "Pardon?"

"Nothing. Anyway. It's better than the arguing."

He seemed to deflate at this, and he sat heavily on the edge of my double bed. "Point taken."

For the next few minutes, Brougham contentedly scrolled through his phone while I finished off my last response. Luckily this one was easy, and it didn't require research to figure out the best approach. When I was done I grabbed my own phone to respond to a few messages Brooke had left about her vast, unending boredom.

Brougham cleared his throat. "I was wondering something."

"Hmm?"

"Could I . . . I'm just really curious to see how your whole setup works. Do you reckon I could check it out?"

"You mean, read my emails?"

He shrugged, waiting.

It wasn't what I was expecting, and I almost said no. But then, it was nice to have someone to share this with. No one but Ainsley had ever seen me do this. "Um, sure. But let me find one that's vague, okay? No names or anything."

"Fair."

I flicked through the last few emails and brought up one

that was sufficiently anonymous. Brougham took over my seat and got comfortable, flicking a stray piece of hair out of his face to read through squinting eyes. He didn't have his reading glasses with him today.

"What's the basis behind this one?" he asked, waving the cursor over the screen.

It was a message I'd sent the day before. "I based it on the no-contact rule."

"Which is?"

Even though he asked it innocently, I sensed he was gearing up to tear it apart. The first outsider to see my stuff, and instead of praise I got critique. Fucking excellent. "Basically what it sounds like. After a breakup, you don't contact them for a while. Usually about thirty days. About how long you gave Winona, incidentally. And if you can't avoid talking, because you're working on a project together or something, you keep it professional and distant."

Brougham nodded slowly. "And you use it when you want to get someone back?"

"You can. Or, like I said in the email, you can use it to get over someone as well. It's a win-win."

"And girls use this?"

"Anyone can use it. It's not gender-specific."

"Right, right," he said at the screen, before looking up at me. "I have a question, though."

"Of course you do," I muttered.

"You told me the other day *He's Just Not That Into You* reckons if a guy doesn't chase you, it's because he doesn't want you."

"True."

"And that, if that happens, you should move on."

"Ideally, yeah."

"But what if he's not ignoring you because he's not into you? What if he's just following the no-contact rule?"

He looked triumphant as he swiveled around in the chair, crossing one leg over the other. But I was nonplussed. "Well, if he's doing that, what does he want from you?"

"For you to want him back."

"And why does *He's Just Not That Into You* exist?"

"To scam money from desperate, lonely people who think following a one-size-fits-all rule will help them land a complex individual as a partner?"

"The reason it's able to *make* money is because people need to be *told* that if they're ignored, they should give up. And that's *because* lots of people like the chase. Which is exactly why the no-contact rule works so often."

"Sure, but what if both partners are following different rule books?"

I blinked. "Sorry?"

"Well, what if I'm following the no-contact rule, hoping that it makes my ex fall for me, but she's reading *He's Just Not That Into You* and deciding that my thirty days of silence mean she needs to meet someone else?"

"Well, she—"

"Or what if I know about the no-contact rule, and can't move on when they go silent, because I'm low-key hoping they're using it on me because they want *me* back? When actually I *should've* been listening to *He's Just Not That Into You*? They can't both be true all the time."

"No. That's why you have to take in other information. Like, how invested was the partner during the relationship? Do they usually use silence to show anger or disinterest? Who broke up with who, and why?"

"So it's not one size fits all," Brougham said with an air of triumph. Like he'd somehow backed me into a corner here. Not even close.

"Agreed. That's why I base my advice on personal situations, letter by letter."

"Right," Brougham said. "And *that's*, of course, why you never take someone's money before you get all of that information. Who broke up with who, the history of the relationship, yadda yadda. Even if they don't include any of that in the initial letter."

I faltered.

His eyebrow quirked the tiniest bit. He seemed quite pleased with himself. The annoying thing was, he *had* backed me into a corner. Except for one tiny detail. "I have a ninety-five percent success rate, don't I?" I asked. "I can tell everything I need to know from the vibe of the letter."

"You know all the information without having all the information?" Brougham said, before standing up to face me at eye level. "Miraculous."

Amazingly, I did not murder him. "Can we get started?"

"Sure. One quick, teeny question first, though?"

I mean, he was gonna ask anyway, right? "What?"

"If someone sent you a letter and said, 'Help, my boyfriend ignores me for days on end if I say or do something he doesn't like,' what would you say?"

I could already see where this was going, but my mind couldn't function effectively with him *staring* at me like that, so I gave in and let him lead me into his trap. "I'd say that the silent treatment to punish or manipulate is emotional abuse. But that's different, this isn't to punish—"

"But it *is* trying to manipulate someone into changing their feelings, right?"

Well, yeah, kind of, but—but it was different, wasn't it? It was more about getting space from someone than winning them back. And even if someone *did* use it to get someone back, it was okay to do something if the aim was good. And what could be more "good" than rekindling love and affection?

Sure, maybe part of that was to make the other person feel lonely, or miss you, or uncomfortable, but . . . Actually, if I thought of it like that, maybe Brougham had a point. It didn't seem the same, though. It was *not* emotionally abusive to create boundaries and space after being dumped by someone. What a ridiculous thing to imply.

How did he get me *doubting myself*? Who was the expert here?

"Can we just . . ." I trailed off and waved my hand around in a circle.

"Just what?"

"Just *not* right now? It's too early, and we don't have much time to get you ready for today."

He wanted to push it. *Ooh,* I could see in his eyes he wanted to push it. And I had the horrible feeling if he did, he'd have me scrambling to type out a new email response imploring my customer to ignore the initial advice.

Instead, he flopped backward onto the bed and spread his arms to the sides, chin up and self-assured. "Rain check on that one, then. Hit me, Phillips, what have you got?"

I went under the bed and fished out the bulletin board. "I realized your timeline with Winona is missing something important."

Brougham shook his head in amazement. "You dragged that all the way from your mum's for this?"

"You're welcome. We know a lot about what was working

for you guys, but I'm unclear on what wasn't. So: first fight?"

"Jesus, I don't know," Brougham said as I got my pen and paper ready to add to the board. "How am I supposed to remember the *first* one?"

"Lots of fighting," I murmured as I wrote the words down for a caption.

"We didn't—it wasn't *lots*."

"Whatever helps you sleep at night, buddy. Okay, how about the most common fight?"

"We mostly fought over how often we should be messaging each other."

I nodded, and started the picture above the caption. A male and female stick figure, both with angry eyebrows. I drew a speech bubble over the female figure and wrote "Text me more" in it.

"No," Brougham said.

I glanced up at him. "It's close enough, it doesn't have to be word for word."

"No, I mean . . ." He suddenly looked uncomfortable. "I was the one who wanted to be talking more often. Not her."

And for once, I had no words. How was I supposed to speak when my whole view of Brougham was crumbling into a thousand pixels and rearranging itself to tell the story of a person who looked nothing like the version of him I had in my head? That version of Brougham was a commitment-phobe. He pulled away when people got too close. He was aloof where others were clingy. He had a closed-off heart.

But this, apparently, was false.

The words sat in my mouth for a while before they forced their way out. "O-oh. Got it." I scribbled out the arrow of the speech bubble and connected it to the Brougham figure instead.

"You sound awfully surprised."

I pressed my lips together and kept drawing.

"You shouldn't be so sexist, Philips," Brougham continued lightly, picking a lint ball off his sweater. "Assumptions like that'll keep me trapped in the claws of toxic masculinity."

A throbbing in my jaw warned me I was clenching my teeth. I ran my tongue around my mouth to loosen everything up and gave Winona's stick figure a new speech bubble: "No!! I hate your face!!"

"How did you know she said that?" Brougham asked in mock amazement. "You *are* a miracle worker."

"Did a fight lead to the breakup?" I asked while I stuck the new picture on the board.

"More or less. I guess I gave her an ultimatum."

I dropped my hands to my sides and turned around on the bed. "You *didn't*."

"I wish that were true."

"Why didn't you just throw a fucking grenade between you while you were at it?"

Brougham blinked, and a perfectly placed lock of hair fought its way free to fall into his face. "Come on, *that bad*?"

I shook my head in disbelief. "Yes, Brougham, that bad. What was the ultimatum?"

"Well . . . I said if she couldn't be bothered to talk to me, she obviously wasn't invested in the relationship, and I didn't want to be with her if she couldn't bring herself to do something that simple."

"And she said?"

"I was smothering her and she didn't want to be with me anymore anyway."

I feigned stabbing myself in the stomach with an imaginary sword and flailed about in mock pain.

"Yeah. Basically."

I hopped to my feet and crossed the room to start another picture. "I take it you regretted it?"

"Honestly, I didn't mean it to begin with. I think I just wanted her to know how serious I was, so she'd worry and get her act together."

"So, to recap, you thought that by threatening your girlfriend, you'd fill her with so much love and affection for you she'd want to speak to you *more*?" I looked up at him.

He twisted his mouth and took a deep, weighted breath. ". . . Yes."

On a fresh piece of paper, I drew male and female stick figures with a heart above their heads while Brougham watched. "What's that I'm aiming at the heart?" he asked.

"A bow and arrow."

"Ah. Of course."

"Okay, this is useful. Now we know you have to focus on not smothering her!"

"Wow, gee, why didn't I think of that before?" Brougham glared. His attitude couldn't affect me right now, though. I was simply brimming with confidence.

"Okay, let's practice. What are you gonna say to her when you see her?"

"I dunno. Hi, I guess?"

"No! Don't say hi, because then if she just says hi, the conversation dies and it gets awkward and it's all downhill from there. You need to ask open-ended questions."

"Like what?" Brougham asked, lolling his head back. God, is this what it was like to be a teacher when kids gave sass in class? I reminded myself to tell Mom how much I admired her when I got home, because if I were her, I would've marched out of class mid-lesson, driven to McDonald's, and eaten some chicken nuggets while pretending I didn't have responsibilities long ago.

"How are you, how are your parents, that sort of thing."

"Okay, got it."

"Good, let's go. 'Hi, Brougham!'"

"Oh, brilliant, you're fake Winona again."

"Yup. *Hi, Brougham.*"

"This is stupid."

"It's not stupid, you just don't want to do it. Too bad."

He stared at the corner of the ceiling while he took in a slow, deep breath. I wondered if this was a natural reaction or a planned coping mechanism for dealing with me. "Hey, Winona. It's been ages. How have you been?" His tone was overly chirpy, like he was auditioning for a cleaning-product commercial. He even injected some emotion into his facial expressions.

"That's fine, now let's go bigger. Try kicking things off with something more dynamic this time."

He blinked, all traces of sunshine gone from his face in one hit. "Such as?"

"Like, an icebreaker. Tell her about something funny that happened on the way over, or something you saw that reminded you of her."

"Got it. How about, 'Hey, you! Today I spent the morning being nagged and criticized by this girl I know, and it reminded me of that fight we had in the car the night I met your parents. How are *they* doing, anyway?'"

"If you're not gonna take this seriously—"

"Phillips, hey." He got to his feet and clasped his hands in front of him. "Thank you. But please trust me on this, I know Winona. If I'm in my head about conversation rules, *that's* gonna make shit awkward. I don't need help with this. I need help with later on, once we've been together for a while. *That's* when she starts distancing."

It stung. He'd approached *me*, asked *me* to give up my morning helping him get Winona back, and now he didn't want to hear any of the advice I had. I wasn't just making it up, either. I'd spent all last night combing through YouTube videos, especially Coach Pris Plumber's backlog, finding the basic foundations of seduction. And none of it was good enough for him.

But I guessed it wasn't up to me. I just had to trust him.

"Okay," I said. "Got it."

"Awesome. So, should we get going?"

"One sec. Just . . . let me . . ." I ruffled my fingers through his hair to fluff it up. "There. Now we can go."

I could've sworn, just for a moment, he *almost* grinned at that.

EIGHT

Character Analysis:
Alexander Brougham

So scared of rejection he lashes out to remain in control.

Parents didn't give him consistent love as a baby, so he doesn't believe love is limitless and unconditional. He doesn't withdraw because closeness overwhelms him: he withdraws because he desperately wants to be followed.

Has an anxious attachment style!

There was something unknowably perfect about Disneyland.

It's hard to say if the magic came from the environment, or the contagious excitement emanating from hundreds of bouncing, buzzing kids filling the crowded lines at the turnstiles, or pure nostalgia. If I had to guess, I'd put my money on all three. Standing on these orangey-red bricks, surrounded by families posing for photos in front of manicured grass beds filled with purple and white flowers in the shape of Mickey Mouse, breathing in the scent of corn dogs and recycled water, I was four again. Ainsley was six. She held Mom's hand. I held Dad's. No one was fighting, I couldn't even conceive of my family being split down the middle, and the only thing that mattered was getting the next FastPass.

I guess that's what nostalgia really meant. Even though I'd been to Disneyland dozens of times since then, my first memory was the one that bled into today.

The morning was warm—I'd already shoved my sweater into Ainsley's backpack for safekeeping until I needed it after dark. A gust of wind whipped my hair around my face. To the far right, a girl entering the park with her parents lost her Elsa baseball cap in the breeze, and she broke into a run to chase it, as strangers made mad dashes to grab it for her.

It really was a stroke of genius for Brougham to bring Winona here. It was impossible to hold a grudge in the Happiest Place on Earth.

Brougham and Winona were waiting ahead, closer to the turnstiles. Winona seemed to be in good spirits, and she was chattering away at Brougham while digging through her blue-and-purple paisley tote bag. The material was covered in flowers; squiggly, colorful designs; and Mickey and Minnie in various poses. That, along with her Tinker Bell canvas shoes and *Beauty and the Beast*–themed crystal rose earrings, told me two things: a) rich kids had way too much money to throw around, and I would never stop being jealous of that; and b) Brougham was observant. He hadn't just taken Winona to Disneyland on a whim the year before. He'd correctly pegged her as a superfan.

Observant was a good sign. All we needed to do was

up the thoughtfulness and reduce the clinginess and we'd make a Disney prince of him yet.

Once we'd gotten through the magical bag check and the whimsical scan for bombs or other deadly weapons, Brougham sent me a text.

Get Space Mountain FastPasses
exactly now.

He'd helped me sign Ainsley and myself up to the Disneyland app and paid for MaxPasses for us, meaning we could line up our FastPasses on our phones instead of sprinting to the FastPass dispensers. If you asked me, that took a lot of the adrenaline out of the day, but no one *did* ask me.

Got it. My entry window is
10:45 to 11:45.

Not too far ahead of us, Brougham discreetly checked my response and typed back.

Done.

And we were off, wandering down Main Street, serenaded by a hodgepodge of cheerful music. Sleeping Beauty Castle loomed ahead of us. While we walked, I sent a message to Brooke, glancing up regularly at Brougham and Winona.

Sorry again about today.

We passed a stall selling Minnie Mouse ears, and Ainsley's eyes rested on them for a little too long. She didn't say anything, though. As cute as they were, neither of us had the money to spend on clothing *that* specific. Even Ainsley couldn't find a way to alter and incorporate those into her everyday wardrobe.

My phone buzzed in my hand.

That's okay! I actually asked Ray to
come to the movies with me . . . 😶

I slowed my pace so I could focus on steadying my breathing. This was my karma for sabotaging Brooke and Jaz. It had to be. Life couldn't be this randomly cruel.

"Red Wagon, Red Wagon, Red Wagon," Ainsley chanted, bouncing on the balls of her feet, and I forced myself to focus on the task at hand. I could not afford to spiral.

Brougham and Winona were already veering to the right in the direction of Tomorrowland. "Oh my god, Ainsley, it's *so* early."

"It's never too early."

They were getting away from us, their bobbing heads blending into the thickening crowds. "Okay, I need to go, though. Can you grab them and text me when you're done? You can meet me."

"'Them'?" Ainsley asked. "So, you want a corn dog, too?"

I blinked. "Well, I mean, if *you're* getting one."

She waved a hand. "Fine, fine, go!"

I didn't need to be told twice. By this point, I'd lost sight of Brougham and Winona altogether, so I broke into a jog and dodged families and children and strollers and balloons, over the gray paved path, and past umbrella-topped tables outside Tomorrowland Terrace. Finally, I spotted them hovering outside the Star Trader souvenir shop. Brougham was saying something to Winona, but he seemed distracted.

Then his gaze tracked over and hung suspended for the briefest moment on me before turning back to Winona. His stiff posture relaxed.

They started moving again, which meant I did, too. Far enough behind them that they didn't notice me, but not so far behind I lost them. So far, there weren't any red flags. The conversation seemed evenly split, with no long, awkward pauses. Winona even threw her head back in laughter once, her chestnut brown hair spilling back over her shoulders. All promising.

We were due at Space Mountain in ten minutes, and we'd started heading in that direction. I sent a quick location update to Ainsley.

She appeared just after Brougham and Winona entered the ride, holding one mostly clean stick, and one corn dog with a significant chomp taken out of it. She passed this one graciously to me.

"*Hey,*" I protested.

"Consider it my driving tax. Oh, Darc, can we go to the Bibbidi Bobbidi Boutique after this?"

"Why?" I asked through a mouthful of mystery meat and batter.

"I want a princess makeover. I didn't get to have one when we were kids."

"I'm pretty sure there's an age cutoff. You're about a decade too late."

Her face darkened. "This is such bullshit."

I offered her another bite of my corn dog in consolation and she took it, plus one more, glowering the whole time. At that moment, I resolved to act as Ainsley's shoulder devil the next time we passed a stall selling Minnie Mouse ears. Who cared if she never got the chance to wear them again? She deserved the commercialized, capitalistic Disney princess treatment that she'd missed out on.

With Ainsley's help finishing what was left of my snack, we were soon heading down a red-lit corridor with flashing galaxy lights on either side of us, while a metallic robot voice overhead pleasantly warned us not to ride if we had a heart condition.

We'd just joined the end of the queue when my phone buzzed with a text from Brougham.

Getting on now

> I'm in the line behind you. I'll
> text you when we're done. All
> ok?

Yup

See? He was fine. Bringing Ainsley and me all the way here as his safety net was nothing but a waste of money.

"How's Romeo?" Ainsley asked, peeking over my shoulder.

"He's doing pretty well. I'm hoping he lets us off early soon."

"Not surprised. His face does half the work for him."

"Still don't see it."

After we finished Space Mountain, Brougham directed us by text to Fantasyland to Alice's teacup ride. Unfortunately, riding a roller coaster immediately after inhaling a corn dog wasn't the best idea I'd ever had, and I told Ainsley in no uncertain terms I was *not* climbing into anything spinning right now.

The sun had started stinging the back of my neck, so Ainsley and I found a nearby shaded spot under a tree. It only took me a few minutes to remember the problem with this ride. It easily competed with "It's a Small World" for the music that got stuck in your head the worst. The same tune—"The Unbirthday Song" from the movie—played over—and over—and over again on a whistling flute-type instrument, high pitched and irritating and squeaky. I'd hoped I might have an update from Brooke by now, but there was nothing. She was probably meeting Ray soon.

As for Brougham, I was feeling more and more confident we had this in the bag. The realization made me shiver with pride and happiness, and something a little profound. I'd helped this happen. I'd directly contributed to the world having a little more love in it.

Even if it *was* my blackmailer I'd helped out.

I sent Brougham a check-in text, and he glanced down, pulled his phone out to check it, then slipped it straight back in his pocket. *Well, gee. Don't mind me, Brougham, I'm just literally here because you needed me to be available for advice at all times.*

Finally it was Brougham and Winona's turn to go on the cups. Winona was saying something to Brougham with an enormous grin on her face, and he pointed at the steering wheel then tilted his head close to hers while he replied in an intimate way.

I was so proud of him.

Ainsley and I wandered over to the fence to watch as the ride started. Now that they were spinning, we were pretty safe from being spotted. Next to us, Alice and the Mad Hatter—or, more accurately, their character actors—approached the fence.

Ainsley shrieked so loudly the poor actors jumped a mile.

"Oh my god, it's Alice!" She gripped onto the top of my arm. "I need a photo with her."

Once the ride finished, and Brougham led an off-balance Winona to the exit, she excused herself to go to the bathroom near Sleeping Beauty Castle. Ainsley had returned, so I took that moment to sidle up to Brougham with her in tow. "You're doing perfectly."

Brougham leaned against a wrought-iron gate bordering a tree that looked like it belonged in a storybook. "So far, so good. We haven't talked about the breakup yet, though. It's a bit weird. Like, we're acting like we've always just been friends. Should I bring it up?"

"No," Ainsley and I said simultaneously.

Brougham's eyes widened. "Okay."

"Be *casual*," I said.

"I'm *casual*!"

"If you say so. So, do you still need me?"

Brougham blinked. "Of course I do. Just because I haven't screwed it up yet doesn't mean anything."

"But what do you expect me to, like . . . do?"

Brougham attempted to share an exasperated look with Ainsley, but she shrugged. She was on my side. "If Winona starts looking smothered, let me know and talk me through fixing it," he said.

"You've been doing great all day, Brougham. I think you're using me as a safety blanket. You need to adjust to being with her alone."

He looked positively alarmed at the idea. "No, *no*. Just because it's fine now doesn't mean it'll stay fine. You don't get it. I always think everything's fine right up until she's overwhelmed by me. I need *help*. I'm gonna fuck it up, I *know* I am."

"Okay, breathe," I said. This baby bird was clearly not ready to leave the nest. Noted. "I'm here as long as you need me."

"Thank you, thank you, but can you go, please, she'll be out in a sec."

Dismissed, Ainsley and I took our leave to a crowded spot over by the Matterhorn waterfall. At least he said "please" this time.

The rest of the afternoon went by in much the same way. Ainsley and I trailed after Brougham, following him on rides and grabbing snacks whenever we had a slow moment by a stall. We even found time for Ainsley to buy a pair of sparkly pink Minnie ears, and honestly, even if they were ungodly expensive and cost the same as several outfits at Jenny's would've, I wasn't lying when I assured her it was a justifiable purchase. You couldn't see the look on her face when she took a selfie with them and think anything else.

As for Ray and Brooke, I was cucumber-cool. I only checked my phone several dozen times for texts. Only let my mind wander to what they might be doing right now two or three times a minute, *max*. By the time we park-hopped to California Adventure in the evening and I'd still received no messages from Brooke, I'd started feeling optimistic. Surely if something had happened between them, Brooke would've gushed to me during a bathroom break or something. Even if she thought something was *likely* to happen, she'd let me know. So, maybe it'd gone down the purely platonic route.

And as for Ainsley and me, we just had to get through a couple more hours, then Brougham and Winona would recreate their World of Color date, and either they'd have a romantic moment or Winona would leave with a positive impression of Brougham. Then I could go home and talk to Brooke for a play-by-play.

Then, when we got to the river rapids ride, things started going spectacularly wrong.

It started with Ainsley announcing she needed the bathroom just as we got close enough to hear the running water. Brougham and Winona went straight in, and the line was surprisingly short, so I tried to talk her into powering through, but she insisted. And, naturally, during the three or so minutes it took us to finish in the bathroom, the line filled with dozens of riders, separating us from our stalkees by a good fifteen minutes on our return.

"We should skip it," I said as Ainsley emerged. "They're going to be finished in a sec."

"But it's my favorite ride." Ainsley pouted. "They've been fine all day. Can't you just text Brougham letting him know we'll be running behind? We deserve a *second* to ourselves."

I couldn't say no to her puppy-dog eyes. And besides, she had a point. Brougham had practically just used me as a security blanket all day. He really didn't need me. So, I took her advice, texting Brougham our whereabouts. It took us about half an hour to get through the line, and by the time we'd finished, half-soaked and smelling like chlorine and shivering in the cooling evening air, I was starting to feel twinges of guilt. Brougham had paid for us to come along, after all. We probably should've spent more time negotiating the logistics of my personal breaks.

Ainsley hummed "The Unbirthday Song" absentmindedly while I rescued my phone from her waterproof backpack— and lucky it *was* waterproof, because it'd taken a hell of a splashing—and I checked my messages.

Five message notifications. The most recent one from
Brooke.

> So, I have a girlfriend. CALL
> ME!?!?!?

All thoughts of guilt, and Brougham's whereabouts, evaporated. My legs went weak, and my cheeks started to tingle.
I felt winded, like I'd walked into a glass door I thought was
empty air.

"What?" asked Ainsley.

I passed the phone to her wordlessly.

"Shit."

I couldn't reply. I was too dizzy. I'd left Brooke alone so
I could follow Brougham around Disneyland for *no fucking
reason,* stalking him and this poor girl so I could give feedback that was *never even needed,* and now I'd lost Brooke.
I'd lost her. It could've been me she was sitting beside, me
whose hand might have brushed hers, me who she might
have turned to in a scary moment and kissed. But it wasn't.
Because I was here and Ray was there. My breathing started
speeding up, and my eyes welled up with tears.

"Okay, time out," Ainsley said. "Let's go find somewhere
to sit down."

"No," I forced out in a strangled voice. "We have to find
Brougham. We have to . . ."

"Brougham can wait. Here, unlock it. I'll send him a
text. We won't be long."

People were glancing at me as I sniffled, tears rolling
freely down my cheeks. I rubbed a fist over them to try to
clean myself up. I must have been the most overgrown child
to ever burst into tears in the middle of Disneyland.

"This calls for bread bowls," Ainsley said, making a beeline for the Pacific Wharf Café. And she must have understood the gravity of the situation, because Ainsley had never particularly liked the bread bowls.

With Ainsley as my guide leading the way, I zombie-shuffled past the red bricks of the Boudin Bakery, and didn't even look up as we passed the enormous windows showcasing the bakers inside. When I was little I used to plant my feet firmly outside these windows and stare inside for what felt like hours, mesmerized by the golden-brown sourdough bread, begging my parents to take us on one more tour inside so I could watch the finely choreographed production process of dough to oven to tray. Even the rich, yeasty smell of the area should've been enough to wrap me in a cozy bubble. But though my stomach growled at the smell as we reached the soft browns and blues of the Pacific Wharf Café, everything from my chest up was numb.

"Are you gonna call her?" Ainsley asked as we joined the cattle-style lineup.

"I can't right now. Maybe later."

"Do you know who she might be dating?"

"Yeah. Raina from Q and Q."

"Raina with the French bulldog face?"

I cracked a tiny smile. "What?"

"She's always frowning like this." Ainsley lowered her eyebrows and scrunched up her face into a dramatic frown.

"Well . . . yeah, that *is* who I mean."

"See? Efficient. If I'd said, 'Raina who's yea high and has brown hair,' we would've been here all night. Besides, I'm sure she has a great personality . . . when you get to know her."

"Her personality *sucks*," I snapped. "She's always competing with Brooke and talking down to her and I've never even seen her have a nice word to say. Not *once*."

"So, what you're telling me is Brooke has inexplicably fallen for someone with a French bulldog face and a Persian cat's personality?"

". . . I mean, yeah, I guess."

"Sounds plausible."

From the tone of her voice, it sounded more like she meant "sounds like you're jealous and skewing Raina into an irredeemable caricature so you can convince yourself the relationship won't last long." Which was simply the rudest, most accurate thing she'd ever said to me. I suddenly hoped her bread bowl was stale.

We carried our orders—mac and cheese for me, clam chowder for Ainsley—outside to sit in the cooling dusk. Instead of eating, I reread the message over and over again, like it might magically say something different on the twentieth opening.

"I'm sorry," Ainsley said as she watched me. "There's nothing I can say that makes this better. Except, maybe, high school relationships don't usually last. I only know one couple who got together in junior year that's still blissfully happy. Everyone else crashed and burned dramatically, usually around the SATs, and—Oh, no, babe, don't cry."

But I couldn't help it. Brooke had feelings for someone else—she was dating someone else—and even though a part of me figured she'd never feel that way about me, another part of me had hoped. I was the best friend, the supportive one, who listened to her and laughed with her and stayed up with her chatting 'til all hours of the morning.

But she hadn't chosen me. She was never going to. And it didn't matter how caring I was, or how much effort I put into my hair and makeup, or how much time I put in. It was me, as I was, that wasn't doing it for her. There wasn't anything I could *do* to change that. And that made me feel like there was something inherently not good enough about me. I hiccupped and sniffled as sobs choked my throat. I wasn't a pretty crier. I was bright red cheeks and wobbling lips and puffy, swollen eyes that looked like I'd smashed my face into a table to test its structural integrity.

"It's okay," Ainsley tried. "You'll find your own patronizing Persian cat one day."

"I . . . don't . . . want . . . my own Persian cat," I gulped. "I want Brooke."

"I know. Life sucks."

"And she'll *marry her*," I spat out. "I bet you anything she'll marry her, because that's just how my luck is going. And they'll go on all these fancy trips to the snow and pose in their fancy ski gear and Raina will propose on top of *fucking* Mount Everest and I'll find out on Instagram and I'll have to pretend to be happy for them."

"That is *so specific*."

"It's just my gut feeling, okay? And Brooke will be all *happy*—"

"Yeah, fuck her, right?" Ainsley deadpanned.

"—and she won't even miss Austin and Ally."

"Who are Austin and Ally?"

"That's what we were going to call our twin babies." I stabbed a fork into my mac and cheese, then stabbed again.

"No, as your sister, I would not allow you to name your kids after a TV couple, that is *wildly* creepy and gross."

"It would've been adorable and nostalgic by then, but you know what? It doesn't matter, because now Austin and Ally are *dead*."

"Dark."

I wiped my nose on the back of my hand. "This is all *wrong*. I hate this."

"I know. Have some mac and cheese."

I did, and it was goddamn delicious, but it didn't fix anything. It just made my throat feel gluggy.

"Maybe we should head off soon," Ainsley suggested. "You look like shit and I don't wanna get home too late. Do you think Brougham will mind?"

Brougham.

Suddenly, I remembered the extra texts that had been sitting on my phone. I scrolled through my messages. There was mine to Brougham telling him we were gonna be behind doing the rapids. A text from him saying no worries. Another text with his location. A third message asking if I was off yet. A fourth message saying things were feeling off with Winona, but he couldn't figure out why. A fifth, with his updated location, and a plea for help. Then a response from Ainsley, telling him we needed a dinner break—she'd obviously not read his previous messages. And, finally, one more from Brougham.

Winona just ditched me

My sniffles cut off as I read his message, and all my sadness was replaced with horrified guilt and frustrated rage. "Are you *fucking* kidding me?" I hissed, then I picked my tray up and slammed it down on the table. "WHY IS LOVE DEAD?"

Now everyone really *was* staring. A few parents were glancing nervously between me and their precious, innocent children. I shot them all a dirty glare. "Don't blame me! I'm not the one who *murdered Cupid*!"

"All right, let's go," Ainsley said brightly, grabbing me by the arm and dragging me, still loudly ranting about the injustice of it all, away from the café before anyone could call security on us.

NINE

It was getting close to dinnertime for regular people now, and the restaurants around us were filled to the brim with diners and people cutting through to get somewhere else, all lit up by warm orange lights. The music from a number of different lands all mingled together at this crossroads, a mishmash of flutes and trumpets, smothered by the chatter of hundreds of strangers. Ainsley and I pushed past several families hovering smack in the middle of the walkways as we fought our way across the bridge to get back to the entrance to Pixar Pier.

Not far from the flashing lights of the Pixar Pier sign, Brougham stood with folded arms, leaning against the stone base of a towering, Victorian-style lamppost. Behind him, flashing lights in every color reflected on the black water beneath the pier.

Leaving Ainsley, I joined him wordlessly and stood facing the water, leaning my elbows on the ornate, swirling metal top of the barrier. "I'm sorry," I said.

"We didn't fight or anything." His voice was measured.

I turned around to face the same way as Brougham and

leaned my back against the barrier. "Oh?" I'd been expecting him to bring up my disappearance. I guessed he had bigger things to worry about.

"Yeah. It was just bad luck. We started running out of things to talk about, and she was doing her one-word answer thing, then she ran into some friends of hers, and they wanted to go on some rides together and stuff. So, she asked if I minded her going home with them."

"What did you say?"

"I said it was fine, of course. What else was I gonna say?"

"Is it fine?"

"Totally. She's allowed to do whatever she wants." His tone seemed a little too airy. Then his eyes caught mine, and a touch of uncertainty flashed across his face. "Do you think I did something wrong?"

The realistic answer was: "*Hard to say, I couldn't hear everything from where I was,*" or, "*Possibly, it's a minefield dating someone you've dated before,*" or, "*Wouldn't surprise me, given my experience with you and what it seems like it would be like to date you.*"

But none of those answers were constructive right this minute, and though he was doing an excellent job at pretending otherwise, I had a feeling he was bruised. So, I said, "Nah, I'm sure it was just what it looked like. She saw her friends, and wanted to hang with them. You couldn't have helped that."

"Right. It's normal to wanna hang with your friends."

". . . Yeah," I said, but I hesitated a fraction of a second too long.

His shoulders dropped. "You think it's a bad sign, hey?"

"Well . . . you're right, it is totally fair to want to see your friends . . ."

"But if she liked me, she wouldn't have wanted to."

I chose my words carefully. "It's pretty rude to walk out mid-activity. It either means she's trying to play a game with you, or that she's . . ."

"Not that keen."

"Basically, yeah."

"Which one do you reckon?"

"Me? I don't know her. What does your gut say?"

He turned his head pointedly to look down the pier. The track of his eyes followed the roller coaster, dropping his gaze in time with the distant screams of terror. "The latter."

"I'm sorry."

"I'm not," he said, a little too quickly. "It's fine. We had a good day, and if she wants to be friends, it's better than being enemies. It's not like I can force her into having feelings for me. And if she isn't interested, it probably wouldn't have worked out anyway."

I met Ainsley's eyes across the pier, and she shrugged at me in a question. I held up one finger. *Give me a second.*

"I mean, it's not like we had some great, epic love story or anything," he went on to nobody in particular. "Like, how's this, right, she constantly talks shit about her best friends, and if I ever *dare* to take her side during her two-hour rants about them, she goes and tells them everything I said and they hold it against me! How fucked up is that? Why do I even *want* to see her?"

Distancing and devaluing. He felt back in control when he was the one who didn't want *her*. Textbook.

"Oh but *now,* now she *desperately* wants to go hang with Kaylee and Emma. The same Kaylee and Emma she told me are histrionic drama queens on *Space Mountain,* but, hey, that's none of my business. Whatever she wants to do, you know?"

"Right," I added. Mostly to pretend this was a conversation and not a one-sided rant.

"I'm just saying I'm not the *only one* with flaws here. I'm not going to degrade myself to beg for her to care about me. It's not like I did her some *great wrong.*"

"Well—"

"I mean, I might not have been perfect but I would never have hurt her, or let anyone else hurt her, not for anything. I'm sick of feeling like I'm the one who fucked everything up between us. She broke us just as much as I did."

It was truly fascinating. Even while descending, Brougham managed to keep his face almost entirely passive. If it weren't for the odd twitch in the corner of his mouth, he might as well have been discussing the humidity levels.

"You're hurt," I said simply.

He scoffed. "Ah, no. I'm fucked off."

"And hurt."

"You have to care to be hurt," he said.

"And you don't care?"

"No. Like I said, it's fine. I'm *glad* she's gone off. Saves me putting in any more time and effort."

Talk about a gentleman who doth protest too much. "If you say so."

His head snapped up and he bored into me with hard eyes. "You can go now. There's no point staying, unless you want to go have fun with your sister. I know you didn't want to be here in the first place."

And there it was. For a moment there I thought I'd gotten

away with losing Brougham and being AWOL when he needed me. "I know I fucked up. I'm so sorry. The timing of that was awful."

The only indication he was irritated was him sucking on his teeth. "It wasn't just at the end. I kept losing you all day."

"Disneyland's a big place," I said, but it was a weak defense. "And, I guess, I didn't think you needed me."

"Well, next time, if you don't think there's any point, don't come. I didn't force you, you know. But you said you'd be here, so I was relying on that."

Okay, no. Not fair. "Well, blackmailing someone in the first place makes them feel pretty forced into whatever you ask them to do, even if you say they can say no."

A frown creased the top of his nose and his mouth dropped open. "What are you on about?"

". . . You blackmailed me."

"I did *not*!"

"You did! You said, 'Oh, I'd hate to tell everyone in the school who you are.'" I helpfully mimicked his accent to jog his memory.

"You're twisting my words. I said I figured you wanted to keep it private. As in, don't worry, I'm not gonna go around telling everybody you're working with me!"

I paused, suddenly as baffled as he looked. Was that . . . no, that's not what he'd meant. Was it? He'd said . . . the vibe of what he'd said, anyway, had been . . . but then, he hadn't threatened me since. Even slyly.

"I *thought* you got shitty at me out of nowhere," Brougham added, linking his hands behind his neck and shaking his head.

"Well, yes, I thought you were threatening me."

Brougham dragged his fingers over his mouth and jaw. "I didn't mean it to sound like that."

I didn't know what to think anymore. My head hurt. Suddenly I wasn't sure how much of my behavior toward him had been unwarranted. My cheeks flushed at the realization. "I guess it was just a misunderstanding," I said softly.

We fell into silence while I tried to replay our interactions in my head to sort through it all. "I'm sorry I was checked out today," I said. "I guess I was sort of resentful because I did feel forced, and then everything fell apart, and—" I broke off as a warning lump appeared in my throat.

"Hey, what's wrong?" His voice was surprisingly gentle, given that he had every right to be annoyed at me.

I flapped a dismissive hand. "I don't want to talk about it right now. Just . . . it's been a hard day. I'm sorry."

While I took some deep breaths to collect myself, Brougham kept his eyes locked on me. "Yeah, my day wasn't in my top five, either. I think I'll head home. I'm sick of it here."

The thing is, I wasn't sure I believed him. If I was right about Brougham having an anxious attachment style, then when he shut down, he actually wanted someone to urge him to open back up. If he pushed people away, it's because he wanted to be approached.

Luckily, Oriella had taught me exactly what to do in a situation like this. And I'd taught *others* what to do in a situation like this.

"Honestly," I said, "all I want to do is eat junk food and go on some more rides and not worry about shit for an hour."

"So do it."

I looked over at Ainsley. She'd lost interest in Brougham and me, and was scrolling through her phone while she leaned against a trash can across the bridge. "I would, but Ainsley was talking about heading home."

"Oh." Brougham rocked back and forth on his heels, like he was debating something. Then he gave me a one-sided shrug. "If Ainsley wants to head off now, I could always give you a lift home later?"

I broke into a slow smile.

Forty minutes later, Brougham and I were sitting across from each other in a carriage on Pixar Pal-A-Round, my personal Disneyland must-do, and the perfect thing to distract me. Because Pixar Pal-A-Round, or "The Mickey Wheel" as Ainsley and I had called it as kids, was less like your standard Ferris wheel and more like a thrill ride hidden under a calm, unassuming exterior. At least, if you chose one of the moving carriages, it was. And if you asked me, it was nonnegotiable to do so. Basically, you'd be gently cruising upward, gazing at the lights and crowds beneath you, when the carriage would suddenly slide down several feet like you were falling to your death, and swing back and forth using the momentum of your terrifying plummet.

It seemed Brougham hadn't bothered trying the Mickey Wheel before, because the whole "unexpected plummeting" thing caught him off guard. The first time we went down he screamed like he'd been shoved off a building. Once the carriage stopped swinging—or, at least, stopped swinging quite so *ferociously*—he turned large, accusing eyes onto me like I'd tricked him.

"You don't like it?" I asked through a torrent of giggles.

He took a moment to catch his breath, pressed back firmly against the caged wall, his hands splayed out to touch the carriage on either side of him while we rocked. "This is not safe, this is not safe, I want to get off."

"It's Disneyland, it's safe."

"People *have died here*!"

"Shout that a little louder, I think some of the small children up there didn't hear you."

"Is it too late to get off?"

"'Fraid so. But you get used to the rocking, I promise."

He looked doubtful. Slowly, but surely, though, I was proven correct. By our third fight with gravity, Brougham was down to a single scream of fear per fall. Calm enough to bring back up something he'd apparently really wanted to discuss. "Hey, so. You know how this morning you said using silence as a weapon is emotionally abusive?" he asked. "It's complicated, I think."

I smiled and pushed a waving strand of hair out of my eyes. "Maybe not so complicated."

He looked over the park below while he spoke. "It kind of is, though. I never knew who was in the wrong with Winona and me. But sometimes—actually, often, I guess, I would feel her withdrawing. And I'd try *so hard* not to freak out, because I *knew* she thought I was clingy and the last thing I wanted to do was make her withdraw even more, but literally no matter what I did she would just go quieter and quieter until she'd totally ignore me for days. One time it was two weeks. Like I wasn't there, you know? Then I'd get in this fucking *spiral* where I'd try to stop myself from reaching out, but I'd convince myself she was about to dump me and come up with a good reason to text or call casually, and she'd ignore *that*, and I'd blame myself for reaching out and getting in her space. I just never knew what to do. And everyone around me would be like, chill *out*, she doesn't owe you her attention every second of the day, you don't own her. And I'd be like, I'm not trying to own anyone, I swear, but I just . . . isn't it normal to want to hear from your girlfriend literally *once* in a two-week peri-OOOODDDDD?"

Our gondola plunged again and Brougham's hands went right back to the metal mesh so he could steady himself. I tried to hold in my laugh of delight at the thrill of the drop. On the one hand, this was a serious conversation. On the other, it wasn't exactly my fault Brougham brought up such a serious topic halfway through an amusement park ride.

When Brougham's breathing returned to normal, and the rocking evened out, he continued on gallantly. "Then she'd come back every time, and she'd act like it didn't happen, and she'd say she was just busy. And on the one hand, I'd hate myself for being so demanding when she was just trying to live her life. But then I'd wonder how much she actually cared about me if she couldn't find thirty seconds to reply to a text in two weeks while she was on vacation."

The last bit he directed at me. He sucked his lips in and shrugged. It wasn't a question, but it definitely seemed like an invitation for advice.

"It doesn't sound like she was doing it to be cruel," I started. "Like, it wasn't following a fight or to make you give in to a demand or anything, right?"

Something funny flashed over Brougham's expression. "No, totally," he said. "She wasn't doing anything wrong. I never meant to say she was. I *know* I was the one being demanding, it's *obviously* okay to take time to yourself. She didn't owe—"

"Well," I interrupted. "Not really. Because it's actually not unreasonable to ask for communication from your girlfriend."

From the look he gave me, you'd think I'd just told him the ocean was made out of hot chocolate and the grass was peppermint sticks.

"Maybe she has the right to be busy, but when you're in a relationship with someone you sign up to respect them. She could've communicated with you that things were hectic. She could've told you when things should be back to normal. In Western society, you know, we value independence *so much*. But you're not the bad guy if you want closeness. You weren't being clingy, or hurting anyone. You just weren't having your needs met."

He was gripping the edge of his seat with white knuckles. I wondered if he noticed. "She's not a bad person."

"I know. But neither are you."

Suddenly, his eyes were glassy, and his teeth clenched. It seemed like something I'd said there had struck a chord. I wondered whether Alexander Brougham heard that very often. *You're not a bad person.*

Brougham was confusing. It seemed bizarre that the same guy who walked around with a grating level of swagger, proclaiming he was a catch, and intimidating, and knew all there was to know about flirting, could now be so vulnerable and uncertain.

He tipped his head back and took a deep breath, like he was trying to suck the emotions back into hiding. "So, where do I go from here, Coach?"

There was only one option for either of us. "Well, there's not that much you can do except feel it."

One eyebrow went up. "Feel it?"

"Just let it out." I threw my hands up. "Say fuck this, it *sucks*."

Because it fucking did. It sucked, it sucked, it sucked.

Brougham stared at me. "You want me to shout, 'Fuck this, it sucks,' in the middle of Disneyland? The Happiest Place on Earth?"

Well he didn't have to say it like *that*.

Right next to us, the Incredicoaster shot out, and the people riding it let out bloodcurdling screams as they hurtled to their doom in the middle of said Happiest Place on Earth. We were up high enough that the whipping wind ran off with our words as soon as they left our mouths, making us shout to be heard. As weird as it sounded, this was about as private as it could get around here. "There's too many people screaming for anyone to hear you. Stop stalling. Come on!"

Brougham glanced around us—into midair, I might add—then shifted in his seat. "It sucks," he mumbled.

"It *sucks*!" I spat it out, all the poison I was feeling about being dragged away from Brooke today, and about Ray swooping in, and about my utter inability to fix my own love life.

"It sucks," Brougham echoed, a little more loudly this time.

"IT SUCKS!" I shouted, getting to my feet to make a point. The carriage chose that moment to tip and slide down to the end, and I screamed bloody murder. "OH MY GOD, NO, HELP," I yelled, gripping onto the bars near the door. My body was thrown against my seat, and I toppled backward so I was splayed awkwardly across the bench. I'd almost certainly bruised a butt cheek, and maybe also a spot on my back that'd crashed into the back of the carriage.

"Hey!" Brougham rose up with his hands outstretched, his face stricken, but I waved him off, laughing so hard I fell off my seat and onto the floor with my knees up as the carriage swung violently back and forth. "IT SUCKS," I shouted again, this time directing my yelling at the ceiling.

Brougham sat back down and shook his head at me, then, amazingly, cracked a smile. A real, actual smile, honest to god. I felt like I was probably the first person to ever witness this. I couldn't have been more amazed if it were my own kid taking their first steps. "*It sucks,*" Brougham cried, halfway to a yell.

"Louder."

"IT. SUCKS." He slapped both hands down on the bench he sat on, and I applauded, still on the floor.

"You know what else sucks?" I asked.

Brougham stuck out a hand and helped me back onto my seat. "What?"

My laughter trickled into a drip, and my voice came out tinny. "I'm in love with my best friend. And she's got a new girlfriend."

"Wait, Brooke?"

I nodded.

"Shit, Phillips, that *does* suck. We're as screwed as each other."

I laughed despite myself. "Nah, you're less screwed. You have me, and we're not done yet. How about—"

"Actually, I need some time to think."

My first reaction was surprise. Then it shifted into something more akin to offense. What, one strike and I was out? Hadn't I said they'd need to be friends first? Did he think I wasn't worth the money just because they weren't passionately kissing on the Mickey Wheel right now?

Worse than that, worse than him feeling that way, was the fearful little voice in the back of my mind whispering *he's right*. I had failed. I was no Coach Pris, no Oriella.

I couldn't see myself, but if I could, I was pretty sure dismay would've been carved into every feature. And it only took Brougham glancing at me for him to add a hurried addendum. "I'm really grateful for everything you did. And honestly, I'm impressed. You're good at this. Better than I expected." He shrugged. "And I'm not saying I'm calling it quits. But maybe . . . a hiatus?"

Okay. Well, that was fair. Because hearing Brougham talk about his relationship with Winona? Put it this way: if he wanted me to help him, I would, and I would do my *best*. But I couldn't say I was convinced either one of them were all that healthy for each other. Maybe I was wrong. There was probably lots and lots I didn't know. But I did know some things.

If Winona was as Brougham described, withdrawing into silence whenever she felt smothered, and shutting down emotionally, immune to his pleas for empathy and affection, I'd put money on her being a dismissive-avoidant. Honestly, it made sense. The avoidant and the anxious often found each other. Maybe because the highs and lows felt like love. And maybe because people loved the familiar, and finding someone who was inherently wrong for them reinforced all the negative views about relationships they'd grown so comfortable holding: that they will suffocate you and steal your independence, or that they'll leave you alone and bleeding.

An anxiously attached person who feared rejection and a dismissive-avoidant who feared being consumed by closeness would constantly overwhelm each other unless they both put a lot of effort into understanding their triggers and learning coping techniques. Ultimately, if Brougham wanted things to work with Winona, they'd both need to unlearn their views. And from where I was standing, she didn't exactly seem to be seeking help in rekindling their romance.

But it wasn't the time or place to dump all these what-ifs on Brougham. So I just leaned forward to rest my elbows on my knees as the wheel brought us back to where we started.

"Well, if you decide you want to try again one day, you know where to find me."

CHAPTER TEN

Dear Locker 89,

It's me again. You were such a help last time,
thank you so much for your advice. I struggled
with writing this letter, because, in a weird way,
it feels like you know me and you were rooting for
me. I hope this won't change that.

I have a confession. The girl I wrote in about
last time? She's now my girlfriend (yay!) but I've
been hiding a secret from her. Last year we were
in competition for something (I don't want to say
what because it'll give me away), and I wanted it
so badly I did something awful. Long story short,
I rigged it so I won. This was before I liked
her. The problem is, I told a couple of my friends
about it this week (I cracked from the guilt), and
it's not necessarily that I think they'll tell
on me? It's that I know if they _did_, she'd never
forgive me.

I guess what I'm asking is . . . do you think I should tell her myself? I'm terrified of how she'll react, but more terrified of her finding out through someone else. Just . . . please tell me if you think I'm making a huge mistake.

Thank you,
ray_of_sunshine001@gmail.com

The letter, which had made me see red, sat hidden in my desk drawer under three textbooks back at home.

Right now, all I could see was black, as I sat motionless on Brooke's bed with my eyes closed and my head tipped back, waiting for Brooke to finish my eye shadow, her warm hand resting on my forehead. "Cut-crease time," she'd declared ten minutes ago, pulling out her kit. It was pathetic, but I was thrilled to hear those words, because it meant I got a solid ten minutes of attention from her.

When she let me open my eyes again I blinked, and Ray came into focus. She had a curling iron in her hand, and was methodically working through strips of her hair, styling them into tight curls. She started them higher than she should've, though, and it gave the top of her head a bumpy, uneven finish. I could've given her a hand, but after *that* letter, I wasn't feeling generous. If she wanted to go to tonight's mixer with a head full of regency curls, it was none of my business.

She seemed casual, and chirpy. If my disgust had slipped and shown on my face at any point this evening, neither she nor Brooke seemed to have noticed. At least, they hadn't mentioned anything.

I wondered how she would react if she knew her letter was sitting back in my bedroom. If she'd notice my expression then.

Satisfied with my makeup, Brooke headed over to fuss over Ray, leaving my forehead cold in her hand's sudden absence.

We had about half an hour before Brooke's mom was due to drop us off at Alexei's for a gathering of kids from the gay–straight alliances at various schools, organized by the Q&Q Club. Of course, when Brooke had asked if I'd come over and get ready with her, I'd known Ray would be there. Ray seemed to have gained a VIP pass to literally everything Brooke and I ever did together, and she'd even ended up at *my* house without me explicitly inviting her a few times. Since they'd started dating I'd caught up with Brooke alone exactly once. *Once.* At school, Ray was there. After school, she was working or hanging out with Ray. On the weekends, homework and Ray.

Usually I did my best to be optimistic about it all, and convince myself I would learn to love Ray, and I should be happy my intimate dyad with Brooke was expanding.

Today, that was not about to happen. Because yesterday I had discovered Ray was a sea witch, a siren, a freaking chupacabra. I focused on my breathing, because I had asked God this afternoon to grant me the serenity to accept things I could not change, and acceptance meant slow, meditative breathing.

On Brooke's bed, Ray pouted in front of the mirror and held the curling iron out to Brooke. "Can you do it, pleeeeease?"

Brooke rolled her eyes, but it was affectionate. "You know I love a damsel in distress," she murmured, taking it from her. She threaded her fingers through Ray's mousy hair, shaking the curls out slowly, lusciously, in a way that screamed sex.

I awkwardly averted my eyes, fully aware that if I weren't here, they'd be making out. And that they'd probably prefer it that way. Instead, now that my makeup was done, I grabbed my outfit and ducked out to the bathroom to change. Another annoying thing about Ray crashing literally everything these days: I was not comfortable enough to change in front of her.

In the bathroom, I put on my dress for the night—a turquoise sack of a thing I'd bought at Jenny's because of its cute three-quarter sleeves, which Ainsley had then nipped in at the waist to turn into a skater cut—and finished my hair in privacy so I didn't have to soak in the weird couple-y vibes emanating off Brooke and Ray. I wished Ainsley were here. I'd begged her to come along—she'd founded the club, after all. But she was out with some college friends at her own get-together. She'd also added a comment about how it couldn't live up to the one she'd organized last year, anyway, because *that* mixer had a jumping castle, which honestly just made me think she was more bummed about the conflicting plans than she'd let on. At least she'd let me borrow her car for the night—she'd assured me she had no intentions of staying sober enough to drive.

When I finally headed back to the bedroom, I walked in as Brooke and Ray were mid-kiss. They ended it, giggling into each other's mouths, then went back to fixing Ray's hair without even acknowledging me. I wandered over to Brooke's desk and picked up my phone, while Ray started telling a story about some senior Brooke seemed to have heard of, but I hadn't. Then I dug through Brooke's perfume collection and sprayed myself, while Brooke asked Ray to make her promise not to drink any shots. Then I doodled on a spare sheet of paper while Ray invited Brooke to a family barbeque that weekend, and, *come on,* wasn't it rude to invite someone to something within earshot of someone who *wasn't* invited?

I tried to tamp down my glower and checked my phone. We were supposed to leave ten minutes ago now. Brooke's mom would be somewhere downstairs waiting for us. I got to my feet and stretched. And this, finally, got Brooke and Ray's attention.

"Are we ready to go?" I asked.

Brooke and Ray exchanged a glance, and it was a *loaded* glance. A glance that said something about me, and I didn't think it was something I'd like.

"We don't even have our shoes on yet," Brooke said in a long-suffering kind of way.

"Okay, cool," I said, and an awkward layer fell over the room.

"Well," Brooke said with a light laugh, turning to Ray. "Guess we'd better get our shoes on, huh?"

Another *look* I was left out of.

Tonight wasn't going to be much fun for me, was it?

Brooke had forgotten me again.

We'd finally had a moment to ourselves without Ray linking their arms together or hooping her arms in a noose around Brooke's neck or spidering her fingers up Brooke's back, and then Brooke had excused herself to the bathroom. She'd said she'd be right back, so I'd stayed in my spot by Alexei's living room window, half-blended into the curtains. Then I'd watched Brooke return from the bathroom, sway her hips to the blaring pop music as she walked through the dimly lit room, find Ray where she was talking to Jaz and an unfamiliar girl, and slide on into their conversation.

I'd expected it, but it still felt like a slap.

I scanned the room for someone to talk to. I'd already worked the room about a billion times tonight, and I was getting sick of injecting myself into conversations. My first urge was to find Finn, but he'd disappeared with a short redhead about twenty minutes earlier.

Ray laughed at something Brooke said. Her face was alight and soft. She looked innocent, there in the half-shadows. Like someone who hadn't rigged an election she was going to lose, and then hidden it from her girlfriend, even when they started dating.

Too bad that, as of a few days ago, I knew better. Too bad for Ray. Too bad for Brooke. Too bad for me. Because now I knew Ray was wrong for Brooke, knew it with a fierce certainty. She'd hurt her, stolen something from her, and she hadn't done a thing to fix it.

Even in the letter, she wasn't certain. The only reason she even wanted to confess was to save face, just in case the secret came out through someone else. She didn't want to confess for Brooke. If she loved Brooke, it shouldn't be a question.

But what could I do with information I shouldn't have?

I tore my eyes away from Brooke and spun my empty cup between my fingers, then wandered over to the occupied couch and slumped down in a free spot. I aimed it wrong and my hip bumped against Hunter, Brougham and Finn's friend. Finn had brought along both Hunter and Luke. He said it was because they were allies, but I suspected it was more to do with how those two preferred to party. "Oh, sorry," I said.

"It's cool," Hunter said, distracted, as he shifted over to make room for me. He was leaning forward, holding his phone between his knees as he composed a text. I glanced down at his screen, tipsy enough that I'd read his message before I realized how rude I was being.

> just at the party with luke and finn, i'll message you when I get home. cant wait to see you tomorrow. thinking about you 🖤

Hunter shoved his phone in his pocket and hopped to his feet to clap Luke on the back. I hadn't even noticed Luke approach, what with the lack of light and the swarm of bodies. There must have been at least thirty people in the room. "Hey, Finn's in the yard," Luke said. I couldn't hear Hunter's reply, as they turned to walk off together, leaving me alone on the couch.

He hadn't even said bye to me. And there I'd thought we were couch buddies.

I also wondered if he happened to be the guy who'd called his girlfriend a psycho once. If so, I hoped Finn and Brougham didn't let that shit slide if he said it out loud. But, on a positive note, if it was him, at least he had the ability to learn. His message couldn't have been more suited to soothe an activated attachment system if I'd written it myself. The thought injected a little warmth into my otherwise sour mood.

Even still, I was out of emotional energy to do anything but sit alone and observe.

Which I did. I observed Brooke and Ray get into some sort of chugging competition with Jaz acting as referee.

I observed Alexei working the room, dropping in on various conversations and making sure the living room stayed reasonably clean and tidy, which made sense given their parents were just upstairs. While they were obviously in the running to win the "most chilled-out parents" award, I'm sure they wouldn't appreciate a trashed house, and it wasn't like Alexei could do a quick cleanup to hide the evidence if things got out of hand.

I observed Finn glide into the living room from the direction of the backyard, look around slowly, then sort of drift unsteadily down the hall. He might have been going to the bathroom, but he looked . . . odd. I wasn't otherwise engaged, so I followed him, half out of concern, half out of curiosity. He wandered down the hall ahead of me in no great rush, taking in the family photos hanging on the wall, and the ceiling, and his own feet. He paused at the bathroom, looked in, then kept walking. He found a door, pushed it open and slid inside, leaving it open behind him.

I peeked around it. I half-expected to find someone else in there, but it was just Finn, spinning around slowly in the center of the room on top of a cream shag rug. The room was a sort of second living room/study combination, with a heavy chestnut desk, a ceiling-high bookshelf running along half a wall, and a maroon sofa and armchair set up by an expensive-looking coffee table.

I knocked to announce myself and walked in. "Hey, dude. I'm not sure we're meant to be in this end of the house."

Finn looked positively delighted to see me, and he held out his arms for a hug. "Darcy!"

I came closer to him, crossing my arms uncertainly. We'd never hugged before. But he kept his arms out, so I cracked and gave him a quick embrace. "How's your night?" I asked.

"Oh, it's great. It's *awesome,* you?" Before I could reply, he went on, pulling back from me but keeping his hands firmly on my shoulders. "I've met *great* people, everyone here is *great*. My friends are all here! Well, not all of them. But Hunter and Luke are here! Isn't that great?"

"So great," I agreed, equal amounts amused and confused. "How come Brougham's not here?"

Finn waved a hand, then looked at it for a long moment, and waved it again while he narrowed his eyes in suspicion at the limb. "He has a swim meet in the morning. Besides, he doesn't drink."

"His body's a temple," I said wryly. I didn't know why I was being mean about Brougham. He was all right, really. We hadn't talked at all since Disneyland, but we'd ended our business relationship on okay terms. And he *had* kept my secret for me. I was just mad at the world after reading about what Ray had done to Brooke, I guess.

Finn shook his head. "No, it's not that. It's—*what* is wrong with my hand?"

He held it out between us, wide-eyed. It seemed standard, as far as hands went. "I don't know, what's up?"

Finn shoved it in his back pocket, then sat down hard on the sofa, pinning his hand under his body weight. "Oh," he said vaguely.

"Finn?" I asked, uncertain. How much had he drunk? "You okay?"

"I did a thing."

"What did you do?"

He shifted to release his trapped hand, then slowly tipped backward on the sofa until he and the sofa had all but become one. "I had some gummies."

It took me a second. "Wait, like weed gummies?"

His eyebrows drew together, and he adjusted his glasses while he focused in on something in the distance. We sat in an endless pause. Then he blinked slowly and sighed. "Pardon?"

". . . I asked if you ate weed gummies."

"Oh. Yes. I did that."

Uh-oh. I had approximately zero experience with this kind of situation. I was only recently getting used to how to support drunk people, and it involved way too much vomit for my liking. Was Finn going to vomit? Should I get him to the bathroom?

"What?" Finn asked sharply.

"I didn't say anything."

"Oh." He looked relieved. "I thought you said 'chicken nuggets.' I was like, *what*?"

Why—but—*what*?

I decided to go into nurse mode. Which was difficult, given that I had no idea what red flags I was looking for, but Mom, ever the schoolteacher, had drilled drug safety into my head constantly since I hit puberty. Find out what they took, when, and how much. Just in case someone needs to know at some point. In case something goes wrong.

"Is that what you were doing outside?" I asked. "Eating gummies?"

"No. How long do you think it takes to . . ."

Sentence over, apparently. I pressed him again. "When did you eat the gummies?"

"Before the party."

I checked my phone. Three hours ago? "How many did you take?"

"Two, then I took another an hour later because I didn't . . ."

End sentence. Okay, so he had three, two to three hours ago. That didn't seem like an awful lot. And surely it wouldn't be hitting him *now,* three hours later? Did that mean something else had happened? Was something wrong?

I didn't want to make a huge scene out of things, not yet, in case Alexei's parents left their bedroom to see what was going on. I'd involve them if I needed to, obviously, but I didn't want to throw Finn under the bus just yet. Not when all he was doing was sitting on his hands and hallucinating talk of nuggets. I mean, who among us *hasn't* hallucinated someone promising us chicken nuggets at some point in our lives?

I sent Brooke a text to ask her to come to the study—alone—and put a hand on Finn's shoulder. "Are you okay? Do you feel sick?"

He concentrated very hard on his answer. Good to know I was getting quality, thought-out content here. "I feel . . . like my throat has become an icicle. My throat is just all . . . ice."

Finn took his glasses off and, purposefully and methodically, slid them underneath the sofa.

At that moment, God sent me an angel in the form of Brooke Nguyen. I beckoned her in as I rescued Finn's glasses from their hiding spot.

"What's going on in here?" she asked.

I glanced at Finn. "My face is falling apart," he informed Brooke solemnly.

"He ate three weed gummies."

Brooke gaped. "*Three*? You're supposed to have *one*! Or, like, half of one, really. They don't regulate the doses properly, it's *so* easy to take too much."

"He said he took them hours ago, though," I said. "Are we sure it's that?"

"Yeah, Darc, they get digested, then they hit. Digestion takes time."

Oh. Now she said that, it made perfect sense.

On the plus side, Brooke didn't seem concerned. A little worried, maybe, but there was enough humor behind the worry that I didn't feel the urge to race for Alexei's parents, or 911.

"Brooke," Finn said, a sudden urgency in his voice. "Brooke, Brooke, Brooke. Brooke."

"Yes, Finn?"

"I figured it out. I died about half an hour ago! I'm *dead*. That's why."

Brooke shot me a sideways glance. "Oh dear."

"Is this bad?" I asked. "Can he die?"

"Nah, you only die from edibles if you do something stupid while you're high and *that* kills you," Brooke said. "He'll be fine if we keep an eye on him. He might green out, though, if it gets any worse."

Well *that* sounded ominous. "Which means?"

"Puking, sweating, all the fun stuff."

"I'm not nauseous," Finn said. "It's just that . . . existence itself is . . . existence is a vacuum of bleak despair." He touched his chin with hesitant fingers, like he half-expected it to have vanished.

Brooke climbed onto the sofa, trying and failing to contain a giggle. "Oh, my poor bunny," she cooed as she wrapped her arms around Finn.

How were we supposed to keep an eye on him until he sobered up? What if he ran away or something and danced through the freeway traffic or tightrope-walked along a canal? All at once I was horrifyingly aware we were responsible for a human with the memory span of a blowfly, the critical thinking levels of a distracted three-year-old, and the speed and strength of a seventeen-year-old boy.

Well, okay, who could we trust to keep him safe until he sobered up? Hunter and Luke were downstairs, sure, but they'd definitely been drinking, and, now that I thought about it, had probably eaten gummies right along with Finn, given they all came together. Group effort where the Q&Q Club shared joint responsibility for him? Nope, even worse, then everyone would assume someone else knew where he was if he disappeared.

Could we just . . . barricade him in here with some food and water and hope for the best?

Then, with a relieved rush, I realized the best option here was obvious.

"Hey, Finn, I'm gonna call Brougham to come and get you, all right?" I said.

"Oh, *Brougham*," Finn breathed, cupping Brooke's cheek as he spoke. "I *love* Brougham."

"Why do you have Brougham's number?" Brooke asked while Finn caressed her face. The phone was ringing already, though, so I held up an apologetic finger as an excuse to dodge the question.

When Brougham answered with a surprised, "Hey, Phillips?" my first thought was it was odd to hear his voice again after acting like we didn't know each other.

"Hey, um, so don't freak out but something's happened with Finn."

Brougham's response was sharp and sudden. "Is he okay?"

"I don't know. Apparently, someone gave him some edibles, and they got the dosage wrong or something . . . he's really out of it. I've been drinking so I can't take him home, and—"

"Yep, yeah, I'm coming. You guys still at Alexei's?"

"Yeah. Do you know where they live?"

"I'm the one who dropped the guys off. I'll be ten minutes, max. Can you keep him safe in the meantime?"

I glanced up at Finn, who had stopped stroking Brooke, wandered across the room toward me, and started the process of climbing up one of the bookshelves like it was a ladder. I grabbed his arm and held him steady, and he looked at my hand in confusion, like it was attached to nothing and shouldn't have been there. "No guarantees, but I'll do my best."

"Wait, I didn't make myself clear enough. Keep him safe, *totally* guaranteed, no buts."

"Better get here fast then," I said. Brougham started replying but I hung up on him and shoved my phone in my pocket so I could use both my hands to guide Finn back down.

Ten minutes.

We just had to keep him safe for ten minutes.

With a sigh, Finn walked with great purpose toward the center of the room, stopped in the middle of the shag rug, then lay facedown with his arms straight by his side. Brooke and I looked at each other.

"Do you think his friends are this bad?" I asked.

"They were fine when I was downstairs. I'll text Ray and check. Also, um, why do you have Brougham's number?"

Damn, so I hadn't dodged the question after all. I decided

to tell half the truth. "He uses the pool after school to train, and we've chatted a few times while I waited for Mom to finish up."

"Oh, random," Brooke said, but she didn't look particularly perturbed. "You've never mentioned that."

"Never came up."

"Brougham is the best friend," Finn piped up from his spot on the floor. The words were muffled by shag rug, but still comprehensible. "You guys don't even . . . know. You don't even *know* him."

"Darcy knows him, apparently."

Finn lifted his head—and from the stiffness of his neck, that was apparently a ten-ton feat—and shook his head with a stern expression, eyes squeezed shut. "Nope. Nope."

"You stand corrected," I said with a grin.

"I think *Darcy* is The Best Friend, actually," Brooke said, and I suddenly realized just how much I'd been wanting her to say something affectionate like that lately. I could forgive her for ditching me a million times over, I felt, as long as I knew I was still her best friend. Still important to her.

My phone buzzed. "Brougham's here," I announced. I was a little disappointed he'd arrived so fast. I'd been enjoying the quality time with Brooke. Because, yes, compared to how things had been recently, pairing up to watch Finn was practically a weekend getaway for two.

"Hurry back," Brooke said. "I—*Finn Park, don't lick the carpet,* oh my *god*."

I hurried.

ELEVEN

Dear Locker 89,

I (17yo F) broke up with my boyfriend (17yo
M) about a month ago, and ever since he's been
orbiting me. Liking all my stuff on Instagram,
viewing every single story, opens every
Snapchat etc. But he's the one who told me he
didn't want to stay friends. I figure if we're out of
each other's lives, we're out of them. I don't want
to block him or anything because we ended
on ok terms (he just said he wasn't feeling it
anymore :( ) and it's not *bothering* me that he
keeps popping up. But I wonder what it means.
Should I reach out to him and ask why he's up in
my shit? Or try to start a conversation? Do you
think this means he wants me back and is too
scared to ask?

HadleyRohan_9@gmail.com

Locker 89 <locker89@gmail.com>   7:53 p.m. (0 min ago)
to Hadley Rohan

Hey Hadley!

Orbiting is a great term here. He's keeping himself in your orbit, and it's also a sign you're in his. While I can't say it's necessarily a sign he wants to get back together, or he still has feelings for you, I can certainly say you're on his radar. He is aware of you, and notices your presence. The only time this observation might change is if he's the type of person who views and likes every single thing that comes across his feeds. You know the answer to that better than me!

Regardless, I don't advise you to reach out. If he dumped you, and he hasn't made an effort to get back in touch, then it means that, for whatever reason, he does not want to be in touch right now. Not only that, but if he *does* want you back? After getting dumped, you absolutely deserve to be re-courted with fervor. Don't take on the emotional load of fixing what he broke, especially given it sounds like the breakup wasn't any fault of your own. If he does reach out, I recommend you be pleasant, but don't jump into anything too fast. You have every right to take your time to decide whether your heart is ready to try again, and to ask him what's changed, and how you're supposed to know he won't change his mind again in a month.

Brougham spotted me instantly, and plowed through the crowd to approach me with brisk strides.

From the looks of things, I'd caught him as he was getting ready for bed. For a start, he smelled like apricots, like he'd just gotten out of the shower, and his hair was messy and standing up at odd angles. Instead of his usual casually preppy style, he'd thrown on sweatpants and a wrinkled, baggy white tank top that showed off his bare arms. He looked, in the weirdest way, sweet. Cuddly, even.

Until he spoke in a clipped, no-nonsense tone. "Where is he?"

"Down the hall, come on."

He glued himself to my side as we skirted around the living room, weaving in and out of small groups of chatting, drinking people, guided by the soft blue glow emanating from the television.

"Thanks for coming," I said. "I know you have swimming in the morning, but I—"

"Hey," Brougham cut me off, grabbing my lower arm. I stopped and faced him straight-on, and he took a step toward me, deathly serious. "It's Finn. If something happened to him and I found out you hadn't called me? I would hate you until the day you died, then I'd crash your funeral and tell everyone how much you sucked. And if I died first? I'd haunt you until you wished you'd gone before me."

I wrenched my arm away from his. So much for gratitude. "If you go anywhere *near* my funeral, I swear to god you won't have known the *meaning* of haunting before then."

Brougham shrugged. "No worries, we've avoided all that messiness because you had the sense to call me when you did. Aren't you glad?"

"Ecstatic."

Ray and Brooke jumped apart when I opened the door. Because of course Ray had darted in to fill in for me the moment I left the room. I didn't want to know, so I didn't think about it, didn't think about them *making out* while their friend was sick and in need of help and support, lying only feet away from them, possibly still licking the rug with zero intervention. Didn't think about how shitty that was, and how Brooke would never have done anything like that before Ray, and how Ray made everything, and everyone, worse, because she was a liar and selfish and did cruel things to people she was supposed to love.

Didn't think of it at all.

My self-control was really improving these days, I was so proud of myself.

"You're an absolute numpty," Brougham said in a fond voice, crouching down in front of Finn so they were face-to-face.

"I want it to stop. Make it stop?"

"You're stuck riding it out now, mate." Brougham hooked his hands under Finn's arms and hoisted him easily to his feet. "Can you walk? You okay?"

"Yeah, I . . . yeah."

Finn was standing without noticeable difficulty, but Brougham grasped his upper arm anyway. "All right, come on then, druggie. You can sleep at mine tonight."

Brooke, Ray, and I followed them, Brooke laughing silently as Brougham steered a very off-balance Finn down the hall toward the living room.

"Give him *lots* of water, Brougham," she said through her laughter, trying to clear her throat and get serious.

"Someone check on Hunter and Luke," Brougham ordered. "I couldn't find them when I got here."

Ray nodded, and turned on her heel. It made sense for

her to go, I guessed. She was in the same grade as them, after all.

But, most importantly, she was gone. And I might not have another opportunity to speak to Brooke in person without her hovering. It was now or never.

"Hey," I said to Brooke. "Can we go in the backyard or something for a sec?"

Something wary flashed across Brooke's face, but she agreed. Brougham seemed to have the Finn situation well under control, so we excused ourselves and headed off. When I looked back over my shoulder—just to make sure Finn hadn't somehow died in the last two seconds—I found Brougham watching Brooke and me as we retreated.

He held my gaze as I caught his eye. "Thank you," he mouthed.

It was an uncharacteristic moment of gentleness from him, accompanied with that intense stare of his, the one I'd noticed that afternoon at his house. The one that'd made his eyes seem bluer. Now I felt doubly bad for taking a dig at him earlier.

Outside on Alexei's patio, the music was reduced to a muffled thumping. Brooke and I sat on decorative wrought-iron dining chairs on either side of a matching counter table. String lights wrapped around the patio fence in a weaving pattern, glittering on and off.

I fought the sudden urge to skip having an uncomfortable conversation and propose an Instagram photoshoot instead, so we could be happy and have fun and I wouldn't risk pushing her away.

"What's up?" Brooke asked, and, well, here went nothing.

"I miss you."

She broke into a grin. "What do you mean? I'm right here."

"I know you are, now. But come on. When's the last time we hung out, Brooke?"

"We got ready together today!"

"Alone."

She gave me a look that quite plainly said: *Are you serious right now?* "Come on, I don't know. Like, the other day when I came over and we helped Ainsley hem that dress?"

"That was *weeks ago.*"

At this she sighed at me, and I shrank into myself as my chest clenched. She'd never sighed at me before. *To* me, to make fun of someone else, maybe. But this? This was disdain, directed right at me, not even tempered by a soft smile. "I've been busy, I'm *sorry.*"

"You're not too busy to see Ray."

"She's my girlfriend."

"So? I'm your *best* friend! Why is it important to cram Ray into your schedule but not me?"

Inside, a cheer rang out. "It's not that I'm avoiding you or anything. It makes it hard that you two don't get along, though, you know. If I could invite you out with us this wouldn't be an issue."

"So, you're saying it's my fault?"

"*No*, I'm just saying . . . can't you try to be friends with her? Then I won't have to choose between you two."

"Not that it's seemed like much of a choice lately," I said.

"That's not true."

"Well, I don't know what you want from me," I snapped. "I'm not trying to not be friends with her. It's not like I'm rude or mean or anything."

"I can still tell, though. You should see your face every

time you're near her. It's like you give her daggers twenty-four seven, and she hasn't ever done anything to you, Darc. It makes her uncomfortable."

I pictured Brooke and Ray snuggled up on the couch, while Ray badmouthed me, told Brooke how cruel I was to her, how *mean* I was, and Brooke agreed with her. Both of them saying how horrible it was to have me around. Like a joke I was the only one not in on.

I'd had no idea Brooke felt like that.

And, why? Because I didn't light up with joy every time Ray burst in to stand between Brooke and me? Seriously?

I swallowed the lump forming in my throat and spoke with a worryingly shaky voice. "It's not about what she's done to me. I feel weird about her because she was always so mean to *you*."

"That was in the past," Brooke said in a firm voice. "I appreciate that you have my back, but you have to trust my judgment. If I think she's changed, she's changed. I need you to support that."

"I'm not in love with the idea of unquestioningly supporting you if I don't like a situation you're in," I said.

"Don't do it unquestioningly, then. Do it logically. When was the last time you saw Ray be anything but gorgeous to me?"

I bit my lip. A little too hard.

Brooke took my silence as agreement. "See? She's sweet, Darc. She's fun, and supportive, and understanding. She'd never do anything to hurt me, never, and it's ridiculous for you to be suspicious of her still."

I crossed my arms and legs and scowled. How had we started out with me begging for my best friend back, and ended up here, with the Brooke-and-Ray team versus evil

Darcy? Like I was the only one who made things weird—Ray had given me *plenty* of salty looks when *I* came in the room. So why was I completely at fault?

And as for "sweet," and "supportive," and "never doing anything to hurt Brooke"?

Hah. *Hah.*

"You have rose-colored glasses on," I said stubbornly, "and you just can't see you're punching below your weight."

I meant to say that she deserved better, but somehow those words had come out instead. Before I could backpedal, Brooke scanned my face up and down. "Seriously, *what* is your problem with her? I know you, Darc, and the person I'm friends with is not a catty bitch who makes other people feel awful. It's like I don't even know you."

What?

"*Wow*," I cried. "I'm a catty bitch? Because I'm not as madly in love with Ray as you are? It doesn't make me *evil* if I don't share your *opinions*, Brooke. Do you even like me anymore?"

"Well, I don't kno—" Brooke started, but she cut herself off straight away as I wilted. "I didn't mean that. I do like you, of course I like you, I *love* you. But I'm pissed off at you right now."

My laugh was cold and harsh. "All because I'm the horrible bitch who sometimes gives Ray weird looks, and she's the bundle of happiness and sweetness who never did a single thing wrong to anyone and so desperately needs your defending."

"Yeah, you just about summed it up."

"I am *not* the only shitty person in this situation, Brooke."

"And yet I'm still waiting to hear a good reason to believe that."

"Maybe you just need to trust me and my judgment."

"Trust you? Just trust that you have a good reason for treating my girlfriend like a pariah? No, nope, doesn't work like that. Either you don't *have* a reason and you need to grow up and cut it out, or you know something I don't and you're not telling me."

I bit my tongue so badly I cringed.

"You don't *have* a reason," Brooke said in a low voice, tinged with disdain.

I couldn't help it; she was looking at me like I was nothing, and it wasn't fair, and I hadn't *done* anything, it was Ray who'd done something wrong, and it wasn't *fair*. "I do."

"You have a good reason?"

"Yes."

"Then *what*?"

I hesitated, because I couldn't, I shouldn't, this was a bad idea, but Brooke shook her head and threw her hands up. "Knew it."

"I can't tell you."

"Oh, *that's* convenient. Well, guess what, Darcy, if there *is* something I should know, then you're being a crappy friend right now."

How did I get myself out of this hole? I hadn't even meant to dig myself into it. I just—I just didn't want her to look at me like that. Ever again. "I'm sworn to secrecy, and you know what? It's fine, it's something that happened ages ago, it doesn't affect anything now, and—"

Brooke stood up now, though. Turned to leave.

My hand shot out of its own accord. "Wait, wait—Brooke, she rigged the council elections."

And the words were out in the world. And I couldn't swallow them back inside.

Brooke froze in her tracks, then swung around, her face emotionless. "What?"

"You were supposed to win. She rigged it."

Brooke processed this. Pursed her lips. She was handling this so well, I wondered if she already knew. Maybe Ray's fears had come true, and she'd already found out through the rumor mill. Maybe she genuinely didn't mind. Water under the bridge.

"How did you find out?" Brooke asked.

Well, funny story. A funny story I had no intention of sharing. "A few people were talking about it yesterday," I said. "It might just be a rumor . . ."

"But you don't think it is a rumor, do you? And you've only known since yesterday?"

"Yeah. I didn't want to hide it from you, but I wanted to wait and see if she told you herself first."

"Well," Brooke said. The sentence didn't get finished, though. Suddenly, she was all but jogging inside. I got up with a scrape of my chair and chased her. Through the door. Through the living room. Past Callum and Alexei. Over to the kitchen archway. Over to Jaz. Over to Ray.

Everything inside me was wary, and freaking out, and my brain raced trying to find a way to erase all of this.

But it was too late for that, wasn't it?

"Hey," Brooke said over the music, in a voice that screamed *run, shit's about to go down, retreat*. "I heard a really *interesting* story. Apparently, I was meant to win the council race until you rigged it?"

All the color drained from Ray's face. She just stared at Brooke, almost as though she hadn't heard her. As blank as Brooke had looked a minute ago.

Now Brooke turned her attention to Jaz. "And not only

that, I'm *also* apparently one of the last to know. Did *you* know?"

Jaz looked helplessly at Ray. Ray didn't—maybe couldn't—react, though, so Jaz gave the meekest, sorriest nod I'd ever seen.

And Brooke laughed. Wildly, hysterically, bending over a little. Then she stabbed a finger toward Ray's chest. "What did you do, steal the voting ballots? Incredible. *Fuck* you."

Ray recovered a little, but not enough. "I—I wanted to—I can fix this."

"This," Brooke said shrilly, "is not fixable! I *earned* that position. I needed it for college, and you took it from me. And you *lied about it.*"

Ray looked at me, scanned my face for—for what? Triumph? Laughter? But I was getting no entertainment from this. This was not satisfying. I just felt sick.

Jaz placed a hand on Ray's arm to comfort her, and Ray covered her mouth with a hand. "Brooke, I—"

"We're going," Brooke snapped to me.

We.

So, she wasn't mad at me, suddenly.

I hardly had time to process this before she'd grabbed my wrist and led me through the living room. Pretty much everyone had stopped to stare at us by now. Looking between Brooke and me, and Ray and Jaz. Forming theories in their heads about what it could be, what could've *happened*.

Someone turned the music down.

Then we were outside. Brooke stopped. I stopped.

And she promptly burst into tears, gripping my wrist with both hands like she needed me to stay upright. So, I grabbed her right back, and helped her stay upright.

TWELVE

Dear Locker 89,

I don't want to have sex with my boyfriend.

I've done it with him a few times, and I gave him my full consent, so don't worry about that, but I did it because I felt like that's what people should do in relationships, not because I wanted to. My friends told me I'd change my mind once I did it, but I didn't. Then they said I didn't like it because sometimes it hurts the first time, and it'd start feeling better. But it didn't hurt. I just didn't like it. I'm pretty sure it's supposed to feel different to this. And it's not my boyfriend's fault, I absolutely adore him. And I'm *attracted* to him, that's the confusing part! I think he's the most beautiful guy I've ever laid eyes on, I *love* looking at him, and cuddling him, and being around him is my favorite thing to do in the world. And I've always wanted a boyfriend, I've been a hopeless romantic for years, I consume romance books like they're my oxygen, etc. etc., so I know I'm not asexual. I don't know what it is! I guess my question is, what do you think might be wrong with me? And is it fair to ask my boyfriend to hold off sex while I try to figure out what's going on? What if it takes me forever to figure out?

EricaRodriguez@hotmail.com

Locker 89 <locker89@gmail.com>   6:12 p.m. (0 min ago)
to Erica

Hi Erica!

I want to be clear here. There is nothing wrong with you. Also, it is absolutely okay to ask your boyfriend to hold off sex. You do not need a reason to say no to sex. There is no time limit after which point it's been "too long" and you should resume sex. The answer, for you, might be "never," and that's perfectly okay. You should only ever, *ever* have sex with someone if it's something you decide you want to do, not because you're afraid you'll be dumped, or out of guilt or pressure.

In saying that, I recommend that you try to have an open conversation with your boyfriend about how you're feeling, and why you would prefer to "hold off," as you put it. For some people, sex is an important part of a relationship. For others, it's not crucial at all (or wanted!). Everyone is different, and giving your boyfriend the opportunity to express his own wants, and understand where you're at, will help you both make an informed decision about whether the relationship continues to be a good fit for both of you.

But again, I must stress, please do not act out of panic or guilt. You should make this call for you, based on what you want and need. It's no one else's call to make. Some people firmly don't want sex. Some are indifferent. Some choose to have it for certain reasons such as conception. Some choose to not have sex under any circumstances. All are fine and valid. The key is it should be your choice, based on what you want, period.

Also, I wanted to note that in your letter you seemed to be saying you cannot be asexual because you feel romantic toward your boyfriend. There is a difference between being asexual and being aromantic. Asexuality refers to sexual attraction (and not necessarily whether you like sex itself: some ace people enjoy sex), and aromanticism refers to romantic attraction. In fact, there are so many different experiences and identities here, and I'd encourage you to explore it further. I will say, though, you can be asexual while experiencing romantic attraction. You can be aromantic while feeling sexual attraction (and you can like romance without experiencing romantic attraction yourself). And the romantic attraction you seem to feel toward your boyfriend is not the same as being sexually attracted to him. Have you ever attended the Q&Q Club? They meet on Thursdays during lunch in classroom F-47. It's a safe space to go if you have questions, or are confused about anything regarding sexuality and gender. It's a judgment-free space. And you might meet someone who's experienced something similar to what you're experiencing.

Good luck!
Locker 89

———

"It's fitting for it to be raining," Brooke said.

She sat on the sofa drowning in an enormous black sweater left behind by her older brother Mark when he went out of state to college. Her hair still fell in sleek curls, and her knees were neatly tucked under the sweater so only her calves and matching socks poked out. Her eyes were puffy from crying half the night, but she'd still found the energy to remove her makeup and apply a full skincare routine before going to bed and upon waking up. Brooke mourned like an Instagram model.

The weather had taken a note from her book, but it'd missed the part where it was supposed to be miserable, but in an aesthetic sort of way. Instead, it just went from zero to a hundred, the wind tossing rain-drenched leaves against the window in a howl, rain slamming against the parched ground and overflowing from drains that weren't designed for this weather, and plummeting the thermometer down *far* lower than any self-respecting California day should ever be, even in February.

"I'd say you have climate change to thank for it," I said, working a comb through my matted waves.

Brooke cuddled herself into an even tighter ball. "It's convenient."

"Well *that's* the first nice thing I've ever heard said about climate change."

"Yes, well, everyone deserves to hear something positive about themselves every now and then. Even climate change."

"And now you're talking nonsense."

She shrugged one shoulder. "Whatever, who even cares?"

I dropped my comb and crawled onto my knees to sit in front of her. I gently poked her calf with one finger. "You okay there, bud?"

She let out a breath in a gush of air. "It's not that she sabotaged me. I mean, it *is*, but it's not just that. I deserved to be council leader. I earned it. And she *kept* what she did from me. What does that say about her?"

We'd been back and forth over this all night, starting the moment Brooke's mom said good night (we'd stayed relatively silent as she drove us home: Brooke didn't want her to know all the details just yet). Hashing and rehashing and badmouthing Ray and rationalizing her behavior and deciding that no, it was *definitely* unforgivable. There was nothing I could say that hadn't already been said. And with every rehash, my stomach twisted more and more.

I hoped my cheeks weren't as red as they felt.

Ray wanted to tell Brooke, I reminded myself. A fact I'd conveniently forgotten in the heat of things last night.

Right, but would she have set things straight at school? I thought back. *The letter said nothing about that.*

Well, anyway. It was done now, either way. Even though I hadn't really expected Brooke to break up with Ray over it. Or . . . had I hoped?

I didn't even know anymore. I'd gotten very skilled at lying to myself recently.

"And you know, if she's the type of person to be *that* threatened by someone?" Brooke went on. "We wouldn't have worked long term. I'd always have to make myself small to avoid making her jealous. I don't want to be small."

Now I nodded more vigorously. This was a much better train of thought, because it came free of the niggling voice that said *you still know something Brooke doesn't*. Maybe Ray *was* going to tell her, but it certainly didn't change that she was the kind of person to sabotage someone else to get her own way. "You shouldn't ever be small. You weren't meant to be."

Brooke gave me a watery smile. "I love you. You know that, right?"

I returned the smile, but it felt taut, like pants that refused to button. "Yeah, I know."

"So," she said in a purposefully perky voice. Subject changed, apparently. "When are you safe to drive?"

"I have to be under point-oh-one." I took out my phone to do some calculations. "Technically I've probably been safe all day, but it's scary. Like, girls metabolize so much slower, and it changes depending on your weight and your body, and I don't know if my liver's very *good* at this yet . . ."

"I know, I know," said Brooke. "Like, you're probably fine, but if a cop pulled you over, you'd still have an anxiety attack."

"*Yes*, exactly! I got told once we shouldn't drive at all the next day if we were drunk the night before."

"But I don't know if you were *drunk* drunk."

"I felt drunk drunk for a half hour, though."

"What does 'drunk' even *mean*?" Brooke complained. "It's *so* vague!"

"*So* vague. It's like they *want* us to fail."

"Just eat some bread." She grinned mischievously. She knew perfectly well bread didn't do shit to sober a person up. "Come on, you've had lunch, it's almost three in the afternoon, you stopped drinking at, what, midnight? I think you're fine."

"I know, I probably am," I grumbled. "I just wish cars

came with Breathalyzers." I started gathering my stuff, then paused to look over at Brooke.

"Hey . . . Are you gonna be okay?"

She burrowed even farther into her sweater. "Yeah. Thanks for checking. But I will one hundred percent harass you for the rest of the day with whining and mopey messages."

"I look forward to them."

So, over the limit or not—and I very much hoped it was a *not* by now—I climbed in Ainsley's car, double-checked my vision and balance, and set off. A minute in and I was fairly sure my reflexes were up to their usual standards. That, plus the fact that the calculator predicted I should've been at zero somewhere around sunrise, made me relax a little. Although next time I felt I might just ask Ainsley or Mom to play pickup and drop-off to save me the headache.

It was pretty rare that I hung out at Brooke's house— she usually drove over to visit me. Rare enough that I'd forgotten the route from hers to mine took me right past Brougham's. It wasn't until I was on his street, trying to figure out where I recognized all the fancy town houses and mansions from, that I realized where I was.

When I drove past Brougham's house-mansion, I slowed down to admire it again instinctively. The first thing I noticed wasn't the aesthetic, however. It was a figure sitting on the porch, leaning against one of the columns with their legs drawn up to their chest. Brougham.

Now, Brougham and I hadn't exactly spent much time together lately, and you couldn't count last night as a hangout sesh. Not to mention that the night on the Mickey Wheel was the first time we'd ever actually been around each other without bickering, and it was probably just a fluke. All in all, me stopping to check in on him was probably super weird, and I should definitely not do it.

But honestly, I just . . . couldn't justify driving past without at least slowing down to make sure everything was fine. When I was younger, I was the kind of kid who spent hours fishing ladybugs out of the pool so they didn't drown, and who invited the kids sitting alone to play, and who went door-to-door knocking if I found a stray dog to reunite it with its owner. It just didn't sit right with me to ignore someone who might need help.

So, like the creep I was, I pulled to the curb and rolled my window down. Luckily, the sheet of rain was falling on an angle against the passenger side so I stayed dry, but even still a gust of air *much* too cold for California entered the car. *Nope, nope, nope.* It was a sign I needed to leave, right?

I could still half-view the porch through the gaps in the iron gate, but as far as I could tell Brougham hadn't noticed me yet. His attention seemed focused on the house. Just as I went to put my window back up, I made out a woman shouting at the top of her lungs from inside the house, followed by a retort from a man. There was a crashing sound, loud enough for me to hear it all the way over here, and Brougham winced.

All right. Okay. Window back up.

I pulled the hood of my jacket over my head, got out of the car, and hurried down the driveway, ducking to avoid the rain.

Brougham sure as hell noticed me then. "What are you doing here?"

Well, it suddenly seemed a bit rude to say I'd heard his parents screaming at each other from my car and wanted to rescue him. "Ice cream," I said instead, raising my voice so he could hear me over his father asking his mother exactly *how much* she'd had to drink.

"Pardon?" Brougham asked.

"*Do you want to go grab some ice cream?* Sorry, it's a bit loud."

He looked at me like I'd sprouted three noses without noticing. "I heard you fine. What I'm not getting is why you've randomly appeared on my doorstep during the pouring rain wanting to get ice cream?"

Now that he mentioned it, it probably wasn't the weather for it. "Coffee?" I suggested weakly.

He looked at me. I looked at him.

Another crash inside, followed by two voices swearing over each other. We both looked at the house-mansion.

Brougham sighed, got to his feet, and pushed past me to walk into the storm. "Fuck it, whatever," he muttered.

Hey, "Fuck it, whatever" was only a few degrees off of "Hell yeah, let's do it!" Unless I was mistaken, I was starting to grow on him.

Once we ordered and sat down in the café, a small place with only a few tables, exposed brick walls, and suspended maidenhair ferns spilling foliage, I was overcome by a horrible feeling the roof was about to cave in on us.

The rain had started pelting with even more ferocity than earlier, and honestly, this place didn't exactly look structurally sound. By the doorway, the ceiling was dripping brown water onto the floor, and the two waitstaff were eyeing it nervously. One of them put a WET FLOOR sign up. A bucket would've been better, I felt, but hey, what did I know.

"So, was Finn okay?" I asked, the same moment Brougham burst out with, "I'm sorry you had to hear all that."

We paused, and Brougham took the reins. "Yeah, Finn's fine. He didn't even have a hangover, just popped up out of bed like nothing went down last night. I was surprised—I figured he'd be stuffed after the way he was carrying on."

"Oh, good, great." The silence returned. It was broken by a low growl of thunder in the distance. Brougham became inexplicably interested in the salt and pepper shakers—little ornate ones carved from chestnut—and I tried to figure out if he'd prefer me to pretend the whole scene with his parents hadn't happened, or if he'd rather talk about it.

Well, I figured finally. *He* did *bring it up.* "You don't have to apologize for your parents. It's fine."

Brougham spun the salt shaker around between two fingers. "It's embarrassing."

"What is there to be embarrassed about? *You* haven't done anything wrong."

"Doesn't matter. It still sucks. That's exactly why I don't let people meet them."

I leaned back in my chair. "You let *me* meet them."

"Yeah, that was urgent, though. And I felt weird about going to your house when your mum's one of my teachers."

"Couldn't have been *that* urgent," I said lightly.

"What?"

"You kicked me out after, like, five minutes! You barely even gave me a chance to get it right first." I raised my eyebrows at him. Checkmate. "Not that it made much of a difference in the end, but you get my point."

Brougham pushed the salt shaker away and straightened to look me in the eye. "That wasn't about you."

"Then what was it about?"

Brougham's sharp, fine-boned face was perfectly still, and his eyes locked intensely on a spot near my shoulder. Then the corner of his mouth twitched almost imperceptibly, and he took out his phone and started using it in his lap, the table blocking it from my sight.

Outside, the rain picked up, smashing against the ceiling in a flat roar. It sounded less like individual raindrops, and more like the ocean had been tipped over our heads. It drowned out even the conversation in the room, and the couple at the table beside us started shouting to each other to be heard.

But Brougham didn't need to speak to be heard. He just had to pass me his phone.

On the screen was a picture of his mom in a bikini, on a beach. It was a selfie, taken by the man sitting next to her in the photo. He had brown skin, deep dimples, and thick eyebrows. He had his arm around Brougham's mom, his fingers curling around her waist. It wasn't a platonic pose.

The rain lowered to merely a monsoon, and Brougham leaned over so he could view the screen with me. "This is the guy Mum's cheating with right now," he said. "There's been a few."

Shit. "Oh no. I'm so sorry."

"Don't be, I'm not looking for sympathy. It's just relevant." He shoved the phone in his pocket. "Don't just blame her, either. It's like a chicken-egg thing. Dad's an asshole to her, she drinks to deal with it, drinking makes her horrible, too, they blow up, she cheats on him and doesn't even try to be subtle about it, he finds out, they blow up more. It's been like this for years."

"That's awful."

His face was blank. "I'm used to it. But that's what was happening when I had you over. He came to visit Mum, and Dad came home. He does that sometimes, to try to catch her doing something wrong."

"She doesn't try to hide it?"

"Nope." At this, he actually smiled. But it was cold and humorless. His eyes were devoid of any light. "Maybe she wants him to crack and ask for a divorce. Maybe she wants him to get jealous and act better. Who the hell even knows?"

Coach Pris Plumber probably would, a voice piped up in the back of my mind, but I decided not to bring that up. It seemed rhetorical.

"Anyway," he went on, "they were about to kick off, so I got you out as quick as I could."

Holy shit. I was an absolute idiot. How had I bought his weak excuse that easily? I guessed him being needlessly cruel fit the narrative I'd created for him, so I hadn't questioned it like I should've. That, and I'd gotten so fixated on Brougham criticizing my skills that all reason had gone out the window.

Huh. There was a mild possibility I had an issue with taking criticism.

I felt a wave of shame for how annoyed I'd been that afternoon. "Why didn't you tell me that's why you wanted me out?"

"Because it's embarrassing. Plus, I thought it was sort of obvious?"

Touché. "Fair enough. But, like, I wouldn't judge you. Just so you know. My parents had a really messy divorce. I get how much it sucks."

"Yeah?"

"Yeah. I mean it was *messy* messy. They're pretty good with each other now, but it was about two years of arguing *all night* every night before the divorce. Then after it, they'd argue over Ainsley and me. If they weren't mad because one of them wanted us for an event and the other wouldn't switch weekends, they were mad because one of them wanted to *lose us* for the weekend so they could do something and the other wouldn't take us. It was like they each just figured out whatever the other one wanted, then refused to give it. And the whole time Ainsley and I were bargaining chips. Like the only cards Mom and Dad had left to hurt each other, and they were gonna fucking *use those cards*, you know?"

Brougham's face was solemn. "That's fucked."

"It was. But it was also years ago. It's been pretty good for a while."

"I'm glad." He paused thoughtfully. "Sometimes I wish they would just get divorced, but I don't know if it'd make it any better. Mostly, I'm just glad I'm heading to college this year."

"Do you know where you're going?"

He nodded. "UCLA."

Oh, that wasn't far at all. I'd half-expected him to say he was heading back to Australia. Or at least the East Coast. For someone who wanted to escape his parents, he wasn't running very far. "Fancy."

"In some ways I probably have Mum and Dad to thank for it," he went on. "Outside of the whole finances thing, I mean. I used to swim a lot when I was younger because it got me out of the house, but it's more than that now. I like how predictable it is. You put in effort, and you get results. If you train, you improve. And then I joined a school team when I was younger and found out I was really *good* at it. Plus, it's nice to feel useful."

I got it. After seeing the way his mom looked at him, I completely understood the appeal of performing well and impressing a coach, and his teammates.

Everyone wanted to feel like they were worthwhile at the end of the day.

There was a lull in the conversation, and Brougham excused himself to go to the bathroom. Part of me suspected he didn't feel comfortable sitting in that vulnerability, but I didn't call him out on it.

I pulled out my phone to check it as the waitress brought over our coffees. I had one message waiting from Brooke already.

My life is a black hole.

Something very much like guilt pattered against my stomach. At the same time, I couldn't help noticing how much more attentive she suddenly was. I'd never have heard from her so soon after a catch-up when she was with Ray.

Maybe Brooke messaged me when she wanted to stop herself from messaging her.

I love you. I'm sorry.

Did you get home safe?

Actually took a detour.
I'm getting coffee with
Brougham?

Brooke is typing.

Brooke is typing.

Brooke is typing.

Ok back up. In less than 24
hours we've gone from you never
mentioning Brougham, to you
having his number and chatting
with him after class, to COFFEE?
Are you guys dating and you didn't
want to tell me because my love
life is up the river? Because that is
completely unnecessary and I want
to know these things!!!!

Brougham was heading back to the table now, his hands
shoved in his pockets. I typed out a quick reply.

It's nothing like that I swear.
I'll explain later. I'm being
rude right now though.

I flipped my phone facedown as Brougham sat. "So,"
I said, searching for a topic. Then an obvious one came
to me. I hadn't had an update from him since Disneyland.
"How's the whole Winona situation?"

Brougham tipped some sugar into his coffee and stirred
it. "We haven't really talked since. She liked one of my photos
the other day. Nothing else to report."

"And you're still okay with that?"

"Not that I have a choice. But, yeah, I am. How about your Brooke situation?"

Hah. *Hah.* That was the question of the year. "Well, we were . . . fine. Last night she and Ray broke up, though."

"Oh shit. What happened?"

I wouldn't have expected Brougham to be the best person to discuss this with, but in a way, he kind of was. He had more background information on the situation than anyone I knew, bar Ainsley. "I found out Ray did something really awful to Brooke before they got together, and I told Brooke."

"Shit," he said again. "Can I ask what she did?"

I shook my head at my iced coffee. After all the messiness of last night, I didn't want to add to the complexity by spreading gossip. Even if I doubted Brougham would go home and share it.

Brougham was staring at me with a curious expression. ". . . Can I ask how you *knew*?" I met his eyes, and my guilt must have betrayed me, because he rested his chin on one hand and bobbed his head. *"Shit."*

"I know, I know. I don't usually use the locker for that kind of thing, I swear."

"Usually?"

"Almost never. Just once before, and that was Brooke, too."

He didn't react, but that in itself was a reaction. "Yes, I'm hearing myself," I said. "But I was just trying to look out for Brooke."

Brougham widened his eyes at the table and took a sip of coffee.

"What?" I asked.

"Nothing."

Oh my god, he was judging me. Considering that his opinion didn't exactly mean much to me, I was surprised how much the realization stung.

"I wish I hadn't told you," I said to my knees. "Now you think I'm a terrible person."

"You're far from a terrible person. But it sounds like you know in your gut you didn't do it for Brooke's sake."

"Can't you just tell me it's okay to go a little overboard if you're in love?"

Brougham's eyes crinkled, and he gave a lazy, long shrug. "Is that what you'd tell someone if they wrote in to the locker?"

My head hurt, and I felt like someone had tied an anchor around my waist and let it drop in the middle of the ocean. Because Brougham was right, and he was often right, and I kind of hated him for that. Smug asshole.

It was so much easier to be angry at Brougham than at myself.

Brougham seemed unperturbed. "You're not the first person to do something shit in the great, noble pursuit of love here."

I caught his eye and cracked a reluctant smile. "You've never ruined anyone's relationship, though."

"Well, no, I'm not a *supervillain*," he said lightly, but the glint in his eye told me he was teasing me. "But I'm not perfect, either. You should see how passive-aggressive I can get. I can be a massive—"

The next word that came out of his mouth was so unexpected I sucked my iced coffee down the wrong hole, and broke into a very graceful run of coughing and spluttering for air.

Brougham looked mildly alarmed as I got my breathing

back under control. "Sorry," he said. "I keep forgetting the effect that word has here."

I wiped my mouth with the back of my hand to check for coffee splatter. "Good *god*, is there anywhere that word *doesn't* have that effect?"

"Does my entire country count as somewhere?"

"Depends who you ask."

"Rude."

"So, what, it's not a bad word there?"

Brougham wrinkled his nose. The effect on his normally serious face was comical. "Um, I wouldn't say it to anyone over, like, thirty, but outside of that it's complicated. Like if it's said, you know, *fiercely* enough it could be offensive, but it can be a compliment, or something you call someone if you're mucking around. It's a multitasker."

"I'll allow it, then. But *never* in front of my mom, okay?"

"Don't worry, already learned that one the hard way. I got a detention out of it."

I cackled. *"Really?"*

"Yeah, it was my second week here. It didn't have the desired effect, though, because it was just a novelty to be in a Real American Detention, like on *Riverdale* or something."

"Oh my god, *don't.*"

"I'm dead serious. We all grew up with your movies and TV shows and books, but most of the things in real life were nothing like them. It was *so much fun* moving here. Like, 'Holy shit, all the car seats are swapped around, and there are *cafeterias*, and *Twinkies*!'"

I twirled my straw around and poked at the ice in the glass. "You don't have cafeterias?"

"Nope. Most people bring lunch from home, or there

are a couple of things you can buy from the canteen, but they're not full meals, and there are no trays or anything. And you usually eat outside."

"Like, outdoor dining?"

"No, like, on your lap on the grass, or sitting on a brick wall or something."

If my grin was nearly as big as I thought it was, I should probably restrain myself, but I didn't quite care enough to. "*Oh,* I wanna go."

"You should. Go to the Gold Coast or Adelaide."

"Are you from one of those places?"

The very corner of his mouth curved up. "Adelaide. That's why I have the accent."

"*Yes,* I've been meaning to ask you about that!"

"Well, long story short, when Australia was invaded and colonized they decided it'd be a good idea to chuck all the convicts in Britain over there, so most of the eastern side of the country developed an accent that was influenced by a lot of British accents, especially the ones more common in the working class."

"You know how you just sounded, right?"

"The British class system's problematic; don't shoot the messenger. Then when Europeans started coming over to South Australia a little later, they were free settlers, so there was a lot more *received pronunciation.*" Here he put on an exaggerated, snobbish accent to illustrate. "Like the *Queen's English,* you know? Then that accent mixed with the other accents and had a bastard baby that sounds like me. So, most of the country says 'dance' and 'chance' kind of like you guys, but we're 'dahnce' and 'chahnce.' That kind of shit."

My iced coffee was forgotten on the table, getting more watery by the second, but I wasn't even bothered. It was the first time I'd heard any of this. It struck me I didn't really know that much about Brougham's country at all. I mean, I'd thought I did, but . . . "Are there other differences?"

"Well, you know, regional ones, but nothing that'd mean much to you, I guess. Like, some states say 'bathers,' some say 'togs,' some say 'swimmers.'"

"'*Bathers.*'" I snorted.

"Is the *correct* term," Brougham said calmly. "Oh, and, we do a weird thing with our *L*'s most of the country doesn't do. Like, we don't pronounce them if they come before a consonant or at the end of a word. Like 'milk' or 'yell' or 'talkative.'"

I listened closely as he spoke. "Miw-k." "Yeh-w." "Taw-ka-tive." "I feel like a nerd right now but this is kind of fascinating."

Brougham leaned forward. "No, it's nice that you're interested, actually."

ACK-shuh-lee.

His weird little bastard accent had already been growing on me, but now that I was aware of its history, even more so.

And maybe the same could even be said for him.

THIRTEEN

Locker 89, I have a crush on a guy I've never spoken to. We're in so many classes together, but he hangs out with a totally different crowd, and I'm sure he'd never be interested in me. But I want him to be. Will you be my fairy godmother?

Marieleider2003@hotmail.com

Locker 89 <locker89@gmail.com>   3:06 p.m. (0 min ago)
to Marie Leider

Hi Marie,

Eye contact, eye contact, eye contact. Now I don't mean follow him around staring at him without blinking. But I do mean glance at him, and if he meets your eyes, hold that gaze for at least a couple of seconds. Looking away quickly can make it seem like it was an accident (we don't want that—we don't want him doubting your interest; we want him sure that if he comes up and says hi he won't be rejected!) or like you lack confidence. And confidence is the sexiest thing ever! It says I love me, and if you know what's good for you, you should too!

If he starts a conversation, smile, be pleasant, engage, and ask open-ended questions. Nothing that only needs a yes or no answer. That'll keep the conversation flowing. And don't be afraid to approach him to start a conversation first! Just keep it casual and ask if he remembers when that book report is due, or if *he* was the one who got an A+ last year, and how did he manage that? Not necessarily those word for word, but you get me. Just show you're friendly, and easy to talk to.

Honestly, don't be afraid. Most people are really nice, and they wouldn't have an issue with someone striking up a friendly conversation (and seriously, if this is one of the few guys in school who would give you hell for asking a simple question, maybe you should have a long think about if that kind of guy deserves you anyway?). At best, he was hoping for an opportunity to get to know you and was too shy to approach (guys can be shy and nervous too!). Worst, you might get a new friend / friendly acquaintance. You have nothing to lose.

Good luck!
Locker 89

Brougham and I stood outside the café, ducked under the awning for protection from the rain.

"It's not gonna stop raining anytime soon," he said.

"Nope."

"Make a break for it?"

I nodded at him with gritted teeth and we darted down the sidewalk to my car while I pounded the unlock button on the car keys. *"Get in, get in, get in!"*

We were soaking wet by the time I slammed my door closed, water dripping down our hair and from our clothes all over the car seats. Brougham's green sweater was almost black with rain. He smoothed a hand over his hair to slick it back out of his face. "Now what?" he asked as I started the engine, windshield wipers kicking into gear.

I'd kind of assumed he would want me to take him home. But now that I thought about it, of course he wouldn't want that. Not if *that's* what he had to go home to. But at the same time, I got the feeling that the last thing Alexander Brougham wanted was to be labeled a victim. He wouldn't ask for help. He wouldn't admit he hurt.

Well, if the Disneyland trick had worked once . . .

"Do you have to get back just yet?" I asked carefully. "There's something I'd like to do."

A rivulet of water dripped down Brougham's forehead and along the bridge of his nose, and he pushed his hair back once more. It didn't stay slicked back for long. "Sure, I'm not in a rush."

Bingo. And in one sentence, I was framed as the one asking for a favor. Brougham didn't need to reach out, or feel pitied.

"Where are we going?" Brougham asked as we crossed the border of the city and started down the highway. "This seems ominous."

"Regret getting in a car with me now?"

"Now you mention it, I might just shoot my GPS location across to Finn."

"He won't make it in time to save you," I said in a low, gravelly voice.

"You're a massive creep, Phillips."

I drove carefully, well aware of the dangers of highway driving in weather like this. There were barely any other cars on the road. Just us, the bruised sky, rain thundering on the roof of the car, and drowned fields of grass stretching into rolling hills.

Brougham grabbed my phone, which was plugged into the car's USB port. "Can I be DJ?"

"Sure."

He scrolled through Spotify and I tried not to take my eyes off the road, but it was hard not to glance sideways to try to catch his reaction. Music taste always felt so personal. Like if someone judged your playlist, they were really judging your soul.

"Dua Lipa . . ." he murmured to himself. "Travis Scott. Lizzo. Shawn Mendes. Oh, Harry Styles *and* Niall Horan? Where are the others?"

I felt like he was making fun of me, but it was hard to tell. "I'm sure Zayn and Louis are on there somewhere. I'm not a Liam fan."

"Oh, come now, poor Liam."

"Don't give me any 'poor Liam' shit. He knows what he did."

I didn't want to say I was surprised Brougham knew the members of One Direction, just because he was a straight guy. But a part of me *did* wonder if he got his base knowledge from Winona by any chance.

Brougham settled for Khalid. "I know, I know, I like top forty stuff," I started. "But it's good. Sue me."

"Totally. Just because something's popular doesn't make it bad."

I couldn't help but look over at him at this, but he didn't notice. He was too busy delving deeper into my playlists.

"You know, though," he started, and as soon as I heard the tone of his voice I hit the steering wheel.

"Here it comes! I *knew* I was gonna get roasted!"

"What? I said I like your music."

"So you *weren't* going to get all indie and suggest something better?" I asked.

Brougham hesitated. "Kind of . . . sort of . . . 'better' is a strong word, though."

"Hah, I'm sure."

A Jeep took a break in the oncoming traffic to overtake us, followed closely by a sedan. Apparently I was the only person in California who followed the suggestion to drive slower in the rain. Even if the rain was getting lighter the farther away we drove, as far as I was concerned, that was no excuse for driving at the speed limit like a reckless hooligan. Mom's words, not mine. She had a real thing about hooligans.

"No, I swear, your stuff is good! But before I was saying how fun it was to move here, because we get all of your media. And the thing is, we get all of yours and you get *so little* of ours, and honestly you're missing out."

"Is that so?"

"Yes, it is. Like, classic rock, for one. Have you ever heard of Midnight Oil or Cold Chisel? Jimmy *Barnes*?"

I shrugged. Honestly, I wasn't that interested in what I was missing, but Brougham seemed passionate about this so I let him run with it.

"Jimmy wrote, like, Australia's *theme song*," he said, half to himself, while he started searching on Spotify.

Good-bye, Khalid. You were wonderful to drive to while you lasted.

As predicted, Khalid's smooth tones were snatched away from me, and they were replaced with some eighties sounding piano chords. "Woah, *that* was a vibe change." I grinned.

Brougham was unswayed. "'Working Class Man,'" he said, like that was meant to mean something to me. "You've *never heard this?*"

"You know I haven't—" I started, but the music picked up in pace and volume and Brougham began honest-to-god *bopping in his seat* to what seemed to be Australia's take on Bruce Springsteen. I was so stunned my train of thought evaporated.

He turned up the volume for emphasis and started mouthing along to the words, hands fisted and eyes closed. Then he began singing, in an over-the-top gravelly, growly voice to mimic the singer, soft at first but growing in volume, laughing as he sang. By the end of the song he was shout-singing at full volume, and I was giggling so hard I was worried for our safety. He held his hands out to the windshield like he was performing to a sold-out crowd at Madison Square Garden, chin lifted and face scrunched up with put-on emotional intensity.

"Who *are you?*" I howled, gasping for breath. "What is *happening?*"

"*Musical genius is happening,*" he cried over the closing bars of the song.

"I'm *terrified!*"

"That's just your mind struggling to catch up with how much it's missed out on."

"Oh my god."

Brougham was out of breath and panting, but giggling right along with me. "Okay, I'm done. We can put on your music again."

"Thank god, I'm not sure I could've kept the car on the road through an encore."

Khalid wasn't able to serenade us back to earth for too long before I pulled off the highway and onto a smaller country road. A few more turns, then we'd reached my goal: the base of Mount Tilda.

In all fairness, "Mount" was an overstatement. It was really just a glorified hill, given its dramatic name by some kids at school who wanted an Instagram hashtag for their hiking pictures. But it was large enough to boast its own steep, rocky road winding around and around its body, and that suited our purpose. I started up it, and Brougham gripped the center console with white knuckles, all light-heartedness vanished. "Don't kill us, don't kill us, don't kill us," he started chanting.

"You sound serious."

"I'm *perfectly serious, Phillips, if you kill us I'm going to kill you.*"

"It's nice to get some emotion out of you, Alexander."

"Is . . . terror an . . . emotion?"

"Of course it is." I shifted gears, and the car rolled backward barely a foot or two while it adjusted. Brougham's head hit the back of the car seat and he pinched his eyes closed and moaned.

I took my hand off the gear and squeezed his shoulder briefly. His eyes flew open, and he looked down at my hand in mild alarm. "We're fine." I giggled.

"Keep your eyes on the road," he ordered faintly.

"Yes, sir, sorry, sir."

We reached the top of the hill, and I pulled into the lookout area. Below us were sprawling fields in a vibrant green, rolling hills, and trees scattered in clusters. The horizon was foggy and grayed out with rain, but, as I'd hoped, it was lighting up every few seconds with sheet lightning. The center of the storm was too far away to make out the thunder, but the lightning entwined with the twilight to produce purple, pink, and yellow flashes across the vast expanse of sky. From here, we could see all of it through the rhythmic back-and-forth sweep of my windshield wipers.

Next to me, Brougham had calmed down somewhat, though his hand was still gripping the glove box like it'd somehow save him in the event of the car tipping over the edge of the hill. At least the color was returning to his cheeks.

"We all used to come here," I said. "Back when my parents were together. Anytime there was a storm."

Another flash of lightning lit the sky up in a pale peach, before dimming back down to deep gray. Brougham's hand relaxed its grip and he drew it back into his chest to massage the tension from his long fingers. Then he looked sideways at me. "Let's go."

"What, already?"

But apparently he didn't mean home, because he'd unbuckled himself before I'd gotten the question out. Then he opened the door, letting in an icy gust of air and rain, before launching himself outside and slamming the door shut. "Brougham!" I called, but there was no way he could've heard me.

There wasn't much to the lookout. Just space for a few cars, a low barrier made of interlocked logs, and a couple of trees. Beyond that was just the sharp drop-off.

I wasn't going out there. There was nothing out there except a hell of a lot of water, and freezing cold wind, and regrets.

Through the rain-soaked passenger window I watched Brougham, now drenched, make his way over to the nearest tree and inspect it.

Why?

Why *anything* with Brougham, truly?

Against my better judgment, I yanked out the car keys and stumbled outside to join him.

The rain hit me with gale force, no buildings or valleys to protect us from the worst of it. My hair whipped around my face in wet tendrils, and my denim jacket was water-logged and heavy within seconds, making my shoulders feel as though they weighed a hundred extra pounds.

Brougham, for reasons known only to him, had started climbing the goddamn tree. With the grace of someone naturally athletically talented, he pulled himself up branch by branch.

"What are you *doing*?" I asked. I hadn't meant my voice to be filled with quite so much despair, but there it was.

"I've never been on a mountain in a rainstorm before," he called back.

"It's a *thunderstorm,* Brougham! You know, the kind with *lightning*?"

"The storm's ages away, don't be a wuss."

"What the *fuck* is a 'wooss'?" I stood at the base of the tree, hugging myself against the rain and frost.

"Scaredy-cat." He hauled himself onto a thick branch, jiggled into a comfortable sitting position, then leaned forward to see me through the leaves. "You coming or not?"

I let out an exasperated sigh and looked around. There was no one, nothing, not even a bird. Just us, and Ainsley's car.

It'd be awkward if I didn't, now, wouldn't it?

I shot Brougham a look of pure disdain and started the painstaking process of hauling myself up a damn tree, on a damn mountain, during a goddamn lightning storm.

Branch by gradual branch, with the grace of someone so naturally athletically untalented I couldn't successfully cross monkey bars, I dragged myself up. When I got close enough, Brougham stretched out a hand to help me climb the last few feet. Warily—and more than a little worried about the weight-bearing properties of this branch—I lowered myself to sit.

"You did it," Brougham said. He was grinning at me, properly. Nothing fake or forced about it.

I couldn't help but grin back. "I hate you. Why couldn't you just watch from the car like a normal person?"

"Because now I can say I've done this."

"We're soaking!"

"We were already soaking."

I opened my mouth, then caught myself. He wasn't exactly wrong.

The wind howled with a special kind of fury up here, and the leaves rustled back and forth with it, small branches hitting against my head rhythmically. The air smelled washed clean. Rain and the now-familiar musk of Brougham's cologne. In the far distance, the storm had grown close enough that we could make out the first rumblings of thunder. And the lightning show flickered on.

"Didn't you ever do this as a kid?" Brougham asked, turning to look at me. His face was shiny and wet, raindrops splashing on his skin and pouring down his hair, over the bridge of his brow.

"Can't say I did, you weirdo."

Brougham turned back out to the storm and swung his legs out. "New memories, then."

"I guess. I definitely won't forget this. It's a bit of a departure from my usual thunderstorm routine."

"What's that?"

"Phish Food, blankets, horror movies."

A clap of thunder over the steady hum of the rain pelting the cliffs. That one was closer, but not so close I worried.

"Horror movies! Great choice," Brougham said approvingly.

Well. *That* was interesting. With Brooke's taste in movies— or lack thereof, really—I'd been long deprived of a movie buddy who wasn't Ainsley. I cleared my throat. "Um, when did you say you needed to be home by, again?"

"Hot cocoa or hot chocolate?" Mom asked, hovering halfway between the kitchen and the living room. In this case, "hot chocolate" referred to a particularly indulgent recipe she'd picked up from one of the teachers at school a couple of years back. I personally thought of it as "rich people hot chocolate," but wasn't going to call it that with Brougham in earshot.

I pretended to think about it. "Well, given Ainsley polished off the Phish Food, I vote hot chocolate." I turned to Brougham, who had just tucked himself in on the sofa, cocooned in what had been my favorite fluffy turquoise blanket as a kid. "Agreed, or . . . ?"

Brougham pulled the blanket tighter around him. Mom

was notoriously stingy with central heating. She believed there was never a need for it in California. "I didn't know there was a difference."

"In this house, you can have powdered hot cocoa," Mom said. "Or *decadent, creamy,* real dark chocolate *slowly* melted over a saucepan and stirred in with *full-cream* milk."

"Settle down, Mom." I grinned. She should've worked in marketing.

"Well, I would also like a hot chocolate, and I want Alexander to make the *right decision*. But it's up to you." She gave him a megawatt smile.

Brougham looked between us then shook his head. "Well, how could I say no when you put it like that?"

"You couldn't. I'll be back in five."

"Wait, are you watching the movie with us?" I called after her.

"I wish, sweetie, but I have tests to grade."

"I think one of those is mine," Brougham said to me.

"It is!" Mom's voice rang out, distant but audible. "I've already graded it. You did very well, you just need to tighten the paragraphs a little next time, hon."

Brougham stuck out his lower lip. "No worries. Thank you!"

Well, if Mom wasn't joining us, and Ainsley was upstairs editing a new video she wanted to upload in the morning, then it was just Brougham and me. Which meant we had full control of the TV. Just the way I liked it.

"Any suggestions?" I asked, scrolling through the list of available movies with the remote.

"Hmm, depends. Are you more into jump scares, or generally unsettling shit?"

"I *do* love being unsettled."

"There's a new one out that's supposed to be creepy. *Poppy,* I reckon it's called. But I don't think it's got the best reviews."

"Sometimes things that aren't the critics' favorite turn out to be pretty okay," I said.

"Totally agree. So I'd be down for that. Otherwise . . . wait, have you seen *Respawn?*"

I blinked. "I don't think so."

"*Really?* With the Pincers, and the moving objects, and . . ." He trailed off at my blank expression. "You *have* to."

"It sounds terrible."

"It's campy. It has a cult following!"

"Oh my god."

"I am *insisting* right now."

Well, given how the last time he'd insisted on sharing something with me turned out, at least it was likely to be entertaining. I giggled. "Fine, fine, okay, but if your taste in horror sucks we can't be friends."

"Can we still be colleagues?"

"As long as the price is right, I'll happily sell out my integrity for you, Brougham."

"That's all any guy ever wants to hear," he deadpanned, holding his hand out for the remote. I passed it over, and he promptly found the movie buried in the library. The display image was a teacup sitting off-center in a saucer.

"Ooh, very unsettling," I said. "Grandmas everywhere are quivering in their crocheted cardigans."

"Shut up and watch, Phillips."

"Oh and *talk* about intimidating, you're so dominant, I'm terrified of you."

"You're not one of those people who talks all the way through the movie, are you?"

"*No*. But the movie isn't on yet."

Before Brougham could retort, Mom brought in the hot chocolates, which she'd topped with a generous amount of whipped cream and a marshmallow she'd browned with her little handheld kitchen torch. If I didn't know any better, I would've thought she was trying to make an impression here. Maybe she just felt the need to show off when one of her students came over?

She flicked the light off as she left for the study, plunging Brougham and me into near-darkness, broken only by the dim bluish glow emanating from the screen. I set my cup down on the side table to cool and Brougham clutched his between both hands, blowing on it gently. "I like your mum."

"If you didn't, I'd have to assume there was something wrong with you. You gonna press play or what?"

He side-eyed me and turned the movie on.

Like he'd promised, it actually wasn't bad. Maybe it was even kind of good, in an atmospheric sort of way. The movie followed aliens called Pincers that were either invisible or existed between dimensions—hard to say—and hunted their prey for days before turning them inside out, cell by cell, gradually at first then exponentially, until organ failure. The only sign of their presence? Objects would start to move, ever-so-subtly, as their molecular structure was rearranged and put back together.

Brougham was lucky he hadn't gone into detail on the premise, because the cinematography was the only thing that saved this film from being cheesy and ridiculous. But as it stood, it was weirdly engaging. It even got a choked scream out of me following an unexpected shot of an exposed, decaying jaw turned inside out. Brougham only laughed out loud at my reaction. It seemed we'd found the one thing guaranteed to get a smile out of him: schaden-freude.

I managed to resist messaging Brooke until about half-way through the movie. When I absolutely couldn't take it anymore, I whispered, "Will I miss much if I run to the bathroom?"

"Nah, you're good, go."

I had my phone whipped out before I'd even reached the room. I probably could've checked during the film, but Ains-ley *hated* people going on their phones during movies, to the point where physical violence wasn't out of the question from her to get the phones put *away*. Now I'd learned that lesson the hard way, I couldn't really unlearn it.

Two messages from Brooke.

I feel like absolute shit.

Wanna do something tomorrow?
Sushi or an escape room or literally
anything?

Did I *want* to? After two months of scrounging around for any free scrap of time Brooke had left over, this was the most beautiful text I'd ever seen.

But, man, it felt really fucking dirty.

Hear me out: Sushi AND
escape room?

I love you so much. Yes please. 12?

How was it possible to be both filled with remorse and simultaneously happier than you've ever been regarding a decision? It *wasn't* possible. And yet, here I was. I felt like I'd finally defeated the boss in a game I'd been playing for months. Ray was gone and Brooke was back and *why did I sound like a psychopath—it wasn't okay to be so self-satisfied after doing a shitty thing.*

But it wasn't *super* shitty, right? I mean, I was just looking out for her.

Wasn't I?

Brougham's comment earlier today about gut feelings popped into my mind. Something told me he was right. If I'd done it for the right reasons, I wouldn't feel so terrible about it all. I might as well be honest with myself.

Brougham had thoughtfully paused the movie when I left the room, so I hadn't missed anything. I sat back down in my warm spot, and my shoulder bumped against Brougham's. Had he been sitting this close to me before? No way, there'd been like five inches between us. He must have readjusted his blanket while I was gone. To my surprise, even though our arms were all but mashed together now, he didn't make any move to pull away. He must have been as cold as I was.

He stayed right where he was for the rest of the movie, in fact. The warmth of his body made me feel snuggly and cozy, even with the light drizzle outside. Every now and then he glanced sideways at me with a funny expression, like he was expecting me to do or say something, but god only knew what.

When the movie finished, he stretched out like a cat, then climbed to his feet. "I hope I didn't overstay my welcome."

"What? No, not at all."

"I just realized you've been putting up with me for almost seven hours now. I've just ordered an Uber."

Wow, seven hours? It hadn't felt that long. Was this some sort of rejection preempt? Like, criticizing himself so I couldn't do it first? "No, I enjoyed it. It was fun. You should've let me take you home, though."

He shook his head. His shoulders seemed to lose some of their tension, though. "Nah, it's late." He folded the blanket while I got up to walk him to the door. He passed it back to me, and I took it, and he held onto it for just a second too long. He must really be dreading going home.

"I hope everything's okay back at your house," I said.

He seemed surprised. "Oh, yeah, it'll be fine. No stress. I'd almost forgotten about that, actually."

"Let me know if you need anything."

"Darcy, thank you, but honestly, I've been living with them for seventeen years now. I know the ropes. I'm fine."

"Okay. Well. I'll see you, then, I guess."

"I'll let you know if I need any advice," he said. "And . . . good luck with Brooke. I know advice isn't exactly my area of expertise, but if you do need to talk about it, I'm an okay listener. I think."

I smiled. "You are. 'Night."

It wasn't until I closed the door behind him that I realized he'd called me Darcy.

Back in the living room, everything was normal, until it wasn't. The first thing I noticed that looked off was that the box of tissues that usually sat on top of the coffee table was now on the floor, slotted in behind one of the wooden table legs. That wasn't that weird, I figured—maybe Brougham had grabbed a tissue without me noticing. But on a hunch, I scanned the rest of the room.

It was the same, but different, in small, subtle ways. The patchwork blanket we kept folded at the unused end of the sofa had been turned so it faced the armrest in a diamond. The coffee table had been moved out by about half a foot, leaving deep tracks in the carpet from where it'd sat stationary for the last several years. Our hot chocolate mugs were now perfectly back to back so they formed mirror images of each other, and the curtains were drawn just enough to let a sliver of streetlight through, and the floor lamp was shining light into the hall when it was *definitely* facing the sofa this afternoon.

Nope, no, no, no, fuck this, this was creepy as *shit*. Even though my mind jumped straight to Brougham—that asshole—something small and secret whispered, *"But what if it's real?"* What if the Pincers were real and they knew I was in the room alone? Mom and Ainsley were both fast asleep by this point, and I couldn't wake them up for this, could I? Wasn't that a little hysterical? *Was I hysterical?*

I squished up against the arm of the couch and sent a text to Brougham demanding an explanation. When two minutes had passed and he still hadn't responded—and something scraped against the window that *might* have been a tree branch but also might have been a Pincer searching for a way inside—I called him.

He answered in a breathless voice. "Hey?"

"Did you move everything in my living room?"

"Why would you think that?"

Oh no, oh god, it *wasn't* him. At least if I died now, I'd have him on the phone to witness my screaming. He could tell my parents what happened. "Because everything's *moved*."

"That does make sense then."

"Did you or not?"

"Well, let's see. Did I have any opportunity?"

Oh, of course he didn't. He'd been right there with me the whole time. Unless . . . "I went to the bathroom halfway through," I said triumphantly.

"Right. Well, logically, the evidence does point to me."

"I'm only going to ask you one more time. Did. You. Do. It?"

"Before I answer, I'd like to clarify real quick, why do you feel the need to ask that question at all?"

"What do you mean?"

"You *do* know Pincers don't actually exist?"

Was that amusement in his voice? "Brougham, I am *the only one awake in this freaking house, and*—"

"Come on, Phillips, you told me you had a strong stomach for horror."

"I'm going to kill you. I'm going to get in my car, find a hacksaw, and break your window to—"

"Calm down, calm down," he said. "It was me, I promise. There aren't any Pincers. I thought you'd notice while I was there."

"You're *not funny, Brougham.*"

"Incorrect. I'm heaps funny."

"I'm hanging up now."

"Don't forget to close your curtains. The Pincers can see auras in the dark, remember?"

I rolled my eyes, then hopped up and did what he said. Just in case. "I hate you."

"I don't think you do."

I went to retort, but then remembered something I'd forgotten in my panic. "Hey, um. Is everything okay over there, before I go?"

"Oh." His voice dropped to a whisper. "Yeah, it's fine. Dad's gone out and Mum's passed out on the couch."

"Is she okay?"

"Yeah, she sleeps there sometimes. Usually when—" He broke off, but my mind filled in the blanks for him. *When she's been drinking.* "Anyway, no worries. Thanks for asking. Send me a text if anything tries to eat you."

"Likewise. But I just want a text with their address. So I can send a thank-you card."

"Rude. 'Night, Phillips."

"'Night, Alexander."

Character Analysis:
Alexander Brougham

Is complicated.

FOURTEEN

Spotify gave me recommendations after you put that song on in the car. I'm learning about your culture.

HAHA ok I'm worried. What did spotify suggest?

Umm so far we've had run to paradise, bow river, the boys light up, khe sanh, the horses . . .

THE HORSES!!! Why didn't I show you the horses? That's the REAL national anthem

Am I Australian now?

You're Australian when you
instinctively yell "Alice? Who
the fuck is Alice?" and "No way,
get fucked, fuck off" at the right
moments at the pub. Until then
you're a welcome visitor.

I am . . . so confused right
now

Good

"Do you think we should be more involved in the school?"
I asked Brooke after the final bell as we hovered in the halls
one Tuesday.

Brooke tugged on her skirt—today's was a *very* short tan
cord that showed off every slant of her thighs. She'd been
really pushing the boundaries on what she could get away
with within the uniform policy these last couple of weeks;
I guessed she was planning on making Ray jealous through
the power of raw sexuality. That's not the advice I would've
given her if she'd come to the locker for help, but she
hadn't. Not that I blamed her, after the advice she'd gotten
last time.

"Really?" she said as we moved through the crowd of
navy. "*More* involved? I'm already doing Q and Q Club and
student council."

"Yeah, no, I don't mean formally," I said. "Just, you know,
around the place. Like, when's the last time we went to a
sporting thing?"

"Like a football game?"

"Yeah, exactly. Or, like, a swim meet."

Brooke's sharp eyes snapped onto me. "Is this a Brougham thing?"

"*No!* Not exactly. But when he was talking about swimming yesterday I realized we never go to any of that stuff."

"Right," Brooke said. "Because we hate it."

"Do we?"

"*Darcy!*"

"I'm just saying, we've never talked about it. I didn't think it was active avoidance."

Brooke gave a melodic laugh, pulling me against the wall by one arm so we were removed from the crowd of students. Funny. Only a month ago this would've made my knees buckle and sent a shiver up my arm. Today, it only caused a mild stirring in my chest. It wasn't nothing, but it wasn't an overwhelming longing like it'd once been.

"Okay, I know you said it's not a Brougham thing, but if it *were,* I would *die.*"

"Die?" Of . . . jealousy? The stirring perked back up, hopefully.

"*Yes.* It's been *forever* since you liked someone"—false, but I guessed she didn't know that—"I feel like we never get to gush over you."

The stirring returned to hibernation.

"I didn't really see you with a guy," Brooke went on, "but I guess a het relationship would have its pros. Not that I know why you'd opt for a guy when there are perfectly good women around, but I'm biased."

"Well, it wouldn't be a het relationship, would it?" I asked. "Because I'm not straight."

"No, obviously. That's not what I meant. I just mean you wouldn't have to deal with homophobic bullshit."

"Yeah, I know what you meant." But it still didn't sit right.

By the lockers, Marie Leider, a girl from my history class, stood clutching her books to her chest and grinning, red-cheeked and wide-eyed, while Elijah Gekhtman waved his hands around in excitement. ". . . know there was someone else at school who'd even *heard* of it," he was saying. "What episode are you up to? I got to seventy-something last year, but then . . ."

"Anyway, do you need a lift home?" Brooke asked, and I dragged my eyes away from Marie as a warmth simmered around my heart. Seemed like Marie had found common ground with someone.

"Nah I'm good, I'll just wait for Mom."

Brooke widened her eyes at me with a knowing smile. "Okaaaay."

"What? What was that?"

"Nothing." She grinned and walked off, clasping her hands together behind her back. "Have so much fun hanging around here talking to *only your mom* for the next hour."

"You're reading into it," I called out after her, and her laugh echoed in the emptying halls.

I rolled my eyes and headed through the hallways to Mom's classroom. It was empty, which either meant that today's last class had been exceptionally tidy, or, more likely, that she'd gotten annoyed with them and forced them to stay back for a few minutes and clean it up at the end of class as punishment.

So I wandered upstairs, through the teacher's lounge— where I paused to greet Sandy (Ms. Brouderie), Bill (Mr.

Tennyson), and a teacher whose name I couldn't remember (but who clearly knew me)—to reach Mom's office.

She was surrounded by messy stacks of papers and typing away at her laptop on a long bench-desk that accommodated three other teachers. None of them were here, though.

Above her desk, Mom's bulletin board was covered, as usual, with sticky notes and photos of Ainsley and me, along with a few group photos of her with teachers or students at events like prom or field trips. One of the newer additions to the board was a to-do list, on which I spotted my name.

"Darcy's birthday," I read out loud.

"Surprise," Mom joked as she paused typing. "What would you like this year? Big party or big present?"

That had been the rule for Ainsley and me for as long as I could remember. A big party usually meant a group gathering at a venue, maybe at home, with food provided for everyone, as well as stuff for us to do. If we chose that option, we still got a present, but it was something a bit more modest. Or, we could choose for our parents to splurge on a present, and the celebration itself would be more along the lines of a store-bought cake with candles at the kitchen counter, along with pizza or Indian food or something. Unluckily for us, having divorced parents hadn't resulted in twice the presents on birthdays and Christmas. Our parents managed to put aside their differences twice a year to collaborate on this.

"Um, I hadn't really thought about it," I said.

"Well, it's only three weeks away now. You've gotta give us some warning."

"Can I let you know in a couple of days?"

"Sure thing."

She was obviously distracted by whatever email she was

replying to, so I took the opportunity to head back down to the locker. Once I was sure there was nobody around I retrieved the letters and let myself into an empty classroom, locked the door, and sat against the wall so I wouldn't be caught while I went through them.

The first couple of letters were standard.

The third one was unusual. It had fifty dollars in it.

I opened it, frowning. I'd had more than one letter with no money in it, sent by someone who, for whatever reason, couldn't afford the ten dollars. And, of course, in situations like that I was happy to waive the fee. I of all people understood the feeling of needing help but not having the means to pay for the service. But I'd never seen a tip like *this* before.

Dear Darcy,

Even though we've been working together for a while now, it's the first time I've put in an actual letter. I figured I should probably try to follow the rules for once.

Yesterday, my ex-girlfriend texted me out of the blue. Then long story short we spent the evening together, and I think she wants to give us another shot. So, basically, no matter where it goes from here, I think we can count this one toward your 95% success rate. And I did promise the other half when it worked out, remember?

From,
Me

I stared at the letter, and shoved the remaining unopened ones in my backpack. I stood up to leave, then remembered as an afterthought that I shouldn't be carrying *any* letters around in my hands, so I stuffed this one in the backpack on top of the others. Then I walked straight to the pool, my stomping feet thudding on the floor.

A *letter*? That's how he let me know? A *letter*? Where was the celebration? The "thank you so much, Darcy"? The "we did it, yay"?

Thankfully, Brougham was the only one in the pool today, so I didn't need to worry about subtlety.

"Um, hi," I called out, competing with the splashing and the hum of the pool heaters.

For once he heard me the first time. Brougham stopped mid-stroke and bobbed in the water, pushing his hair out of his face. "Hi. You got it?"

"Yeah, I got it," I said, hovering by the pool's edge. My voice came out funny. I didn't know if I was angry at him, per se, or even fully hurt. It was just a little weird. It was a weird way to let me know. "I wasn't expecting it."

"No, I know," he said. "I asked her where this was all coming from, and she reckons nothing happened. She just missed me, apparently."

"Oh." I cleared my throat to get rid of the funny tone. I didn't want to ruin Brougham's moment over a petty annoyance about his news delivery method. "Good of her to finally see the light!"

"Yeah, I guess."

Brougham hadn't come over to the side of the pool, so I got the feeling he didn't want to talk about this, for whatever reason. I was so curious to know exactly what had gone down yesterday, though. Why was he choosing *now* to be so nonchalant about it all?

Maybe this very nonchalance was what had changed Winona's mind. That thought worried me a little, because I wasn't sure how long Brougham would be able to keep his investment at arm's length like this.

But at the end of the day, it wasn't my place to bring up that concern. He didn't need me anymore, so that was that, right? I'd done what I set out to do, 95 percent success rate retained. And it's not like we were ever friends. Colleagues, really. And I'd still see him around school. There were still several months until summer.

So why did I feel like this? Like vines had grown around my heart and compressed it, and snaked up into my throat to choke my airway? Like something awful was coming, only I didn't know what? Was it really a gut feeling about Winona? Was I worried for Brougham?

Brougham tipped his head to one side as I hesitated. What was he thinking? Did he want me to leave?

Why *was* I still here?

I guessed, if I was being honest with myself . . . I guessed that I *had* sort of considered us friends. Newly minted ones, maybe, but still. Was that just not a thing anymore, now that I'd served my purpose?

Finally, Brougham broke the awkwardness. "You waiting to walk me to my car?"

It was hard to tell from his tone if he was teasing. My cheeks burned. "No, just waiting for Mom to finish. Sorry, I'll—"

"When does she finish?" Brougham interrupted, kicking his way to the edge of the pool and propping himself up on folded arms.

"About thirty minutes or so."

"Bear with me? It'll only take me a couple to shower."

I nodded, and some of the tension left my shoulders.

Brougham reemerged from the changing rooms wearing fresh, casual clothes and carrying his bag in front of his chest.

"I'm sorry," I said. "You didn't have to cut your training short for me."

He shrugged. "It's chill."

We walked, side by side in silence, through the halls and outside. The sun glared down onto us, and I ducked my head to let my eyes adjust.

"Is everything okay?" he asked, his tone cautious.

Not really.

I'm worried you aren't going to be okay.

I don't know if I'm happy you're with Winona, after our talk at Disneyland.

I want to tell you that but I don't want to be responsible for breaking up another friend's budding romance, because I don't trust my biases anymore.

I forced a smile and nodded. "Yeah," I said in the chirpiest voice I could muster. "Totally. I'm thrilled for you."

Brougham shrugged one shoulder. "It was touch and go for a minute there."

I grinned. "Not really. I knew from the start you'd be able to get her back."

He almost smiled at this. "Because of my charisma?"

"No, because of your modesty."

He shifted his backpack. "Is that what you would've written in my email? Be charismatic and modest?"

"Nah. I would've told you to stop trying to preempt people's rejection of you."

With a short laugh, he bumped his shoulder against mine. "Way to call me out."

"I tell people what they need to hear. It's why it works so often."

We reached his car, and he unlocked it to throw his backpack in the passenger seat. Then he shut the door and leaned his back against it, facing me in a lazy, languid pose. "There's only one issue."

"What's that?"

He cocked his head. "Well, Winona and I aren't officially back together, yet. So, it's too early to call it a perfect win. It was just good enough for the sake of our agreement, I figured."

God, anything to be contrary, right? It just *killed* him to let an argument go by unexplored. I gave him an exasperated look. "Come on. You obviously think she wants you to ask her back out."

He swallowed. "But what if I didn't?"

What did *that* mean? I blinked at him, uncomprehending. Was this more of Brougham just trying to be a pain in the ass? Surely not. No way would a person as smitten as he was jeopardize his reunion just to win an imaginary point against me. "I'm not following."

"What if I didn't get back with Winona? Would you consider it a failed venture?"

Seriously? How could he look at me so innocently, with those unfairly blue eyes, with his funny little half-smile, and threaten me? And for *what*? If he thought I was the one who stood to lose more in this situation, he had another think coming, stat. "Uh, I think I'd survive, somehow. You'd lose a lot more than I would."

He pushed himself away from his car, and toward me, with one foot. "You know? I don't think so."

And once again, I felt like we were having two conversations. The one we were having, and the one he *thought* we were having, where I inexplicably understood what cryptic nonsense he was hinting at. "You're going to have to be a bit clearer with me."

He dropped his voice to a murmur, even though we were the only ones in sight, making me lean forward to hear him. "You want me to spell it out?"

"Yes, please. Spell it out."

And it wasn't until that very moment that it clicked. I couldn't say whether my suddenly thudding heart tipped me off, or if the thudding was in response to my realization. It all happened in one dizzying, thrilling moment, one messy tangle of conscious and subconscious. Brougham's eyes were heavy-lidded, his chin had tilted, and his mouth was slightly open so I could hear his breathing. The air between us was buzzing with unseen energy, jumping and sparking off my skin and willing me to get closer to him. And we both hung suspended in time and space, and the moment that was about to happen came into sharp focus. Like I couldn't stop it if I wanted to.

But I didn't want to stop it.

His hands came to my waist first. Warm and large and gentle-pressured. He pulled me, just slightly. A question. I answered it by moving with them.

Then his face was only inches from mine, and all I could feel was his body heat and a shuddering *something* thundering around in my torso and all I could see was his lips, then my eyes closed of their own accord.

And he kissed me.

He kissed me.

He kissed me, and his lips were pillow-soft, and his mouth was gentle against mine. Warm.

He kissed me, and he tasted of chlorine, and I was vaguely aware of his hands still on either side of my waist, and as soon as his lips met mine, they squeezed and tensed, grabbing onto me like I was the only thing keeping him upright.

He kissed me, and it was hesitant and questioning. *Is this okay? Do you understand now?*

I didn't. I didn't understand anything. But the only thing that mattered in that moment was keeping him close. And then I was kissing him back, pushing into him until his back collided with the passenger door of his car. My fingers slipping up his neck, tracing his sharp jawbone. My other hand finding his on the warm metal of the door, resting over his smooth skin.

He gave a small moan against my mouth and suddenly all rational thought vanished. My hands flew up around his shoulders and pulled him in harder, deeper. I was flush against him, his chest against mine, my fingers threaded through his damp hair, his tongue running along my bottom lip. He let out a thick breath as his hips lifted to meet mine, and I almost lost all sense entirely.

And this was Brougham.

It was Brougham.

It was Brougham.

I pulled away and scrambled backward, my hand flying to my lips. And suddenly, all I heard were alarm bells. And everything was tumbling, and this wasn't right, and something was wrong, and I didn't know what, but it was, it was wrong, and I'd done the wrong thing, and I had to go, *go, go.* He was staring at me in confusion, and his funny smile was gone, and he was saying my name, but it was distant and distorted. I think I said I'm sorry. I think I said it three or four times, in fact.

And I ran away, back toward the school, and my mom, and the empty halls, my hand still on my mouth. My head shaking. My brain screaming words I didn't understand. I didn't know what was wrong, but all of it was. All I needed was space. This was too unexpected. It didn't make sense. I needed more warning than this. Where was the warning? Where was the buildup? Where had this come from?

How had I missed this?

I didn't dare look back as I ran. I didn't know if Brougham was following me, or if he was still standing, stunned, by his car. I didn't know which thought was worse, so I didn't, I didn't think of him, I didn't.

My eyes burned with tears as I pushed through the double doors into the school hallway. It was deserted. Not a person in sight. I power-walked along the linoleum floor, putting as much distance between Brougham and me as I could.

I didn't want to see Mom. I didn't want her to know, to look at Brougham differently, to form an opinion on all of this. Not when she didn't know the full story.

With shaking hands, I pulled out my phone and went straight to Ainsley's contact name. Somehow managed to press call.

Pick up, pick up, pick up.

Did this mean Brougham liked me? What if he did, and he'd kissed me, and I'd run away from him? Literally run from him, the way he was always terrified everyone would do. Maybe I—

Ainsley answered in a bright voice. "Hello?"

"Hey," I said. "Are you in class?"

"I'm just walking out now—wait, what's wrong?"

"Can you please pick me up from school? Now? Now now? As quickly as you can?"

"Yeah, of course. Are you okay?"

"Um, yeah, no, not really, kind of. I'm safe. Something happened. I need to talk. But I need to get out of here. Now."

"Meet me in the parking lot. I'll come right now."

I got to the front doors and peeked out into the parking lot. It was deserted. Brougham was gone. With an exhale, I texted Mom that I'd gotten a ride home with Brougham. Hopefully Ainsley would arrive before Mom finished up.

The day was normal out here. Cloudy skies, a little gray, a cool sixty-five degrees. A slight wind. Just as it'd been when Brougham and I had walked outside barely ten minutes ago. But nothing was the same. Nothing was ever going to be the same.

Maybe I should message Brougham.

But oh, oh no, what could I say? That I didn't like him? Because maybe that wasn't true. What if I said I *did* like him? What would that mean for us? I wasn't ready for it to mean anything. Thirty minutes ago, I'd accepted the idea that he was Winona's boyfriend. And *Winona*! What would happen there? What if he was just intending on stringing us both along? If he liked me, why was he talking to Winona at all?

And *Brooke*.

Not that Brooke should matter. Brooke was not going to happen. But was I ready to move on from her yet?

Yes.

No.

Mostly.

But it was one thing to be mostly there, and another thing to date someone else. To close the door on her completely.

Even if I did like Brougham.

Oh no. What if I did like Brougham?

Why hadn't he given me a warning? Now my brain was all scrambled, and I didn't know what I thought, or how I felt. I couldn't talk to him like this. I might spontaneously combust.

But I couldn't just leave him in silence. Because that would hurt him. And I didn't know what I wanted, but I *did* know I didn't want that. He didn't deserve that.

So. So. Um.

I took some deep breaths, and glanced around to check he wasn't sneaking up on me. Nope. All clear. Just swaying palm trees and the empty parking lot and a plastic bag tumbling in the distance along the asphalt.

I took a few minutes to compose a text.

> I am so, so sorry. Please don't take me running away badly. I just need some time to think. I'll message you soon, okay?

A few minutes later, during which I paced about three full laps of the parking lot, I got a response.

> It's fine. Don't worry about it.

I let out a sigh of relief. Okay. This was okay. It was fine. Fine was good.

Okay.

Where was Ainsley?

I chewed on my finger. I had to talk to someone now. *Now.*

So, I dialed Brooke's number.

She picked up on the fourth ring. "Hey, what's up?"

Down the far end of the street, I could make out Ainsley's car pulling up at a red light.

I opened my mouth to reply to Brooke. To say *nothing much*. To say everything had changed. To say I didn't know what to do.

But instead of speaking, I burst into tears.

FIFTEEN

Self-Analysis:
Darcy Phillips

Did my parents fail to respond to my crying as an infant? Probably. I remember when How I Met Your Mother was on, Mom and Dad would flat-out refuse to let me talk as a kid. I had to go to my room. Well, now look, you guys made me terrified of vulnerability, thanks a lot! Assholes.

I do start feeling panicky when I think someone wants to kiss me. Remember Sara in eighth grade? If she'd tried, I might have bitten her tongue off I was so stressed out. All because my parents wouldn't take two seconds away from watching their stupid sitcom to parent me my whole infancy. Wow. Really, it's a miracle I survived this long.

Has a fearful avoidant attachment style?

Probably needs therapy.

Definitely needs a hug.

Ainsley knocked on the door and poked her head around the gap. "Want some Phish Food?"

I met her eyes with a pitiful frown and pressed my hands together, waving them like a fish swimming, like we'd done as kids. She rushed in with a mostly full pint, sat cross-legged on the bed, and handed me a spoon. Mom, presumably, was grading papers or something. She hadn't noticed me holing up in my room to mope, in any case. She hadn't even noticed I hadn't grabbed any leftover casserole from the fridge for dinner.

While I dug through for a chunk of marshmallow fluff, Ainsley glanced at my notebook. "You did a profile on yourself?" she asked, reaching for it.

I nodded and stuffed an overloaded spoon of ice cream in my mouth. "I've been reflecting," I said through a mouthful of goo.

"I can see that," she said, scanning through the words. "They *were* assholes about *How I Met Your Mother*."

"Right?" I asked, passing her the pint. "And now I'm damaged. Which is *great*."

"You should sue," she agreed, then bit her tongue in a goofy smile. "So, explain this one to me?"

"It's kind of like a mixture between anxious and dismissive-avoidant attachment," I said. "It's rare."

"Like *you*!"

"Thank you. Basically, they're ambivalent. They want to be close to people, but they're also really scared of being close to people. And their emotions go all scrambled, and they want to be closer and further away at the same time. Like, if you feel rejected, you want to get closer, but then when it's all working out, you suddenly feel trapped."

Ainsley stared at me in amusement, then something like thoughtful contemplation crossed her face. "Well, it'd explain Brooke, I guess."

"What do you mean?"

"You've been obsessed with her for ages. You never felt trapped, right?"

"Right."

"Well, she wasn't into you. No offense. So you were always in the 'I want to get closer' phase, right?"

I stared at her. "Oh my god. You're a genius."

"Correct." She waved her spoon at me, before digging it back into the pint. "But where do Mom and Dad come in?"

"Oh. Well, you get your attachment style from how you were raised. And fearful-avoidants wanted to go to their parents for comfort, but their parents were the ones that made them need comfort to begin with."

"That makes sense. So, you think you needed comfort from them because they wouldn't let you talk during *How I Met Your Mother*?"

"Yup."

"And not because they'd scream the house down every second night when we were trying to sleep?"

"Hmm. Could also be that, I guess."

"Could be." She passed the ice cream back to me, and I dug straight into it. "Damn. Now what?"

I placed the ice cream on the floor and she opened her arms for me to fall into. "Gosh, you're a handful." She laughed into my hair as she rocked me. "Such a heartbreaker."

"What do I do?" I asked into her chest.

"You're asking *me*?"

"Well, I can't ask locker eighty-nine."

We pulled apart, and giggled together. "Do you like Brougham?" she asked.

With a groan, I threw myself backward and bounced on the mattress. "I don't know. Maybe."

"Okay. Well. What color are his eyes?"

"This really pretty dark-blue color. Navy, I think."

"What does he think of Phish Food?"

"He prefers tiramisu."

"When was the last time you saw him smile?"

I responded without missing a beat. "When he asked if I'd be upset if he didn't get back with Winona."

Ainsley went silent for a while. When I peeked back at her, she was staring at me with one knowing eyebrow raised.

Then I got it. "Oh *wow*. I might like him."

"Yeah, I think you might."

Okay. Shit. I might.

I might like Alexander Brougham.

I had feelings for Alexander Brougham.

Alexander Brougham, with his arguments and his perpetually serious face and his rudeness.

Alexander Brougham, with his vulnerability, and his perceptiveness, and his ability to make everything I said feel weighted and important.

Alexander Brougham with his too-blue eyes and the prettiest, rarest smile and delicate fingers.

Alexander Brougham, with his wild car karaoke, and his love of horror movies, and his impulsive decisions to sit in a tree on a cliff in the rain.

But if I did like Alexander Brougham, what did that say about me?

I tried to picture Dad's reaction to Brougham, a *guy,*

coming over again. The Q&Q Club's reaction if I announced I was a girl dating a guy. The world's reaction if I sat down at queer events and told them about my boyfriend.

I hadn't even realized I held that fear before. But now I thought about it, my stomach turned so violently that it was clear it'd been sitting in my subconscious long before this moment.

I picked up my notebook and reviewed my entry, my head spinning. But I shut down all the stirring, confused thoughts with one neat, safe, objective realization. "Well, you know," I said. "This is definitely not going to work, anyway."

Ainsley, ever patient Ainsley, nodded. "Why not?"

"Well, because he's got an anxious attachment style, and if I'm fearful avoidant, which I might be, it'll never work. It'll just be toxic, like he and Winona were. We'll drive each other up the wall. I'll freak out and my freak-outs will freak him out and then he'll freak out, which will freak me out even more."

"Are you sure you're fearful avoidant?"

I shook my head. "I need to do some tests to be sure. But if I am, it's all over. Unless we're both able to work on our coping mechanisms, but that's a *huge* effort, and really, I've invested nothing at this point so it's probably a lot easier to walk away while it won't hurt."

"Darcy?"

"Hmm?"

"Don't take this the wrong way, but I had a thought. I know you're really into all of this relationship advice stuff. And you're great at it, don't get me wrong."

I didn't love where this was going. No compliments ever started this way. "Okay?"

"But . . . do you think there's a chance that—with Brougham and Brooke, anyway—you're intellectualizing things so you don't have to, you know, feel them?"

I puffed out my cheeks while I thought about that one. Was this what it was like to get blunt feedback from locker eighty-nine? Because it was *confronting.* "Maybe?"

Maybe Brooke was a fantasy for me. One that felt exciting, and a little breathless, but, most of all, safe. In real life, though, she wasn't my imaginary wife. She was my best friend, a real person. And in real life, I didn't challenge her, or light a fire in her the way she needed and deserved.

And if I was honest with myself, I could say the same for me. Only I'd ignored that in favor of fantasies about how she *would* challenge me, how she *would* set me alight—when, if, maybe. Ainsley grabbed a pillow and fluffed it in her lap before resting her elbows on it. "Don't be afraid of hard emotions, okay? Maybe just let your feelings happen, even if it's just for the night. See how that goes?"

On an intellectual level, I knew Ainsley might be right. Maybe I wasn't fearful avoidant. Maybe I was just . . . fearful. Because if I liked Brougham, and he liked me, I could get hurt, the kind of hurt that unrequited love couldn't compare to. Right now, I was sitting in the space between a sound and its echo. Brougham had asked a question, and I had to answer it.

It was that, or keep dreaming about love, and working toward helping others find it, while never letting myself risk it.

Despite making my decision with Ainsley, I put it off for longer than I intended. Throughout the next school day, I kept waiting to run into him in the halls, but the one time I caught sight of him he was so far away there was no point trying to get to him. Then, that night after school, I kept starting and erasing texts. Finally, I decided I needed to talk to him in person, and resolved to find him the next day.

It was easy to find Brougham on a Thursday, at least.

I stood in the empty, abandoned halls after school, not far from locker eighty-nine, working up the courage to go and speak to him. Apparently, at some point, talking to Brougham had become terrifying. My hands were trembling. *Trembling.* Over Alexander Fucking Brougham.

It occurred to me as I started to pace in front of the pool entrance that I didn't know Brougham's middle name. Just that it was, almost certainly, not "Fucking."

I glared at my hands until they stilled, then pushed open the door.

Brougham was swimming freestyle in the lane closest to me, with another student I didn't recognize over in the far lane doing a backstroke.

Brougham slowed to a stop as soon as he noticed me, and swam over to the edge of the pool. "Hey."

I dropped down to a crouch, careful not to let the hem of my skirt touch the wet ground. "Hey. Can we talk?"

He bobbed in the water, considering. "Yeah, I can spare a few minutes."

Gee, how generous. I hopped backward while he hoisted himself out of the pool, and did my very best not to stare at the water droplets dripping down his torso, running over the smooth curve of muscles on his slim back.

He snatched a towel from the stands and rubbed it over his body haphazardly before slinging it over his shoulders. If this is how he dried himself off, no wonder his clothes were soaked through the day I'd met him. "What's up?"

I lowered my voice. It was an unnecessary precaution,

given I was pretty sure the person swimming in the far lane couldn't eavesdrop with his ears underwater, but it felt respectful anyway. "I'm sorry about the other day."

Brougham's face was, as usual, expressionless. "You don't have anything to apologize for."

He paused, and I realized after a beat he was waiting for me to say something. That was fair. I had told him I'd get back to him, after all.

But instead of speaking, I totally froze.

He was looking at me, and the tiniest fleck of hope or expectation flickered across his features, and words failed me. It was like preparing to give a speech to a crowded auditorium, then freaking out at the mic. I had no clue where this fear had sprouted from. All I knew was it was paralyzing.

Brougham's face went default blank again, and he cleared his throat before speaking in a dull tone. "Just . . . to check in, to make sure we're on the same page . . . The other day was weird, but I don't think it meant anything to either of us, right?"

So that hadn't been hope on his face. I'd just been reading what I wanted to see again. As quickly and as enthusiastically as I could, praying my face didn't betray my bewilderment, I nodded. "Right."

"Okay, good. Because, um, Win asked me to go to prom with her. As her date. I wanted to make sure it wasn't weird." He searched my face.

Win.

Since when did he call her Win?

And since when was he back on the *Win* train?

It was weird it was weird it was weird it was—

"Not weird at all," I squeaked, twisting my face into what I hoped was a delighted smile. Because I was *happy* for him.

I'd helped him, and I'd gotten him what he wanted, and I was *not going to embarrass myself* by admitting I thought the other day meant something. *Why did you kiss me, if you still wanted her?* I wanted to ask. But I already knew the answer. I was there. I was a distraction. I was a stand-in. I knew how he felt about Winona. I couldn't be surprised, could I?

I almost tried to figure out a way to change the subject, to confirm that everything was okay between us, that we hadn't broken something that should've been unbreakable Tuesday. But he'd set his towel down and turned back to the pool, impatient. He wasn't in the mood for a chat. So, instead, I said, "I'll leave you to it."

And he nodded. "Cool. See ya. And thanks again."

Thanks again.

Thanks again.

There was nothing else I could do except duck my head, shove my fisted hands inside my blazer pockets, and walk back to Mom.

I spent the next two weeks flatlining.

Even though Brooke and I hung out as often as we ever had—before Ray, anyway—our conversations were falling to listlessness. We didn't talk about Brougham, and we couldn't talk about Ray without Brooke getting emotional and me inwardly disintegrating from guilt, so we avoided the subjects.

Honestly, I disintegrated into guilt several times a day as it was. It was getting harder and harder for me to look Brooke in the eyes and pretend her heartache had nothing to do with me. I'd ruined things between Brougham and me, and I *knew* I had to tell Brooke what I did to her, but I couldn't bear to ruin us, too, so I kept putting it off, day by day. I kept telling myself the timing didn't feel right, but, honestly, it was mostly that I didn't want her to know I was a terrible person who did awful things.

I didn't want to think of myself that way. In my own head, I was the hero, a good person. I'd always been the hero. I was nice (wasn't I?) and I tried my best to do the right thing (usually). But you weren't a good person because you wanted to be. You were a good person when you did good things. And I'd done some bad, bad things to the people I was meant to care about most.

To add to my self-made purgatory, every time I caught a fleeting glance of Brougham, it felt like getting an electric shock. Brougham mediating a game of keep-away between Hunter, Luke, and Finn in the halls. Brougham chasing down a teacher between classes to clarify something, his face earnest and posture respectful. Brougham grabbing books from his locker, lost in his own thoughts.

He never looked at me. I might've been invisible. Just an ornament decorating the halls, blending into the navy.

One afternoon, as Mom drove me home from school, even she caught on to my foul mood about it all. I didn't want to dump on her with all my shit: she dealt with high school drama all day every day. The last thing she needed was me piling it on more when she got home. But honestly, it hadn't occurred to me that she'd notice—it's not like she usually did—so I hadn't put on a convincing act.

"I'm fine, honestly," I protested when she started pressing, but all she did was raise her eyebrows.

"I carried you in my womb for nine months, I raised you, I've lived with you for almost seventeen years, and you don't think I can tell when something's wrong?"

In response, I curled into myself, pulling my feet onto the car seat and hunching my arms in tight. She said it like we were constantly opening up to each other. But sure, I'd bite.

Obviously, I couldn't tell her everything. But maybe I could find a way to tell her what'd happened, without telling her.

"It's about Brooke and Ray," I said.

Mom nodded, sympathy flitting across her features. "Having a hard time with it, huh?"

She knew how I felt about Brooke. Or, *had* felt about Brooke, anyway. "No, it's not that. Actually, they broke up. And it was sort of my fault."

An eyebrow raise, but silence. My invitation to go on.

"So, Ray did something pretty bad to Brooke," I said. Best not to tell Mom about the whole "rigging the election" thing. I didn't want to risk her involving the staff in all this messiness. "And I found out, and I knew Ray wanted to tell her, but I told her first. And then she dumped Ray."

There was no point sugarcoating it, or trying to paint myself in a better light. If I couldn't be honest about my ugly parts with my own mom, who could I be honest with? It was a sobering thing, realizing that in an equation where a few people weren't innocent . . . I was the most wrong.

To her credit, Mom didn't seem shocked or judgy. But then, she didn't seem much of anything. She barely took her eyes off the road as she replied. "So, tell Brooke that Ray wanted to tell her, honey. You shouldn't lie, even if it's by omission."

"But . . . if I tell Brooke the whole story, she'll be pissed at me."

Mom shrugged. "Maybe. And maybe she'd have a right

to be." Hah. She didn't know the half of it. "But since when is that a good enough reason to not do the right thing?"

"I get it, I get that, but . . . I don't know if I can."

Mom slammed on her brakes to stop at the traffic light. "Hold on a sec, hon, this guy won't get off my butt." She wound down her window and stuck her head out to direct a nasty look at the car behind us. Well, gee. It was good to know she was emotionally invested in my struggles, here. I mean, *she'd* asked me to talk to her.

The light turned green, and Mom started driving again, but she kept shooting glances at the mirror. Finally, the car behind us sped up and overtook us. "Yeah, you do that, hope you get home a whole five seconds faster," Mom snapped.

I stayed silent. Mom muttered something to herself. Eventually, she remembered I was pouring my heart out to her. "Sorry, Darc, what were you saying? Oh, Brooke. Honey, she'll be madder at you if she finds out you knew and kept it a secret. Plus, you'll feel relieved if you get it off your chest. You're better off getting it out of the way now."

Was she right? Would it be better for me and for Brooke in the long run if I told her everything now? So she could know that after months of making the wrong choices over and over again, I was at least determined to change that pattern now?

At the thought, the brick that'd been sitting in my stomach for weeks vanished.

Simultaneously, all the hairs on my body stood to attention in terror.

I knew the right thing to do. But that did not mean I relished the thought of doing it.

SIXTEEN

Self-Analysis:
<u>*Darcy Phillips*</u>

Is a good person who did ~~a bad thing~~ two very bad things.

Would do anything to protect Brooke, especially when Brooke gets rose-colored-glasses syndrome when she's in love.

Is wondering if it's okay to hurt someone to save them from worse hurt?

Isn't that called "The Greater Good"?

Isn't that the motivation behind every movie villain ever?

Is <u>not</u> a movie villain. Is not <u>any</u> type of villain. Right?

Is trying her goddamn best, okay?

(Are you sure about that?)

I waited until lunchtime the next day, when Brooke and I had settled in at our table. Brooke's spirits seemed okay, at least, compared to the last few weeks. I only noticed her staring in the direction of Raina's table once.

I'd been rehearsing this all morning. I knew exactly what I was going to say, and exactly what Brooke was going to say back, and how I would respond to that. I'd prepared for at least fifteen different possible Brooke reactions to my news. Nothing could take me by surprise, right? I just had to do it.

"So, as far as I know, Ray doesn't have a date to prom," Brooke said. She seemed pleased. "I don't know if she asked anyone or anything, just that she's going with a group of girls. Jaz told me. And I doubt that'll change in the next three days."

Just do it. I forced a smile. "That's good."

Brooke hesitated. "Did you know about Brougham?"

I snapped out of my pump-up mantra. "What about him?"

"He's going to the prom with his ex-girlfriend."

"Oh." Brooke had been Team Brougham ever since I'd called her after the kiss, and had inexplicably remained so even after it went nowhere. "Yeah, he told me a while ago. I don't think she's an 'ex' anything anymore, either. It's fine."

"Wow. I'm really proud of you, Darc. I can only imagine how weird it must feel, but you're totally being the bigger person here."

Just do it, just do it, just do it.

"Why are you staring at me?" Brooke asked.

Just—"Because I did something really bad and I have to tell you and you're going to hate me forever."

Well, her expression was closer to wry amusement than fear or fury. For now, at least. This was a good start. "Um, okay, I doubt that, but shoot."

And even after all the rehearsing, the words fell right out of my head. I tried to wave my hand around, but it didn't achieve much. It only made Brooke look kind of confused. Then the words came back to me.

"I'm the person who runs locker eighty-nine," I said. "It's always been me. I started doing it a couple of years ago. I got the locker combination from the master list in the admin area the first year, then erased it from the records."

Brooke's mouth fell open, and she glanced around us to check for eavesdroppers. Everyone else in the cafeteria was minding their own business, totally unaware that the biggest secret of my life had just been revealed for the second time this year, feet away from them.

If they'd known what we were talking about, I had a feeling not many of them would keep minding their own business.

"How . . . but . . . why didn't you *tell me*?" Brooke asked, eyes shining. She looked equal parts astonished and impressed.

She didn't seem mad at all that I hadn't told her. I'd kept this enormous secret, and her immediate reaction was to ask for more information, but only in order to *understand*.

But the penny hadn't quite dropped yet.

"I didn't tell anyone," I said. Best to leave out the whole Brougham thing, for now. "It started small, then when it got big so quickly I didn't know when to tell you, and I also didn't want to put anyone in a weird position."

"Oh my god. I mean, I hate you for hiding this, because

what? This is the coolest news ever, I can't believe it was *you,* but I'm not *mad.*"

Hah. "I'm not finished. Ray wrote in about you a few weeks ago. A couple of days before Alexei's mixer."

Brooke took a second to process this news. "And that's how you knew?"

"Yeah. She explained what she did, and said she was thinking of confessing to you."

"Wait . . . and you told her not to?"

"No." I hesitated. "I didn't reply at all."

"But when you told me, you said *nothing* about her wanting to tell me. You made it sound like she was never planning on letting me know."

"I know," I said simply. I didn't make any move to defend myself, to say I only wanted to look out for her, because, honestly, I didn't know how much of that I believed anymore. And Brooke would see right through that if I tried it. If I wanted her respect, I had to own my shit. Even if the way she was looking at me right now was straight out of my worst nightmares.

"You wanted me to dump her."

"Yeah, I did. And now I regret that. I was angry at her for what she did to you, and I didn't think she deserved you, and I was jealous you thought she was perfect. I wanted you to see she wasn't."

Brooke had forgotten all about her food by this point. All she could do was sit and stare at me. "Wow."

"I am so sorry that I didn't tell you. It was wrong, and so selfish, and I can't even say I didn't know what I was doing, because I *did.* It was really manipulative of me, and I'm fully aware of that, which is why I'm telling you now."

But Brooke had torn her eyes away from me to frown at the table. "Wait, you were running the locker when Jaz and I got those weird responses telling us to stay away from each other."

And as much as I knew she'd realize this sooner or later, I truly felt that I would've rather been shoved inside the locker and left there to starve to death than face Brooke with this. If time travel existed, I would grab hot coals or swallow wet concrete or rip my chest clean open in exchange for the chance to take it back.

"Yeah," I whispered.

"You were jealous," Brooke repeated. There was an understanding beneath her words. I couldn't meet her eyes, and my cheeks were burning so hot they were surely only moments from blistering. It had clicked. It'd finally clicked. And she was looking at me with something that could only be described as disdain. Time seemed to be warping, going simultaneously slower and faster. "Okay. To clarify. You didn't tell me about the locker, let me write to you with private information not knowing it was you, abused that position to wreck something I had going with someone else because you were *jealous*, then did it *again* with Ray because you were *jealous*. And at no point did you tell me you were jealous, or why that might have been. Have I missed anything?"

"I am *so* sorry, you have no idea, I can't even *begin*—"

"I'm not mad at you," she said over me, raising her voice. "Because mad would be the understatement of the *century*."

"If there's anything I can do, anything, I swear—"

"I don't even *know you*," she cried, standing up. A few people looked over at us curiously. "Who *are* you? How could you *do that*? I don't . . . I just . . . I can't believe this. I can't *believe* it. You liked me, and instead of telling me, you ruined all of my relationships?"

I couldn't get words out anymore. My throat had completely closed over. I gritted my teeth and tried to keep the tears from spilling.

"You must really not give a shit about me, huh?" Brooke said, still standing. "Because as long as you get to control my life so it's convenient for you, who the fuck cares how I feel? You watched me, you have *watched* me, for weeks. And you. Said. *Nothing.*"

"I'm saying something now."

She laughed, and it froze me. "Well, thank fuck for small mercies."

Then, with half the freaking cafeteria gawking at us now, she flipped me off while walking backward, then turned on her heel and left me.

Alone.

SEVENTEEN

Dear Locker 89,

My boyfriend and I are in a fight because he's refusing to come over my house anymore. Basically, my dad and brother have a dry sense of humor, and they make a lot of jokes about what my boyfriend wears or says or does, and it's been hurting his feelings. I keep trying to explain to him that that's how they are, and they've been doing it to me my whole life and I just try to brush it off and laugh even if it's not that funny because it's not worth the drama. I feel like it shows a lack of interest in me / my family that he's not willing to even try to go along with the jokes. It's causing problems for me at home now, too, because my family has noticed he won't talk to them and it's making them think he's wrong for me. I don't know what to do, and I'm resentful that I'm being asked to pick sides.

Please help,
mrs_shawnmendes2020@gmail.com

Locker 89 <locker89@gmail.com>   7:32 p.m. (0 min ago)
to Mrs. Shawn Mendes

Hi Mrs. Shawn Mendes!

Ok, so. Real talk, here. From the information you've given me, I don't think your boyfriend is the one putting pressure on you to unfairly choose sides here. A huge part of a strong relationship is being able to view your partner as a safe base to explore the world: you might go out and get bruised and battered, but when you return to your partner you should feel unconditionally accepted, loved, and supported. We call this safe base "the couple bubble." When your boyfriend tells you these "jokes" are genuinely upsetting to him, and you invalidate his feelings by telling him to just put up with them, he can't view you as a safe base anymore, because you don't have his back when it counts.

Now, I'm not implying you must choose your partner over others in every situation! There are many times when you may prioritize your family and friends. But your boyfriend isn't asking you to miss a special celebration, or to not be there for someone when they're sick or in need of help, or to sacrifice something important for him. He's simply asking for basic respect and dignity in a situation where he's been made to feel unsafe, and he does not feel supported by you.

From your letter, it seems to me that your dad and brother are failing to respect basic boundaries here (and it sounds like they may also do this with you, which is not something you are required to accept). You don't need to start a fight with your family members to have your boyfriend's back. Some solutions might include having a talk with your dad and brother and requesting that they cool it, or saying "that's not funny" if they make hurtful comments, or assuring your boyfriend that if he comes over and they start making digs that you will go with him into a private area of the house. The key here is that your boyfriend should feel that his hurt feelings matter to you, and that you're willing to compromise and stand up for him if he is being unfairly disrespected by people around you.

Good luck!
Locker 89

Brooke wouldn't speak to me the next day. She hadn't responded to my texts or DMs the night before, so I guess I'd kind of expected this, but it was still another level of horrific to have her look me in the eyes coldly and then move her gaze right past me.

I was used to being alone at school, but not while there were other kids here. This morning, while I floated awkwardly waiting for the bell, pretending to busy myself at my locker or walking with purpose like I had somewhere to be, it felt like everybody was staring at me.

Then, around the time I doubled back and started retracing my steps, still walking with purpose, I realized everybody *was* staring at me. As I passed Marie, she opened her mouth like she was going to say something, then closed it and looked away. A group of girls whispered among themselves, and I *definitely* heard my name, and all of them looked up as I passed with all the subtlety of a viral Tik-Tok.

I slowed my pace and stared around the hall, my neck prickling with the stares. How could it be that so many people knew Brooke and I had blown up the day before? More importantly, how could it be that so many people *cared*?

Then a girl I only barely, *barely* knew approached me. I only recognized her because of her impeccable taste in hijabs, which she always coordinated with her eye shadow. But I couldn't have pulled her name out of a hat with a single slip in it.

"Hey, can I talk to you for a second?" she asked.

All eyes were on us. A hit new Broadway show, starring me and brilliantly pigmented eye shadow girl. There was nothing bizarre about this whatsoever.

We walked a few steps down the hall until we were away from the main hub. Even then we didn't exactly have much privacy, so we angled toward the wall and spoke in whispers.

"So, what's . . . how can I help you?" I finished haltingly.

"I wanted to ask you to please keep my letter quiet," she said. "I thought it was confidential when I sent it, and it's really, really important it stays between us."

And finally, I realized what was going on.

Pins and needles flooded my body, and the world seemed to desaturate. "How did you know about that?" I asked, thinly.

But I knew the answer, didn't I?

"Oh. Everyone knows. I figured you'd . . . Sorry."

Somehow, I managed to stay upright, and semi-steady. "Okay, I see. Um. Right. I don't know who you are, and I don't know what letter you mean in particular, but I haven't told anyone anything. It's totally confidential."

Oh, the *skepticism* on her face. "Really? Because I heard—"

"Yes, one incident happened yesterday, but I promise you, it was isolated. I will never, ever tell *anyone* what you wrote me . . ."

"Hadiya." She didn't look convinced. "I'm serious, though, it really can't get out."

"Hadiya, I swear on my sister's life I will not tell a soul about your letter. Please don't worry. But I . . . I need to go."

Everyone *was* looking at me.

I *was* the star of the show. The surprise villain revealed.

I needed to find Brooke, because even though there was nothing she could say that would make this better—I already *knew* what had happened here—it was the only obvious next step. And I needed to have a next step. If I didn't, I would have no choice but to stand alone, helpless in the middle of this crowd while accusing stares were directed my way.

So, step one. Walk.

My feet cooperated.

Step two. Locate.

She was already outside the classroom, waiting to go inside and bag a seat as far away from me as she could. At least she didn't try to get away when she saw me storm up.

"You told everyone?" I hissed as soon as I was within earshot.

She stood her ground and spoke in a firm tone. "I told Ray. She had every right to know what happened."

"Everyone knows."

She shrugged. Not her problem. "I imagine Ray told her friends what you did to her. Why shouldn't she? She doesn't owe you anything."

"But . . ." But what? "It was my secret. I didn't want anyone to know."

Brooke was unmoved. "Yeah. It sucks to have your private shit handed out to people you didn't want to know it, huh?"

Somehow, a part of me had figured telling Brooke was the right thing to do, and people didn't get punished for making the right decision, so therefore I wouldn't have to face the consequences. It was wrong to lie about what I'd done, so therefore, choosing not to lie about it should've absolved me, right?

Of course, that was ridiculous. Admitting I did something horrible didn't magically erase the horrible thing I'd done. Neither did an apology. Owning the situation might have stopped the fallout from being worse than it otherwise could've been, but I still owed a karmic debt. My biggest sin here was not covering up what I'd done. It was doing it in the first place.

So, next step?

Pretend people aren't staring at you. Go into class. Let Brooke sit as far away from you as she wants. Concentrate on the teacher. Survive.

Right now, that was my only option, wasn't it? I'd let the wave dunk me, and pull me under, and hold my breath and wait it out. Hopefully, by the time I resurfaced I'd have a clearer idea of how to swim back to shore.

As it turned out, surviving class wasn't my boss-level challenge.

It was surviving the period break.

I'd barely made it out of the classroom when a girl I'd

spoken to a few times named Serena fought through the crowd of students to find me.

"I want my letter back," she said.

My heart started racing. "I don't have it. I rip up all the letters and throw them in the trash after I respond."

"But you haven't responded to me. I want my money, and my letter."

For a moment I didn't understand. I was almost certain I'd never missed a response. I systematically tore up the letters after I pressed send. Then—"Wait, when did you write in?"

"The day before yesterday."

"I'm so sorry, usually I'm on top of it, but it's been a crazy couple of days."

She folded her arms. "I don't care. I just want it back."

Well, that was reasonable enough. "Sure. Can you meet me after school?"

"*Now.*"

Fucking—argh, okay. Fine. We had a couple of minutes. I sighed deeply and prayed to the maker for patience. "Come with me."

Students jumped out of our way like we were on fire, torn from whatever had held their attention seconds earlier. A small, quiet sort of guy named Justyce broke away from a group of kids and fell into step beside Serena and me. "Are you two going to the locker?" he asked. "I wanna get my shit back from it."

"Join the queue," I muttered. I felt like a freaking shepherd with a flock of angry sheep.

Along the way, two girls I didn't know silently joined us. By this point I didn't even have the energy to greet them.

They could all take their fucking letters, and I . . . well, I'd just have to sit with the shame of it all.

By the time we reached the locker, we were surrounded by a semicircle of spectators. I entered the combination, doing my best to shield it from the many, many eyes, and opened the door. "Okay, if you—" I started, but Serena darted forward and started digging around through the letters. One of the girls joined her, and Justyce hovered behind them, trying to see through the gaps in their shoulders.

"Can you give them to me, please?" I asked.

Unsurprisingly, no one gave any indication they'd heard me. I was shut out of the group completely as they fought to find their letters. A few envelopes escaped the shuffle and fell to the floor, sliding a little on the linoleum.

"Hey," I protested, reaching a hand out. "Stop."

A couple of students surrounding us let out cries of alarm. Suddenly, several students pushed ahead to examine the envelopes, both on the ground and in people's hands. Snatching, and grabbing, and trying to figure out which letter was the one they had sent.

Then the several turned into dozens. Paper tore as people dug through the envelopes, some making off with the letters inside, some pulling out the bills stuffed in. It was a feeding frenzy. More and more people were joining, and I was pushed farther and farther back, and I cried out for people to stop, stop, *stop,* but my voice was smothered under the ruckus.

One guy grabbed an envelope and started backing away, and another lunged for him, shouting that it was his. They collided against the locker door in a crunch of metal, the first guy hitting it hard with his shoulder and letting out a yelp of pain.

"Hey!" Mr. Elliot materialized out of nowhere and stormed toward us. "Break it up. Enough."

Kids scattered in various directions.

The envelopes were gone.

The locker was empty.

And its door was bent very slightly out of shape. I tried to push it closed, but it no longer fit snugly into its hole. I took my hand away and it sadly swung a few inches outward.

"*What* was all that about?" Mr. Elliot asked. I wasn't sure if he directed the question at me, or the remaining spectators, but thankfully none of them ratted me out.

"Long story," I said. "We're fine. Thank you."

"Yeah, well." He gave me a suspicious look. "Save the bloodshed for Black Friday sales, got it?"

He continued on to class, and I turned to look at the last few students.

One of them, a girl I didn't recognize with curly black hair and glasses, raised her eyebrows at me. "I just got here. My letter was in there," she said, nodding at the empty locker.

Ah.

This.

Wasn't great.

When I was called to the principal's office halfway through next period, I was expecting it.

My history teacher, Joan (Mrs. Lobethal to everyone else), came over to my desk and told me to pack up and head over there as quietly as she could. That's how it was done at our school: the teacher would get an email, and they would tell you to head on over. No P.A. announcements. They didn't want to shame anyone, as a general rule. I'd agreed with the approach before, but now that it was applying to me for the first time, I was especially grateful for it. The last thing I wanted was for the rest of the school to know my shame.

For Brougham to know.

The classroom burst with whispers as I stood up. Brooke glanced at me sideways, but she didn't show any emotion. The embarrassment might have been bearable if she'd cared.

In his office, our principal, Stan, sat at a large, cluttered wooden desk on a cushioned leather desk chair, going through his emails on his desktop computer, which sat on one side of the curved desk. When I knocked on the door, he minimized the email screen and swiveled around, gesturing for me to take a seat on one of the two blue fabric chairs.

No sooner had I sat when Mom walked through the open door behind me without knocking and stood behind the spare seat, resting her hands on its back. "What's going on?" she asked Stan.

Stan was one of those people who had no business being called Stan. When I pictured a *Stan,* my mental image was of someone kind of weedy, nonconfrontational, maybe with a handlebar mustache and a nervous sense of humor. But our Stan was a tank who wouldn't look out of place in the marines, a stocky, Terry Crews lookalike. His eyes were usually kind when he saw me in the halls or the staff room, though.

Today they weren't looking awfully kind. They looked *pissed.*

"Please, take a seat," he said to Mom. She shot me a concerned glance and sat as Stan went on. "It has come to my attention Darcy has been running some sort of agony aunt advice business on school grounds, and charging students for it."

In my peripheral, I could see Mom turn to me. I kept my eyes fixed on the desk.

"I'm of the understanding that she's been doing so for several years now. This morning there was an incident in which multiple students had their private information stolen after Darcy allowed others to access the locker."

"That wasn't my fault—" I started, but Mom shushed me.

"I've already received several complaints from the students involved, along with a formal complaint from a parent. On top of this, some damage was sustained to school property."

"That was an accident," I said, ignoring Mom's warning look. "And it wasn't even me."

"What property was damaged?" Mom asked.

"A locker door."

"We'll pay for it," Mom said. I let out a cry of protest. *That* was totally unfair. Why should we have to pay for damage I didn't do? Especially when we were one of the families *least* able to afford something like that.

"The damage is the least concerning part, at this stage," Stan said. "Darcy, running a business, a *paid* business, on school grounds is completely unacceptable for a myriad of reasons. When you are on campus you are representing the school, and the *school* is responsible for all activity taking place within its walls. Had something gone wrong as a result of your advice, advice you *charged* for, the school would be liable. Our reputation would be on the line."

Fear clenched my chest, squeezing out every trace of breath until all I could do was gasp. Of course I could be held liable if something went wrong. I hadn't thought of it, because it'd started out as some fun. I'd felt protected by my anonymity. And no one had raised any concerns to me before.

Not that many people had exactly known.

"What are you proposing?" Mom asked in a grim voice. This was her boss she was talking to, I remembered. I was sure she didn't want to throw me under the bus, but she wasn't at liberty to scream or swear or say he was being ridiculous. Especially when I was the one in the wrong.

Stan turned his attention to me now. "Darcy, do you have anything to say for yourself? Is there anything I might be unaware of?"

I swallowed thickly, and tipped my head back to try to suck the welling tears back into my head. "I'm sorry. I was just trying to help people."

Stan sighed and clasped his hands together on the desk, on top of a notepad. "Usually, when a student has a record as clean as Darcy's, we would be willing to let it go with a warning or detention. But not only has Darcy breached multiple rules, she has put the school's reputation at risk, and has put other students at risk. At this stage we have no choice but to recommend a two-day suspension, effective immediately. Darcy can collect her things. We'll see her here again on Monday."

Suspended.

It almost sounded fake to me. Like this was a really bad dream I was about to wake up from. I couldn't be suspended. I'd never even been called in here to be scolded before. I was always so aware of what the teachers wanted from me, of not embarrassing Mom. Of not being the *scholarship kid* dragging down the standard.

But no one laughed. No one said, "Actually, no, that's

too harsh." Even as the bell sounded to signal a change of period, and Mom walked me out to my locker, I half-expected her to whisper that I needed to just wait in the car while she sorted this out.

But she didn't. She just stood there, teeth gritted, while I filled my backpack with everything I'd need for the next couple of days at home.

The disappointment radiating off her settled over me like a fog, clouding my brain and blurring my vision. My back burned with the stares of passing students. I could hear their whispers. No one stopped to ask what was wrong, though. Not that I blamed them, with my mom standing in her power stance, arms folded and jaw set.

My bag wasn't designed to carry this many textbooks. Once I'd loaded it up as much as I could, squeezed in next to my laptop, I was left balancing the rest in my arms. Mom, throwing herself into her drill sergeant role, stormed down the hall without offering to help me carry anything.

The crowd of students parted for us, a Red Sea that only had to take one glance at Mom's face to dive out of her way. Somewhere in the sea, I caught sight of a familiar head bobbing. Alarmed eyes. Mouth opening, saying words I couldn't hear over the usual hallway chatter. Shoving and weaving toward me.

Brougham broke through the wall of bodies and came right toward us, undeterred by Mom. "Darcy, hey. What's going on? What happened?"

The sight of his face, concerned and open, made my heart swell. It was the first time all day someone had looked at me with anything better than disdain. Having someone who got it, someone who was on my side—and who wasn't shocked to find out my secret—felt enormous right now.

"Hurry up," Mom snapped back at me. I picked up my pace, and Brougham fell into step beside me.

"They found out about the locker," I whispered.

Brougham's voice was panicky. "Wait, are you in trouble?"

Mom flipped around to stare Brougham down. "Go to class," she said in a dangerous tone.

"Yup, just a sec, Ms. Morgan."

"No, *now, Alexander.*"

You didn't fuck around with Mom when her voice got like that. It was her "don't touch the hot stove top" voice, her "how dare you throw a tantrum in the supermarket" voice, her "if you ask me to buy it one more time I'm not going to tell Santa you want it" voice.

And Brougham, bless his heart, Brougham who'd grown up fearing what would come next when his parents raised their voices, froze.

Then, amazingly, he unfroze, broke into a jog, and caught back up with us. "Ms. Morgan, wait. It wasn't just Darcy. I was involved, too. And you don't understand, she wasn't doing anything wrong. She was *helping* people—"

If he followed us for much longer, I wouldn't put it past Mom to lash out. I touched his arm to cut him off. "There's no point. Go back to class. I'll be fine."

"But—"

"Go. You'll make it worse." I gave him a pleading look, and he slowed, wounded. By that point, we'd reached the entrance, and he couldn't exactly follow us to the car. So he stayed behind, and I followed Mom out into the sunlight.

We climbed into the car, and Mom let her head fall back

against the seat without starting the engine. "You messed up, kid."

I ran a balled fist under my eyes to get rid of the stubborn tears that forced their way out. "I know. I'm sorry. I'll stop the locker."

"Uh, *yes*, that is a given. And you'll give a refund to everyone you gave advice to."

I blanched. "I can't! I've spent most of it."

"You're just going to have to save up."

"Well, I'll be saving 'til I'm thirty, then, because I've been getting about ten letters a week."

"Ten letters a—a *week*? You've been giving sex advice to ten students every week?"

"Not *sex*," I said. "Relationships. Like Oriella."

Mom barked a laugh. "Darcy, you are *sixteen years old*, you don't know enough about relationships to charge people for advice!"

I was seventeen next week. Mom always did that. Rounded my age up when she thought I wasn't doing enough, and rounded it down when she thought I was doing too much.

"Well apparently I do, because they kept coming back," I said defensively. "I research everything. I'm not just making it up."

"What kind of advice have you been giving the students at our school, exactly?"

I shrugged and looked out the passenger window, even though we weren't moving. "All sorts. How to set boundaries, what to do if your friends don't like your new boyfriend, how to tell your girlfriend you're unhappy without hurting her feelings. That kind of stuff."

Mom shook her head. "Unbelievable. You're not a therapist. You can't counsel people!"

"I wasn't *counseling*. What about advice columns?"

"They're public opinion posts, with disclaimers. That's freedom of the press. There are rules about who can counsel to keep everyone safe, Darcy."

I folded my arms and frowned. "I don't see how I was putting students in danger. Last time I checked, telling someone how to use friendly body language or how to make your partner feel respected isn't high-risk stuff."

"Yes, but you're still giving advice that you are unqualified to give, and accepting payment for that advice with no liability or indemnity terms. Which is, incidentally, why we tend to frown upon teenagers starting their own business while hiding it from all the adults in their lives, because you don't have a *clue* what you're doing from a legal standpoint!"

"Well, it's fine, because nothing went wrong, and now it's over."

"Sounds like a *lot* went wrong this morning!"

"That was not my fault."

"News flash, Darc, when you offer confidentiality in exchange for payment, it becomes your responsibility to ensure that confidentiality. If you didn't do everything within your power to keep that information safe, that's abso*lutely* grounds for complaint."

This was a nightmare. I was going to get sued, and we'd lose everything. That, or someone would involve the police, and I'd get arrested. I didn't know what for, exactly, but there was probably some law I wasn't aware of that covered leaking information. Then they'd find out what I did with Ray and it'd be all over.

I couldn't hold the tears back any longer.

Mom glanced sideways at me, caught sight of my expression, and softened just a touch. "You're right, though," she said, her voice still firm. "You did get lucky that nothing worse happened. It *could've* been a lot worse. As it stands, miss, we will be issuing a notice through the school that anyone who would like a refund can come to see me. I'll organize that, and you can pay me back. If it takes you fourteen more years, so be it."

"I don't see why we need to offer refunds to everyone. I did what they paid me to do."

"Damage control," Mom said simply.

All the work I'd done over the last few years. All of it, over. Everything I'd earned, turned into debt. No more locker. No more advice. No more warm glow when I'd solved a tricky problem. No more knowing I'd helped people with no one else to turn to.

It was all done.

"And it goes without saying that you're grounded," Mom said. "And I'm out of town for the ninth-grade science camp tomorrow night. I don't know if I can trust you anymore. Do we even have trust between us?"

"Of course," I said.

"Well, I don't know, Darcy. You didn't tell me this."

I scoffed. "When was I supposed to do that, Mom? You make me hang around here every afternoon but you're too busy grading papers to talk to me when I need help. I have to go to Ainsley for *everything*—"

"That's not fair."

"It is! Ainsley drives me everywhere, and gives me all the advice, and comforts me when I'm crying in my room, not that *you* ever noticed. You don't even know about *Brougham*, for god's sake."

"What about Brougham?"

"*I don't want to talk about Brougham right now,*" I said.

"That's not the point. The point is that I *did* want to talk about him with you and you were too busy. Like you *always* are."

Mom stared at me with a wounded expression. "I'm always asking after you. How could you say I'm too busy for you?"

"You ask, but when I start telling you, you drift off!"

"That's not true."

"It *is*."

Mom took a measured, deep breath. "You're upset, and you're projecting onto me, and that's not fair."

I wiped away my tears and glared out of the side window. What was the point of arguing back if she was just going to shut down everything I said?

"So, you're telling me that I won't regret it if I let you stay at home on Friday, and I don't need to send you to your father's for supervision?"

"I can guarantee that. Also, Brooke hates me, and I have no friends anymore, so there's nothing I'd want to do even if I was going to break the rules."

"Wait, what happened with Brooke?" Mom asked.

I turned back to give her a *look*. Something akin to horror crossed her face. My point couldn't have been made more effectively if I'd tried. "Why didn't you tell me?"

"I spent all last night crying in my bedroom; I guess I figured you'd notice and *ask*. By the way, *your advice* caused it. And I shouldn't have listened to you, because you didn't know the full story, and it all went to shit."

"Uh, that would be because you didn't *tell me* the full story."

"I didn't feel like I *could*! I knew you'd be mad at me about the locker."

"Well, of *course I am*, I—" She broke off, took a deep

breath, and started the car. "This conversation isn't over, okay? We need to discuss this when we're both feeling calmer. But . . . it's not okay for you to feel like you can't talk to me about things. So."

Yeah. We'd see if she ever brought this up again. I wasn't holding my breath, though.

As she pulled the car out of the parking lot and waited for traffic, Mom's downturned mouth was touched by a tiny smile. "Ten letters a week," she murmured to herself, shaking her head. "Good god, girl."

EIGHTEEN

With Mom gone on Friday, and the house empty, Ainsley and I settled in for a night eating junk food, watching Netflix, and feeling sorry for me.

To add to my misery—something that felt oddly satisfying—I distracted myself throughout the movie by scrolling through pictures of prom as they were uploaded. There was a picture of Winona, looking stunning in a figure-hugging, glittery pink gown. Ray with a group of her friends, wearing a magenta jumpsuit. Brougham, Finn, Hunter, and Luke, posing with a group of senior guys, laughing at a joke I'd never hear.

Brougham's smile met his eyes. I loved how that looked.

He'd texted me the night before to check in on me, and I'd thanked him for his concern and updated him on the suspension thing, but didn't keep the conversation going. I was buried in a cloud of shame and embarrassment, and I just didn't want to talk about it. All I wanted to do was eat junk food and put my social and academic downfall out of my mind, to be dealt with properly next week.

"Your turn next year," Ainsley said as she caught sight of the photos. "Any drama?"

"None that I know of."

"Ah. The stories will start coming out on Monday. Let me know if they involve anyone I might know."

I wondered how Brooke was feeling, seeing these photos of Ray. I wished I could comfort her. I wished even more that I'd never hurt them.

Then, amazingly, my phone started vibrating with a call, and I scrambled to answer it. Brooke? I didn't care what she was calling for, to yell at me, or to cry to me, as long as she spoke to me.

But it was Finn. Ainsley paused the movie while I answered.

"It's Brougham," said Finn as soon as he heard my voice.

I shot up so quickly I pulled a muscle in my neck. "What happened?"

"Some shit went down over here, I'll tell you later, but long story short he's really wasted."

"*Brougham* is?"

"I've never seen him like this. I'm scared what his parents might do if he goes home right now."

Furniture thrown. Insults hurled. Doors slammed and threats screamed. And that's just what I'd witnessed.

No, I didn't want Brougham going home right now, either. "Where's Winona?"

"She went home a while ago. She won't pick up her phone."

Something bitter and jealous kicked against the inside of my stomach at the realization that Finn had called Winona to come for Brougham first, as ridiculous as that was. And then a hurt, mean part of me piped up that I should tell Finn to keep trying Winona. Say that Alexander Brougham was not my responsibility. He had chosen Winona, after all, so who exactly was I to him?

But it was Brougham.

It was Brougham, and I would never, ever do that.

"And your mom is on the trip, right? Can you help?"

Honestly, it was never a question. "Ains," I said. "Can I borrow your car? We have a situation."

The prom after-party was still well underway, with groups of teenagers spilling out into the front yard, standing around on their phones or taking selfies by the string up in the oak tree, or sitting slumped by the porch. The main party seemed to be in the backyard—I could see heads bobbing over the side fence, and the thudding music seemed to be coming from there, too. The house was secluded, at the end of a dirt road lined by houses on enormous properties filled with horses and goats. I could see why they'd elected to have the party here.

At first I'd offered to go alone, too guilty to ask Ainsley to get dressed and leave the house so late on my account. But when she'd pointed out someone needed to ride alongside Brougham to keep him safe on the ride home, I couldn't argue. The only caveat Ainsley had was telling Mom what we were doing, but she took the responsibility for that one, so I wouldn't *technically* be breaking my grounding. Not if it was *Ainsley* who wanted someone to stay over.

I texted Finn as we pulled up. There was no point entering the lion's den hoping to pull off a search and rescue mission; we'd just end up chasing each other all over the house.

Now we just had to hope he remembered to check his phone through the haze of alcohol and god-knew-what-else.

"Is that Luke?" Ainsley asked, sitting up straighter in her seat.

I squinted. "Ainsley, that looks literally nothing like him."

"Well, *I don't know,* it's been a while."

"It's been ten months since you left school!"

"Right." She gave me a grave look. "Ten long months that changed me in ways you couldn't imagine."

"Sure thing, Ains."

"Okay, that's *definitely* him. By the porch."

This time, she was right. There was Luke, dressed in a rumpled tuxedo, walking—or, rather, stumbling, alongside Finn. Between them, they supported Brougham, who was making a frankly pitiful attempt at walking. His hair was messy and sticking to his forehead with sweat, his eyes were glazed over and unfocused, and his posture gave the overall impression of someone whose bones had inexplicably evaporated. He was wearing a dress shirt that'd once been white but was now stained in a medley of yellows and pinks.

He looked miserable.

I practically launched myself headfirst out of the car to run to them. Ainsley followed at my heels.

"Hey," I breathed as I reached the boys. Finn looked relieved. Brougham lifted a heavy head and glowered at me.

"I'm *fine,*" he said, wrenching his arm out of Luke's grip. He wrenched a little too hard, though, and went stumbling into Finn, who'd already braced himself for the impact.

"If even *I* think you're not fine, you're not fine," Finn said. "Hey, Ainsley."

"Hey, you. Up to trouble, as usual, I see."

"Me? I've been on my best behavior tonight, unlike *some people* we won't name," Finn said. *"Brougham,"* he added for clarification anyway.

Brougham wasn't able to form a coherent response, but he did manage a groan of displeasure.

"Has he been sick?" I asked Finn as he and Luke helped Brougham to Ainsley's car. Brougham's head fell forward like all the muscles in his neck failed at once.

"No," Brougham said, apparently still conscious despite appearances.

"A couple times, yeah," Finn said. "You got a bucket?"

"Sure do. Hoping we won't need it, but still."

"I thought he passed out at one point, about thirty minutes ago, but he grunted when we poked him, so I think we're safe. Then we poked him some more for fun, and he kept grunting, so. You know. That's promising. Still, you might wanna keep a close eye on him for a little while. Call me if anything goes wrong, because his parents think he's at my house tonight."

"Wait, what?"

"It'll be fine. I'll text you his mom's number just in case, okay?"

Not exactly, but it was too late now.

"What are the legal ramifications if he dies at my house?"

"Terrible. That's why I'm passing him off to you." Finn grinned and bent his knees to hoist a very floppy Brougham into the backseat, with Ainsley holding the door open for him. "*There* you go, bud. Comfy?"

Brougham squeezed his eyes shut and tipped his head back with a drawn-out moan.

While Finn tried to operate Brougham's seat belt with drunken fingers, I went around to the other side and slid into the backseat beside him. Brougham watched Finn's hands with a measure of interest.

"You okay?" I asked him over the revving engine.

He emerged from his daze and looked at me like he'd only just noticed I was there. Then his eyelids drooped, and his head tipped again. "I mmm sleep."

"You can lean against me if you need to."

He didn't need to be asked twice. His cheek went straight to my shoulder, his hair tickling my collarbone and his breath warm against my chest as he began to breathe deeply and methodically. The way people tended to breathe when they were trying their hardest not to vomit.

I reached for the bucket and pulled it into my lap for safekeeping.

At home, it took both me and Ainsley to haul Brougham out of the car and all the way into the living room. Keeping him upright while also opening doors and fiddling with locks was no mean feat, either. By the time we deposited Brougham unceremoniously on the sofa, I was out of breath.

Ainsley sprinted to the car to fetch the bucket while I watched him. He slumped to one side, but stayed on the sofa.

"What happens if he starts throwing up?" I asked Ainsley when she returned.

"Why do you *think* we have the bucket?"

"Right, but wouldn't it be, like, cleaner to take him to the bathroom?"

Ainsley shook her head as she plopped the empty bucket down by the sofa. "No. That's how you get broken teeth."

"*What?*" I was aghast.

"True story. It happened to a guy in my class. He was leaning over the bowl and his head dropped down and—"

"*Don't* finish that sentence," I cut in. "Do we have anything we can give him to sleep in?"

"Um . . . god, this would be easier if we had Dad. How about Sparkly Sweater?" she said, referring to the oversized, cream wool knit sweater covered in glittery golden polka dots I'd worn to death in sophomore year.

"Why can't he borrow something of *yours*? You're taller than me!"

"Yeah but you're wider, Miss 'Child-Bearing Hips.' Sparkly Sweater's the baggiest thing either of us owns."

Brougham had shuffled backward to lean heavily against the couch. "Would you like a glass of water?" I asked him. He didn't seem to hear me. ". . . I'll get you a glass."

Ainsley traipsed into the kitchen with Sparkly Sweater while I was filling the glass. "Do you think he can dress himself right now?" she asked.

I regarded the sweater in horror as blood rushed into my cheeks. "Oh."

We gave each other a stricken look.

"I'm not doing it," she said.

"I'm not doing it! He's my friend."

"Uh, yeah. That's exactly why it should be you."

"Friends who *made out* a few weeks ago, might I remind you? Besides, you're older than him, it'll be like a big sister–little brother situation."

"We don't have that kind of relationship!"

Awesome. It seemed like my choices were: a) put Ainsley in an uncomfortable position, b) leave Brougham to marinate in his sweat-alcohol-and-vomit-soaked shirt all night, or c) systematically and platonically assist a friend of mine in changing his shirt.

I was making way too big a deal out of this. Why was I doing that?

Because, a voice whispered, *he is not just a friend, and you know it.*

Well, tough. Right now, he was just going to have to be.

And, frankly, I wasn't trying to cross any lines on purpose here: I would have by *far* preferred Winona to be the one looking after her boyfriend tonight. If she called Brougham's phone in the next thirty seconds or so, I'd *happily* pass the job off to her to avoid the sheer awkwardness of it all.

"Okay, fine. *Fine.* Can you grab some sheets or something for the couch then?"

"On it."

I knelt in front of Brougham with a glass of water and Sparkly Sweater while Ainsley traipsed off to the linen closet.

Brougham was propped up against the couch, motionless and eyes closed. I shuffled forward and gave his upper arm a small squeeze. "Hey, you awake?"

He opened his eyes with a start and nodded.

"I have something for you to sleep in."

Unfocused eyes took in Sparkly Sweater, and he nodded with a renewed determination. "Thank you." His words were already resembling English more than at the party. He started unbuttoning his shirt, and I rocked back on my haunches, hopeful that maybe I wouldn't have to intervene after all. Unfortunately, he got three buttons down and gave up, pulling the shirt over his head instead, where he got promptly stuck.

"Help," he said in a pitiful voice, as I assisted him to shimmy the shirt over his face and off his arms. I did my very best

not to look at the smooth muscles of his arms, or the un-
blemished, soft skin of his bare chest, or the small folds that
creased across his belly button as he hunched forward. Or
the light patch of fuzz near said belly button. Or the sharp
jutting of his collarbone.

Apparently, an attempt did not equal success.

I fixed my eyes firmly on his face and helped him pull
the sweater on. This must be what it was like to dress a toddler. If the toddler was almost six feet tall.

Sparkly Sweater was definitely too short in the arms, but
it did the job. Also, I'd never seen him in anything that
wasn't high quality and curated—yes, including his casual
pajamas look at the mixer—so the overall effect was a little
ridiculous.

He started on his fly button with sloppy fingers, and,
to my intense relief, managed to figure it out and pull his
pants off without the need for my assistance, leaving him
in Sparkly Sweater and boxer briefs. "Ow," he said dully,
flexing his right hand. I noticed for the first time it was red
and puffy.

"What did you do?" I asked.

"Mmph mmm."

Oh, that cleared things up.

By this point he was out of breath at the sheer enormity
of the tasks given to him, and he wilted while Ainsley came
in with some blankets and pillows for a makeshift bed.
Brougham allowed us to help him onto the couch, and, a
few layers of blankets later, he was safely cocooned.

Then Brougham rolled over to lie all but unconscious on
his back. Ainsley shook her head at this and grabbed some
of the throw cushions from the armchairs.

"What are you doing?" I asked as she wedged them in

between Brougham and the couch, pulling Brougham onto his side.

She directed her reply at Brougham, not me. "You're not to sleep on your back tonight," she said, slowly and clearly. "Stay on your side. The bucket's going to be here. Okay?"

Brougham made a noise of acknowledgment, but didn't open his eyes.

Ainsley looked back at me now. "If he's on his side he can't choke on his vomit. Better safe than sorry."

"Jeez, since when are you an expert on treating drunks?" I asked in surprise.

"College has changed me. I've *seen things,* Darcy."

"Damn. Respect."

Given that it was now close to two in the morning, Ainsley, understandably, headed off to bed. And suddenly, it was just me. Me, and a very drunk guy who might or might not be my friend. It was hard to say at this point.

To be fair, that *did* describe most people in my life now, though, so.

Sighing, I sat on the floor in front of the sofa. I should probably have been asleep by now, but adrenaline had woken me right up. Besides, I wanted to stick around for a little while, just in case.

Brougham was fast asleep already, his cheek smushed against one hand. He was breathing steadily. That was good, right? Nothing to worry about.

I stuck one headphone earbud in, keeping the other ear free to listen out for any changes, and pulled a movie up on my phone.

About halfway in, just as I was starting to feel sleepy, Brougham stirred.

Through the dark, I could just make out his large,

soulful eyes. Those intense, beautiful eyes. Boring into me. He blinked slowly, long, thick lashes brushing against the tops of his cheekbones. "Darcy?"

"Yeah?"

"Why did you come for me?"

"Because you needed me."

He kept staring at me with wide eyes, his mouth working. All I wanted to do in that moment, what everything in me was *screaming* at me to do, was lean in and embrace him. To stroke his hair and promise him I'd always be there if he needed me. To run the tip of my finger along the curve of his neck down to his shoulder, and assure him there was nothing he could do that would make me abandon him.

But I couldn't promise that, because I'd already left him once.

And the price I had to pay for that was knowing I couldn't do any of those things. I could never touch him like that again.

I could never kiss him again.

And before long, I wouldn't be able to remember what he tasted like. And then it would be like none of this had ever really happened at all.

And, worst of all, was the way he was looking at me, with his mouth slightly open, and his chin leaning forward, and his breathing thick. He looked like he wanted to be kissed. In that moment, in the dark, in the quiet, I felt that if I'd leaned in, he maybe would've closed the rest of the gap between us. He maybe would've pulled me hard against him, kissing me the way I hadn't let him kiss me the first time.

But I just. Couldn't.

"How are you feeling?" I whispered.

"My head hurts."

"Have some water."

He propped himself up, unsteady, and took the glass from me. His fingers brushed against mine. I hadn't done it on purpose, and I felt ashamed of the shiver that ran across my shoulders.

"Did Finn tell you about Winona?" he asked, his words thick and fuzzy.

"Yeah. That's why he called me. Sorry you're stuck with me instead."

Brougham hooked his gaze back onto me, earnest. "I'm not."

Yes, well, I was through criticizing people's girlfriends, so I ignored him. "It's just Ainsley and me here tonight," I said while he took small, slow sips. "There's a towel next to your clothes here. You can take a shower whenever you like. We sleep upstairs so it won't wake us. There should be a new toothbrush in the cabinet, too. Feel free to take it."

He blinked, trying to digest the information. I had to remind myself just because he was conscious now didn't mean he was sober.

Another in a myriad of good reasons to keep my distance.

As carefully as he could, he placed the glass back down on the carpet and managed not to spill it. The act of leaning over the side of the sofa brought his face close to mine, and I wriggled backward quickly, my breath catching. I had to move, because I wanted to stay put so badly. To let our lips meet.

He looked up and took me in as I moved back, eyes unfocused but still sharp enough to notice. He rested his head back down, looking at me without saying a word.

That wasn't nothing.

This wasn't nothing.

So, I got to my feet, swallowing. "I'll be upstairs if you need me. Will you be okay down here?"

He hardened his face. "Yeah," he said in a voice that was too perfectly upbeat to be quite right.

"Okay. Good night."

He chewed on his bottom lip, then, finally, nodded. "'Night."

Poor Brougham spent the better half of the next morning throwing up in the bathroom.

Luckily for Ainsley and me, he was perfectly capable of using a toilet by this point, so there was no bucket to deal with, but it was still pretty awful to hear. After breakfast, Ainsley made one pointed comment about the fact that she couldn't film anything with that kind of background music. I suggested she purposely create something hideous and lean into the ambience. She didn't find the idea quite as funny as I did, but she did soften when Brougham zombie-walked back to the sofa to curl up into a ball wearing nothing more than socks, underwear, and Sparkly Sweater.

"I can run these through the washer and dryer," I suggested, gesturing to his clothes. "You probably don't wanna put them back on as is."

"I can't ask you to wash my shit," Brougham moaned, burying his face head-down into the cushion. "It's humiliating."

"Yeah, well, you might need to rise above it."

"I'm sorry." He peeked over the cushion at me, eyes full of contrition.

"Don't worry about it. I'd rather you be here than at your house."

He cringed, and nodded, and I headed off to fix up his clothing. Finn had offered his own place as a refuge for Brougham as soon as Brougham was well enough to get there. But Brougham hadn't yet made it a full twenty minutes without vomiting violently, so that option was off the table for now.

Speaking of, from the sound of things he was back in the bathroom. I waited in the living room for him, but when he hadn't returned after a particularly long time, I went to check on him. Rapping on the door, I asked if everything was okay.

"Yeah." His voice was small. "You can come in if you want."

He was on his knees in front of the toilet, resting on our fluffy gray mat, his shoulder flung over the seat and his head resting sideways on it. His hair was stuck to his forehead with sweat, and the color had drained from his face. He didn't open his eyes as I came in. "I don't even have anything left in my stomach," he panted. "I'm just throwing up air."

"Since when do you drink so much?" I asked, trying to keep it curious rather than judgy.

All I got in response was a hand wave. None of my business, apparently. Okay, fair.

"I don't think . . . my head . . . has ever hurt this much in my life."

"You took the Tylenol I grabbed you earlier?"

"Yup. Didn't touch it." He squeezed his eyes even tighter, then flipped back around to retch into the bowl. Like he said, nothing came out.

It was okay if I rubbed his back, wasn't it? That was

platonic enough. I gingerly reached out and pressed my palm flat against Sparkly Sweater to make small circles.

When the retching stopped, Brougham gave a frustrated sob. "Knock me out until it's over. It's cruel to keep me conscious right now."

"It's just a bit of poisoning, it'll be over soon. Our bodies don't like being poisoned."

"You don't say." He caught his breath and kept his eyes closed. He didn't shrug my hand off, though, so I could only assume it was helping.

The midmorning sun was streaming through the high bathroom window, casting a warm, bright glow over the gleaming white tiles and porcelain tub and sink. All the white probably wasn't helping his headache any.

"What happened to your hand?" I asked. The redness on his knuckles from last night was gone, replaced by a purply-brown bruise.

"No idea, but it hurts like a bitch."

"Can I help? Ice, or . . . ?"

"No." Something about the tone of his voice told me to leave the subject alone.

"Brougham?"

"Mmm?"

"Can we please be friends again?"

Now he opened his eyes, though he didn't lift his head. "We never stopped."

I gave a dry laugh.

"Okay, fair," he said. "You're right. We stuffed up there, and it's been weird. I'd really like to be friends."

Thank god. Thank god I had Brougham. Knowing that I hadn't destroyed our friendship beyond repair didn't fix everything, but it did make me feel like I had something to hold on to, where before I'd been treading water. "Cool."

"Are you okay?" he asked.

"Oh, you know. Been better, but at least I'm not throwing up in my underwear in my teacher's bathroom."

I got a small smile out of him at that one. "I'm sorry about the locker."

"Well, so am I. But maybe my mom was right. Maybe some of my advice was good, but I probably got it wrong all the time. I'm lucky I didn't *really* screw anything up."

I thought about what Brougham said about me not having enough information from one letter. I thought about my impression of Brougham at the beginning versus now. How my perception of him, and his issues, had changed. My success rate had always been such a source of pride for me. But how could I have been at such a high percentage? Really?

"You probably did get it wrong sometimes," Brougham said, his voice weak from straining. "But that was never the point."

"What do you mean?"

"I mean maybe some people genuinely needed advice. But I'd bet you anything a good chunk of those letters were just people who wanted someone to listen to them without judging them, or to give them validation. It's really powerful to have a safe place to just . . . let everything out."

"Are you saying all I was good for was listening?" I asked, straightening where I sat.

"No. I'm saying you're a genius who gave awesome advice a lot of the time, but the pressure you put on yourself to get everything perfectly right isn't necessary."

Huh.

There was something special about being seen the way that Brougham seemed to see me. Maybe Ainsley understood me in a similar way, but that was different, because she was my sister. This was someone who was a total stranger to me only months ago, sizing me up and listening to what I said—and listening harder still to what I didn't say—and somehow correctly piecing it all together to understand me. And maybe he could do that because in some ways, we mirrored each other. We shared cracks in complementary places.

Brougham made me see the best version of myself, the kinder, wiser, more empathetic version I'd always wanted to be. And that was a hell of a lot to gain, which made it a hell of a lot to lose. And I almost had.

I was so scared to lose him again.

But that felt too intense to share. So, instead, I said, "And now everyone hates me."

"They'll forgive you eventually. Don't worry too much."

"Maybe. I'm not sure."

"Well, if they don't, I know a great school in Australia you can start fresh at."

"Oh, true! And I know that working-class song now. I'll fit right in."

"Yep. Just make sure you call it exactly that, word for word, so they know you're authentic."

We giggled together, which triggered another round of unproductive retching for Brougham so intense he got tears of effort on the sleeves of Sparkly Sweater.

Well, on the bright side . . . at least I could be certain Winona wouldn't be too threatened if she found out how I'd spent the morning with her boyfriend.

NINETEEN

School was fucking terrible.

Brooke still wouldn't speak to me. Every time I saw her, she caught my eye, then looked quickly away and found something, anything else to do.

And the other students whispered. No one outwardly said anything to me, but their eyes tracked me like magnets, and I heard my name weaving in and out of the crowds as I walked through the halls, as I waited for class, as I dug through my locker.

And locker eighty-nine still stood slightly ajar, its frame bent and shelves empty.

By far the very worst was lunchtime. Walking into the cafeteria alone, and scanning the filling tables as I walked past, and knowing there was nowhere for me to go.

Brooke was sitting with Jaz and her friends. I'd sent both Ray and Jaz apology messages over the weekend. Ray had responded by blocking me, and Jaz had left me on "read"— not that I blamed either of them. Brooke pretended she didn't see me, but her face was cold. I couldn't sit with people I vaguely knew, because they might be mad at me.

Maybe their notes were in the locker. Or maybe they just felt uncomfortable. Maybe they thought I'd paired them with a letter they'd written the locker at some point. Maybe in some cases they'd be right.

I wanted to turn around and sprint back out, and honestly, I was only seconds from doing just that. Better than sitting alone and trying as hard as I could not to cry when too many eyes were on me for my humiliated tears to go unnoticed.

And then, like he'd materialized from the air, Brougham pushed past a group of students and touched my elbow. "Come on," he said simply. And for once, the order didn't sound pushy or rude.

He gently steered me through the crowd to his group's table, on an unfamiliar end of the cafeteria, far away from Brooke and Jaz. I was so grateful I could've dissolved into tears.

A few other students sat at the table, along with Hunter and Luke. Next to Hunter sat Finn, who was apparently pleased to see Brougham had rescued me. Now, I guess, all three of us had rescued each other from self-inflicted suffering in varying degrees.

"Thanks for letting me sit here," I said as I slid into the free seat across from both of them.

"We don't have any reason to be mad at you," Finn said. "We've never required your services."

Brougham and I met eyes for a fleeting moment, but neither of us corrected him.

"That makes things easier," I said instead.

"It *does* seem like the majority of the school has at one point or another, though," Finn mused. "I'm impressed. You must have been busy."

"Business was steady."

"Apparently." He took another mouthful and chewed thoughtfully. "I mean, I never put in anything because I assumed it was some straight white girl answering them." He nodded at me, his eyes twinkling. "Half right."

I grinned. "Would you have, if you'd known it was me?"

Finn snorted. "Darcy, I like you a lot, but you don't have the *range*. No offense, but if I've got a question about, like, a guy wanting to come to my cousin's wedding with me when some of my extended family's still in denial about me being gay, I'm not exactly desperate for advice from someone who doesn't know the first thing about my life or what it's like to be Korean American. Like, what the fuck would you know, you know?"

He said it all very pleasantly, conversationally, but it wasn't exactly what I'd expected him to say. For once, though, keeping Brougham's words from the weekend in mind, I clamped down on the instinct to defend myself. Instead, I shrugged a single shoulder. "Well, that's probably fair."

But Finn had already lost interest in the conversation. He'd leaned his head in toward Brougham, whose gaze was somewhere else. I followed their eyes, but I couldn't see what they were looking at. Just students. No one was acting out of the ordinary as far as I could tell.

"Jack's looking over here," Finn said under his breath.

"I noticed." Brougham's tone was light.

I had no idea who Jack was, but I looked again with this in mind. Now I did see a stocky guy with red hair giving Brougham the side-eye. When he caught me looking over, he turned his attention promptly back to his food.

"Still salty about the prom fight," Finn said.

I perked up. This was the first prom-related gossip I'd been privy to, given basically everyone hated me. "Ooh, what prom fight?"

Finn gave me a funny look and quirked his head to the side. "Uh, Brougham's?" he said, the same moment Brougham jumped in with, "Let's not talk about that right now."

I looked between them, my mouth hanging open. "*What? What happened?*"

"Brougham got drunk and punched Jack Miller."

"I did *not*," Brougham said calmly. "It was before I got drunk."

I'd never heard of this Jack Miller before. "Are you serious? What happened?"

Finn answered. "Well, that's the great mystery. He won't *tell us why*, and neither will Jack."

Stunned, I gave Brougham a questioning look. He met my eyes and stayed passive as he chewed a mouthful of lasagna.

"I'm pretty sure I know what happened," Finn said.

"Do tell, I'm fascinated," Brougham said.

"I will. Darcy, tell me if you think I'm hot or cold. Winona and Jack have been carrying on a star-crossed love affair for months now, and they weren't able to commit because their parents work at rival bookstores. An indie and a big chain."

"Presumably, they're the children of Meg Ryan and Tom Hanks," Brougham said dryly. Finn looked blank: the reference obviously didn't hit. "Also, you know Winona's mum works in a bank. Why don't you listen to people?"

"Because I don't retain boring information. Okay, fine. An indie bank and a big chain bank."

"An indie bank," I repeated. "How indie are we talking? Like, someone's stash of money under their bed?"

"Sure, sounds romantic. Anyway, their parents are rivals and secretly in love themselves, so Winona and Jack weren't able to consummate their love."

"And it's become clear you don't have the *foggiest* what 'consummate' means," Brougham added.

"Can you two please stop interrupting? Anyway, Jack, who in this scenario is actually Brougham's secret half brother—way to keep us in the dark about *that* one, Brougham"—Brougham's eyebrows raised almost imperceptibly as he blinked—"is *maddened* with jealousy that Brougham and Winona are getting back together. He finds Winona at prom and tries to kiss her, and she's like, '*No, I cannot, my heart belongs to another*'"—here Finn threw an arm over his head for dramatic effect—"and Jack's like, '*But you'll never love him like you loved me,*' and Winona runs off and hides in the bathroom for a chunk of the night, so Brougham hangs out with me. I'm there, by the way. Picture me as the bard of this story."

"As long as you don't start singing," Brougham said.

"You're no fun at all. Then Winona comes back like nothing happened, and she and Brougham dance, and Jack plots his revenge. Then at the after-party, Jack confronts Brougham and challenges him to a duel for Winona's heart—"

"Because relationships are transactional," Brougham said as Finn ignored him.

"—and Brougham wins the duel! And Winona's all torn and distressed so she runs home and won't answer her phone. So, Brougham gets shitfaced to numb the pain."

Finn finished and waited for our reactions. Well. To put it lightly, it was the worst story I'd ever heard. Brougham fighting over Winona like some damsel in distress. Gag me.

Brougham and I locked eyes, and he shrugged. "I mean, honestly, I don't know why you wanted my side of the story at all. You got every detail exactly right."

My stomach plummeted.

"Really?" Finn asked.

"No, not even close. But I'm curious as to the relevance of making Jack my half brother?"

"Dramatic tension," Finn replied without missing a beat.

". . . Okay, sure."

I snuck another glance at Jack, and waited for him to look up. The eye farthest from me, the one that had been hidden from my sight the first time I'd looked at him, was indeed an interesting purple-magenta color, the lid so swollen it hung down over his eyeball. Oof. What, exactly, could have caused Brougham, who didn't drink, who had all the reasons in the world to avoid alcohol, to get drunk? To have caused Brougham, who loved ribbing but hated true confrontation, to hit someone?

If Brougham wouldn't even tell Finn, there was no way I'd be privy to what had happened to him that night. Still, after the bell rang and everyone started dissipating to class, I hung by his side. "I don't want to poke my nose in where it isn't wanted," I said softly. "So you don't need to tell me what happened at prom. But I wanted to check if everything's okay. If you want to vent, or if you need advice, or anything . . ."

"Nope. Actually, I'm in a really good place right now," Brougham said. "Thank you."

"Oh." It stung, but the important thing was that Brougham was okay. And wasn't the goal of every relationship coach to get their client to a point where they could confidently navigate situations themselves? Not that I would know, this being my first gig and all. But it seemed about right. "I'm glad to hear. As long as you're good, that's all I need to know."

Brougham pursed his lips. "Thanks. Hey, by the way, I told you Finn isn't afraid to tell people what he thinks."

It took me a second to catch up to the topic change, then I remembered the locker discussion.

"He had a good point," I admitted.

"Of course he did. But the look on your face when he said he wouldn't have written to you." Brougham looked almost delighted about it, which, for him, involved the slightest quirk in the corner of his mouth.

"I didn't have a *look*, did I?"

"Oh, you totally had a look," Brougham said, and warmth flooded my cheeks. "Not everything's gonna be your place, you know. It's okay not to always know more than everyone else in the room."

I rested my back against his locker neighbors while Brougham rummaged through collecting his stuff. Now that the surprise of hearing Finn say he didn't want my advice had worn off, I felt like an idiot. Of *course* I wouldn't be the best person to talk him through some of the shit he went through. And the fact that Brougham had noticed my initial shock made me want to evaporate. Both of them probably thought I had the biggest unearned ego in the school. And, honestly, they wouldn't be far off from the truth.

When Brougham reemerged, he took one look at my face and asked, "What's wrong?"

I closed his locker door and started walking. He hurried to catch up with me. "I never had any business giving people advice," I said.

"Why, because of what Finn said?"

"No, god no. Finn was totally in the right. It's just, all

of it. I wasn't ethical with Brooke, I broke Ray's confidentiality, I let all those letters get stolen. I started the locker to help people, and I ended up using it to hurt them. I hurt so many people. What is *wrong* with me?"

"Hey," Brougham said, touching my arm to slow me down. "You stuffed up. That's gonna happen sometimes. It's more helpful to everyone now if you learn from it, and actually do things differently next time, instead of moping about how shit you are. Yeah?"

Half of me knew he was right. But how did I even begin to make up for all the damage I'd caused?

"Yeah?" he pressed.

"Yeah. I owe Brooke the world's biggest apology."

"That's a good start." Brougham glanced around us, then leaned in. "Um, also, speaking of immoral mistakes, I want to tell you what the Jack thing was about."

This pulled me out of my shame spiral more quickly than any lecture. "Don't tell me he *is* your half brother?"

Brougham rolled his eyes. "You're both ridiculous. No. He was one of the people who had a letter leaked."

My laugh faded, and the hallway went fuzzy. "Oh."

"We were talking in a group and it came up, and he was drunk, and angry, and it got a bit personal."

"Personal about me or you?"

". . . You. Like I said, he was drunk and angry. And it doesn't matter what he was saying, but it wasn't . . . polite. I told him to shut up, and he kept going, and I saw red." Brougham stared at the ground. His cheeks were gently coloring. "I've never hit anyone before. I didn't even mean to, it's like my hand acted without permission from my brain."

This. Was a lot to take in. So . . . *I'd* been the unwitting damsel in distress? "Why didn't you tell me?"

"It's embarrassing. I don't want to be the sort of person who goes around punching people. I've just never been *mad* like that before."

I couldn't help it. I was flattered, and a little touched, even if I hated the idea of being any sort of distressed damsel with a fiery passion. "You were defending your coach's honor." I grinned. "That's kind of cute."

"It's not."

"A little. I bet you'd do the same if someone started trashing your swim club coach."

"I—maybe. I dunno. I hope not."

I giggled. I couldn't help it—he looked like a puppy who'd been caught tearing apart a couch cushion. Even though this was serious, and I *got* how weird he felt about violence, especially with the stuff he saw at home, it was hard not to be charmed by someone who'd stepped in to defend me when I wasn't there to defend myself, then had the decency to look so goddamn *contrite* about it. "Well, it's done. Probably not the *best* move, but just . . . try not to do it again."

He kept his eyes fixed on the floor, pressing his lips together.

"And," I said, bending down so I could look him in the eye. "Thank you. That was really sweet of you, in a violent, assault-y sort of way."

He tipped his chin grudgingly. "You're welcome. And I promise I'll never give anyone a black eye on your behalf again."

"Yeah, you probably didn't need to hit him so hard. Or, you know, at all."

"I have weight training three afternoons a week. Apparently I've got some force behind these things," he said, swinging his arm back and forth.

Whether Winona was put off by the punch, or she knew it was related to me and felt weird about it, or whether she went home early for an entirely different reason, who could say. Mind you . . . *should* she feel weird about it? Was it weird for him to defend my honor like that? Should I be wondering what it meant that he had?

No, I decided, a little deflated at the realization. Brougham had said he was in a good place, so whatever had gone down obviously worked out for the best. If there'd been anything more to it, there's no way he'd be so calm and certain about things with Winona.

So, I was happy for him, and his newfound ability to navigate relationship weirdness.

Mostly.

Mom, Ainsley, and I sat in the living room, Mom and Ainsley on the sofa, me curled in an armchair, all three of us staring at my phone.

"I can't do it with you guys looking at me," I said.

Mom and Ainsley glanced at each other.

"I've got a design I can do, I guess," Ainsley said reluctantly, getting to her feet.

Mom took her laptop from its place on the coffee table. "I'm not even here. Just reading some assignments."

"But you're very obviously here, is all."

"You said I don't have time for you, now you're trying to send me away. Which is it?"

Huh. I was surprised to hear her bring this up. We'd had a tentative truce since she returned from her school trip, and neither of us had mentioned our blowup in the car last week.

"I want to help," Mom pressed.

Okay. Fine. "I'm scared to call."

"She's been your best friend for how many years now, Darc? She won't bite you."

"Yeah, but she might say she doesn't want anything to do with me."

"She won't."

"She *might*."

"Okay, I'm gonna play devil's advocate with you. Let's say she does. Then what?"

I mean, really. What the hell kind of question was that? "Then I'll have lost the best friend I ever had. Do you not see how that could be devastating?"

"Sure, but she's not your only friend. The important thing is that you respect her enough to give her a proper apology. Whether or not she forgives you is less important. All I'm saying is," she added hastily as I opened my mouth to protest, "let's say she isn't ready quite yet. That's okay. This apology isn't *about* you. And if you do lose her, which I don't think you will, you'll survive this. It's not like you're relying on this girl for a lung transplant or anything, right?"

She'd had me right up until the end, then she'd lost me. "Way to minimize my pain here, Mom!"

"I'm just putting things in perspective."

"Really? Because it feels kind of like you're saying to suck it up, it's not that bad."

Mom stopped pretending to be on her laptop. "Honey, I don't mean that at all. Friendship breakups are worse than romantic ones. I know it's scary. I just don't want you to terrify yourself into isolation because you're worried you'll get rejected if you reach out."

I flipped my phone over and over between my hands. It

was like having a solid representation of how my stomach must look right now. "She's not just my best friend, Mom, she's my *only* friend at school. I'm friendly with other kids but she's my *friend*, you know? I put all my eggs in one basket then I smashed the basket against a brick wall."

"Oh, *Darc*—"

"And *don't* tell me I can make other friends easily because I have a 'great personality,' okay?"

"Well, actually, I wasn't going to, although I don't like you saying you have a 'great personality' like it's a lie, okay? I don't take kindly toward you being criticized, even if you're the one doing it. I was *going* to say I saw you in the cafeteria today." Oh, *ew*, I hated hearing about her seeing me around the school. It always made me feel like I was being watched from the shadows. "You seemed to be having fun with Finn and Alexander. Don't they count as friends?"

Well, yes, but no, but . . . I mean, kind of. My first instinct was to say it wasn't the same as Brooke, and I was right, it wasn't. Neither of them knew my most embarrassing moments, or my guiltiest pleasures, or which people annoyed me so much I gagged at the sight of them in the hallways. If I wanted someone to stay up with me until three in the morning eating junk food and watching YouTube videos, I wouldn't call Finn or Brougham. We didn't have that level of intimacy. And that's what a best friend was. An incredibly intimate thing.

But maybe Mom had a point. Just because they weren't *best friend* material didn't mean I should discount them altogether. In fact, now that she mentioned it, it was a little funny they hadn't popped into my head when I thought about my friends. Even Brougham.

"Alexander definitely considers you one," Mom went on. "That boy spent half the day petitioning Stan to reverse your suspension Friday. He didn't leave after lunch to get ready for prom with the other seniors. Nancy said she practically had to remove him by his collar."

To say I was gobsmacked would be an understatement here. What was she talking about, and why was this the very first I'd heard of any of this? "Why didn't you tell me that?"

"Well, I was on the trip already, I didn't see any of this go down myself. But they were talking about it in the staff room today." Mom straightened, smiling to herself. "I have to be honest, it won him a few brownie points as far as I'm concerned. Not many kids would stand up to Stan."

Well.

Huh.

I made a mental note to bring this up with Brougham the next chance I had. Why hadn't he told me he'd done that? We'd spent practically the whole day together Saturday, and he hadn't thought to mention he'd fought my case to the principal?

Add that to today's story about Brougham punching—*punching!*—someone at a party over the locker? Well, people always wrote in to the locker asking about mixed messages, and I gave the same approximate answer every time. Mixed messages don't exist: they're telling you the truth clearly through their actions, and you're either believing their honey-eyed words like a lovesick fool, or placing too much weight on the odd inconsistent action. But maybe I'd have to eat my words, because there was nothing clear about Brougham's behavior. Not when he was apparently still happy with Winona.

"Are you calling this girl or what?" Mom asked, snapping me back to the present.

"No," I said. Everything was too confusing and scary and overwhelming right now. A phone call was too much to stack on top of all that. "No, I'm going to text her."

"Don't you dare! A text is *not* an appropriate apology, Darcy."

But I ignored her, because it had just occurred to me that as awkward as I found a phone call, Brooke would probably find it even worse. Put her on the spot and demand a response that instant, or else sit in an uncomfortable, lengthening silence? No, *that* was a rude, emotionally laden demand on someone. A text was actually more polite. It would let her know, plainly and confusion free, where I was coming from, then she'd be free to process it and respond in her own time. Or, not at all, if that's where she was at.

"Your generation is so *rude*," Mom complained as I composed the text. *"Darcy."*

> Hey, so, I was gonna call but I felt weird about it. I'll call if you want me to, I'm not trying to take the easy way out, but I thought I'd rather not put you on the spot. I wanted to say I'm really, really sorry. I was so so so in the wrong with Jaz, and I was in the wrong with Ray. I told myself I was telling you because I cared about you and wanted to keep you

safe. But actually I wanted to
have you back to myself. So I
fucked everything up for you.
I regret it more than anything,
and if there's anything I can
do to make it better, I will.
I understand if that's not
good enough for you, and
you don't have to reply if you
don't want to, but please
know I am sorry. I won't ever
do anything like this again.
Also, I miss you. A lot.

Send.

"Call her, Darc," Mom said.

"It's done. I've texted her. She'll let me know if she wants to talk."

Mom made a big show of rolling her eyes and sighing like I'd just decided to text instead of call the president with news of an impending nuclear attack or something. Yeah, yeah, me and my whole generation were heathens, I got it.

"Thank you," I said.

"For what? You didn't take any of my advice."

"Yeah. But you listened."

Mom held out her hands for a hug, and I went to her. "I'll make sure to do that better from now on. I also need you to promise to come to me whenever you need help from now on. Deal?"

"Deal."

"Are you done?" Ainsley called out from the staircase. "I can't hear weeping or groveling."

"I texted her instead," I called back, pulling out of the hug.

"Oh, great call," Ainsley said, coming back into the living room. "At least that doesn't put her in an awkward spot."

Mom threw up her hands in disbelief.

Ainsley was carrying a dress over one arm. "Okay, two things. First, these sleeves have to go." She unfurled the dress to reveal a cream peasant dress with sleeves that puffed out, then came in to meet a band, several times from the shoulder to the waist. Three puffs per sleeve.

"Um, obviously, they're hideous," I said.

"Of course. But I'm wondering whether to go totally sleeveless or to hem it off under one puff so it's, like, understated poofy."

Mom narrowed her eyes, deep in thought. I did the same.

"Keep one puff," we said at the same time.

"Okay, fantastic, you guys are the best. Um, but also, Oriella just posted a new video, Darc."

"Cool, I'll check it out later."

"No, like, a *big* one. She's just announced a tour. She's coming to L.A."

I yelped and sat up straight so fast I almost careened forward out of the armchair. *"What?"*

"Yeah, like she's doing a whole keynote thing then a workshop with everyone and you can do a meet and greet. You'd get to *meet her*!"

My mouth worked as I tried to come up with the words to describe how badly I needed to go. I mean, I *had* to be there, it wasn't optional, *Oriella* who lived in *Florida* was going to be an hour's drive from me. I'd never have an opportunity like this. And a *meet and greet*? She could meet me, and know I existed in the same realm as her, breathing the same air as her? I could tell her all the stuff I'd learned, and what I did at school, I could even run some advice I'd given past her to see if she thought I'd made the right call.

The room was floating.

Or I was floating.

Ainsley flapped the dress. "Have you chosen party or present yet? Because screw a party, this is *Oriella*."

I only had to briefly glance at Mom, who was cringing and trying to subtly shake her head at Ainsley, to realize it was too late.

"We've already gotten you a present," Mom said slowly.

Ainsley pulled the dress into her chest and gave Mom an apologetic look. "Oh, oops."

"That's totally fine," I said at the same time.

"But we have the receipt," Mom went on. "Would you like me to exchange it?"

Her face was open and kind. There was no trap here, she definitely meant the offer, and a part of me was tempted to jump at the opportunity and thank her through elated squeals. It wasn't a critique of their present-buying skills; this was just poor timing. There hadn't been any way for her and Dad to know this was about to come up.

But at the same time, there was something so dirty about asking someone to exchange a present they'd bought for me. Mom and Dad had spoken—in what was probably a civil conversation—come to a decision, shopped for me, and bought something special for me, from them. It was a *little* less weird than asking for a receipt after opening a present to exchange it . . . but I didn't feel like it was less weird *enough*.

"No, no, no," I said. "Definitely not. Don't worry about it."

"You can just buy it yourself," Ainsley said. "Right? You have money."

"Of course," Mom said dryly. "Your mysterious income source I only recently became aware of."

Well. Interesting point. Only Mom didn't know about the money Ainsley was referring to. My locker money went to various things basically as I earned it: phone bills, foundation, movie trips, self-help books. I'd barely saved a thing from *that* venture, especially after four students took Mom up on the refund option at school and I had to cough up forty to pay her back from my meager savings pile.

But Ainsley meant the Brougham money. The money that came in a couple of lump sum, large bills.

That I hadn't spent.

But it was the only money I was going to have for the foreseeable future, now that my income was cut off.

Before I could come up with a clear thought, my phone buzzed, and everything, everything, vanished except for the fact that Brooke had said her first words to me in days and days.

Hey. Thanks for the apology. I still feel really weird about everything, but it's nice to know you know you messed up. I need more time.

Okay. More time was reasonable. It was better than "never." I would take what I could get for now.

TWENTY

I was on edge throughout the entire Q&Q Club meeting that Thursday. And given that this meeting was chaired by Finn, who'd been defusing tension since the day he left the womb, that was saying a lot. But something was becoming clear to me. Something that had started as a niggling in the back of my mind, so vague I hadn't had words for it at first. The thing is, I'd wrecked things with Brougham romantically, but even if he was out of the picture, I still had to figure this fear out. Because that's what it was, I was realizing. Fear of multiple things.

I needed to discuss it with the only group of people who would get it, first. In the one safe place we'd created where anything could be discussed.

Across the room from me was Erica Rodriguez. She'd poked her head in at the start and asked if she could join in, just to see what it was like in here. She hadn't said a word since introducing herself, but I knew why she was here. I'd kind of sent her here myself. I shot her a smile, but I couldn't seem to make it meet my eyes. She offered me a shaky one in return and shook her long box braids off her shoulders.

Finn cleared his throat dramatically as the meeting started to draw to a close. "As chairman, I've added a few extra items to today's agenda."

Mr. Elliot's eyes widened in trepidation, but he let it go.

"One. Chad and Ryan in *High School Musical 2*."

I glanced at Brooke to share the joke automatically. She was holding in laughter. There were a few murmurs, and Ray hissed, *"Seriously?"*

Finn continued undeterred. "I want the room to take a moment to consider the song 'I Don't Dance,' perhaps the most loaded song lyrics in Disney history, if not the history of entertainment itself. The whole thing is a double entendre. 'I'll show you how I swing'? 'Slide home, you score, swinging on the dance floor'?"

"Oh my god," Alexei muttered.

"And to the doubters, I present the clincher: Ryan and Chad can be seen shortly after, sitting side by side, *now literally wearing each other's clothes*. It's the biggest hidden scandal since Simba wrote 'sex' in the sky with leaves."

"Wasn't that S-F-X? Like, sound effects?" Mr. Elliot asked.

Finn shook his head at him pityingly. "So old, and yet so naïve."

"Old? I'm *twenty-seven*! And don't you talk to me about those movies like I couldn't understand, I was *there*."

"What's your point, Finn?" Ray cut in, her no-nonsense voice back up and running.

Brooke glanced at her, then looked straight at the floor. As far as I knew, she still hadn't worked things out with

Ray. I guess even though I'd set things into motion out of turn, that didn't magically erase Brooke's anger over what Ray had done.

"My point is I'm moving to make Ryan and Chad the official mascots of the Q and Q Club."

"We'll consider it; next item," Mr. Elliot said quickly.

Finn narrowed his eyes at him, then tracked his finger down the clipboard. "Okay . . . here's a submission from . . ." He squinted, then pulled back. "Finn Park."

Ray looked very much like she wanted to snatch the clipboard right from his hands.

"I woke up at four a.m. this morning after an inspired dream and realized—alliteration! We should be the Queer and Questioning *Qlub.* Qlub with a *Q.* Triple Q. That'll *definitely* increase recruitment."

The room fell into silence. Finn looked around, circling his hands in the air to invite feedback.

Ray raised a stiff hand. Finn pointed to her. "Raina, always a pleasure."

"There's one item left and we're running out of time," Ray said.

Finn looked put out. "Fine, but we're revisiting this next week. So, the final topic is . . . biphobia, with Darcy."

He didn't have to make it sound like a talk show.

Suddenly, all eyes were on me. And I didn't want to do this, but I knew I had to.

"So," I said. "I've been feeling really . . . confused, lately. The thing is, I'm . . . really scared to have feelings for a guy, any guy," I spat out. There. Now I'd said the words out loud, I couldn't deny them to myself if I wanted to. "I'm bi. But the last time I liked a guy, I wasn't part of this group, and being bi wasn't this huge part of my identity. But now it is, and, I guess, I feel weird about it?"

"Weird how?" Finn asked.

I swallowed, and scanned the faces staring up at me. No one looked judgy or irritated, even though it felt like such a stupid, trivial thing to bring up. The fear of passing as straight, for god's sake. "I feel like if I'm with a guy, I won't belong here properly anymore. What if I got a boyfriend? I'd feel weird bringing him to pride events, or even telling queer people I have a boyfriend. I'd feel judged."

"Oh my god, Darcy," Jaz said. "We wouldn't judge you."

"You belong," Finn said simply. Brooke nodded, and my breath caught in my throat. It was the first time she'd acknowledged me in person in weeks.

Alexei folded their arms and leaned across the table. "That's all in your head," they said. "You're the only one thinking that, I promise."

"No," Ray said sharply, and I turned to look at her. She didn't look angry, but her tone was firm. My stomach dropped. This was what I'd been so terrified of. That I'd open up, and my fears would be reinforced. But then she went on. "Don't gaslight her. What she's describing is internalized biphobia, and bi's didn't invent this shit. Society sends us that message. We're made to feel like we're not queer enough to hang with queer groups all the time."

Well. Stunned was an understatement for how I felt at that moment. All at once I felt a rush of warmth and gratitude toward her. Gratitude that was instantly tempered by something that felt a lot like guilt. I didn't deserve her backup.

"It's true," Lily said. "Ace and aro people get that sort of shit, too."

Erica whipped her head around to look at Lily, eyes widening hopefully.

"Exactly," Ray said.

"Internalized biphobia?" repeated Jason.

Ray didn't skip a beat. "Yeah. It's when bisexuals start to believe the biphobia they're surrounded by. We're told that our sexuality isn't real, or that we're straight if we're with another gender, and that our feelings don't count if we've never dated a certain gender, that kind of crap. Then we hear it so many times we doubt ourselves."

"Yeah," I said. "That's how I feel. I've been told I was 'turning' straight or 'turning' lesbian again depending on which gender I got a crush on. And a little while ago, someone told me it was good I can date guys, because then I don't have to face discrimination."

Brooke startled in her seat, and it was only then I remembered it was actually her who'd made that comment. I hadn't brought it up to guilt her, and I hoped she didn't take it that way. Now that I'd started letting out some of the anger and frustration I'd barely known was there, though, I couldn't stop.

"And I guess I could *technically* choose to just never act on my crushes when they're not on a guy, but *what the fuck*? And the implication is that I'm less queer than others, because, you know, I can just *go straight* and not deal with any oppression at all, easy. Like being with a guy magically makes me straight. Like it's a competition, or a ranking, and I need to stop speaking on queer issues because am I *really* queer? *Really*, though? And I want to clarify that this person didn't say any of that, but that's just how it felt. And maybe I don't know what it's like to be gay or lesbian, but I do know some people will *never* understand what it's like to be queer and to *blush* every time you join in on a conversation about it because you feel like you're treading on people's toes, because when they say 'queer' they don't mean *you*."

I hadn't meant to yell.

The room fell uncomfortably quiet. Brooke had covered her mouth with her hand, and Ray bit her lower lip. "Once, I had a girl ask me who would I choose," Ray said. "And I was like, well who are they? And she's all oh, no one in particular. And I asked her if she had to choose between girl A and girl B, who would she choose, and she got all grumpy at me and said that was different."

Around the room, the others were starting to break into smiles.

"I'm always hearing that it's suddenly 'weird' if I like one gender after being attracted to another," I said. "Oh, and once, some straight guy asked me how being bi 'works' when I'm in a relationship. And I asked him how it works for him, and he said 'it works in that I'm not bisexual.' Then I asked, if he's attracted to women, how he can possibly stop himself from cheating on his girlfriend with every woman he runs into. Like, for fuck's sake, dude, I said I'm bisexual, not a nymphomaniac."

"Oh my god." Ray snorted.

"I swear, most people think we're either lying about being attracted to multiple genders, or that we must be *so attracted to literally everyone* that we need to make out with every human on this *earth, immediately, damn it*!"

Finn slammed his hands on the table, causing Brooke and me, along with a few other members, to jump. He straightened in his seat, looking grave. "Darcy."

"Yes?"

He grinned. "You're queer."

Ray nodded. "You're queer."

Brooke looked between us, her lips trembling. "You're queer, Darcy."

I loved her so much. I might not be *in* love with her anymore, but I loved her. Was this an olive branch? Did we talk again, now? I would do anything, *anything,* for that.

"You're queer," Alexei echoed.

"You're queer." Jason.

"You're queer." Jaz and Mr. Elliot in unison. Erica whispered it alongside them in a voice too quiet to hear.

"You're queer!" Lily shouted, rising in her seat for emphasis.

I was not going to cry. I was not going to cry. I was—

"Even if I'm with a straight guy?" I asked.

"Yes."

"Yeah."

"Fuck yes."

"Always."

Instead of tears, giggles came out. Happy, giddy giggles. And the others joined me.

For the first time, the very very first time, I really believed them. That my relationship status did not change me. And that even if other people didn't agree, every single person in this room had my back without hesitation. I was with them and they were with me and we were with each other. A community within a community within a community. No questions asked. No proof needed. No valid form of identification required.

We just belonged because we belonged.

After the club meeting, everyone had dispersed, and Brooke hadn't hung back to say anything to me. Apparently today's baby step had been just that. A baby step, not a reconciliation. Ray, at least, had paused to offer me a smile across the room before she left. We hadn't had a friendship to recover in the first place, but it definitely seemed like we'd reached some sort of truce.

Still, neither of them even looked at each other. Which gave me the feeling they wanted to. If you were nonchalant about someone, you didn't put so much energy into ignoring them.

I texted Brougham to meet me by the locker after school before he started his laps. We stood against the wall, out of the path of the last student stragglers leaving for the afternoon, and I summarized my day. Not all of it, of course—I left out the stuff about me feeling like my crush on him had somehow excluded me from my own identity. Even if I was starting to realize that fear had played a part in my reaction when we'd kissed, it wasn't relevant information for him. Not now that he was back with Winona.

But I did tell him about my text to Brooke. And her support today. It was nice to be able to share all of this with Brougham. He gave me his full attention while I spoke, narrowing his eyes in concentration, and "oh"-ing at all the appropriate moments. One-on-one like this, it felt like the two of us up against everyone else. I worked to remind myself that this wasn't the case, though. It wasn't just the two of us. He had a girlfriend. I was his friend, and that was all.

"Do you think she'll ever forgive me?" I finished.

Brougham barked an unexpected, rare laugh. "'Dear locker eighty-nine,'" he joked.

I groaned. "I know, I know. But I'm too involved. I can't trust that my perspective is unbiased here."

"Look. You can't erase what you did," Brougham said. "It's done now. But maybe you could try to patch things up?"

"But how am I supposed to do that?"

". . . Are you serious? Have you not been telling people how to patch shit up for two solid years now, or was that a fever dream of mine?"

Okay. Great point. "I mean, there's a couple things I could probably try," I said. And those things would cost money. But I still had a little of that, if I . . . skipped Oriella. "But I couldn't do it alone."

Brougham drummed his fingers on the locker he was leaning against.

"Good thing you're not alone."

Saturday afternoon, Brougham arrived at Mom's house to join in on my birthday cake holding a plate of white bread coated in sugar sprinkles, for some reason.

Ainsley led him into the kitchen where Mom, Dad, and I were sitting around the kitchen table, which had a supermarket chocolate cake proudly stuck in its center. One of the best parts of my birthday, if not *the* best part, was having Mom and Dad in the same room, at the same time, doing their best not to snap at each other. It was just so rare to see them together, it was basically a present in itself.

Brougham gave a soft smile the moment he saw me and held the plate up in offering, while the rest of us stared at it as one. "I brought fairy bread," he said. "It's not a party without fairy bread."

"Technically, it's not a party at all," Ainsley said, tearing open the package of birthday candles. We'd been waiting for Brougham to arrive to do the cake. Brougham and I had to run off to start setting up in about half an hour, so I'd asked if he could join in on the festivities. Usually Brooke would be the one making a guest appearance, but today that wasn't really an option.

"Do I dare ask what that is?" Mom asked, eyeing the plate warily. What did Brougham do in science class to make her so wary of his cooking, exactly?

"It's bread with butter and hundreds-and-thousands."

"You mean sprinkles?" I asked.

"Yeah, whatever."

"But *why*?" Ainsley asked, picking up a triangle-shaped slice of bread to inspect it. She took a nibble of the corner, then shrugged. "It tastes like you'd expect it to taste, I guess."

That was a good enough endorsement for Dad, who took a slice. But to be fair, Dad also thought pineapple and anchovies belonged in unspeakable dishes, so he didn't have a leg to stand on in terms of food snobbery.

"Happy birthday," Brougham said brightly, holding the plate out to me.

I tried not to laugh as I accepted his offering. I got the distinct feeling he did all this just because he knew it'd throw us.

Dad and Ainsley finished up arranging the candles on the cake, lit them, and then sat me down in front of it while everyone sang "Happy Birthday" to me. Ainsley dutifully filmed the whole thing on her phone. "Don't forget to wish for something," she said at the song's end.

It wasn't hard to figure out something to wish for. All I wanted was for tonight to go well. Looking across the table at Brougham, standing between my mom and dad and smiling his perfect hint of a smile, I was struck that no matter how lucky I felt to have him in my life, even if only as a friend, he was no replacement for Brooke. No one could be.

I blew out seventeen candles in one breath, then raised an eyebrow at Brougham while I got ready to cut the cake. "I'm surprised you don't have a special Australian birthday song."

"Actually, we do. It's quite mean, though, so I wasn't sure if it'd go down well."

Aww, he was learning! "Good call."

My presents were placed on the table by Mom and Ainsley. From Mom and Dad, I got a pair of honest-to-god real diamond studs. "Because those kids at your school might like to show off with all the expensive trends, but that can't compete with something quality and timeless," Mom explained, laughing as I threw my arms around them.

From Ainsley, I got a rosy mauve peasant top that she'd covered in gold and berry-toned embroidered flowers and vines, hundreds of them. It was so intricate I gasped out loud. "Holy *shit,* Ains. I'm going to put it on right now."

"Can I film you wearing it? I've been filming myself making it for ages now. I'm gonna need footage for the video."

The two of us ran upstairs, leaving Brougham to chat with our parents and/or keep them from each other's throats now that they'd lost their witnesses.

"All set for tonight?" Ainsley asked as I tore my shirt off.

"Yup. You still okay for six?" My voice was muffled by fabric as I pulled the new blouse over my head.

"We'll be there at six on the dot."

I smoothed the blouse down over my denim shorts and we surveyed me in Ainsley's floor-length mirror. I looked—

"So beautiful," Ainsley breathed. "I am *so* talented."

"Thank you. Okay, ready to film?"

Ainsley stroked her bottom lip. "Wait, one sec." She opened her desk drawer and dug through her jumbled pile of unorganized makeup samples and brushes—which Brooke would have a coronary over if she ever saw—and fished out the peachy liquid lipstick she'd won over me months before. "This will go perfectly."

Beaming, I applied it, then shoved it in my shorts pocket.

"Hey," Ainsley protested. "Give it back!"

"I need it to reapply later! You'll get it back, calm down."

"I'd better," she grumbled.

We filmed a clip as quickly as we could, then headed downstairs, where Brougham was sitting between my parents, his back unnaturally straight and his hands sandwiched between his knees. Mom and Dad were talking to each other in hushed whispers over his head, and both of them wore a distinct "I'm politely irritated by you but I'm going to be the bigger person here" expression.

Brougham looked relieved to see me, and he jumped up. "We should probably head to mine," he said. "Heaps to set up."

Dad's relief was just as palpable. "Well, that's my cue to go then, I guess," he said, stretching. "Happy birthday, sweetheart."

"Thank you. And thank you for the earrings." I touched my earlobes.

"Good luck tonight," Mom said, pulling me in for a hug.

"Wait, what's tonight?" Dad cut in. He knew bits of background, of course. Like, he knew I'd gotten suspended. He knew about the locker. He knew Brooke and I had had an argument. But beyond that, not so much. Mom knew everything, though. I'd told her my plan, and she'd listened. She'd even offered some suggestions of her own.

"Brougham and I are cooking dinner for Brooke."

Dad gave a vague, pleasant nod. "Oh. That's nice," he said.

As Brougham and I left the house, I made out Mom's chiding voice. "You could stand to act more interested in her life, you know. Ask some *questions* . . ."

TWENTY-ONE

"Okay, ingredients can go in the kitchen," Brougham directed as we lugged the shopping bags in from his car at his house. "Do we start on these first, or the decorations, you reckon?"

"Let's get as much prepared as we can, so we can throw it in the oven on time later," I suggested, dropping my loaded canvas bag on his pristine, glossy countertop.

Brougham hoisted himself up to sit on the counter and took out his phone. I gaped at him.

"Don't sit on the counter! That's so unhygienic."

"What? I'm wearing clean pants."

"Yeah and you've been sitting in *all sorts of places*."

He rolled his eyes and hopped down to sit on a bar stool, like he should've done in the first place. I glared at him then grabbed a cloth from the sink to give the whole countertop a wipe down. God only knew how many butts had been on this thing.

"Okay, hit me with the sexy menu," Brougham said, sliding his reading glasses on. "I'll type it up and laminate it while you get ready."

"Don't title it 'the sexy menu,' though, okay?" I said. "Just 'menu' is fine."

Brougham pulled a face that indicated he disagreed, but didn't argue.

"We're starting with garlic-butter oysters in puff pastry, followed by roast figs, potatoes, and asparagus in chili and lime sauce, and ending with chocolate-covered strawberries."

Brougham noted it all down, then tipped his head to one side. "Are they pescatarian?"

"Nope. I was just on a bit of a budget after I bought the projector."

"Cool, just checking. Hold on. DAD?"

One of the main reasons we decided to do this at Brougham's house—outside of the general ambiance of his backyard, that is—was that Brougham's mom was over in Vegas this weekend at a friend's bachelorette party. I'd been assured multiple times that Mr. Brougham wasn't so bad when he wasn't arguing with his wife. This was my time to find out, I guessed.

In fact, this was my first time seeing Brougham's father in person. As he walked into the kitchen, I was struck by how little he resembled his son. He had thinning, soft brown hair that might have once been curly, and was stocky where Brougham was naturally slight, with a neck that stood like a solid block, not a curve in sight.

Given the arguments over Mrs. Brougham's fidelity, I couldn't help but wonder if the lack of resemblance was a point of contention for the family.

"What's up, mate?" Mr. Brougham asked. Then he nodded at me with a smile as reserved as Brougham's usually was. "Hi. Darcy? Happy birthday."

"Thank you."

"Are we using the duck in the fridge?" Brougham asked.

His dad leaned one hand against the counter. "Not for anything in particular. Your *mother* was going to cook it last night, until she got *busy*."

Reading between the lines, that sounded like another argument had gone down last night.

Brougham pushed past the dig at his mom. "Can we use it?"

Mr. Brougham stuck out his lip and made a show of considering it. "Only if you cook it properly and I can have some for dinner."

Brougham scoffed. "Have I ever *not* cooked something properly?"

His dad flourished a hand in my direction. "Is that a wise question to ask in front of your lady friend?"

At that, Brougham flushed pink. I cut in to change the subject. "If we can use the duck, we'll have *plenty* to go around for everyone."

"Go for it," Mr. Brougham said. "Shout out if you need anything, hey? And don't forget about the dishes. Just because the drill sergeant isn't home doesn't mean you get to slack off."

"I would never."

It was interesting watching Brougham interact with his dad. Unlike when he'd run into his mother, his body language remained relaxed, and even though he was very "polite mode: activate," still, the air of tension that'd surrounded him with his mom just wasn't here. I could see why he was keen to spend time at home while his mother wasn't around. His not-mansion didn't even seem quite as vast and empty to *me*.

As it turned out, Brougham wasn't as hopeless in the kitchen as accused—he just had a bad habit of underestimating the cooking time of things. So, while we prepared the duck and chopped the vegetables, I explained and demonstrated the purposes of a kitchen thermometer to a fascinated Brougham. It took us longer than I'd initially hoped to get everything in the oven roasting, so we split tasks, with Brougham in charge of printing the menus and setting up the projector, and me looking after decorations.

Brougham's backyard patio didn't need much help to become a romantic paradise. Immediately outside the back doors was a huge patio area with masonry stone flooring, decorated with potted plants in stone planters, pastel flowers bordering the edges, and creeping vines spilling down the walls. A four-person outdoor dining setup, shaded by a brown umbrella, stood dead center, overlooking the Broughams' enormous pool. The edges of the patio formed a semicircle against the house, and descended down to the garden in several wide steps, all illuminated by in-ground, warm yellow lights.

I got to work unraveling and tacking up string lights around the columns supporting the patio veranda and in some of the bushes and trees dotting the garden. A lit candle went in the center of the table, and then Brougham gave me a hand hiding the extension cords so they didn't ruin the vibe. We'd *just* finished linking my Spotify to Brougham's portable speaker when Ray walked out, having been apparently let in by Mr. Brougham.

"Wow," she said, spinning around to take in the garden. She was dressed up, wearing a pair of black, skin-tight leather pants paired with a low-cut turquoise shirt and white heels. It seemed Brougham had effectively communicated tonight's theme of fancy-slash-sexy. His words, not mine.

Luckily for us, Ray was 100 percent invested in anything that could help her gain Brooke's forgiveness, and she'd jumped at the chance to come tonight when Brougham messaged her (it had to be Brougham because she'd, understandably, blocked me on everything she *could* block me on, even if we were in a sort-of truce).

"When does Brooke get here?" Ray asked, brushing her fingertips along the surface of the table.

"Ainsley should bring her by in the next few minutes," I said.

"I'm really relieved she agreed to come."

Brougham and I exchanged a glance. "Well," I said. "She doesn't . . . exactly know this is going on. She thinks she's agreed to come see me on my birthday as a surprise."

"Oh." Ray's face clouded. "Happy birthday. But . . . she's gonna leave."

"I don't think she will," I said. "She's been miserable since—" I broke them up "—you guys broke up. I think she just needs a chance to hear you out."

"Speaking of," Brougham said, looking over his shoulder toward the house.

He was right. I could make out faraway voices. I gave Ray a thumbs-up, and followed Brougham inside.

Brooke stood with Ainsley in the sprawling hallway, looking equal amounts exasperated and bewildered. "Happy birthday?" she said when we entered. "I, um . . . I've never skipped one of your birthdays. It felt weird."

"A lot of things have felt weird," I agreed. "I'm really glad you came."

"Right," Brooke said, then added, questioningly, "to . . . Brougham's place?"

"You know," Brougham piped up beside me. "It's just now occurred to me this plan involved you apologizing for a lie by lying."

Brooke whipped around to face him, eyes wide.

Thanks, Brougham. "You're not here for my birthday," I said in a rush. "Ray's outside, and she wants to talk to you. And we've made you guys dinner. And a show, I guess."

Brooke blinked. "Ray's here?"

She didn't look mad.

I perked back up. "Yes, she wants to talk. If you do, too, you can head out and chat for as long as you want to."

Brooke nodded, then dug through her handbag. "I, um, got you a present. Kind of."

"Oh, you didn't have to." She passed me a box, and I opened it to find about two dozen sample skincare and makeup sachets. I broke into a smile. "*Thank you!* My stash is so low." Next to me, Ainsley stuck her head in the box and made an excited gushing noise.

"I bet it is." Brooke giggled. "And you're not gonna have much cash to replace them, either, huh?"

My smile faded, and I cleared my throat. "Yeah. True."

"I'm sorry you lost the locker. And got suspended."

"It's not your fault. But thanks." I turned to Ainsley. "You staying? We have a lot of food."

"Nah, Mom's already ordered Chinese. Good luck, though."

"Hey," Brooke said as Ainsley started moving toward the door. "Those"—she pointed an accusing finger at the box Ainsley held—"are Darcy's birthday present. I have an inventory list and I'm not afraid to cross-check it later."

Ainsley rolled her eyes but grudgingly promised not to steal any. I couldn't have cared less if she did, though. I was too busy drowning in heady delight that Brooke had referenced a future visit to my house. Was she one step closer to forgiving me?

Brougham and I walked Brooke most of the way outside, then Brougham showed Brooke where to go and grabbed my hand to slow me down. I glanced down at it, surprised at the unexpected contact. His hands were softer than I remembered them being. "Let's stay out of their way. We're awkward. We have to blend into the background as much as we can." He steered me toward the kitchen.

"Speak for yourself, I'm not awkward."

"No, you're the person who viciously tore them apart out of jealousy, which is worse."

"If you wanted to be in the background, we should've worn all black."

"Yes, that would've done wonders to blend us into the background on this warm, sunny California evening."

"Do you know arguing with everything people say is not cute? It's insanely annoying."

"Really?" He quirked an eyebrow. "I kind of thought you liked it."

"Did you? So, you're contradictory for my benefit?"

"Partly."

"And what's the other reason?"

"It's great fun."

I rolled my eyes as he bent to check on the oysters in the oven. "You think arguing is *fun*?"

He opened the oven and looked over his shoulder for an oven mitt. It was closer to me, so I grabbed it and handed it to him. His eyes sparkled before he turned back to his task. "When it's with you? Definitely. Isn't it for you?"

I was halfway through retrieving plates from his cabinet, and I paused, still bent over. "Well . . . I . . . it's still annoying."

"Huh. Well, I'll stop then," Brougham said, transferring oysters to the plates I held out.

"You don't have to do that," I said. "Just, do whatever you want. It's whatever."

He met my eyes and broke into a grin. I wasn't even sure if I could call it a rare grin anymore. He seemed to offer them up with more and more abandon as time passed.

Outside, Ray and Brooke were leaning into the middle of the table, talking. Their faces seemed serious. They both jumped back and straightened at the sound of the door opening.

Ray grabbed the menu from the table and scanned it. "Oysters, huh?"

Brougham and I placed the food down, and Brooke snatched the menu from Ray. "Figs, asparagus, chili, chocolate, and strawberries? Darcy!"

"What?" Ray asked.

"They're all aphrodisiacs. Darcy, you're sick." Brooke burst out laughing. Ray went a lovely shade of magenta.

"How am I sick? I'm just setting the mood!" Besides, aphrodisiacs aren't scientifically real. It was just kind of funny.

"Trying to make us horny at someone else's house is *weird*!"

Even Brougham started laughing at this. I rolled my eyes and bit back a giggle. "Grow up, guys. Now eat."

"Yeah, eat your emotionally manipulative meal in silence," Brougham deadpanned, and I dragged him off by the arm.

After the appetizers, it was time to start the show. Brougham and I had set up a projector and screen on the patio, and Ainsley, a video-editing genius because of YouTube, had helped me put a short movie together.

The screen lit up.

PART ONE: THE GHOST OF RELATIONSHIPS PAST

Ainsley appeared on the screen, wrapped in a cream-colored sheet we'd scavenged from the closet. "Ooooooooh. I am the ghost of relationships past. Tonight, you will be visited by three ghosts. They're all going to be meeeeee. I don't get paaaaaaaid enough for thiiiiissss."

"Very atmospheric," Brougham whispered from our spot at the window of his second living room, looking outside. We were kneeling back-to-front on his leather sofa, folding our elbows on its back.

"First, take a look at the relationship that was, so your memories aren't clouded by aannnggeerr. AANNNGGEERRRR! WOOOOOO!" Ainsley waved the sheet around.

"And you approved this," Brougham commented lightly.

"By the time she showed me it was too late for a reshoot, okay?"

Now came a slideshow of photos and videos, set to "Only Time" by Enya. Ainsley's choice. By the time we'd mined Snapchat, Instagram, and Ray's personal collection, we had more than enough happy memory clips to fill a several-minutes-long video. Outside, Brooke burst out laughing as she and Ray watched the video. I wasn't quite sure if she was laughing at the clips and the fond memories, or at the video itself. Oh well. Soldiering on.

Brougham and I moved on to prepare the main course. This one was particularly difficult to set up, as it involved holding the plate just so, and placing it a little closer to Brooke on the table than to Ray. As planned, Brooke, being closer, lifted the silver lid off of the plate, and let out a scream so bloodcurdling I was worried Brougham's dad might rush out. Brooke scrambled out of her seat.

On the tray sat a remarkably realistic black widow spider figurine I'd found on Etsy. I shoved it in my pocket. "Enjoy."

Brooke, gasping like she'd run a marathon, stared at me. "What the *fuck*?"

"Just wanted to liven things up."

"Why are we *friends*?" she shouted, pressing a hand to her chest. "I could've had a heart attack!"

"Brougham knows CPR; you're fine."

Ray and Brooke exchanged an incredulous glance, and Brougham and I returned inside.

There was a reason for the spider, of course. One of the first things I'd learned in my studies: fear and adrenaline remarkably mimic the sensation of falling for someone. Always go to a horror movie on a first date, if possible.

Spiders work, too.

After bringing Brougham's dad his portion as promised, Brougham and I perched ourselves by the window again, far enough back that we wouldn't be noticed staring, and ate our own servings.

"They look a lot happier than they did," Brougham remarked with a full mouth.

"Ninety-five percent success rate," I replied.

"Touché."

"Speaking of, how's Winona doing?"

Brougham looked surprised by the question. But I'd said it as casually as possible. Sure, we hadn't spoken about her much, but she wasn't entirely off-limits, right? "She's fine, I guess. Seemed happy enough the last time we spoke."

"Well that's a glowing endorsement," I said.

"I don't know what you expected. I mean, does she have to be thrilled?"

"Um, ideally?"

Brougham snorted. "That's a very rosy outlook. I don't know how realistic it is, though."

That. Made my heart break a little. And it took every ounce of strength, every little *bit* of self-control in my body not to interfere. If anyone had written into the locker describing their relationship so ambivalently I would've told them something seemed very wrong. Especially so early into its revival. Brougham deserved someone who was fucking *psyched* to be with him, and if that wasn't Winona—

If that wasn't Winona, that was his business. It wasn't my place.

"Can I just check you're okay?" I asked.

Brougham put his finished plate down and stood up. He wasn't smiling, but there was nothing concerning in his expression. "Darcy, I have never been better. Honestly. Thanks for your concern, though."

Well, that had to be that.

Anyway. There was no time to dwell on it, because it was time for the second movie.

TWENTY-TWO

Ainsley's face was projected on the screen again. This time, she wore a red velvet dressing gown and a flower crown prop she kept for her videos. "Hello! Ho, ho, ho! I am the ghost of relationships present!"

"Does she think that's Santa?" Brougham murmured. "Does she know they're different?"

"The past is something that we cannot chaaannggeee, ho, ho, ho!"

"Well, now she's just smashed them all together and made something new and horrifying," Brougham said. I shushed him.

"We're not obligated to forgive the paaassstttt, but sometimes we get so focused on it, we fail to see the present, woooooOOOO! WOOOOO!" Ainsley leaned forward and belted this into the camera, eyes wild.

Brooke was laughing so hard her forehead was pressed against the table. Ray shuffled away from the screen a little, as though she was worried Ainsley would climb out and shout in her face.

"For this task, all we ask is that you listen to what's

being said in the present, before deciding whether the past is worth holding oooonnntttoooo." Ainsley dropped down slowly onto her knees, and kept going until she was out of the camera frame, leaving the camera pointed at her empty bedroom. The video cut out.

For this part of the night, Brougham and I were doomed to be left out. Ray had asked us when we invited her to provide her with an opportunity to apologize to Brooke properly. And that's what she was doing now. We could spy on them through the windows, and try to gauge how we felt it was going. We could watch the tears roll down Brooke's cheeks, and guess if the nodding was a good indicator. But the words were private.

After an eternity, both Ray and Brooke started to look what I interpreted to be much happier. Ray turned to the window—apparently they were both fully aware they were being spied on—and gestured to us it was safe to go out. Brougham and I hurried to the kitchen to fetch the dessert.

As soon as Brooke and Ray had their plates, I brought the laptop as close to Brooke as I could get it. "You're responsible for I.T. operations," I said. "Someone needs to pause and restart the video once you're done answering each question, because we couldn't predict how long you'd take."

Brooke gave me a still-watery smile and nodded.

Ainsley's next outfit was a black hoodie with the hood up, and sunglasses. It was the best we could do on short notice. "I," she wheezed in her best lifelong-smoker impression, "am the ghost of relationships yet to come. I wanted to show you visions of yourselves dying alone, but Darcy told me I'm not allowed to do that, so I drew a picture of it anyway, and I'm adding it in behind Darcy's back."

"What?" I hissed.

The screen filled with a picture done in what looked like Microsoft Paint, showing two graves, each with DIED ALONE written on them, accompanied by BROOKE and RAINA.

"Oh my god," I muttered, rubbing my temples.

"You left her unsupervised," Brougham observed.

I went over to the window as Ainsley's voice went on, losing her wheeze for a minute. "I felt that was important for the theme, but no pressure to get back together or anything; for real, it's *totally voluntary.* Lots of people live very fulfilled lives, single and happy."

I banged on the window and Brooke and Ray looked over, startled. "It's true!" I yelled, before returning to Brougham.

"I mean, I *personally* thought that was obvious, but now that that disclaimer is out of the way so Darcy doesn't murder me again—because I'm already a ghost, get it—the final task for you two is to promote transparency moving forward. You are to be presented with thirty-six questions. Both must answer to complete the final task, or risk painful death."

"Did she add that in last minute, too?" Brougham asked.

"No, she said it was crucial to fit the tone of the creepy ghost."

"She really threw herself into this."

The first question appeared on the screen: *If you could have anyone in the world, past or present, over for dinner, who would you invite?*

"What's this based on?" Brougham asked, shifting so his legs were crossed beneath him.

"Thirty-six questions of increasing vulnerability. It's supposed to fast-track a bond."

"Ah."

We watched as Brooke gave her answer to Ray.

"It's a toss-up between my nanna and the director of the C.I.A.," Brougham said suddenly.

I blinked in surprise. I hadn't expected us to play along. But, sure. Why not? "That's an interesting toss-up."

"I know. My nanna's the best person I know, and I used to get sent to her house all the time when I was little and my parents blew up. But she lives in Adelaide, so we never get to see her anymore. But the director of the C.I.A. would know so much cool shit, and I figure I can kidnap him and force secrets out of him."

"Just casually."

"Right."

"Mine would be Oriella. She's a YouTuber I watch all the time. I'd love to pick her brains."

"I know who she is. You mentioned her to me once, so I looked her up."

"You did?"

"Yup. Her videos are interesting."

Huh.

Hadn't picked Brougham to be interested in something like that. But I guess he *had* sought me out for help in that area months ago.

The next question appeared on-screen. *Would you want to be famous? For what?*

Brougham shot a hand up. "Easy. Freestyle world record."

We went on like that for a while, answering the questions as they came, and trying to match Brooke and Ray for time. Then we came to the first intense question.

"My most terrible memory," Brougham said. "Jesus.

That's not something I try to think about on purpose." He smiled weakly, but I just waited. "Okay, um. Once when I was about ten, Mum got really angry at Dad, and they'd had this massive fight the night before, so she went to drive me to school but then she changed directions and took me to the airport. She said we were going to fly to another country and I'd never see my dad or my friends or the rest of our family ever again. And she bought us tickets—I can't even remember where *to*—and we were lining up to go through security, and I was fucking *terrified*, and I wanted to ask someone for help, but I couldn't, because I was more scared of her and what she'd do to me if I did. But the thought of having no one to buffer her for the rest of my life, and never seeing anyone else again . . . I've never been that scared. Then when we got to the front of the security line she took my hand and led me out, and we left the airport, and she dropped me at school and told me to never tell anyone what happened. And I never did."

I could see it on his face. The terror that a little kid had felt, once, being kidnapped by his own mother and too afraid to do anything to stop it. And holy *shit*, this was intense, way too intense, and I guessed that was the whole point of the questions, but *Jesus*. I hoped Brooke and Ray were okay. "I'm so sorry," I said.

"It's fine. Let's just . . . not talk about that one again, please."

"Got it. Well, my worst memory is easy. We were little, and I'd spent all morning mad at Ainsley for some fight we were having, and our parents both took her side, which made me even angrier. And then we were outside and she kicked a ball onto the roof and decided to climb up to get it, and I didn't tell her not to because I thought it'd be funny if she fell. I don't know why—I was mad at her, and I didn't really get it. I didn't think seriously bad things *could* happen to us. Then she *did* fall and like . . . she didn't bounce, like she did in my head. She got knocked out and I thought she was dead. She woke up after a few seconds but it felt like an hour, and I had to face the thought that she wasn't guaranteed, you know? People can die. *That's* the most scared I've ever been."

Brougham watched me speak with a serious expression, nodding the whole time and not tearing his eyes away from me for even a moment. I hadn't talked about that day in forever. I hadn't *thought* about it in forever. But it was weirdly freeing to tell him about it now.

The questions only got more intense from there. Some things we agreed on, like the definition of friendship. Others, our answers looked very different, like how love and affection looked in our lives (for me, it was the sun everything else revolved around; for Brougham, it was a goal, something he felt might change the way his whole life looked if he had as much of it as he would like to).

The question about relationships with our mothers made the room feel heavy and uncomfortable. Brougham hesitated, so I went first. "I love my mom," I said. "I think our relationship's starting to change for the better, lately. We've been talking more. It was hard for a while, because she's always *so* busy, and I know it's because she has to juggle everything without much input from Dad, but having her ignore me for work hurt more than when Dad does it. Maybe that's not fair, I dunno. But she's the one I live with most of the time, so it was her I wanted more support from. And on the flip side, I guess it's her that I'm closer with in general for the same reason."

Brougham glanced outside at Ray and Brooke. "I'm worried I'm going to become mine, and I won't notice it happening. I keep thinking about how I got drunk after prom, and I didn't do it to have fun or be social, I did it because I was angry, and I didn't wanna be. And that scares me."

Brooke and Ray had moved onto the next question, but I felt like we might need to skip it. Brougham and I needed to linger here for a minute. "Look, I'm not an expert," I said. "But I think you're being really hard on yourself. You're scared of it because you've seen how bad it can get. But you're also really aware of yourself, and you have the ability to reflect, and to change your choices when you don't like how it went last time. You might be more at risk of issues with it because of genetics, but it's not a sentence, you know? You still have control over how your life will go from here."

Brougham looked up at me through his lashes. "You reckon?"

"I do. You're not addicted, and you don't have a history, and you haven't set up dangerous habits. But if it's scaring you so much, maybe you should see someone about it, like the school counselor or something, so you can figure out what to do if you're in that situation again."

Brougham rested his head against his elbow. "That's a good idea," he said. He sounded tired.

We sat in the silence. Brougham was off somewhere else, and I didn't want to push him to make his way back to me.

A few questions later, I sat up straight. "This is a more cheerful one," I said. "Three things we like about each other."

Brougham blinked and shook his head a little. "Ah, yes, better not miss the ego stroke."

"You're damn right. Okay, I like that you're . . . impossible to predict, but I'm starting to anticipate you acting out of the ordinary, so maybe I'm sort of starting to predict you anyway. I like that you're always there for people when they need you, especially Finn. And I like how you insist on letting people in, even though you've been stung for it more times than most."

Brougham's expression was funny as he processed these. Not quite readable. He cleared his throat. "I like that you always have a response, like you're never caught off guard by anything, you just adapt and retaliate. I like that you're so concerned with the happiness of total strangers, and you're happy when other people are happy even if you don't get the credit for making it happen. And I like that you're just genuinely *fun*. People like to be around you."

Well. For all his insistence that I was never caught off guard, I sure felt unsure how to respond. It felt like he'd looked at me, then ripped off my skin and looked underneath that, then dove deeper still.

When the questions were finally done, Brooke and Ray stood up and embraced each other, holding the position for second after second after second. Brougham and I watched them, side by side, our shoulders pressed together. "That looks good," I said. He gave a grunt of agreement.

The sun was beginning to set as we walked outside, and everything was glowing with a warm orange. The yard had a dreamlike feel to it. So did I, come to think of it. I felt completely drained.

"Thank you guys for setting all this up," Brooke said. Her eyes were heavy lidded. She looked how I felt. "It's just . . . you went above and beyond. It was . . . extra. But it was really nice."

"Well, you know. I'm really, really sorry for what I did. To both of you. I know it doesn't make up for anything, but I . . ." I shrugged.

"I'm gonna give Brooke a lift home," Ray said, but she was smiling. Apology accepted? Hard to tell. She placed a hand gently on Brooke's shoulder blade, then let it drop.

"Okay. So . . ." I trailed off.

Brooke held her arms out, and I fell into them.

"I'll text you," she said. The most wonderful thing she'd ever said to me.

As Brooke and Ray headed off, Brougham steered me to the pool. "Let's just chill for a minute," he said.

We were both wearing shorts, so it was easy enough for us to kick off our shoes and sit on the edge of the pool side by side, with our legs in the water. His pool had soaked up the heat from the day, and it was almost warm. The perfect temperature for the evening. I wish I'd thought to bring my swimsuit.

"I got you something," Brougham said. "For your birthday."

I looked up, surprised. "I thought all of this was for my birthday?"

"Nah. That was for them. This is for you." He fished an envelope from his pocket, and for a wild, irrational moment I thought it was a locker letter.

Inside the envelope was a piece of paper. I unfolded it and smoothed out the creases. It was a printout of a ticket.

ORIELLA ORATES VIP PASS
209 SLATER BLVD. SANTA MONICA. CA 90408
ADMIT: 2

I stared at the ticket in disbelief while Brougham spoke quickly beside me. "I know how much you love her, and I was checking out her videos and saw she's coming, and I asked Ainsley and she said you didn't have tickets so it was kind of perfect. And I got two so you wouldn't have to go alone, but you can take whoever you want. And if you can't find anyone I'll totally come with you, like, I don't want you to be alone, and it'd probably be interesting, but I didn't get you two tickets so you'd have to take me. Just to clarify."

This.

Would've cost.

So much money.

Too much money for a friend's gift. Did Brougham realize that? Or did rich kids just not grasp the implications of spending a fortune on someone?

A warm breeze picked up, blowing my hair into my face. The sunset cast a peachy glow over the pool, the porch columns, our skin. A dragonfly darted past Brougham's head and skimmed the surface of the pool, dipping down to the water and sending ripples scattering. He was watching me, a little uncertainly, like he thought I hated it or something.

It wasn't that.

It was just . . .

"Brougham?" I asked, still grasping the ticket in both hands. "Does Winona, um . . . know, we're friends?"

Brougham looked confused. "What are you on about?"

"I'm *on about* the fact that sometimes people hide friendships from their girlfriends because they're worried, and I've never seen that end well. So, does she know?"

"Okay, leaving the obvious problem with that question aside for a second, do you reckon people shouldn't be allowed to hang out with the gender they're into when they're in a relationship?"

I huffed. "Of course not. I mean, I'm bi. If I couldn't, that'd be pretty damn limiting for me."

"You made it sound like there's something wrong with it."

"No, it's about openness and honesty."

"But why would people hide something that isn't wrong in the first place?"

"They just *do*. And I don't wanna interfere with your relationship, but—"

"But interfering in relationships is literally how you made a living," Brougham finished for me helpfully. "Though I don't know what relationship you're talking about."

I smacked my hand on the concrete, frustrated. "You and Winona!"

"What?" Brougham looked briefly amused, then the laughter in his eyes faded to something more quizzical. "Wait, did you really not know we broke up?"

"You *what*? When? Why didn't you tell me?"

Hope sparked in my chest, while my brain scrambled for clarity. None of this made any sense. I would *know* if they'd broken up, wouldn't I? Brougham would share that with me, right?

Brougham wrenched his stare away from me, eyebrows furrowed. He looked about as baffled as I felt. "Honestly, Darcy, I thought you knew. I figured Finn told you. I thought you said he *had*. I broke up with her after prom."

I stared at him, totally lost for words, as I tried to reshuffle the last week in my head.

He'd ended things with Winona at the party.

Gotten into a fight over me.

Gotten drunk.

Slept on my couch, and stared up at me with that aching in his eyes (which I was now certain I didn't imagine) and yet didn't initiate anything. Didn't ask me to stay behind when I left to go to sleep. Didn't reject my offer of platonic friendship. Even when he thought I knew.

"Why?" I asked.

Luckily for me, he didn't pretend to misunderstand the question, for once. He raised his hands, then let them fall in his lap helplessly. "Don't you . . . don't you *know*?"

I was too scared to believe I knew anything right now. But somehow, something within me got brave enough to take his hand.

He really was beautiful. And despite what I'd thought of him when I met him, now that I knew him, I was quite sure he might be the most beautiful person I'd ever met in my life.

His leg bumped mine underwater as he shifted. His hand tightened its grip on mine, and we pulled each other in, and our lips met in the middle softly, and Brougham drew in a sharp breath.

He tasted just as I remembered. He unthreaded his fingers from mine and rested them on my temple, before walking them backward to both push my hair back and pull me in to deepen the kiss.

I didn't want the kiss to be gentle anymore. I tugged him into me to press his chest against mine with one hand, and the other I weaved up and around his neck. Then I shifted and pushed myself up and around so I was straddling him, my knees against the concrete. He kept kissing me, and grabbed my hips to move me into a comfortable position. We were getting water everywhere, but it barely mattered.

All I could do was kiss him for all the times I'd wanted to but couldn't. Letting my hands roam wherever they ended up. Letting him run his hands under my shirt to touch my shoulder blades, and rake his fingertips down my skin when I sank low into his lap, drawing a moan from somewhere guttural. He broke his kiss away and moved it to my neck, holding me in place so I could arch my back without crashing into the pool. The warmth of his mouth and the sweep of his tongue against my collarbone almost made me lose my grip on everything completely, and I fought to draw myself back into the present before I gave in to abandon and pulled us both underwater.

Because we—

His hair was so soft and thick, and the bit by the nape of his neck was like touching a mink blanket—

—couldn't do anything but kissing—

—and I felt myself slipping, or maybe Brougham was sliding forward, but my feet were in the water now, and I wanted to let him—

—because his dad was in the *house and could be watching us right this second.*

I wanted to, but I couldn't. I steadied us by bracing my knee against the pool's edge, and broke away, panting. "Brougham."

He froze. A flash of panic swept over his face, like someone sobered by ice water. Straight into sharp focus.

He thought I was going to run off again.

I cupped his jaw with my hands and tried to give him a reassuringly warm look. "Your dad is right inside."

Everything relaxed, so intensely I could physically feel the shift of his body beneath mine. "Right. Yup. Duh."

I stayed in my position while we caught our breath and

tried to bring things back to more of a three out of ten on the intensity scale.

"I wanted to tell you I had feelings for you," I said. "But you'd already picked things back up with Winona. It happened so fast."

Brougham tipped his head back in frustration. "Of course. Of *course* that happened. Fuck me. It's what I do, I convinced myself you didn't feel the same because you never reached out like you said you would, so I threw myself into Winona so I could try to get over you and go back to the way I used to feel about her. I thought it'd work. I just didn't want to deal with having feelings for someone who didn't like me back, so I tried to change them."

Because that's what *happened* when someone who was anxiously attached felt rejected. And I knew this, and yet I couldn't logically apply it to Brougham at the time, because I was too close to see things clearly. "It's okay. I get it."

"I fucked up."

"I think it's fair to say we both did."

His hands drifted lazily to my thighs, where his thumb started tracing circles over my skin, sending a rippling shiver up to my shoulders. "Today's been a lot," he said. Then he pulled his hands away, and leaned back from me, giving me full control over our position. "I'm sure you have a lot you wanna think about."

"There's nothing to think about," I said.

"You have to get home," he added.

"Not for a while still."

"It's kind of happening out of nowhere."

"You call that out of nowhere?"

He shrugged. Because he knew it was bullshit. He just wanted to protect himself by giving me an out. Any out.

"I don't have anywhere else I'd rather be," I said.

I touched his arm. Looking up at me, not taking his eyes away, he shifted his weight so he could lift one hand to take mine.

We laced our fingers back together and rested our hands between us.

He looked at our hands, then back up at me.

And then he smiled. Soft. And really not rare at all.

"Okay."

TWENTY-THREE

Self-Analysis:
Darcy Phillips

Is not set in stone.

The swim meet was indoors, but the upper half of an entire wall was a grid of windowpanes, allowing the morning summer sun to stream through and glint on the pool's surface. The effect was a little like a greenhouse, and combined with the heat radiating from the water and the strong smell of chlorine, it was hot, muggy, and stifling.

Our spot in the bleachers was behind the lifeguard station, where a girl in an oversized T-shirt kept an eagle eye on all the swimmers. On the ground was a line of white plastic tables where people with pens, papers, and timers sat watching the endless parade of swimmers. Along the sides of the pool, girls and guys hovered with jackets thrown over their swimsuits or towels wrapped around their shoulders, cheering on their teammates or awaiting their own races.

The bleachers we sat on were fairly empty, with only a smattering of family and friends from each team sitting at either end. But those of us who were there were enthusiastic enough to make up for the sparseness, getting to our feet and shouting for our team in every race. And there were a *lot* of races.

A few families down from us, one particularly engaged mom was playing "We Will Rock You" by Queen through her phone speakers and waving it from side to side. Near the pool, her daughter kept sending stricken looks and widening her eyes before pointedly looking away from the bleachers.

Even Brooke, whose idea of a good time was practicing with new makeup or sitting in a clean meeting room planning to organize a school event, stomped and cheered and held out her hand linked with Ray's in a victory punch when we were winning.

Brooke, Ray, and I really were a trio these days. Months ago, I could barely imagine tolerating Ray joining us every time I did something with Brooke, but now I more than tolerated. I loved having her here. She balanced out Brooke's sweetness with a brash, confident energy that made me feel we were sort of invincible, all together. And if it weren't for Ray, I'd probably be here alone today, but Ray insisted we stick together for this kind of stuff, every single time.

And in even better news, it seemed Ray would be hanging with Brooke and me for the foreseeable future. A few days after my birthday, Ray had sincerely offered to tell the school about the rigged votes, which was enough to clinch Brooke's complete forgiveness. Brooke wouldn't let Ray do it, to be clear. I think, for Brooke, it was enough that Ray offered to, and seemed to mean it. So as far as I was concerned, they were endgame at this stage, and I intended to do whatever I could to support that. Minus any meddling.

Even though we were reaching the end of the meet now, Brougham still checked on us at regular intervals while he stood with the rest of his team on the ground, kind of like a toddler checking their family was watching them on a jungle gym. Every time he caught my eye, his expression softened, and he'd look away with a glow about him. It wasn't the first time I'd come to one of his meets, but the novelty of having someone there to watch *him*, to support *him*, had yet to wear off for Brougham.

We only had the relay to go when a girl with long, straight blond hair and a pointy face I vaguely recognized sat next to me out of nowhere. I didn't mean to give her such a startled look, but to be fair, random people who don't know you didn't usually come up and sit in your personal space with several feet of bleachers free for the sitting.

"Hey, you're Darcy, right?" she asked.

My shoulders tensed of their own accord. Straight away my gut told me this was locker related. I'd finally gotten to a point where I didn't feel judged by half the school, and now someone was here to bring it all back up. "Yeah, I am."

"I'm Hadley. My brother's on the team with your boyfriend."

"Oh, nice. They're killing it today." Hadley, Hadley . . . I vaguely recognized the name, but I couldn't match it to a letter. Or maybe she was one of the unlucky few who got her letter snatched during Lockergate.

"Yeah, I'm really proud." Hadley hesitated, and Brooke looked over in interest to eavesdrop. "Hey, I came over because you helped me out a while ago. I wrote in about my ex-boyfriend . . . the orbiting . . . ?"

I blinked, then it all came back to me. "*Oh*, he was liking all your posts, right?"

"Yes! I loved your response so much. Especially the line about deserving to be courted with fervor. *So* Jane Austen. It's, like, my life motto now."

Okay. This didn't seem to be going the route of righteous indignation. The tension flurried out of my limbs. "What ended up happening?"

"*Well*." Hadley folded her arms and leaned forward, storyteller mode activated. "About a month after that he started texting me all like 'I miss you, I've been thinking about you, I saw your photo with the Rollerblades and I haven't gotten your smile out of my mind all night.'" She pulled a face.

"Too little too late?" I asked.

"Oh, completely. By that point I'd started realizing he was kind of shitty as a boyfriend, you know, like he wanted to talk about himself all the time, but if the conversation came to me I might as well have been talking to a Magic 8 Ball. 'Yeah, nope, maybe, hmm, wow that's craaaaazyyy,'" she said in a flat-toned, robotic voice.

"I'm proud of you!"

"Thanks. You helped a lot. I was losing it by the time I wrote to you, I was about five minutes away from bursting in on him in class and demanding an explanation. But, um, I wanted to ask. With the locker broken, no one seems to know how to send you a letter anymore?"

Brooke *and* Ray were listening in now, leaning forward blatantly.

"They can't." I shrugged. "The school said I can't run a business on campus."

"Okay, so, do you have a Patreon or a Ko-fi or something?"

Come again? I gave a short laugh. "I don't think people really want my advice anymore."

Hadley looked taken aback. "Um, *yeah*, they do."

"Come on, I was a pariah after . . ."

I didn't need to spell it out. Hadley shook her head impatiently to cut me off. "People were pissed off that their letters got leaked. But that's got nothing to do with you giving bad advice. Like, my friend Erica said you helped her with her boyfriend, too, and they're in a *great* place now. And if it's all online it's safer anyway, as long as you use a VPN, right?"

I hesitated, totally caught off guard. I mean, right . . . maybe . . . I guess? I hadn't thought about it?

Hadley bounced on the spot. "I mean, I'd use it. Hey, the relay's about to start; I gotta get back to Mom and Dad. Good luck, though."

"Thank you," I said, watching her as she hurried back to her seat a few rows back.

Brooke, Ray, and I exchanged glances.

"That's interesting," Ray said.

Yeah. It really was.

After the final relay race—which we won by a heart-poundingly close margin—Brooke and Ray headed back to Brooke's place, and Brougham announced, rather concerningly, that he was close to death from starvation. We made a pit stop at Subway on the way to my dad's, and Brougham begged to stay and eat there quickly, because he was more likely than not to pass out at the wheel on the four-minute remaining drive.

As he took a dramatic mouthful—or, more accurately, throatful—of his loaded footlong, I crossed my legs at the ankles. "So, I had a girl from school come and chat today. Hadley something?"

Brougham had the sense to swallow before replying, although there was a startling moment when I wasn't sure if he could fit that much food down his throat in one hit. "Oh, Hadley Rohan? With the blond hair? She was in a class with me."

"Yeah, her. She said I should consider giving advice online."

Brougham paused with his sandwich halfway to his mouth, then lowered it. "What do you reckon?"

"I don't know. Do you think people would use it?"

"*Yeah,*" he said without hesitation. "You're amazing."

But something had been niggling at me. The multiple times that Brougham had pointed out I'd probably messed up my advice. Even though he'd insisted it was fine, a part of it still didn't feel fine. I felt phony.

But bringing that up again felt like compliment-fishing, even though that's not what I was looking for. "I keep thinking about all the things Mom said when I got caught with the locker," I said instead. "Like, I'd need insurance or legal advice, and I'd need to keep her involved. And it'd need to be public posts only, with disclaimers. Stuff like that."

Brougham considered it, squinting in thought. "Do you think she'd have a problem with you doing it?"

"Not really. Not as long as I'm not lying."

"Then don't lie. Simple. You don't have to rely on just yourself anymore."

The gentleman madeth a good point. These days, Mom and I talked regularly enough that I felt she'd be reasonable if I came to her with this. There was no *need* to hide it. I rocked from side to side as a hesitant sort of excitement shot through my chest. "I think I kinda wanna do it."

This time, he spoke with his mouth full, because it was one of Brougham's ongoing life goals to be as endearingly irritating as possible. "We coo shet roo up wiv a webshite."

"Do you know how to do that?" I asked, unwrapping my own sandwich at last.

"Yeah, easy. We just need a web host and a URL; there's a bunch of hosts that have simple site-building tools. I know a little HTML, that should get us most of the way there."

"And could we do a little section where people can send in anonymous questions for me to post? And maybe even like a donation section?"

"Definitely. We're not here to fuck spiders."

I stared at him for the longest pause on record. ". . . *What?*"

He rolled his eyes like *I* was the one who didn't know how the English language worked. "If we're gonna do it, we're gonna do it right."

Huh. Do it right . . .

Then it hit me. "I could ask for feedback," I said slowly. "All I had to go off to know if I'd messed up was my refund rate, but I never found out if I'd messed up little things that weren't worthy of a refund. But if I left a section for complaints, or reviews, or something, I could learn from my mistakes. Actually improve, instead of just assuming I nailed it."

Amusement touched the corner of Brougham's lips. "How do you think you'll do if someone writes and says you got it wrong? Can you handle that?"

He had a point. A few months ago, I probably couldn't have. Maybe even as recently as a month ago. But these days, getting something wrong didn't seem like the catastrophe it used to. And it definitely didn't seem as bad as messing up and never fixing it. "I think I can handle it. Maybe I could do blog posts, too. Like, a general advice sort of thing, as well as personalized responses."

Brougham nodded, eyes widening. "I *love* that. And you know, being online means you'll have a *way* bigger reach, too. It could get big. Maybe Ainsley could even push you on her channel?"

"Maybe. She *has* been begging me to join in on a video sometime." The more I thought about the idea, the more excited I got. This was actually achievable. And I'd been missing the letters, badly. The rush of realizing I knew exactly how to help someone. The fulfillment I got as I saw my demand increase, as word of mouth snowballed. The sense of purpose.

And the extra cash hadn't hurt, either.

Brougham and I finished our lunch as quickly as we could, then hurried to my dad's.

"Hey guys," Dad said as we burst through the front door. He was sitting at the kitchen counter eating his own lunch, a turkey and pickle sandwich, because he had the same taste in food as Satan himself. "How was the race, buddy?"

"Really good," Brougham said. "I shaved a second off my two-hundred-meter freestyle."

"Hey, great job." Dad held out his hand for a high-five, and Brougham met him in the middle.

After Dad adjusted to the idea of me dating a guy instead of a girl—and honestly, for a minute there it looked like Dad was adjusting to the *disappointment* of me dating a guy instead of a girl—Brougham and I had made a point of spending as much time with him on Dad weekends as we could. I saw Dad so little as it was that if he was ever going to have a relationship with the people in my life, we had to be kind of a package deal.

Thankfully, when Dad found out about Brougham's commitment to swimming—the day Brougham picked me up to go see Oriella live, in fact—he revealed he'd been on the swim team back when *he* was in high school, which I hadn't even known myself, and the two of them were off. Sometimes I had to tear Brougham away from talking to Dad when he came around so we could get some alone time. I got it, though. Brougham didn't get many chances to speak to an adult who had the time of day to hear about, let alone validate, his achievements. I was hardly going to begrudge him that.

. . . Like now, for example.

"That reminds me of my senior year," Dad was saying to my enraptured boyfriend, who'd just finished recounting the final relay. "I knew the guy next to me would be far and away my biggest competition, so I ignored everyone else and stuck neck and neck with him the whole way, then with the last few seconds to go, *boom*, I sprinted with everything I had, and got in front of him by a hair. And, of course, it turned out we'd been in the lead, *and the crowd went wild!*" Dad waved his half-eaten sandwich in the air for emphasis. A pickle fell out the bottom and landed on the floor.

"That's awesome, Dad, but can we please continue this in a bit?" I asked, grabbing Brougham's arm to steer him away. "We were *just* about to do something."

"You have my blessing as long as 'something' is PG-13 or lower."

Brougham snickered as I flung around to glare at Dad. "Um, can you *not*, please?"

"Go, get out of my hair, you're bothering me," Dad said with a mischievous grin.

Brougham's smile faltered, and he scanned my dad's face. To make sure his lighthearted tone wasn't hiding a threat, I guessed. I was getting familiar with Brougham's micro-expressions—with a face like his, I had no choice but to get fluent in them. I squeezed his arm reassuringly, and we headed to my bedroom. "He's joking," I whispered as we got inside my room.

He waited in place as I turned around after closing the door, and his hands went straight to my waist, his eyelids lowering. I was also becoming well-acquainted with *this* expression. My breath immediately started feeling thick in my chest.

"You did so *good* today," I gushed, cupping my hand around his cheek. He leaned into my touch and kissed me. Though I kissed him back, my mind wandered instantly.

How would I get the word out about it, I wondered? Maybe I could do a mass BCC email with my locker email to all my previous contacts. That way, everyone who ever cared would know, and word of mouth would do the rest . . . but was that ethical . . . ?

I didn't even realize my body language had changed as I drifted off, but Brougham pulled back. "Are you all right?"

I cringed and gave him an embarrassed smile. "Yes, totally. I was just thinking about my website."

Brougham touched his head to mine and groaned, laughing. "You're dying to get started on it, huh?"

He took my laptop to the bed, and I nestled in beside him and leaned against his shoulder to watch as he worked.

"What are you doing now?" I asked.

"Just . . . registering you . . . a domain name." He navigated to a search tool with a flashing cursor. "Any idea what you wanna call it?"

"Is Dear Locker Eighty-Nine free?"

He typed in www.dearlocker89.com. The name flashed green. Available.

"You want it?" he asked.

"Yes, quick, take it before someone else does!"

"A veritable race against the clock," he murmured. "And . . . it's all yours."

"Is that it? Do I have a website now?"

"You have a *domain name*." He grinned. "Setting up the website will take a while. I'm gonna message Finn and ask which one he used for his—he said it was really good."

"Finn has a website?"

"Yeah," Brougham said, eyes on his phone while he wrote to Finn. "It's something like 'Ryan Chad Truthers dot com,' I think?"

Of course it was.

Brougham locked his phone. "Done. Hopefully he replies soon."

I dragged my fingertips lightly over his shoulder blades. "I guess it wouldn't hurt to take a quick break while we wait."

Brougham didn't need to be told twice. In one movement he'd flipped the laptop shut and turned around to kiss me again. This time I pushed him backward on the bed before quickly moving the laptop to safety on the floor.

And these days, that taste, that smell, made me feel warm, and safe, and infinite. In fact, as it was turning out, upon reflection, maybe I wasn't avoidant after all. Because despite my fears and doubts and confusion at the beginning, now whenever Brougham looked at me, or I looked at him, there was no part of me that felt smothered.

We had our couple bubble. He was my safe base. I was his. I didn't fear engulfment. When his life merged with mine? My life simply grew bigger.

So, maybe I didn't always get things right, about myself, or about others. And maybe a part of learning my place in the world was about accepting that I wouldn't always have the answers, and I wouldn't always be the hero in every scenario, and maybe I wouldn't win everything I attempted.

But I was pretty sure about a couple of things.

Whether I was changing lives through my advice itself, or just my willingness to listen, I'd made a difference with the locker.

And I could make a difference again. Maybe even a bigger one. Especially with Brougham's help.

Speaking of Brougham? Of all the terrifying decisions I'd had to make this year, among all the missteps and bad calls and failed attempts—agreeing to help Alexander Brougham was the most perfectly right decision I'd ever made.

ACKNOWLEDGMENTS

Every book I write is close to my heart, but *Perfect on Paper* is, I think, especially so. There were many important topics I hoped to explore while writing this book. Bi erasure and internalized biphobia are probably the most obvious ones, and I believe my stance here is quite clear if you've made it this far: bi people are part of the queer community, and their identity does not change depending on who, if anyone, they happen to have feelings for or date at any given moment.

When crafting my two main characters, I first created two distinct personalities, then topped up those personalities with my deepest vulnerabilities. Unlike Darcy, I was never a blond, California high school student with a penchant for horror movies, a relationship-advice business, and a love of chart-topping music. But I was the sort of kid who latched on to something I was interested in and educated myself on it for hours a day until I knew the topic inside and out and could write at a professional level on it. And, just like Darcy, I discovered that it's one thing to have knowledge and another thing to successfully apply that knowledge to navigating your own life. The timeless tale of the high achiever who initially stumbles when the theoretical becomes the practical, am I right?

Unlike Brougham, I am not particularly athletic, and if anything, my emotions show on my face *too* easily. But, like Brougham—I'm from South Australia! (I'm kidding, that's not the point I was about to make here . . . but in all seriousness, having the opportunity to share snippets of Australian—and specifically South Australian—culture with international readers was hands down one of the most special things ever for me.) I was *going* to say, like Brougham, I have an anxious attachment style. It took me until adulthood to understand what it means to be anxiously attached, but having this knowledge changed everything. Suddenly, I understood some of my most painful, confusing experiences in a different light. Creating Brougham, a character who has flaws, but whose need for security and stability isn't viewed as one of them? Allowing him to be understood, and supported, and allowed to relax enough to give the best of himself without fear of rejection? Writing this was, frankly, a powerful healing experience for me.

My hope is that this story reaches someone who needs it. Who sees themself in these characters and what they face. Who maybe comes away with a new spark of understanding about themself, and why they feel the way they do.

To Moe Ferrara and the team at Bookends, thank you for your support and passion in championing my work.

Thank you to Sylvan Creekmore, who continues to be the absolute best. Thank you so much for your editing wisdom, for putting up with my early-draft nonsense, and for helping me chip away at what I wrote to get to what I *meant*. I'm so very lucky to have you!

Thank you so much to the team at Wednesday Books, for your continued passion, experience, support, and love. I'm so blessed to have a team so committed and talented. Special thanks to Rivka Holler, DJ DeSmyter, Dana Aprigliano, Jessica Preeg, Sarah Schoof, Sara Goodman, Eileen Rothschild, and NaNá V. Stoelzle!

Thank you to Jonathan Bush, my cover designer and illustrator, for giving me this coral dream!

Thank you so much to my authenticity readers Angela Ahn, Mey Rude, Meredith Russo, and others for their thoughtful feedback.

Also, a big thank-you to the readers who assisted me with high school and college swimming research, as well as other American school-life facts, so I could nail the setting: Don Zolidis, Amy Trueblood, Mel Beatty, Emma Lord, Harker DeFilippis, and Sammy Holden.

To the friends who read the earliest, roughest versions of *Perfect on Paper*, Julia Lynn Rubin, Cale Dietrich, Ashley Schumacher, Ash Ledger, Emma Lord, Hannah Capin, and Becky Albertalli: thank you all so much for your notes, wisdom, and feedback.

To my amazing friends, Julia, Cale, Claire, Jenn, Diana, Alexa, Hannah, Ash, Cass, Sadie, Astrid, Katya, Ella, Samantha, Becky, Ashley, and Emma: thank you for talking me off ledges and sharing joy and struggles with me from all over the world.

Special thanks to Emma Lord, Erin Hahn, Kevin van Whye, and Becky Albertalli for their early support of *Perfect on Paper*. You're all amazing!

To Mum, Dad, and Sarah: Thank you for all of your endless support, encouragement, and love.

Cameron, thank you for learning hundreds of publishing

facts and names and roles for me. And thank you for all the chocolate, and for always knowing when to say, "You stay there, I'll go get dinner."

And to the person reading this: thank you for reading my words. I may not know you, but for a moment we were connected through this story, across time and space. Wherever you are, and whoever you are, I wish you all the love and happiness in the world.